A Forbidden Fate

A Forbidden Fate

Kaven Hirning

This book is a work of fiction. Names, places, and incidents are products of the author's imagination or are used fictitiously. Any resemblance to actual events or locales or persons, living or dead, is entirely coincidental.

Trigger Warnings

Death and Murder

Gore

Kidnapping

Thoughts of self harm

Religious Disputes

Mentions of intended assault

Adult language and Themes

Sexual Conduct

Alcohol and Drug Consumption

To every person who screams when Mr. Darcy helps Lizzie onto the carriage and does his infamous hand flex...

This one's for you. Cheers.

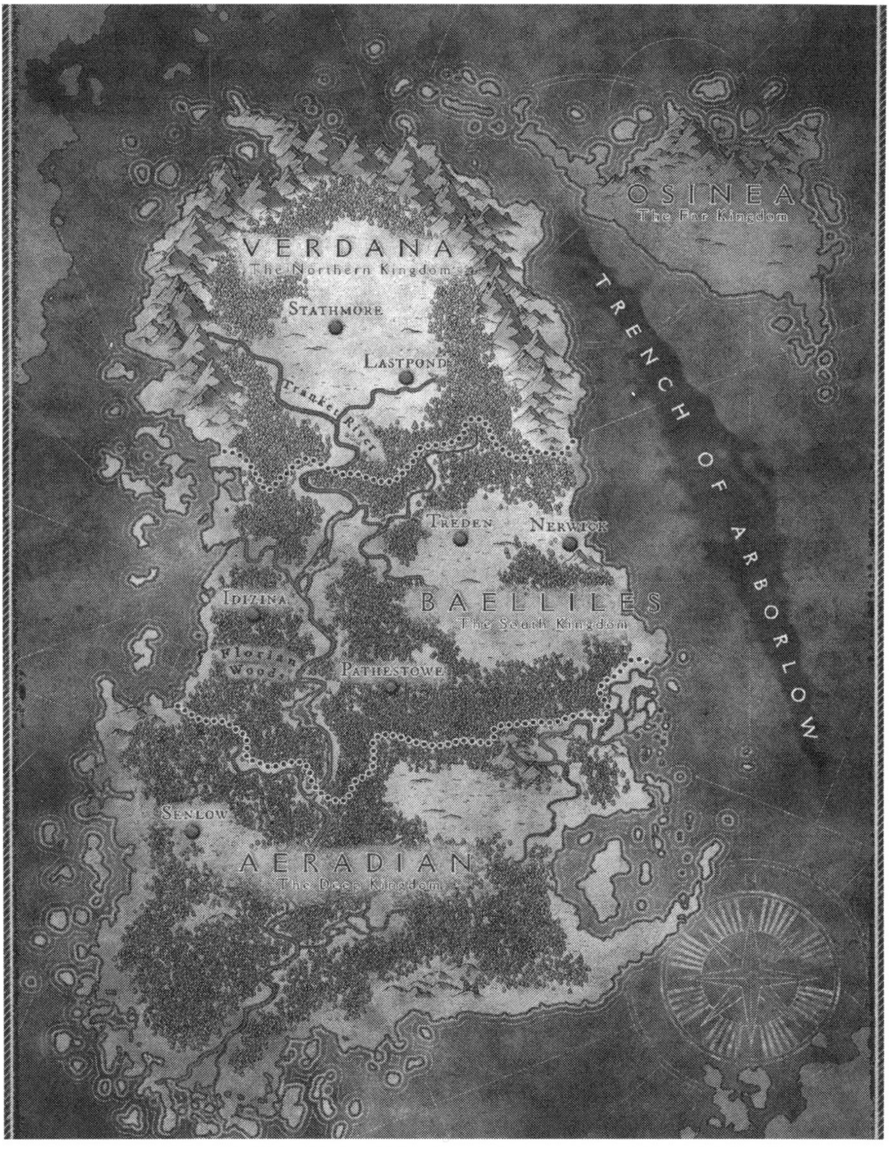
VERDANA
The Northern Kingdom
STATHMORE
LASTPOND
Tranket River
OSINEA
The Far Kingdom
TRENCH OF ARBORLOW
TREDEN
NERWICK
IDIZINA
BAELLILES
The South Kingdom
Florian Wood
PATHESTOWE
SENLOW
AERADIAN
The Deep Kingdom

World Map

Pronunciations

CHARACTERS:

Idalia: Eye-Doll-Yuh

Lachlan: Lock-Lin

Eveline: Eva-Lean

Braizen: Bray-Zen

Rianne: Ree-Anne

Cyra: Sigh-Ruh

PLACES:

Verdana: Ver-Don-Uh

Baelliles: Buh-Lie-Ills

Aeradian: Air-Uh-Dee-In

Idizina: Eye-Duh-Zeena

Table of Contents

Prologue

We flee the castle immediately, leaving everything we brought behind. My father pulls at my arm, yelling at me to get in the carriage. So many things are happening at once, and I can't understand any of them. Adults scream in terror or angrily shout and block our way. I can smell their sweat mixed with the sweet, exotic perfumes they applied for the banquet. Servants careen into each other as some try to enter the great hall and others flee the scene.

Where is my father? He is no longer in front of me. He dropped my hand. I stumble across the cobblestone courtyard; my soft slippers slide on the wet stones. The screams and shouts gradually fade until I can only hear my heart pound and the anxious whines of the carriage horses as they sense our fear.

My father stands at the carriage door shouting at me to enter. I reach his side and gulp for air. Our outriders are all displaying their weapons and strain to hold their mounts in place until father and I enter the carriage. I cannot understand what my father is saying. He is babbling in some strange language and his eyes rake across my face, although he does not appear to see me. He is frightening me.

I place my foot on the first step and my father shoves me up the rest of the way. I look up.

Then I scream and scream.

Chapter One

Idalia

Present Day

Each time I see a dead body in the street, I want to burn Baelliles to the ground. And when another pile of emaciated corpses is hauled off to the Burial Ground, I remember the first pair of lifeless eyes I ever saw. My mother's.

I don't remember their color. Twelve years with her should've been enough time for me to savor such details, but time has a funny way of making us forget. Many memories of the dead elude my mind to make room for the living. Only two memories of my mother are forever preserved in my mind. The first is the sound of her ethereal voice as she sang to me each night. The second is her ashen face pressed against the marble.

Once, when I was young and full of adolescent self-regard, I asked my father which of my mother's attributes I possessed. I desperately wanted to know. Were her eyes an endless brown like mine? Did she detest cold weather, too? I quickly learned that I should only ask him such questions if I were prepared to hear him rage about our war with the South Kingdom.

"They killed her! My precious Revna," he'd fume of his Queen. "Murdered her in cold blood! The Braders are nothing more than ruby-covered snakes. They ensnare you with their charms and coax you with their deceit, and once you are close enough, they swallow you whole!"

Then after his rant, he'd call for his advisers and discuss possible attack strategies against Baelliles, even though our people know he'll never strike first.

Verdana suffers. Verdana is weak.

Our army shields the river and sends scouts on suicide missions to find a way to break our enemy's defenses. Still the people whisper. Still they chant. They crave Baelliles' destruction, and no one craves it more than I.

"Lady Idalia, you must go to the oratory at once," Nurse Lydia exclaims as she flies into my room.

I jerk upright in my bed, clutching the sheets over my bare breasts.

"Lady and Shield, Lydia! The moon is still out! What brings you to my chambers this early?"

She clicks her tongue, unfazed by my frustration, and pulls at the covers. "His Majesty insists upon seeing you. Immediately. He has important news. I don't know any details beyond that."

I groan and reach for my stolen bedding. Lydia easily thwarts my attempt. She balls more of the sheets into her fists and shakes her head.

"The King has ordered me to retrieve you. The message is urgent, so you should meet him with equal urgency! Would you really have me return to him empty-handed?"

"Inform him that I'm much too tired to venture as far as the oratory. Explain that I require a full night's rest before receiving *important* news. Trust that he'll be less than surprised to know I say so."

My nurse scoffs. "Nonsense. He'll never accept such a slothful alibi! I'll ask you once more to get up. Should you refuse, I'll be forced to resort to dire measures."

I lift a vexed brow. "Just how dire?"

Nurse Lydia swats at my legs. Her thick, blond braid swinging in effort. "Get up! Get up from this bed at once!"

A laugh rolls up from deep within me as I throw both palms in the air in surrender. I should've known better than to think she'd give up easily. More of a parent than a handmaiden to me, she never cowers before my stubbornness. I sigh and admit defeat. Despite my best efforts, I'm up before the sun. As my eyes adjust to the sconce's flickering candle, the weight of her message sinks in.

My father has never called a meeting this early, not even with his most loyal retainers. A wave of unease ripples through my gut.

My father has *never* called a meeting with me.

As I ascend the spiral staircase in the north spire, worry almost cripples my steps. My mind races to find any matter that requires my presence, at this hour, in the oratory. I come up short. So, I prepare for the worst and mumble a silent prayer to the gods. I approach the ornate wooden door framed in golden stone. Two sentries bow and open the door. One last deep breath and I cross the threshold.

My father, the King of Verdana, stands silently at the altar, his head lowered as he prays to the statues of the Lady and the Guard looming above him. I stop halfway up the aisle and lift my chin.

"Father," I announce myself as solemnly as I can manage. "You called for me?"

A long moment of thick silence fills the space between us, and then he slowly lifts his face to the statues. "Yes, I have news. Something that requires your immediate attendance. Pray, forgive me for disturbing your sleep."

"It must be of grave importance then," I say, hiding the fear that threatens to glide off my tongue. "For you, above all, know how important my sleep is to me."

He huffs a laugh of sorts, then faces me. "Just like your mother," he says. He meets my gaze and half smiles.

I muster a weak grin, still mentally preparing myself for whatever harrowing news he's about to announce.

He pivots and reaches for a packet, its crimson wax seal already broken. Red. Then it's from Aeradian, the Deep Kingdom.

I'm unsure of what a message from that court could mean. Last year Aeradian's king died in a hunting accident. We'd certainly been expected to attend his funeral. But with most of our army protecting the river, our vital trading route, it would've been almost impossible and irresponsible to gather enough men to protect us adequately. My father had decided it was not worth the risk. Despite that grim reason for a journey, I'd been excited at the prospect of leaving Verdana.

Our kingdom is beautiful. However, it's bordered on three sides by treacherous mountains that make travel in any direction but south impossible. To travel south requires entering Baelliles, the South Kingdom, our enemy's territory. Instead, to leave Verdana, we're forced to take a perilous route through the Florian Wood that borders Baelliles on the west. And traveling through The Wood requires protection.

My father holds the contents of the packet high. "The gods have bestowed upon us a miracle, Idalia. King Lachlan's wife has died of the Gray."

"She died?" I exclaim, raising a hand to my throat.

"Yes! Is it not wonderful?" He beams as he waves the paper. "The gods have not forgotten Verdana! We are saved!"

King Lachlan, a name I'm still not used to. And his wife, the poor girl, was barely even twenty. Taken by such a vicious disease.

"Why are you not celebrating?" My father finally notices my distress.

"Why should I celebrate the death of anyone? Especially the wife of a dear friend?"

"You silly girl! Do you not understand? Lachlan is without a bride! He seeks to remarry!"

My breath halts. "Remarry?" As I repeat the word, it sounds foreign to my ears.

"*Now,* do you see why this is such joyous news?" he asks. "King Lachlan is remarrying, and he has asked for your hand."

I stumble to the nearest bench and sit, rubbing my fingers deep into my temples.

"Lachlan has asked for me. But, no…. he wouldn't," I murmur in disbelief. "His father said he must marry a girl from Aeradian. He declared it so."

"His father is dead," my father interrupts. "As is the Aeradian girl his son married. So, it is of no consequence what he declared when he still walked the earth. Lachlan has requested you as his new bride. It should come as no surprise! The two of you were always friendly. Too friendly. I saw the desire in his stare when you were barely older than children! He has wanted you all his days but was forced to marry another while his father lived. But he is a king now, Idalia. The power lies with him."

"If this is true, then it will seal an alliance with Aeradian," I say slowly as the full import of my father's words hits me. "They'll be forced to take our side and will no longer stay neutral. They'll fight with us against Baelliles."

My father throws the paper into the air with a howl of celebration. He lowers himself to his haunches and places a hand on my knee.

"We will finally know the time of retribution. Your mother shall be avenged; Baelliles will fall," he says.

And I will marry Lachlan, the Prince—no, the King—of Aeradian. I've seen him only a few times since we were children. I remember a sincere, soft-spoken, and humorous man. Though truthfully, what I best remember are his sage-green eyes. The way they brightened when he looked at me. The way they burned against his dark skin and vermilion clothes. Yes, I'll gladly marry King Lachlan. I will save Verdana.

"Where will the marriage ceremony take place?" I ask as reality pulls me from my love-laced daydream.

"In Aeradian, as quickly as we can get you there. I will send you through the Florian Wood with a troop of our best men. It is worth pulling them from the river. Should you reach the Deep Kingdom and marry, we will no longer trouble ourselves with defense."

"When do I leave?" Excitement and a growing trepidation about the dangerous journey bubble beneath my skin.

"We waste no time. You leave tomorrow."

His answer propels a wave of nerves through my chest. Tomorrow? I'm to leave everyone and everything I know, marry, and be in my new home all before week's end? Though I know, I'll only safely reach Aeradian if Baelliles scouts aren't swarming the Florian Wood.

Verdanians haven't traveled that route in years due to the war. While it's possible, it's unlikely that Baelliles has positioned scouts on the road.

I swallow hard and nod. A nod that signifies my acceptance. A nod that means goodbye.

"For the Lady and Shield," my father intones.

"For the Guard and Sword," I pledge back.

Chapter Two

Braizen

"How long are we to sit out here in this blistering heat?" Torrent complains as he wipes sweat from his brow and shakes his thick blond hair. I shoot him a look, one that suggests he stay quiet, but he throws up a careless hand. "Don't start with me, Braze. You know I don't care what you have to say."

Against my better judgment, I laugh. He's right. Torrent doesn't care about what I have to say or what anyone has to say, for that matter. Ever.

He's also right about the gods' damned heat. We're used to waiting in the hot sun but are *not* accustomed to sitting still for so long. We're all sweating and smell stagnant on this last day of summer, the day before the wicked cold pours from the north.

We've never trekked so deep into the Florian Wood. Childhood tales and some common sense have always proved warning enough. Terror supposedly lives within these trees.

Once again, I pat the pocket in my cloak and am comforted to feel the map of The Wood. It isn't an entirely accurate chart of this place, but it's as good as we've got.

"You know, Braizen, you could try pulling rank every once in a while. You'd do us all a favor if you'd shut the big oaf up," Lin says as he stands and shakes the dirt from his rear. "We knew it would be a long mission. The waiting is half the battle. Keep blubbering on about how uncomfortable you are, and you risk sabotaging the entire assignment," he says to Torrent.

Torrent grunts, rolling his hazel eyes at the jab. Lin is the careful, rational, albeit verging on annoying, one in our group. But this care has saved our asses more times than I can remember.

"Well, if I'm forced to sit here all day with this tiny speck, at least hand me the goatskin." Torrent reaches his thick arm across me and violently shakes his palm.

Lin grimaces but reluctantly reaches into his satchel and pulls out the leather pouch. Before handing it over to the man built like a mountain, he takes a generous pull for himself.

Torrent snatches the pouch and proceeds to dump most of its contents into his mouth. Liquid runs down his chin and seeps into his blond beard. He smacks loudly and wipes the remaining liquid from his lips with the sleeve of his dark green tunic.

"Well, has the wine offered you a better outlook on the day?" I ask.

My large friend shakes his head and passes me the pouch. "Hardly," he says and burps. Lin groans, repulsed. "But it does make the two of you more tolerable."

I chuckle, shake my head, and take a swig of the grape. I gasp and cough.

"This is *not* wine," I choke out.

My comrades exchange grins before Torrent slaps my back. "It sure isn't! Hope you don't mind. We swapped the wine for whisky before we left."

I hack through the burn and nod. "No problem at all. Barely even noticed."

"See, Torrent! I told you, our Prince can't yet handle what we peasant folk drink with ease," Lin says.

"You're not wrong about that," Tor agrees. "It's why I suggested we bring it in the first place. We gotta train the boy's liver. How else will he survive a lifetime with us?"

I take another gulp. The sting coats my tongue in an unpleasant greeting, but this time when I swallow, my throat gladly welcomes the heat.

Lin folds his arms across his chest, and his angular brown eyes narrow. "You are mistaken, friend. It was I who suggested the exchange."

"*You?!* Lady and Guard, that's hilarious! I'm the one who supplied the drink!"

"Only because *I* instructed you to bring it in the first place."

Torrent stands, his girth almost matching Florian's massive trees. He towers over Lin, who's only an inch shorter than my own six feet. But then, Torr towers over everyone. He rests his hands on his hips and peers down at Lin. "Maybe it's because of how pathetically small your head is that your memory so easily balks! *I* packed over a dozen goatskins, all whisky-filled, on my own. You merely carry them around. A humble occupation, really. I supply the ideas, and you supply the pouches to keep them in."

Lin shakes a finger up at Torrent. "Perhaps it's because there's only a walnut-size brain rattling around somewhere in that mammoth head of yours that you can't seem to think straight. It was at the Smoky Tavern seven nights past when *I* came up with the idea. You grunted, which we all know is your native tongue, and agreed."

The two continue their quarrel above my head. I sip and revel in the all too familiar badgering. Torrent and Lin have been friends since childhood. Both were orphaned at birth, and both were forced to steal to eat. I met them when I was thirteen, and my wanderlust was high. I refused to stay within the castle grounds and regularly slipped off into neighboring villages. They tried to rob me; I offered to pay for their drinks for an entire night. After that, they considered me a great friend, and I was quickly swindled by their *charming personalities.*

It wasn't long until we formed a coterie of sorts, and I began to aid in their interactions with the rich. Our reputation has grown over the last decade, and we now even boast a name: The Cloaked. Many men and women have since joined and left, but we're the trio who lead the pack—always. We've managed to keep my identity a secret. To anyone outside our close-knit band, I'm just another bandit, stealing for sport. We've never failed, and we've never been caught. Our jobs have always been simple. Pickpocketing in taverns, ambushing traveling carriages and fleecing nobles out of a great deal of money. But last week, a new kind of opportunity presented itself. One none of us foresaw.

King Vaskis of Baelliles, my own father, sent spies across the kingdom searching for The Cloaked. They lurked in every bar, brothel, and village from our southern border within the Deep to the northernmost perimeter near Verdana. One of Torrent's friends caught word and sent us the King's message.

'Let The Cloaked bandits know I have a rather unorthodox errand and can use their assistance. Tell them that it pays prettier coins than their eyes can imagine and more than their hands can hold,' the instructions began.

At first, I was wary. Performing a job for my father ran the risk of my identity being flushed out. The King has no idea that his son is part of a criminal assembly, let alone one of its co-founders. But when Torrent relayed the rest of the message, I knew we had to accept. This was no small job, nor was it a ruse to catch The Cloaked. This job could very well save Baelliles from destruction.

My father needed thieves.

My father needed us.

"There's movement north, at least twelve marks away," Lorna, arguably the best-looking member of The Cloaked, warns. Her emerald-green eyes glisten in the patchy light the tree canopy offers.

I slap the pouch against Lin's legs, who stuffs it into his knapsack. Standing, I send a nod of approval to Lorna, who silently slips back between the trees.

"Are we ready, boys?" I ask, flashing a smile that does not match the severity of the situation.

"Born ready, boss," Torr grins.

Lin picks up his enormous crossbow, which swallows half his body, and props it onto his arm.

"Not in the slightest," he says with a wink.

I run my fingers through my hair, pushing the loose wisps from my brow. As I reach back for my bow, I contemplate the risk ahead for a final time. This time we won't steal money or cozen an insolent nobleman. This time, if we fail, we won't lose a deed or coin purse. My life and my kingdom are on the line.

The band knows how little I can help them should our attempt fail, and they've agreed to do this anyway. The sound of horses' hooves trampling the dirt and the muffled voices of what sounds like a few dozen men grow near. Then the sound of her carriage, the wheels clomping and clunking on the rock-strewn road. I pull an arrow from my quiver and nock my bow.

There are only fifteen of us; we'll need to move fast. I dart a glance at Lin, who's aiming his weapon vertically. Then to Torrent, who has a feral smile twitching on his lips and is caressing the hilt of his long sword. Lorna will give us the signal any moment now, and then, it will be left to the gods to decide our fate.

The horses are so close I can hear their snorting. I roll back my shoulders to shake the anxiety that suddenly flushes through me. They're coming closer. Closer. Closer…

A round object rolls onto the road. The guard walking in front of the blue carriage signals the party to stop. The coachman pulls on the reins. The guard unsheathes his sword and assesses the foreign object. He leans down but doesn't touch it.

"*Come on,*" I whisper soundlessly. My palms are clammy, but I take steady inhales, focusing on my aim. Waiting for the signal.

"What is it, Bernard?" Another guard calls from somewhere behind the carriage.

"I don't know. Looks like some strange animal shell," he shouts back.

"Well, kick it out of the way, and let's keep moving. We need to make camp soon. The sun will set in two hours or less."

The front guard shakes his head and then scans the woods. His eyes slowly survey each tree till they land on the one I'm hiding beside.

He won't see me. We're called The Cloaked for a reason. Another long moment passes, and the guard sleeves his blade. He looks more annoyed than suspicious as he rears back his leg to knock the object out of their way.

As his toe lands, Lorna shouts, "Now!"

The ball explodes in smoke, and Lin fires a bolt into the canopy. I release my arrow, and the coachman grunts in agony as it buries itself deep in his chest. A fleet of arrows follows mine, slicing through the air in a fatal unison. Through the smoke, I see bodies tumble to the ground.

A snapping cracks through the screams; Lin has hit his mark. Large sacks of rocks fall onto the road, crushing some of the guards. Though the smoke soon dissipates, the guards run blindly, shouting hysterically.

"Save the princess!" One yells before more rocks descend and break his neck.

Beside me, Torrent laughs wildly, almost unable to restrain himself from charging.

I ready another arrow and wait for the carriage door to open.

"Thirteen, fourteen…" Lin counts the bags as they fall. "Fifteen! That's it. Go!"

They launch themselves towards the carriage, Torrent leading the group with vast strides. I long to join them, but I know I can't. This is the way it must be.

From the opposite wall of trees, more of our band flow onto the road. The ill-prepared guards are now wailing.

"It's an ambush!"

"Lady and Shield, save us!"

"Save the princess!"

Lin stops his sprint and rapidly sends a pair of bolts straight through the armored chests of two guards. Another sneaks behind him and readies his sword to swing.

I quickly pivot and, from my position in the trees, release. The guard's body stiffens, and his sword topples to the ground. As he falls backward, the arrow impales itself deeper into his neck and pierces the front of his throat. Lin half turns to see who almost claimed him and then sends a fast smile towards the trees.

Torrent is a madman, running and flourishing his sword with such a fervent desire to inflict damage that I can't follow its motion. He drives his shoulders into the guards who dare stand in his way and knocks them to the ground one after the other.

One coward unties the horses and hoists himself atop one to flee. Before I can even pinch another arrow from my quiver, a hatchet spirals through the wind and catches the man just beneath his helmet. He slumps to the right, then slowly falls from the steed. As the animal runs away in fright, Lorna races onto the road, retrieves her weapon, and wipes its bloody blade against her trousers.

I quickly take out a few more scrambling buffoons, making sure not to take my eyes off the carriage for too long. I know she's inside, terrified for her life, as she watches her protectors fall one by one.

Lorna continues to fling her hatchet with deadly precision at the men who dare approach her. Torrent's face is splattered with crimson victory, and I see him work to release the remaining horse from its harness.

Typical. Torrent, the great hulk of rage and death, with the blood of his enemies dripping from his sword, freeing an animal caught in our mayhem. He always does this and, when questioned, only shrugs. "Why should they suffer for the sins of their riders?"

The fight continues until there are only dead guards piled on the road. No—one is wounded; he's the only one left alive. Verdanian defenses are still good for nothing, I notice. He throws off his helmet and clings to the side of the carriage.

"Mercy! Please, have mercy on me! Take the girl! Take her!" he shouts.

I shake my head. Pathetic.

Lin approaches the miscreant with his bow strung and ready. The lone survivor trembles and falls to the ground. "I beg you. Let me live! Let me live!"

"Silence," Lin commands. "It's sad enough that you're willing to betray your king and country by giving up your princess so easily, but to grovel for your life is an embarrassment too pitiable for even a thief to witness."

The guard now sobs, his eyes squeeze shut. "I just want to live. Please… *Please.*"

Lin signals to Torrent, who grabs the man by the breastplate and hauls him to his feet.

"Consider this your lucky day, halfwit," Torrent says. "We need a message returned to your king, and it just so happens that none of us are willing to travel to that rocky hells hole you call home to give it to him."

"Yes, yes! I will deliver your message. Anything! Whatever you want!"

Torrent pulls the guard higher until his feet dangle. "You're going to tell your king that Baelliles sends its warmest greetings. Tell him the summer has passed nicely but that we're ready for the cold." The message is hidden in the wording. Verdana is a barren wasteland, cold and brutal. We are ready for *them.*

"Yes! Yes, sir. Of course, sir," the guard babbles.

"Tell him that we have his precious daughter, but not to worry. We'll treat her as any good Baellilean would." Torrent spits on the ground with those last words and lowers his victim. "And tell him if he ever wants to see her again, he'd better come back to us with an offer our King can't refuse."

He releases the man's breastplate, and the guard stumbles back a few steps. "Of course. I'll go right away. Your message will be delivered with haste."

His armor clanks as he races past his fallen company and back towards home. Torrent sneers and shouts insults after him.

Even though we've dispatched King Ivar's guards, the real risk still lies inside the carriage. Lorna approaches it and readies her hatchet.

The door flies open. A heavily cloaked female lunges out and, pushing past Lorna, runs down the road.

"Don't do it," Lorna advises, her voice dripping with annoyance. "You'll only make this harder on yourself."

Lin throws his bow over his shoulder so it hangs down his back. "I'd listen to her if I were you," he calls to the cloaked figure, then lifts one hand high and swishes it through the air. "It really is easier to do as she says. Lorna isn't known for her patience."

Our band answers to Lin's hand signal and swarms the woman. Dasin, one of our newer members, gets closest and attempts to wrap his arms around her. We hear the sickening sound of a blade entering flesh, and then Dasin clutches his bleeding stomach.

Others pull their weapons.

"Don't hurt her," I sound off loudly from my position. I remind myself I can forge ahead if I keep a safe distance between us. I slide down the hill and stride towards the commotion.

She's threatening my armed comrades, whose eyes anxiously bounce from me to our near captive, waiting for my order to strike. I motion for the captive female to lower her blade.

"Now then, I think we can both agree there's really no place to go from here. Why don't we calm down and have a nice conversation—"

The hood of her blue velvet cloak rapidly shifts as she considers which direction offers the best escape.

"By all means, run if you wish. I'm sure sitting for so long in a carriage must cause one's legs to become restless. However, you might not enjoy the aftermath of that decision," I call.

As more of us circle in, she swings the dagger wildly.

"Oh, and I must ask you kindly not to stab any more of my friends. I rather enjoy them, and it puts a real damper on my day."

I glance at Lin, who again swishes his hand through the air with another command.

The female hisses as she breaks past our party and hurls herself down the road.

I sigh. *So stubborn.*

Three men carrying a net bolt past us and sprint after her. They launch the net into the sky, where it spins through the slight breeze and drops neatly down on her even as she tries to scurry into the protection of the trees. She fumbles to the ground and groans, futilely thrashing against the weighted mesh.

Seeing that she's trapped, I move closer. "Is this what you wanted? To look like a flailing fish? We can avoid any future scenarios like this, but you'll have to listen…"

"Don't come any closer," she cries, trying to cut herself free. The others hover over her. She slices enough netting to squirm her upper body through, but I see her expression change as she realizes she's cornered. There's no way out.

"Look," I say. "We don't need to make this any more dramatic than it already is."

She pushes back her hood, and I'm momentarily stunned as it falls past her hair. She's…gorgeous. The kind of beauty that knocks a grown man to his knees. The kind a kingdom would worship.

Once again, I'm a thirteen-year-old child, ensnared by the fawn-like innocence of her eyes and the curiosity that blooms behind them. Oh yes, I remember this feeling.

Those brown eyes, now frenzied, lock on mine. Her thick, dark hair is disheveled, and it swings as she flings her body around in another attempt to free herself. I remember where I am. What she is to me.

Then she yells, "Don't come near me, you plebeian thief! I mean it! Stay where you are!"

I cock my head to the side, her words pulling me away from her beauty. "Oh, come now, Idalia. Surely you know who I am?"

She stops writhing long enough to glance at my face. Her own fills with confusion.

I click my tongue. "Am I truly that forgettable?"

"I don't waste my time memorizing the features of crooks. Especially ones that hail from Baelliles," she spits and resumes her struggle.

"What about the ones who are extremely handsome?" I flash her a mirthless grin. Her eyes latch onto mine, and for a brief second, I sense she might agree with my quip.

Instead, she scowls, an interesting sight on such a beautiful face. "Touch me, and I'll kill you."

This makes me laugh. Her expression tightens. She must think I'm making light of her threats. I step even closer, leaning down so she can get a better look.

"Touch you, and it will *kill us both*," I say quietly.

Her features still, and her eyes race between my own as if she sees a ghost. Her head knocks back in disbelief; her mouth falls open.

I nod with an amused smile.

"That's right, Little Sparrow. It's the man you almost married. Have you missed me?"

Chapter Three

Idalia

Twelve Years Previous

My mother paces the corridors, mumbling prayers to the gods. Seven times she's ordered Nurse Lydia to change my dress and is wholly unsatisfied with each choice. I love all the dresses, though the third option is my favorite. The bigger the skirt, the prettier I feel. And option three provides not only the big skirt but all the frills and lace I could ask for.

"What of this one, Queen Revna?" Nurse Lydia pleads, her voice wavering. She's even more tired of dressing me than I am of being dressed. My corset squeezes my ribs and prevents me from taking deep breaths. My mother enters my chamber and begins flapping her hands.

"Twirl for me, darling," she instructs and whirls her finger. I spin a few times and giggle as the fabric billows around me. I look like a loose flower petal floating through a light spring breeze. My mother peers at me and places a tired hand on her chin when I stop. Her eyes rove over my body, observing every inch of the dress that clings to it. Then she sighs. "It is hopeless! Have all our seamstresses caught the Gray!?"

Nurse Lydia raises her hand. "There is another option, Your Highness. Let me just take Idalia back into her room…"

"I do not need to see another wretched creation," my mother frets. "They are giving me the most atrocious headache."

Nurse Lydia nods then sends her a worried frown. "Shall it be this one then, Your Highness?" Her voice is timid, as if my mother is made of glass, and she's afraid to crack her.

"I cannot concern myself with this for one moment longer," my mother breathes in defeat. "Choose whichever garment you see fit. Perhaps my sweet Idalia's charms will be enough to sell the Braders, or perhaps they will not mind that she looks like a cheap waif. Let us hope both, or may the gods save Verdana." With that, she leaves.

I run to the door and watch until even her shadow disappears. My nurse releases a strained laugh; her cheeks are stained red.

I tug on her apron. "Do I look terrible in every dress? Is that why she's so angry?"

"Of course not, dear!" She soothes. "Your mother just needs to ready herself for the journey. It's a very important occasion, after all! Come, we'll choose the rest of your attire and worry ourselves with the dress later." She places a light hand on my shoulder. "How would you like a caramel tart and milk?"

Caramel tarts are my favorite treat in the world, and Nurse Lydia rarely lets me have them this late at night. I wrap my arms around her and squeeze in delight. I'll miss her on our trip to Baelliles.

The carriage ride isn't fun at all. My mother complains of her headaches the entire time, and my father spends most of the long travel days lecturing me on how to act properly. Even though my mother is Verdana's ruler, and he's her King consort, my father seems to make the rules. I'm miserable. I've never been confined to such a small space for so long in my life, let alone with both of them.

I stare out the window for days and do my best to block out their dreadful chatter. In Verdana, the treacherous mountains block my views from the castle, and snow covers every inch I can see. But once we're a few days into our trek across Baelliles, we're greeted by lush fields of golden wheat, rolling grassy hills, and tall green trees that seem to reach all the way up into milky white clouds. We shed our fur-lined cloaks, and I revel in the feel of the warm air against my skin. The sky shifts between blue and lavender hues, and soon, the scents of lemon and sage flood the carriage. These small joys are enough to carry me through the long trip.

We finally arrive in Nerwick, the town where our enemy's castle stands. Before I can rise, my father is already glaring at me.

"Idalia," he says coldly, "You must remember all we've taught you. It is *you* who must save Verdana, and it begins today." He doesn't wait for a response, he's already scuffling around in his seat, preparing to exit the gig.

My mother grabs my hands. I fear I'm in trouble, but she softly smiles. "You look beautiful, my sweet Idalia. They'll be fools to not fall in love with you." Her palm cups my cheek, and a tender thumb strokes it gently. "Don't be afraid, do you hear me? I know that your father has told you how important this visit is, but we mustn't be afraid. Let wisdom be your staff; grip it firmly. Let compassion be your crown; wear it proudly. And above all, bring joy with you wherever you go. Cling to it with all of your might. For fear is the enemy of the Hyland women."

Her eyes pierce mine with such intent I wonder if her headache is back. Before I can respond, my father raps on the carriage roof, the door opens, and servants are helping us alight.

"Welcome to Baelliles, Your Majesties. I speak for our entire kingdom when I say that we hope you found no trouble during your travels." A lean man with fair skin bows low and greets us as we descend. "I am Horrick Ferdun, a dear friend and the trusted advisor to King Vaskis. Allow me to show you to the wing where you will reside for the next few days. Please, let me know if there is anything I can do to make your stay more comfortable."

My father inclines his head, and the two begin chatting incoherently, using words I don't understand. My mother squeezes my hand, then straightens her back and stiffly trails behind the men. I remember my lessons and mimic her.

'Keep a straight neck, Idalia!' Nurse Lydia's reprimands ring loudly in my head. *'Chin up! Chin up! Smile and walk slowly. Let the men lead, always.'* I want to run and play with the children who line the streets to watch our entrance, but I know better. My mother will have my head if I

dare to do such a thing. So, I walk slowly and smile, trying not to drop my jaw when I see the castle.

It's not much larger than ours but made of darker stone. Giant trees bend over its central tower, seeming to offer protection from the elements that would seek to wreak havoc upon it. Across each turret creeping vines sprawl like small eager hands that can't seem to grab enough stone.

No cold jagged mountains loom in every direction. Only more trees and beautiful plants playfully swaying in the wind's call. I catch a glimpse of the ocean. I'm in awe, and even from this distance, I can feel the freedom it possesses.

At Stathmore, our castle, there are no changes in color because there are no trees with leaves that grow at this height. We live in a plain, white stone castle surrounded by much taller, whiter stones that make up the craggy mountains. There's no chance of swimming in the sea.

I like it here. Even the flag that snaps in the breeze is richly colored. I'm glad my father says this will be my future home.

Once in our chambers, my father lies on his back on the bed and hurls curses at the ceiling. My mother holds out her hand. "This is not where you will sleep, Idalia. Follow me." She opens one of the last doors on the corridor, and two handmaidens stand to greet me. They're both dressed in bright green, and for a moment, they remind me of the trees. They smile warmly and curtsey. My mother leans down to kiss my forehead. "I will see you tomorrow, my sweet. Get some rest now."

I lean back and look up at her. "Mother, do you have a headache?"

She doesn't answer; she only laughs. With a parting tap on my head, she's gone, and the handmaidens take over.

First, they dunk me in a tub and scrub at my skin so harshly that I fight back tears. "We must rid you of that vile Verdanian stench!" One complains, then scrubs me harder. Next, they pull a silky chemise over my head and spray me with scented tonics. The smell reminds me of the roses that grow in our castle's glasshouse, which my mother orders to be kept warm with fires throughout the year. They put me in bed without even asking if I'm tired, as Nurse Lydia always does. One fluffs my pillow and arranges my neck upon it; the other swaddles me tightly beneath the linen blanket. They seem satisfied with their work and curtsey before slipping out the door.

I lie still and uncomfortable for what seems like hours before I toss aside the blanket. I'm not tired; I'm bored. I search the chamber for games or dolls. My mother says a girl my age should be done playing with toys, but I don't care. I like toys. It's too bad there aren't any here. They've trapped me in what seems to be a room for elders. There's only a bed, a dresser, a mirror made of silver, and a globe.

I huff and fold my arms across my chest. I consider returning to bed. But then I hear faint sounds in the corridor. Multiple voices and titters of hushed laughter pass. I can't bear this dreadful room any longer! Even with the threat of my mother finding out, I slowly open the door and peek out.

Two boys and one girl, all of whom appear to be my age, laugh as they turn a corner. I tiptoe into the corridor, quietly shut my door, and follow. I straggle at a safe distance as we sneak through several candlelit passages. Eventually, they stop before a large door at the end of a hall.

The girl is the tallest, though she looks younger than the boys. No older than nine or ten. She wears a red nightgown, much fancier than my own. It's embroidered with gold lace, and the cuffs are a shimmering opal fabric. Black curls spill from her coif.

Her appearance and red clothes match the boy next to her. Their rich brown skin is much darker than that of the other boy, who stands closest to the door. His skin is bronze, and he's dressed in green, the same shade the handmaidens wear. He bends over the lock while the others hover.

I quietly glide closer, heel to toe. With my next step, the wood floor groans in protest. The boy in red whips his head around, too fast for me to run or hide. I'm paralyzed, and sure he'll call for my mother or another adult to come to retrieve me. Instead, he smiles. His teeth are fascinatingly white against his skin, and I can't help but smile back. His eyes are kind.

"You must be the Princess of Verdana," he says. "My father has told me all about you." He sticks his hand out towards me. I'm not sure what to do with it.

"Lachlan, you toad! She's a lady! She's not going to shake your dirty hand!" The girl intervenes, shoving him aside to stand in front of me. She shoots the boy a stern look and, with a scrunched nose, turns to me and beams. "Sorry about my brother; he hasn't yet learned how to properly introduce himself to a girl. I'm Princess Theodore of Aeradian. It's a pleasure to meet you, Princess." She bows her head as regally as my mother does. I raise a brow.

"Theodore?" I giggle. The girl is very pretty, but I've only ever been introduced to older men who shared that name. Her eyes are a dazzling topaz and framed by long, curly lashes like her brother's. She's far too beautiful. Who burdened her with an older man's name?

"My father wanted all of his heirs to be sons," she says and rolls her eyes. She digs an elbow into her brother's ribs. Lachlan, I think she called him. "So, when our mother popped me out, he didn't think twice about what to call me. Theodore Thrope is the name, but you can call me Teddy." She rests her fists on her hips and grins proudly.

I nod, as I've been taught to when introduced to other royalty. "Hello, Teddy. I'm Idalia. You may call me … Idalia."

Teddy snickers then tucks her arm around me. "Well then, *Idalia*, since you've already met my dumb brother, allow me to introduce you to the owner of the place." My feet drag as she pulls me towards the other boy, busy picking at the lock. "Meet Prince Braizen of Baelliles. It's the two of you who bring us all together." She releases her hold on me and smacks her lips. "That's what my maiden told me! She says we're all here because the two of you are supposed to *kiss*."

I wrench back. "What?!"

The Prince doesn't seem fazed by Teddy's words; he keeps working away at the lock as if nothing was said.

A mischievous grin lights up Teddy's face. "You must kiss! It's what ladies and gentlemen do to make babies. That's how heirs are born! Or at least, that's what my maiden says. I'm not too sure. My mother died shortly after I was born, so I've had to ask around. What do you think, Lachlan? Don't they have to kiss?"

Her brother examines my horrified expression, then shrugs. "I don't think a princess has to do anything she doesn't want to do," he says.

I sigh in relief, but Teddy swats at him. "That's not true at all, Lach! Haven't you heard a word Father says? That's *precisely* what a princess must do." She turns to me with an intense look.

"What's that?" I ask hesitantly, still eyeing the boy picking the lock. "What's a princess to do?"

Teddy looks at me very seriously. "What she doesn't want."

I swallow the thick lump forming in the back of my throat. I can think of nothing more disgusting than a kiss. It's the very last thing I want to do with a boy, let alone a stranger!

Click. "Got it!" Prince Braizen cries in victory. I glance over Teddy's shoulder to see that the Prince has indeed triumphed over the lock.

Lachlan jumps up and down, clapping his hands. Teddy stomps her foot. "Well then, it's time you show us all the things you promised!" she says.

The Prince proudly gestures for us to enter before him. Lachlan and his sister bound into the doorway, pushing against each other to be first.

Prince Braizen turns to face me for the first time, and my breath catches as I meet his eyes. They're the cool blue of a frosted winter's sky in Verdana. I've never seen anything like them. He stares at me as if he has seen a ghost. Or something far more shocking. I shift uncomfortably, and my cheeks flush; I obviously stared at him for too long.

He shakes his head, clears his throat, and tightens his lips.

"Well? Are you coming or not?"

"That depends," I return as boldly as I can. "What's going on in there?"

He lifts his shoulders, and a smile spreads across his face like oil over bread.

"Come in and find out."

I contemplate my next move. If my father catches word of what we're doing, he'll shout at me for months. No proper princess roams the corridors late at night. Or ever. And if my mother learns of this? Her headache will rightfully devour her sanity. I've already endangered myself by following them here. To enter a previously locked room without permission or supervision? *Lady and Shield.*

Prince Braizen crosses one foot over the other and leans against the doorframe. "So, what'll it be?"

I clench my fists. Teddy ran in without a second thought, and she's a princess. Why shouldn't I do the same? I lower my brows and try my best to sound confident.

"Hold the door. I'm coming." With heavy steps, I walk towards the mysterious room.

As I pass him, the young Prince leans in close to my ear and whispers.

"By the way, you really shouldn't listen to Teddy. That's definitely *not* how heirs are made."

I'm inside what appears to be a small cage. Beyond the iron bars lies a huge space I can barely fathom. A domed glass ceiling arches high above tall trees loom amidst a riot of plants that grow everywhere. Butterflies swarm in every direction, and my ears fill with the cacophony of hundreds of chirping birds. Teddy shakes with excitement; her brother's eyes widen in pleasure.

"This is the aviary," Braizen says. "My father has filled it with every known bird species in Baelliles. It was a gift for my mother." As if planned, a flock of blue birds flies in perfect unison near our heads. They race up and trace the dome's perimeter before swooping low into the trees and out of sight. I laugh in delight. This is the last thing I'd expect to find in a castle.

"Open the door, Braizen! I want to run around!" Teddy demands.

"I will," he says. "But we stick to the plan. We explore until you hear my whistle, then we meet back here. We can't stay too long; if anyone finds us, my mother will ship us all to the Crescent Trench."

I gulp. The Crescent Trench of Arborlow. My father tells stories about that trench. It's why no one travels to the Osinean Kingdom. People who dare to embark on that journey are never heard from again.

"And remember," the Prince resumes as he unlatches the cage's hook. "Some birds are friendly; others aren't. Be careful of how close you get to them. They don't mind being watched, but should you try and touch them… Well, you've been warned." He pushes the creaky gate.

Teddy sprints through and takes the first dirt path. Soon, she vanishes behind a plant with giant green leaves that look like the ears of an elephant, an animal I saw in a book of drawings in my father's library. I almost laugh aloud at the thought.

Lachlan offers me a timid smile and then chases after his sister. I eye Braizen, who's waiting for me to exit, and I slowly step onto a path. As my bare feet hit the warm dirt, I catch my breath and curl my toes in delight. There's no place in Verdana where I can feel the dirt beneath my feet; our land is frozen and snowy year-round. I wiggle my toes, reveling in the soft soil between them, even if the soil is inside a castle. The aviary is so vibrant, loud, and colorful; it's as if it had been designed by the theatre troupe my father brings to the court to perform on my mother's birthday. I'm content to stand here and feel no need to explore further. But the Prince grabs my hand and sprints down a trail.

"What are you doing?" I yell as we blaze past a small coppice of trees.

"I want to show you something!"

I try to take in everything as we run. Enormous plants, the sharp, heady scents from the multicolored flowers bloom everywhere in the warm air. The unfamiliar squawks and chirps from birds. When I glance up, I see a colossal bird hovering above us. It looks larger than some of the trees, and its beak dips at the front.

"What's that?" I cry, pointing with my free hand. Prince Braizen briefly looks up.

"What?" he calls back.

"That!" I scream while still pointing. But when I look again, the bird is gone. It must have flown back to whatever massive nest it rests in.

I'm out of breath by the time we stop, but he's almost buzzing with energy. Suddenly, he squats and waves his hand at me without looking back—a signal to do the same. I hunch down next to him.

I start to speak, but he presses a finger to his mouth, a gesture I know all too well from Nurse Lydia.

"We have to be quiet, or it won't come." His voice is barely a whisper.

What won't come? But I wait and don't speak. A strange feeling begins to brew inside me, one I don't recognize. I like the way it feels to be next to the Prince. I like how he unlocked the door to bring us here, despite it being against the rules. And I *really* like his pretty eyes. I wonder if he thinks mine are pretty, too.

"Look," he breathes, pointing. My eyes break free from his profile and follow his finger. An obsidian birdbath lined with jewels sits a few yards away. In and of itself, it's glorious, but as we watch, a small bird lands on its rim to sip from its pool. It could easily fit in my hand. At first glance, its feathers appear to be a dull, grayish brown. Then it puffs its chest, and its feathers shimmer like gold in candlelight, sparkle like they've caught starlight.

I turn to find his cool blue eyes staring at me. He grins and explains in a low voice. "That's the Little Sparrow. It's the rarest bird in all the kingdoms. My father searched for years to find one."

"How did he ever manage to catch it?"

"He didn't. I did."

"*You*?" I say in disbelief. He's a child, like me! I could never catch a bird, not even the magpies that relentlessly knock at the castle's windows.

"How!" It's more of a command than a question. His eyes twinkle as he turns his focus back to the bird.

"I like their world. I'm more at home in the trees than here in this castle. Last year, on my thirteenth birthday, I was in some woods lying in a patch of grass, and it landed on my hand. It was like the trees sent me a present. I didn't move; I just watched it. The sun began to set, and I knew it was time to return home. Only, when I got up, the bird didn't move. It stayed on my palm, unafraid. So, I brought it here."

"You walked all the way from the woods to the castle carrying the bird, and it just … it just *let you*?" My whisper intensifies.

"Yes," he says plainly. "Honest to the Guard and his Sword, it just let me."

I draw a deep breath. We're not to swear on the gods; he must be telling the truth. "What did your father say when you told him? Is your mother happy to have such a rarity in her castle?"

Braizen rubs the back of his fingers against the bottom of his chin. "I never told them."

"You never told them!" My voice rises far above a whisper, and the bird perks its head up from the water.

The Prince swats his hand. "Shh!"

I cover my mouth and peek through the leaves to make sure the bird didn't fly away. After a few seconds of looking around, it continues to drink. "Why didn't you tell them? Your father searched for years to find that bird!"

The Prince seems to consider his answer before looking straight into my eyes. "Because the bird found me. It *chose me*. Not my father or my mother. That's what I like about her. She doesn't show up for just anyone. She's very selective."

"She's female?" I smile as the bird's brilliant feathers shimmer against the black stone.

"I'm not sure," he admits. "But when something is as beautiful as that, I have to assume it's a girl."

The bird hops in and out of the pool to bathe herself, soft chirps that sound like happiness leaping from her beak.

"Have you named her?" I ask.

He doesn't say anything for a long moment. He runs a hand through his brown curls and flashes me a smile.

"You know, you kind of remind me of her," he says.

My heart skips, and I focus on the golden-winged mystery. What in the four hells am I feeling? My stomach turns, but I don't feel sick. I feel light and *excited.*

"There are a lot of pretty birds in here, but this one is different. This one stands out," he says.

"I, well, that's very nice of you. I think?" I don't even know what I'm trying to say. It's as though all the butterflies that flutter around us are trapped inside me. Is he calling me beautiful? Rare? Or picky?

His eyes watch me with unwavering intensity. Can't he feel what rushes through me? Isn't he nervous? He doesn't seem to be. My cheeks are now so warm I can barely endure the unexpected heat.

"I'm glad you are here, Little Sparrow." A loose brown curl droops on his forehead. I forget to breathe. I'm too busy drowning in his ice-blue stare. Only moments ago, I was disgusted at the thought of kissing him, and now? Am I even old enough to kiss? I don't know. My mother hasn't prepared me in the slightest for this. I may need to curse Nurse Lydia for not telling me what to do in situations like these.

I want to kiss him. Even if I'm not sure how.

His hand slides beneath my chin, and my palms grow damp. He leans in so very, very close. "I just hope you don't fly away," he whispers.

The gods can't help me now. I'm certain that whatever it is that I'm feeling has *never* been felt before. It's reserved for only me and him. I float, drift away, and try not to think about what I'm supposed to do. His lips near mine. I close my eyes.

"Help! Help!"

My eyes shoot open. Braizen drops his hand and stands before I realize it's Teddy who shouted.

"Help me! He's hurt! Braizen, help!"

Braizen helps me rise, but he runs towards the call as soon as I'm steady. Before I follow, I scan the birdbath and the surrounding plants. The bird is gone, as is the swirling sensation in my belly.

We find Teddy standing above a fallen Lachlan, who's clutching his cheek and sobbing. "What happened?" Braizen demands, dropping beside his friend.

Teddy stammers. "I saw a green and yellow bird with a large tail. I just wanted to touch it! I wasn't going to hurt it!"

Lachlan hisses in pain. I grow uneasy, afraid. A quake rumbles through my chest and lances through my arms.

"What did I tell you about touching the birds?" Braizen lectures. "What did it do?"

"It started to chase me! Lachlan stepped in, and it…it pecked him!"

With that, my nerves rapidly manifest into a fit of laughter. The mere thought of a bird conquering the boy is too funny to resist.

Teddy faces me, her stare filled with disdain. "You dare laugh at my brother's bravery? He stood up against that beast to defend me, and now he's gravely injured!"

I only laugh harder. Brave? For fighting a bird?! The Aeradian army must be a wretched sight indeed!

"He's fine," Prince Braizen interjects, "It's just a scrape. It'll heal soon."

"And what are we to tell our father?" Teddy demands. "He'll want to know how his son received such a wound!"

Braizen cuts a look over to me and grins at my inability to keep a straight face. "I don't know. Tell him he got into a fight with a vicious kitten," he says.

I snort, then hide my mouth behind a hand. Teddy stomps her foot and glares at us both.

"I think it's time we go back to our rooms," Braizen says. "Sparrow over here needs her beauty sleep, and we wouldn't want anyone else getting *gravely injured*."

"Sparrow?" Lachlan questions as he peels himself off the floor, one hand still slapped to his cheek.

Braizen winks at me before stalking ahead, and the swirls return to my stomach. Though I fear this time they might not ever leave.

Chapter Four

Idalia

Present Day

My heart pounds out of control. We were assured we wouldn't encounter Baellilean scouts. Aeradian assured my father that I'd have safe passage in their letter. How did these bandits learn that I'd be on this road, and why is *he* with them? Surely King Vaskis didn't send him? No king would hire thieves, let alone thieves led by the one man who can't touch the person they kidnapped.

What do these bandits want? I inhale and suck moist fabric back into my mouth. I froze when I realized who'd caught me; I was too stunned to fight. I might as well have been captured by a memory that came to life.

His men shoved a sack over my head and threw me over a horse before I could even utter his name aloud. Now I bounce, as I have for what must be hours, held close by one of the freebooters. I don't know where we're going, but I can't imagine the destination is a pleasant one.

"Braze," the rider who holds me calls out. I recognize her voice; it's the red-haired female with the hatchet. "What about here?" The clomping hooves ahead of us slow.

"This is fine." It's Prince Braizen. His voice has barely changed in all these years. But why did she call him *Braze*? It's disrespectful enough to drop his title, but to address him so? Who *are* these people?

"Greggor, you and two others take the wounded to the nearest medic. Grab some food and fill your canteens. Have Heran draw up a small map from my own, so you'll know where you're going. Don't return unless they're healed. If the wounds take Dasin, bury him next to the others. Lin, start a fire. Lorna, you and some others watch the perimeter. We'll take turns through the night."

I gulp.

"What about the cargo?" Lorna spits out. Her hand lands hard on my shoulder, and she shakes me. I've squirmed my head enough so that the gag has finally fallen from my mouth. Now to just get this horrific sack off my head.

"Torrent, grab the girl. Keep her on the opposite side of the camp. We'll take shifts watching her, too." I hear a few grunts indicating that they're following his orders, and then a pair of ungodly-sized hands grab me. They must belong to that ogre with the ridiculously beautiful blond hair and snow-colored skin. He's entirely too savage, too large, to be considered human.

The sack is unbearably hot, and I kick out against the man's firm grip. "Take it off! I can't breathe! Take it off now!"

His hold tightens. He must be waiting for Braizen to decide. Mercifully, someone pulls the sack from my head. It's now dark. My hair sticks to my cheeks, and sweat beads across my face from my forehead to my lips. The cool air feels like a miracle against my skin. For the first time in my entire life, I give thanks for the cold.

Still firmly in the giant's grasp, I survey my surroundings as best I can. We're camped at one edge of a large clearing, a rough meadow of sorts, surrounded by trees. A tall, thick canopy of leaves hovers over us. The night air is filled with the smells of wet grass and pine. We must be deep in the Florian Wood. A bright moon casts silver rays, and when I look down, I meet a severe stare from a familiar pair of ice-blue eyes. Braizen.

Still every bit as handsome. His brown curls are longer now and wildly unkempt, his eyebrows much thicker, and he sports a light stubble of facial hair. His eyes are the same. Glacial, a frost-bitten blue that pierces my very core.

Never breaking my gaze, I shake my head and spit, reminding myself that this isn't the boy from my childhood memories. He's Verdana's enemy. He and his entire line are snakes, and no amount of attractiveness or jarring stares will ever make me forget this. I can't forget this.

"What do you want me to do with her?"

The giant's huge palms are wrapped snugly around my waist. Even as I stare down Braizen, I wonder what they feed people in Baelliles to produce such a monster. Braizen finally looks away.

"Tie her up over there. Make sure she has a blanket. The wind's growing stronger; the cold will likely come tonight," he says.

"Tie me up? You can't be serious!" But I'm already being carried away as I speak. We pass a dark-haired woman gathering rope from her satchel.

She begins to wrap it around my body. "As if the tethers around my wrists aren't enough!" I hiss back at Braizen. "Are you going to bag my head again while I sleep?"

He smiles lightly. "Your face is fine; it's your mouth that seems to be the trouble." He whistles and the woman who's now tying my feet looks back at him. She nods, then pulls out her knife and cuts away a strip of her tunic.

"*Again?* Seriously?" I shout. Without a word, she shoves the gag into my open mouth and uses a short piece of rope to hold it in place.

I curse vehemently, but my anger and words are as useless as my attempts to speak. I need to concentrate on not gagging. Torrent, the giant, laughs at me. Glowering, I shoot him a dark look.

His eyes flash wide. "She's a feisty one, huh, boss?"

Braizen looks at his friend sharply, then chuckles. "Even more so than I remember." For a fleeting moment, he seems almost forlorn. Then one of his men strides toward him and offers him a drink. Instantaneously, he's back to broad smiles and cocky laughter. He doesn't look at me again for the rest of the night.

My stomach growls as I toss and turn, trying to find comfort on the hard ground. The coarse woolen cloth Torrent threw over me falls to one side, and I can't pull it back up because I'm tied up like cattle. Braizen was right about the cold. I'm in a frozen daze despite my struggles. I've grunted and produced dozens of muffled pleas to whichever guards are on watch, and they've all blatantly ignored me. Some even mocked me.

"Pretty princess isn't used to the dirt now, is she?" "What's the matter, Your Highness? No servants to answer your every beck and call?"

Others opt for shorter insults. I hear that I and all Verdana are the enemies of Baelliles. That my people deserve an icy death for the suffering we've caused.

How moronic these brigands truly must be to believe such lies. Twelve years ago, Baelliles started the current war, the latest in the centuries-long conflict that brings our kingdoms nothing but pain. They solidified a barbaric course that no diplomacy could ever change. They're monsters, all of them. And their rulers, the Brader line, are the worst of all.

Braizen must be deep in the woods that lie across the clearing. He replaced Lorna about an hour ago, and I suspect he won't return for a while. Torrent and his friend are watching me now. The friend is called Lin. Or Speck. I'm not sure.

They whisper to each other, laugh every few minutes, and then gaze at me only to laugh harder. I hate feeling so weak. How much weaker are these people, though? There must be ten of them and only one of me, and yet, they act as if I'm an entire army by myself. I straighten my shoulders against the rough ground. I shuffle again, and the cover completely drops away. I groan and curl my fingers underneath me. Gathering strength, I flip myself onto my side, push my rear back, then thrust forward. I inch along like a pitiful worm, determined to get the blanket. The men are now howling, but I don't care. I'm enraged, and I'm cold. I inch further… further. I touch the cloth.

My fingers stop as I hear a distant crack. I arch my head and peer past the firelight, past the clearing, and towards the distant dark tree line. The trees stand silent and still. The men continue to hurl insults my way. I squint into the dark for a long moment but don't hear anything. I lower my head, trying to relieve the pressure on my neck. Once again, I contort myself in my vain attempt to cover myself. I concentrate all my will on my fingers.

Another crack. This time it echoes across the far tree line. Jolting my head back up, I see Lin and Torrent stand, immediately alert. Lorna shifts, and her eyes slowly open.

"Think it's lightning?" Torrent asks Lin, who's pulling his crossbow into place.

"Never heard any lightning like that. Wake the others."

It's the dead of night. My breaths are now labored and not from my efforts to retrieve the blanket. Waking the others means they're worried. Which means I should worry.

Torrent quickly begins to shake his comrades from their slumber. I grunt and try to make as much noise as possible by shifting my body on the ground. What if there's danger? Am I to lie here with no means to defend myself?

Lorna yawns, lifts herself, then drapes a lazy arm over one knee. "What's that?" she asks, rubbing her eyes with her free hand. "Sounds like the sky's splitting. See anything?" she asks Lin, who's circling with his bow aimed.

"No. Nothing. Nothing from Braze either…"

"*Get up*!" A shout rings in the distance. "*Everyone up*! We need to move *now!*"

I crane my neck and see Braizen galloping towards us across the clearing and away from the dark tree line. Frenzy breaks loose as the bandits curse, grab saddlebags and satchels, and brandish their weapons. I scream, but no one can hear me through this cloth or over their whines. I lash out like a living scourge in a futile attempt to be noticed.

Now others emerge from the woods, whipping their steeds as if they can't run fast enough from whatever lies behind them. My breath hitches as a rolling black mist breaks out from the trees. Are Braizen and his bandits outrunning a fire? Panic sweeps through me as I see the two riders nearest the trees swallowed by the vapor and hear their screams cut short. A sick dread grows alongside my panic as another rider is taken, and then another. In the strange glow from the tree line, I see that it's a sentient shadow, a mist that seeks to devour.

Lin unleashes an arrow. It glides into the mist, and we watch it shred. "Oh, that's not good," he says.

Torrent races past him straight towards the onyx cloud and braces himself before bellowing a barbaric cry.

Now almost in the camp, Braizen waves his hands above his head, shouting. "No, go back! Retreat! Torrent! We can't fight it!"

Tears stream down my cheeks as the horror unfolds. The dark mist engulfs another rider, and I know this will also be my fate. I can't move. I can't run. I can't even speak a prayer aloud to the Lady and the Guard.

I'll die in this obsidian murk, a captive of these Baellilean crooks, and I'll die unheard.

Chapter Five

Braizen

Present Day

I splash my face with cold water from the small stream that flows in an intricate web between the tangled nettles and briars. We've patrolled for more than an hour now, and I know some of my band are already tired.

Braxton dips his head low to take small sips from the stream. I pat his flank in approval. He's barely rested over the last week and yet, has stayed obedient and true. Perhaps Torrent's outlandish beliefs that animals are better than most people contain some truth. They're better than Verdanians, at the very least. Marian and Godie, a pair of friends who joined us last year, lean against a nearby tree and gossip quietly in the dark. Despite their dropped voices, I overhear most of their conversation. They are speaking of *her*. Idalia.

"I didn't expect her to be that good-looking," Godie admits. "You hear such foul things about Verdanians, you know? I half expected her to look like a dog."

Marian laughs softly. "Agreed! And did you see how quick she was with that blade? Poor Dasin! Thwarted by a princess! Could you have ever imagined?"

"She wasn't going to give up; I'll say that much. She only stopped because of what Braze said! Did you catch her expression when she saw his face? It's as if she saw a dead person!" Godie pops a piece of dried meat into his mouth, then tears off more for his friend.

"Well, apparently, she *did* try to kill him all those years ago," Marian says. "My friend from home has spoken to a castle servant who was there, and he said that when the gods cast their curse, the Princess rushed Braze and tried to kill him! Right then and there!"

Godie grunts. "Gods damn Verdanians. A nasty lot, all of them."

I slide my hand over Braxton's leg and sigh. I buried the memories of that day deep enough, never again to be unearthed. At least, I thought I had. But when I saw her, every detail of our time spent resurfaced. The way I felt when I first laid eyes on her, and she stared at me for far too long. The way we danced so slowly together, and…

I laugh softly, and Braxton briefly pauses. Perhaps the cold water didn't do its job of shaking off my grogginess. We were children. And we felt things the way children feel things. Exaggerated, overwhelming feelings that were not based in anything real.

I watch the water glide by and remember. I was a thirteen-year-old boy with nothing more than an infatuation for a girl I thought would be my bride. It's possible my memories aren't the truth. Maybe the servant Marian's friend spoke to has a clearer recollection of what happened. It is likely that Idalia *was* involved in her father's plan, and that she did try to kill me. Verdana was—and is—still desperate. It's not hard to believe that they'd do something drastic. End everything, just to see us fall with them. They still want this.

"Did you hear that?" Godie's voice is sharp. I walk in the direction he's facing. The tree branches no longer sway in the wind. Everything stands eerily still. Braxton backs away from the stream and paws the ground. I run back and grab his bridle, bring his head down, and hold his nose beneath my palm.

"What is it, Brax?" I whisper. His eyes gleam in the moonlight, and he bucks his head. Now I hear it too—one of my men, Klark, crying for help.

I hoist myself into my saddle, kick lightly, and we head in the direction of the cry. "What is it?" I shout. "State your position, Klark! Is it Verdanian troops?"

A shrill shriek of wind whips through the trees. More silence.

"Braze! Help!" Another desperate cry, this time Franden, but from a different direction. I pull on the reins, and Brax trots in a tight, confused circle.

"Franden!" I yell, recognizing the voice. "Where are you? What do you see?!"

Again, silence. A nasty chill lances up my spine.

If it were Verdanian troops or bandits, I would've heard something. *Anything.*

But the silence is too loud. Too strange. I bring my thumb and finger to my mouth and send a loud whistle into the night. Furthest from me but still in sight, Regan, a young woman of nineteen, draws her blade and faces the trees.

"Can you see anything?" I cry, but she doesn't respond. Her sword is shaking, and she turns quickly to face the rest of us and screams. Before the echo of her scream ends, an inky pall of mist rolls over her and engulfs her in its darkness, then spits out her bloody limbs from its sable mouth.

My heart drops. This is no enemy we've ever faced. "Retreat to camp! Go, now!" I command. Whatever is here, in the thick of the Florian Wood, we have no business introducing ourselves.

"What about Franden and Klark?" Godie shouts as he mounts.

"Whatever that is, it's already claimed them. If we search for them, it will surely take us next." I sigh heavily, then clench my jaw.

Godie's shoulders droop, but he nods and kicks his steed's sides. Marian joins him, and they gallop away from Regan's body and towards a break in the trees.

I follow and swoop my head back to see what's left of our band. Four or five riders appear on the rutted path. Leaning down to Braxton's ear, I instruct softly, *"Fly."*

His hooves kick up dirt as we race towards camp. Braxton passes Godie and Marian with ease. Together, we'll guide the others back to the camp.

I slip an arrow from my quiver and turn in the saddle. With one swift pull, I release it into the menacing blight. My panic rises as the black haze splits the iron tip from the wood. What sorcery breathes in these woods? We were warned, and I've seen what the gods can do, but this black shroud of evil is something I can't comprehend.

Desperate screams pierce the air as the mist rips apart another rider. I don't look back. I force myself to focus only on what lies ahead.

We finally break through the trees, and across the clearing, I see our camp's flickering fire. Torrent's massive body plows towards us; the wind flings away his shouts. Lin is close behind him. He fires one of his bolts, and watching his reaction, I know he's seen it destroyed by the malevolent force behind me. I drop my reins and wave my arms as Torrent continues to charge. The bastard believes he can take on whatever this is with his bare fists.

"No! Go back! Retreat, Torrent! We can't fight it!"

His face elongates in fear. He must've seen the mist take another rider. More leg pressure, and Braxton gallops even faster. Torr turns to run alongside me. "Grab the girl!" I yell down at him. No matter who else makes it out of here alive, she must. All those who've been taken can't die in vain. I see Lorna cut our horses loose before she mounts her own.

As I approach Lin, I lean down and extend my hand, which he grabs. I swing him onto Braxton and gripping my waist, he steadies himself behind me.

"What in the four hells is that?" he shouts into my ear.

I keep applying pressure, willing Brax to run faster. I've no idea what this unholy terror behind us is, and I'm not stupid enough to want to find out.

Torrent grabs Idalia and runs at full speed, even with her in his arms.

Lorna sees Torr and pulls on her mare's mane to slow her pace. When Torr is close enough, she leans down. Torr grabs her arm and leaps onto her mount. Once he's secure, Lorna stands on her mare's back and leaps onto another horse galloping away from our camp. She lands gracefully, digs her heel into its side, and yells a command. We're now riding abreast, five riders and three horses escaping across and into unknown territory. Don't look back, I remind myself.

The sinister force crawls toward us, but I won't encourage it. We must ride as fast and as far as our horses can stand. The Florian Wood is home to many mysteries, and I'm sure we just faced one.

The black fog. The Obsidian Mist.

The sun teeters on the horizon, and I've sensed that Braxton is near collapse for many miles. I can only imagine the exhaustion the lesser mounts must feel. For the first time, I look behind me.

A heavy release of tension rushes through me when I see nothing but dark green leaves and tree trunks glowing in the early morning light. The insidious murky darkness is gone. *For now*, I think. I pull back on the reins and signal a stop. Braxton almost collapses, and I leap off before his knees drive towards the ground.

We care for our mounts as best we can. These horses saved our lives. Lorna leans in close to her mare, whispering her appreciation. Lin walks a few steps into a small clearing and begins to gag, then vomit. Torrent still has Idalia tucked under one arm. She's sobbing, from what I can hear. At least he took the gag from her mouth.

"Is anyone hurt?" I call, inspecting the trees behind us. Everyone but Idalia shakes their head. Then I hear it clearly. I whip my neck around to face her.

Idalia isn't crying; she's laughing.

Lorna, Lin, and Torr gaze at her as if she's gone mad, but I manage a wry smile. I remember this about her. She's a princess who laughs at inappropriate times and when she doesn't know what else to do.

Torr unceremoniously drops her. He races between our horses, holding their muzzles between his giant palms. He appears to sense how hard this journey was for them. Despite their exhaustion, they relax in the sunlight at his touch.

"What can we do for them?" Torr asks in a low voice.

I know his heart aches for them, and I can't bear to tell him there's nothing we can do but let them rest. The horse won't survive long without water or food.

"Everyone empty your packs; let's see how much we have," I say. No one had time to collect our larger supplies, but we must have a few items we could survive on.

We look at the small pile: a few pieces of dried meat, some apples, many daggers, and the small mirror Lin keeps wrapped in a soft cloth. Like Lin, it's come in handy. When I first saw it, I teased him about his vanity until he immediately caught the sun's rays with it and set the leaves at my feet aflame.

A far greater concern sharpens the ache in my chest. Eleven of The Cloaked fell to the Obsidian Mist. Only four of us stand in a circle with Idalia. I stifle a hot breath and brush the end of my nose with my thumb.

"We'll take a short rest, and then we'll look for water. If we can get the horses water, they'll have a better chance of survival," I say. I reach deep into my pocket and feel the crumpled map. Thank the gods.

Everyone agrees except Idalia. She's stopped laughing and carefully looks at each horse with a worried frown. The animals' fate and the night's horrors have worn at her face, but she's still beautiful. Unfortunately.

"So, I guess the childhood tales are true," Lorna sighs, dropping onto her haunches. "I mean, we know the gods possess magic, but these woods… and *that*…"

Lin exhales loudly. "These damn trees could give the Lady and the Guard a run for their money. *That* was pure evil, a blanket of darkness. Cold and unremorseful." His body shakes, and he flings his hands away from him. "Scariest thing I've seen in my life."

"Braze," Torrent cuts in, looking pointedly at me. He says nothing else, but his gaze conveys everything. I nod, and he turns to the others. Their mouths pull into a straight line before they nod back.

Torr steps into the center of our circle and looks up to the trees. He clears his throat and begins to sing:

"Oh, Brethren, the sun has burned out,

and the stars are shining bright.

Brighter they may still when you join them tonight."

Torrent uses the back of his wrist to wipe away a rogue tear that drops down his cheek. His voice resonates; its low tones carry the words miles away with the rolling wind. I struggle to hold back my tears. I knew this mission would be difficult, but to lose so many, so soon.

"The ship to the Great Lands is leaving,

So, Sister, climb aboard.

And be granted safe passage by the Guard and his Sword.

To the Lady, she waits for you; all sorrows be healed.

And may you finally find rest behind her mighty Shield."

As the last word lingers in the air, I place a hand on my chest, bring it down slowly in front of me, then raise it to the sky. The others do the same as we honor those taken from us. Anger stains Lorna's face. Lin wipes tears, and Torrent's head hangs low, his chin facing the ground.

She watches me. I sense her stare more than see it. Her hand isn't raised; she doesn't care to pay tribute to our dead. I finally meet her eyes under their furrowed brows.

Her stare is a threat. Her glare, a warning.

"So, what are we going to do about food?" Lin asks, taking a sip of water from the pond we found nearby. I fill my leather pouch and scan the curtain of trees.

"What we have will only last us a day or so. We need to find the nearest village. Then we can plan."

"*Village*?" Torr mocks, laughing at his own words. "You think we'll find anyone anywhere in this haunted death trap?"

Lin nods in agreement, sipping more water from his cupped hands before answering.

"I hate to admit it, but the blubbering buffoon is right. Your map doesn't show any sign of civilization within these trees. Besides the army outposts on the Verdanian border, there are only the bandit camps near the river; nothing else."

Torr grunts in displeasure, but Lin resumes. "And save for our horses, I haven't seen one creature; there's nothing to hunt in these woods. If a village exists, the people must only eat plants."

"Even if this place *did* have creatures, I wouldn't risk eating one," Torr says. "Who knows? What looks like an innocent bunny could turn into a man-eating goblin." He strokes his thick beard and grimaces.

I take a final pull and swish the tepid water around my mouth. They're right. I haven't seen one animal since entering The Wood. Perhaps the mist devoured them, too. Or maybe something worse happened.

"What about the girl?" Torr shoots me a grin. "Does the curse still count if we roast her up first?"

"That's disgusting and shameful, Torrent. Even for you," Lin groans.

Torr shoots up his hands and shrugs. "What? The King can't pay any coin to a bunch of starved corpses in the woods! I was only giving you an option, that's all."

"That option is called cannibalism, you idiot."

"That would suggest that girl is human. She's not. She's Verdanian, Lin. Which means she's more of an animal than the stray dogs we feed back home."

"There's only one filthy dog here," he scoffs and rolls his eyes.

Torr slaps Lin's back with such force that he barrels forward.

"Don't worry, little Speck. I'll use you as the toothpick when I'm done."

The two begin to punch each other, and as much as I want to enjoy the show, I can't. Not yet. Not with so much uncertainty and our very lives hanging in the balance.

"My father told me many stories about The Florian Wood," I say calmly, rising to my feet. The two quit quarreling and turn toward me. "Some stories are about the tribes that live here. The Tribe of Black, the

Tribe of White and the Tribe of Brown. Then, there's the Tribe of Many Colors. Heretics, my father calls them."

Torr spits a wad of saliva on the ground. "Color-coded tribes? In a haunted forest where no animal dares to live? Braze, this is a little hard to believe."

"No less believable than gods who curse kingdoms and mist that eats flesh." I counter back.

Lin's brows shoot up, and he nods. He knows I'm right.

Torr shakes his massive head. "It's *because* of that mist that I can't believe it," he says. "You mean to tell me there are multiple tribes that have survived it for this long?"

"Well, *if* the childhood stories of the tribes are to be believed, most horrors of the Wood come out at night. Maybe the tribes have found a way to outrun them. We did."

Torr contemplates, then says, "Even if what you say is true, and tribes do roam these lands, what then, Boss? How many days will you have us search to find them? How long can we go without food before you lead us back home?"

I run my hand through my hair. "The journey home takes several days. Even if we start now, we'll be too weak to make it. Our best chance is to find a village."

"Or a noble," Lin says so quietly I almost don't hear him.

"What?"

Lin crosses his arms. "I said we could rob a noble."

"A noble? Here? Guard almighty, Braze. I think we've lost him for good. His small body couldn't keep up with his insanity," Torrent mocks, flipping a long lock of hair from his face.

Lin glares at Torrent. They appear on the verge of another quarrel.

"Lin, what do you mean?" I ask slowly.

His eyes flare in anticipation of sharing his idea. "I didn't mention it before because it means trekking dangerously close to the Deep Kingdom's border. And with the Princess with us, I didn't want to risk any of their troops rescuing her. Or anyone possibly recognizing Braze."

"Spit it out, Speck." Torrent grunts impatiently.

"Before we left, someone in the Smoky tavern shared that Tawdrey Lannex would be traveling from Aeradian to Verdana through the Florian Wood in five days. I only half-listened because we weren't going to be anywhere near Aeradian. But after our all-night ride, we must be near their border. And the time is right. The real question is why Lannex would take the Florian route? Why not just send a messenger to brave the river? Baelliles doesn't prevent Aeradian's people from crossing our border. We do, however, always check what they carry with them. So, if Lannex opts to travel through the Florian Wood, then…."

"He must be carrying something incredibly important," I finish for him.

"What's more, he'll have food! And alcohol! We're saved!" Torr cheers. He picks up Lin and swings him around.

Lin pushes against him and turns his face away. "I still say it's easier to eat the horses," he grumbles.

At that, Torrent stills. He then heaves a frustrated breath and tosses Lin into the pond.

"You idiot!" Lin screams as he flails in the water. "We're in the Florian Wood, you empty-headed barbarian! Who knows what lurks in here? Twenty-foot snakes, a squid with blades for tentacles! Leviathans!"

"Let's all pray at least one of those swims in there! If not, I'll jump in and finish you off myself," Torr jests, brushing his hands together in satisfaction.

"I'm going to grab Lorna; you two try not to kill each other," I announce. Neither hears me. Lin is too busy shouting curses, and Torr is too busy laughing at them.

As I swing around a tree, I stop short. A voice. No, a siren's call comes from my left. It sounds like angelic harp strings plucked by the Lady herself. I duck under a limb and nimbly sneak from tree to tree until I'm close enough to see her. I stay hidden, press firmly against the bark, and peer around the trunk.

Idalia runs her fingers through the ends of her long hair; her legs are crossed over to the side as she sings. I have heard the song, though I am not familiar with the words. It's a hymn chanted to bless the dead.

Her voice flows like a soft current of honey. Sweet, smooth, and soothing all ailments. I can barely stand it. Why should the holies bless her, a Verdanian, with such an instrument? *A Verdanian.* The traitors of both the Lady and the Guard.

Her voice trails upwards, hitting octaves that not even our finest choirs could match. It would be a lie to say I'm not awed by the sound. It would be an even greater lie to say it doesn't also bring me an elusive peace. She turns her head slightly, revealing her profile. Such a delicate face, such creamy, unblemished skin. Her hair drapes around her high cheekbones. She was Lady kissed; that much is undeniable. Her beauty knows no bounds and her voice…

Gods damn that voice. Gods damn that face, and gods damn that woman. I shake myself from her spell and turn to leave. My foot snaps the first twig it lands on.

She whips her head around and immediately spots me. Her doe-like eyes, soft and enchanting only seconds before, instantly harden. She grabs her skirts into her fists and stands.

"Spying on me now, are we?" That entrancing voice is gone. In its place is her insufferable, insolent tone. She lifts one brow and waits for my answer.

I manage a chuckle and mirror her stance. "Oh, don't humor yourself, Sparrow. Spying would require having something worthy to watch. I was looking for Lorna, who wasn't supposed to let you out of her sight. Where is she?"

"Why? Afraid I might run away into The Wood I know nothing about? Do you think I'm a fool?"

"Yes, actually. I do. I'm so glad we had this talk." I turn to go.

"Lorna is right over there; she's making a shrine of sorts. For The Cloaked." She points to her left.

"See, Sparrow? Is it really so hard to answer simple questions?"

"Is it really so hard to use your own eyes? Tell me, Prince, do you often rely on others to do *everything* for you?"

I sigh heavily. "I'm finding it extremely difficult to believe you can play nice for even a moment."

She tucks a curl behind her ear. "I'm finding it extremely difficult to believe you can wipe your own ass."

A laugh escapes me but stops when I notice her surprise. She now knows she's brought me an ounce of joy; this is a betrayal to my own that I won't soon commit again.

"I'm going to retrieve Lorna," I say. "You stay there and continue to pay homage to The Cloaked while I do so."

Her head rears back. "I'm not paying homage to those *scoundrels*. If anything, I should sing to celebrate their deaths! They deserve what happened to them."

My jaw clenches at her slanderous words.

She sits, crossing her legs as before and doesn't look at me when she says, "I was paying respect to *my* fallen, lest you've already forgotten the many souls who met their untimely end at the hands of your people."

I'm tempted to throw a disparaging comment, but I won't waste time arguing with the enemy. That's all she is, I remind myself. The enemy—a poison.

If she can't touch my skin, I won't give her the satisfaction of getting underneath it.

Chapter Six

Idalia

It's growing dark, and we haven't moved. I thank the Guard for the small pond and its water, but my stomach growls violently, desperate for even a crumb. We've already eaten the small bit of food that the bandits had in their saddlebags. And Torrent divided up the apples he had between the horses. I've scoured the shrubs, the trees, and even the dirt path for anything remotely edible. A berry, a nut, even an insect of some kind. Anything to stop raging hunger, but there's nothing. The Wood produces nothing good. Its trees harbor no food, only evil. I'm to starve with the robbers. The gods were right; Braizen will be my undoing.

Earlier, when Braizen left in search of Lorna, I considered running. I might have if not for my palms beginning to burn. Heat crawled through my limbs when I thought about taking the first step. When I discarded the thought, the heat faded.

It's a heat I'm growing all too familiar with.

It was strong when the bandits attacked my carriage and again when the mist attacked. It's the same heat I felt when we were children, in the aviary when I thought Lachlan was hurt.

Whatever this sensation is, something about Braizen causes it to flare. Along with other more tantalizing sensations, it stands as one more reason to hate him.

That, and I'm now tied to a tree, as he directed an hour ago. He's yet to send one of his lackeys to release me. I'm convinced the Baellilean Prince leads a cult of fanatics. An imbecilic cult with a thirst for the insane. He likes to tempt fate and ignore rules, and I'm nothing but another lock he craves to pick open. A door whose knob he cannot turn.

The four huddle far enough away that the wind muffles their voices and makes their words unintelligible. I watch Braizen draw lines in the dirt with a stick. Is it a map? A route? Every so often, one of them turns their head to check that I'm still here. Yes, I'm still captive, still helpless, still tied to a damn tree. *I hate Baellileans.*

"Now, how in the four hells will that work?" Lin finally blurts loud enough for me to hear.

Lorna's eyes skirt over to me, but I pretend to struggle with the rope, too occupied to give a damn about what they're doing. She squints hard at me, then looks back to Lin, clutching his hair.

"He'll never go for such a stupid plan! Torrent can't play that character," Lin says.

"And why not?" I hear the burly man's haughty question just as clearly.

Lin throws up his hands. "Because it requires Lannex to be dumb enough to believe it! No noble will think *this* obtuse whale is someone of worth."

"Braze, maybe you should be the one he stops for," Lorna suggests.

"He knows Braizen," Lin shoots back. "They've met before."

"Well, either you or Torrent play the part, and I don't think Lannex will find you intimidating enough without your weapon," Lorna states.

"What's that supposed to mean?" Lin demands.

"It means that he might mistake you for a child, Speck. Why don't you leave the big roles to the big boys?" Torrent sneers.

Lannex. Tawdrey Lannex. One of Aeradian's highest noblemen. They're planning to meet him somewhere. I'm elated that they've all forgotten to whisper. As subtle as possible, I lean my head closer. What on earth do they want with Lannex, and why would they seek to intimidate him?

"All the roles are of the utmost importance," Braizen intervenes. "We need everyone to play their part perfectly if we want this to work. If Lin's right, then tomorrow, Lannex should be right around here," he says and points to a spot in the dirt.

"That's where Torrent and Lorna will flag him down. Lin, I need you to stay at a high vantage point. Somewhere you can unleash your wrath from, should we require it," he continues.

"Gods, I wish I had my rock sacks," Lin mumbles, almost too low for me to make out his words.

"Then, *Lorna* will create a distraction of some kind. That's when I'll grab whatever I can from the transport. We need a big one this time, Lorna. Something to draw him away from whatever he's hiding. I can't be seen." The Prince instructs.

"What about his men, which I'm sure he'll have?" Lorna contests. "Am I to try and distract them all? By myself?"

"That's a death sentence if things go awry," Lin cracks.

Torrent scratches his head. "So, when Lorna distracts all the men, that's when I assist you? Or do I wait?"

"Torrent could help me distract while you and Lin do the plundering," Lorna suggests.

Braizen rubs his eyes. "I need someone to be the lookout. We can't afford things to go sour and not have someone on higher ground. Besides, Lin isn't good at stealing. We know this."

"Well, I can't afford for things to go sour when I'm distracting an entire fleet of men all by myself with only my hatchet. Better Lin proves himself a pitiful thief than me becoming a dead one," she bites out. Even from my vantage point, I see her brows slant towards the bridge of her nose.

"I should do the stealing, Braze should be the lookout, Lin and Lorna do the distracting," Torrent says. He rests his hands on his hips and smiles.

"You idiot," Lin snaps. "The lookout must remain by the Princess! Braizen can't be that close to her. It must be one of us, and I say it should be Lorna. Then, I'll do the distracting, and you two can do the stealing."

"How would you distract them? You think that if things go bad, you'll clean them all out with your big crossbow?" Torr snickers. "We all know that I'm the only one who could take them all on and live to tell the tale."

I almost cough, trying to stifle the scathing words that threaten to spill off my tongue. What an absolute mess they are. I wonder if I'm the first kidnapping they've managed to pull off, and I'm instantly filled with shame. Gods, I hope not. I can't stomach the thought of all those Verdanian soldiers dying at the hands of these feeble first-time kidnappers.

They break their circle and pace in different directions while shouting at each other. They no longer try to hide their plan. Or lack thereof.

"We don't even know if he has men with him!" Lin huffs, poking Torrent's chest.

The giant grabs hold of his smaller colleague's wrist. "We don't know that he doesn't!"

Lorna slaps her palms to her cheeks and lowers herself to rest on her haunches with a groan. "We need more people," she says. "The four of us will kill each other before any nobleman gets the chance." They continue to shout over each other.

"Look, Lorna can be on the lookout. I'll leave her my bow, and she'll give me her hatchet. Then—" Braizen is immediately cut off.

"What? I'm not giving you Nedson!"

"*Nedson?* Oh gods, Lorna, don't tell me you named your weapon!"

"Why shouldn't she? I've named my sword! Brazard!" Torrent bellows.

"Brazard? What in the four hells—"

"Okay, what if Torrent is the lookout, Lin is the distraction, and Lorna and I…"

"I don't understand why Braze isn't the distraction! He's a handsome devil. Maybe Lannex will be smitten by him," Torrent says, folding his stocky arms over his chest.

"We already explained why, you massive twit! Lannex has met Braizen; he'll recognize him, and all will be over!" Lin jabs back, shaking a finger under Torrent's nose.

"Well, then why don't we just lay waste to them? I don't understand why we're doing all this pretending anyway."

"We don't lay waste to nobles, Torr. We *swindle* them."

"Oh? Then how did we get her?" Torrent points to me. "By *swindling* those guards?"

"That was different!"

"How so!?"

"They were Verdanians. They're already our enemies! We aren't trying to make more!"

I can't stand it one moment longer. Their shouts, their petty jabs, their incomprehensible planning. I clear my throat and yell from the tree.

"Excuse me!"

They continue to argue and scream over one another. I shout louder this time.

"Hello! Listen to me! Over here!"

Nothing. These idiots won't stop. I murmur words that a lady would never deign to speak aloud and then cry out a final time.

"Oh, no! The mist! It's returned!"

At once, the quartet of bumbling imps falls silent. They form a tight circle and face outward, bracing themselves for imminent danger from any angle. They turn to me when they finally realize that the sun hasn't yet fully set and no baleful mist is barreling towards them.

I smile at their stupidity. Braizen puffs himself up as if to reprimand me, but I speak before he can open his mouth. "So, the rumors are false then? Baellileans *do* know how to shut their mouths. My father will be shocked to learn this!"

They're unamused. Lorna begins to stalk towards me, probably to shove more cloth down my throat.

I lean my head back against the bark and continue. "Not that I'll ever be able to tell him again, seeing as your atrocious plan will get us all killed."

Lorna pauses and turns her head back towards Braizen. His icy eyes lock in on me. A slight smirk pulls on his lips as though he won't give me the satisfaction of revealing an outright smile.

"Our atrocious plan?" He drawls, running a hand through his hair.

I can't stand his hair—those beautiful brown curls against his bronze skin. I straighten against the tree and beam at them.

"Unless what just passed was a theatrical piece you perform in pubs, and gods, for all our sakes, I hope it was. Because if not, whatever you're planning will surely fail."

Torrent steps forward and points his sword at me. "As a Verdanian, you must know *all* about failing, right? Well, forgive me if I don't give a rat's ass what you say about our plan."

"Not that we're planning anything in the first place!" Lin tries to recover, shooting a worried finger into the air. Lorna rolls her eyes.

"Fine," I huff. "Have fun dying if you like. But please, leave me tied to this tree. I think I'd rather take my chances with the mist."

Braizen spits on the ground and stares at me. His eyes gleam with curiosity. "Is this your way of feeling included, Sparrow?"

Lorna darts him a nasty look then flashes her green eyes at me.

I roll my neck and sigh. "This is my way of telling you that the only thing worse than starving, freezing, and dying in a black mist of carnage is listening to the four of you try and come up with a plan for one more minute."

Torrent's lip twitches.

"Especially a plan that will require five participants," I add with a charming grin.

Braizen's brows shoot up. "Five?"

"Five," I affirm.

"Tell me, Sparrow, do you suggest we search for another person to help us with our situation?"

"Yes, I suggest that. And, oh! Would you look at this! Right here in front of you, a person tied to a tree!"

"A *Verdanian* tied to a tree," he shoots back.

"Then the gods have truly granted you a great favor," I say and wink.

He shows his teeth. I hate that I like how he looks, even when he's wearing a false smile.

"So, what does the Little Sparrow have to add to our discussion? I'm dying to hear."

Lorna bounds forward. "Braizen, you can't be serious…"

He holds a hand up and signals. She stops.

His eyes devour me, and a savage heat runs rampant through my veins. I work to keep my face expressionless, unmoved, despite what my body tries to convince me of otherwise. I twist my wrists in discomfort.

"I'll be the distraction."

"What!?" Torrent rages and stalks past Braizen. "Braze, don't you dare humor this conniving little *bitch*! She's trying to trick us!"

My mouth tenses at the word, and Braizen notices.

He turns to Torrent. "Speak like that to her again, and I'll cut out your tongue," he says in a low growl.

Torrent stops, almost falling back on his heels. His hazel eyes fill with confusion.

"Boss?"

He's met with silence. "I only meant that, well… If she's the distraction, she'll just run away with Lannex. She'll betray us. Why wouldn't she?" Torrent is almost stammering.

Braizen doesn't answer; he only turns to study me again. "How will you distract them?"

His three companions all slump in disbelief, but I don't dare break his stare.

"I'm Princess Idalia of Verdana. I was on my way to visit Aeradian when your band…" Here I pause and let the full force of my disgusted glare sweep over them. "Your band so graciously postponed my trip. My father is well acquainted with Lannex. He loves our mountains."

"Ha! Now that's a lie straight from the four hells! No one enjoys those mountains!" Torrent barks.

Braizen ignores the comment; he appears perfectly content to rest his gaze on my face.

"If he sees me, it will prove enough of a distraction. But if I run..." I make my voice trail off in a question like I'm offering a solution to the world's most brilliant puzzle. Which I am. These oafs should now be able to see how this could work.

"Braizen, this is ridiculous," Lin cuts in. "Surely you aren't actually considering her desperate attempt to flee as a plan."

Braizen's eyes leave mine for a moment, and I use the release to catch my breath. He looks back at the others. "Too many times, you've all told me to pull rank, and I've never listened. We lost almost everyone in one day. We have no food or money. Our horses will die before our very eyes, and we will join them shortly after. We *are* desperate. We can sit here and argue and allow this Verdanian Princess to watch us slowly perish over the next few days because we're too proud to listen, or we can at least hear what she has to say."

Lin droops in defeat, and Lorna sucks on her teeth.

Braizen faces me again. "But they're right, Sparrow. I can't have you running away for Lannex to catch. I'm desperate, but I'm not dumb."

There are so many cruel rejoinders I long to voice, but I'm too hungry and too tired. And there's no time for games; the sun drops lower in the sky by the second.

"We stage a kidnapping," I say, jerking my chin towards Torrent. "He steals me *in front* of Lannex, then runs. The noble will be forced by honor to make sure I'm protected. He and however many men he has with him will have no choice but to retrieve me. I'll make sure of it."

Torrent stops grinding his teeth, which I take as a good omen. Braizen slowly scratches at the pricks of his stubble. I wait, still helpless against this gods damn tree.

"Well," Braizen finally breaks the silence and turns to his crew. "What do we think?"

"I think we'd be the stupidest bandits alive to trust a Verdanian. Especially one we've been holding hostage," Lorna hisses. She's been waiting to say this; I can tell.

"I agree," Lin mutters. "However, with Torrent holding her and how fast he runs… It could work."

"Torr?" Braizen asks, turning to his mightiest member.

The blond giant is openly trying to reel in his disdain, and his hard stare almost sizzles against my skin. Just as I think he'll spew some putrid hate against Verdanians, an unholy grin breaks across his face.

Braizen chuckles and offers in a low voice, "It could be fun."

The huge man's eyes glisten as he corrects his Prince. "Oh, it'll be more than fun."

Chapter Seven

Idalia

Nine Years Previous

My blade makes a nasty clang as it hits the stone floor. I hiss and bend to retrieve it, but my lungs heave, and my arms protest. Instead, I sit hard on my rear and swipe at the hair stuck to my sweaty forehead.

"Pick it up, Idalia. Quickly." My father orders from where he stands in the corner. I roll my eyes and shake my head.

"I can't. I'm too tired." I pant loudly to prove it.

He scoffs and rests his hands on his rounding belly. "Nonsense. Pick it up."

My blood boils, and I fling my head back to stare at the ceiling. "I'm tired, Father. We've been at this for hours! Perhaps, if you'd let me rest or eat…"

A rumble escapes his throat as he strides toward me.

He gestures to my opponent, one of the several stone-faced castle guards who rotate through my training sessions. "Give me your blade." The guard immediately obeys.

"Pick it up," he barks.

"Father…"

"I will bring this sword down on you in three seconds, Idalia. You will retrieve yours and fight me, or you will die." He raises the guard's weapon above his head.

My eyes widen. I look up at my father's hands, gripped firmly around the hilt, his fingers milky white from the effort.

The guard's expression doesn't change, and he doesn't move. I know he won't protect me if my father follows through on his warning.

"One."

I gaze at him. He wouldn't.

"Two," he drawls, his voice low and gritty. He breathes in, and I eye my blade, only a few inches away. His chest thrusts as he stabs the sword higher.

"Thr–"

I roll to my left, grabbing my weapon's hilt. I don't even have the chance to scramble up before my father swings the sword with his whole force. His blade crashes into mine. My gasp is more of a squeak as I stare at the sharp edges pushing against each other.

My eyes flick up to meet his satisfied grin.

He steps back, removing his weight from my sword. "Good," he says as he hands the blade back to the guard.

"Now that we know you are not, in fact, too tired to wield your weapon, we can continue." He saunters back to the corner.

"You were prepared to kill me," I blurt out. "You would truly kill me! Your daughter, your only heir! Are you mad?"

My father stiffens. When he's back in his safe little corner, he turns and answers. "You know why it is necessary, Idalia. Do not waste what little energy you have left on these sporadic emotions. Channel that energy into your training. Focus on the goal."

"And what goal is that, exactly?! To train until I die? Or to die as I train?!"

He laughs under his breath, but the sound doesn't convey humor. His stark eyes pierce mine.

"When the Braders murdered your mother, I swore to her—and to the gods—that I would protect you. That you would never be as vulnerable as she was. I swore to make you a woman capable of fighting for her life."

My father rarely brings up my mother or the circumstances of her death unless he's in a fit of rage. But I don't sense anger today.

His expression is colder than the winter winds roaring outside our castle walls.

"You complain of your long hours training here and on horseback because you do not understand their purpose."

I rise, letting my blade dangle, and it scrapes a hollow line along the floor. I rest the point on the ground and lift my chin.

"And what is this purpose that I do not understand?"

"I do not drive you this hard to build skills with a blade or strength in your body. What I desire to strengthen lies within. One day you will be Queen; you cannot afford to have a weak, undisciplined mind." He rivets his attention on me for a long silent moment before abruptly lifting his arm.

The guard immediately steps forward and raises his weapon.

I frown, then hoist my sword.

The guard's beady eyes don't betray an ounce of emotion.

As we parry, I catch a glimpse of my father. I've witnessed that satisfied expression before. At the stables, when someone succeeds in breaking a stallion.

A wild creature forced to obey.

Chapter Eight

Braizen

I wake to see the others already at work. Even Idalia is active, helping Lin move the horses to a shrouded cove of trees. Torr squats nearby and slides a wet stone against his blade; his cheeks are red, and his eyes heavy. Hunger pains him more than the rest of us. Lorna stretches her arms to the sky and spits. Dark circles rest under her emerald-green eyes. She watches Idalia, and I sense her displeasure. She's the most resistant to the plan, and can I blame her? We're half-starved, half-mad from our lack of rest, and reduced to accepting the help of a Verdanian—the Princess of Verdana, of all people.

Her. The reason my kingdom is still at war, and the one who can destroy us all. Yet I can't dwell on that cruel truth. If we fail today, we'll die in these woods. The black mist didn't return for us in the night, but it could have. No one truly slept. Each whistle of wind jerked me fully awake from a sleepy daze. Only when I glimpsed the sun's rim did I allow myself to drift off entirely.

"Look, our Prince! He lives!" Lorna taunts and smiles at me. "I see my prayers have gone unanswered."

Torr snorts, pressing the stone harder against his blade. I rub my eyes to shake the grogginess before realizing my futile efforts. I vigorously knead my head and squint up at my red-headed companion.

"Your jokes are even less funny when I'm hungry."

She shoots me a bleak stare. "Who says I'm joking?"

Torr rises, and his bones make an inhuman creak that only his body can produce. He pulls at the loose waist of his trousers. "Well, today's the day," he says, staring into the trees softly, almost mystically.

"The day for what, exactly?" Lorna asks, grabbing Nedson from her belt.

He flashes a toothy grin. "The day we either make history or the day we die trying."

"Robbing a noble blind is hardly making history, Torr. Especially for us," I laugh.

"I meant Baellileans working together with a Verdanian."

Lorna spits again, this time with more force. After wiping her nose on her sleeve, she pulls back her hair with a strip of leather.

"Speaking of the damned, I'd better make sure that worm hasn't killed Lin." She doesn't wait for a response before stomping towards the thicket.

"If she betrays us in any way, I'll slice her throat," Torrent says quietly. No twitching smile pulls at his mouth. No mischievous glint dances in his eyes.

I nod.

"Lin's in position," Lorna says as she nudges my rib and points. I follow her finger and see the flash from his mirror a few hills over before it's gone.

"Let's go through this one more time," I lean into our circle. Idalia doesn't join us; she stands behind Torrent, her arms folded against her chest, her face complacent.

"Remember, we only have one chance. Don't let our lack of food and sleep cloud your judgment. There'll be plenty of both after the deed is done." They all nod, including Idalia, to my surprise.

"Lorna and I will wait behind those bent trees. Once Lannex's carriage moves four trees past our spot, Sparrow will run out into the road."

I turn to her. "Now, this part is critical. We need you to really sell it," I say.

"You want me to sell the role of a Princess who's been kidnapped by uncouth hoodlums on her way to Aeradian? Oh, dear. However shall I pull it off?"

Torrent chuckles. I ignore her sarcasm and continue. "Torr, as soon as you see one sentry approach, run and grab her. Don't give the guards time to retrieve her or Idalia enough time to change her mind. Then, run like the Lady is calling you home at last."

"If you don't run fast enough, she just might," Lorna adds dryly.

Torr turns to give Idalia a long look, then nods his head. She doesn't acknowledge him.

"After Lannex leaves his carriage, Lorna will take out the coachmen, and I'll start loading the goods. Torrent, make them chase you for a long time. Tire them out. But don't wander off the trail we've set. Lin won't be able to help you if you go off course. He'll flash a signal if he sees something is wrong. Watch for that, too. We'll meet by the horses when it's all over and have a celebration drink. Or two."

"More like seven," Torrent winks.

The sound of men shouting and the rattling of carriage wheels on the bumpy dirt road reaches us, and we scatter like moths. Lorna and I soundlessly slip behind the warped trees and position our backs against their bark. We nod to each other and pull our hoods over our heads. Mine droops almost to my eyes, but it won't affect my aim; I'm used to the shadowy overhang. I ready an arrow; Lorna's palm squeezes her hatchet's handle.

The footsteps and shouts grow closer and louder—multiple guards. I curve my body around the tree to peek. Five men walk on either side of the carriage; likely, there's another, his right-hand guard, inside. None are on horseback, which momentarily baffles me. Is Lannex truly traveling this distance with only foot guards? I wipe the thought; no time for speculation.

Another glance at Lorna, and I tug the tip of my hood. Her powerful leg muscles flex as she readies herself to run. Her feet dig into the dirt.

We wait.

We wait longer.

The carriage and the soldiers, outfitted in Aeradian red, are now five trees past us.

Lorna grimaces, and she throws up an impatient hand. I shrug my confusion in return. Has the Little Sparrow already betrayed us?

Lorna jerks off her hood. "What do we do?" she mouths. "We've been tricked."

I release a huge breath and rub my palm down my face. Why did I trust a Verdanian? She likely ran off, and Torr is trying to decide whether to chase her or create a distraction himself.

My heart thuds.

No.

No, she hasn't forsaken the plan. She hasn't gone anywhere. *I can feel it.*

She's waiting for something.

A scream pierces the silence, and I lift myself onto my toes to look up the road. Idalia barrels out of the trees and throws herself into the arms of one of the foot soldiers.

"Help! I need help!" She shrieks.

He fumbles with her weight for a moment, then signals a stop. The guards gather around the Princess.

"What is the meaning of this?" Lannex pokes his head out the window and scans the woods.

Idalia shrieks again, and the nobleman flings himself from the carriage. He's a short man, apparently with an ego twice his size. He slides a hand over his balding head. "Lady and Guard, is that a woman!?"

"She says she's the Princess of Verdana, my lord."

"It cannot be so," he states. "She looks like a common whore! I know Princess Idalia to be the most handsome woman. Surely this cannot be her!"

He stalks over to Idalia, cups her chin, and pushes her head from side to side. Any moment now, Torrent will come blazing out. I breathe slowly and concentrate on Idalia's every movement.

"Please, Lord Lannex. I beg of you! Sanctuary! I claim sanctuary in Aeradian!" She sobs and flails her delicate hands in his face.

What were you waiting for, Little Sparrow?

One of her hands lowers to a guard's leg, and I see her pull it back with something she tucks beneath her cloak.

Her wails grow louder. "Take me to King Lachlan! I've been kidnapped by bandits! The Prince of…"

Torr bursts out of the woods, flourishing his sword with wild swings. The first sentry launches himself towards my friend, who, even in his worn, hungered state, does appear savage. Torr kicks, and the guard flies then slams into the ground. Torr opens his arms wide, growls like a wild beast, then grins at the guards.

"Well, don't just stand there, you fool!" Lannex cries. "Seize him!"

"Oh, yes. Please try," Torrent says with a low laugh.

Two guards rush him, but this is mere child's play. One fluid swing of his massive arm, and they fall backward with a sickening thud.

Torrent grabs Idalia by her waist and pulls her into his chest. She beats her fists against him and moans in anguish.

I'm unsure of how much of this is an act. Perhaps she believed that Lannex could have saved her, not that it matters now.

Torrent bounds onto the narrow trail, arrows whizzing past his ears. My bolt punctures an archer's shoulder, and he falls with a horrendous yelp. The six unharmed sentries scramble in pursuit, but Lannex remains by his carriage.

His eyes dart between his fallen men, and he hisses, "Stand! Stand you fools!" He kicks one with his boot, then walks over to the man with the pierced shoulder and kicks his ribs.

"Do you know what is at stake? King Ivar will not care about a box of flowers if we let his daughter be kidnapped! Stand and fight!"

The guard Torrent kicked rolls onto all fours and unsteadily braces himself on a knee.

"What if she's a delusion, my lord? The journal warned us of such things. A devil's mirage, she called them. Evil's fantasy."

"A devil's mirage *is* a mirage, you dimwitted fool! I held her face! Felt her skin and looked into her eyes! She is real! That is the Princess of Verdana."

A Devil's Mirage, another childhood tale.

"But what if it is the Dreaded? Or a follower? Didn't the King warn us of that?"

The nobleman lands another kick.

"I know what I saw!" Lannex yowls. "Go and find her! May The Wood kill you before you return without her!"

Wobbling, the wounded men run toward Idalia's rapidly fading screams.

"*Pssst,*" Lorna draws my attention back to her. "He isn't going with them! Now what?"

Any move now is better than no move. I make a fist and release two fingers. *Follow me.*

She slips between the narrow trunks until she's at my side.

Lannex paces by the carriage and then frantically knocks on the door. He doesn't appear anxious; he's angry. The door opens.

I throw up a hand, and we stop.

"What is the meaning of this!?" Lannex shouts into the carriage. "You told me you could assure us safe passage!"

Someone responds, but I can't hear them. The nobleman frantically shakes his head, and the veins at his temples protrude from his skin. "You think I care? You swore your premonitions would lead us safely. Tell me, then. How did you not foresee these events unfolding? Are your visions blinded by gruesome crooks?" There's no answer.

He places his hands on his hips and clicks his tongue sharply. "I want you out. Get out!" Silence.

He thrusts his head inside. I hear a scuffle, and he's pushed back out in a flash, blood gushing from his head, and lands on the road. He doesn't move.

I risk a quick look at Lorna, whose eyes are wide with fear. I wait a moment longer, and we make our way to the carriage.

Lorna's breathing quickens; panic roils in and between us. Whoever or whatever waits inside isn't afraid to kill a nobleman. What will they do to bandits?

There's still no movement or sound from the carriage. Lorna and I stand behind it now. I look down. Lannex's skull is cracked right down one side; thick blood still spurts from the crevice, and soft, pink matter seeps alongside it.

Lorna looks at me and grimaces a bit.

"*I think that's his brain*." She whispers.

I shush her, though my stomach is beginning to turn from the sight. Whoever did this is a threat greater than even Torrent. Stealthily stepping to the side of the carriage, I nock my bow, ready to release an arrow as soon as I'm in front of the door. Lorna creeps close behind, prepared to fling her hatchet should my weapon fail.

“Don’t move!” I yell. My right arm strains as I tug the bowstring back as far as it will go. I angle myself to face the threat and sense Lorna right beside me. I look straight at what’s prompted our dread, and my grip on my weapon loosens. I point my bow down as I rear back, and my face slackens into stupefied astonishment.

A short woman leans against the plush seat cushions and laughs in delight. She’s wearing a white ruffled blouse, a skirt of juniper green, and holds an apple in her hand. Her skin is darker than mine, and her body is quite round. Against one of her crossed legs leans a bloody mace, remnants of Lannex’s skull still attached to its spikes. Blood, still wet and now darkening, stains the floorboards. She calmly takes a bite of her apple and then turns to face us.

“You must be the gruesome crooks.” Her eyes are a strange meld of yellow and seafoam. She stares into mine and smiles so widely that two dimples pop into her ample cheeks.

“I’ve been waiting for you. I’m Nuri. Welcome to one of the four hells.”

Chapter Nine

Idalia

Torrent's wrists are jammed so hard into my ribs I want to cry. He hasn't adjusted his fierce hold since he began running. Part of me is impressed; a much larger part is annoyed and in pain. How am I to scream believably if I can barely breathe? Each bound of his massive legs ends with his feet crashing onto the dirt path; I'm yanked up and then slammed down.

"Scream louder, Verdanian!" He hisses.

I wish he could see me roll my eyes. I truly wish I could concentrate on anything other than the pain in my ribs or his strident breaths warming the back of my head.

I draw in what breath I can and manage another yell, this time louder. I pull on his arm in a desperate hope that he'll understand how hard his hold is making it for me to shout.

"Let her go, foul ogre!" One of Lannex's guards cries from behind us. His voice is far away, but the fact that I can still hear it means he's following the right path. Did I make a mistake in helping Braizen? Perhaps, but what choice did I have? I was sure to starve if I hadn't.

Torrent slows, which eases my pain, but I'm confused. He can't be exhausted; he's not even breathing heavily. A few paces later, he stops.

"What in the gods' names are you doing?" I hiss, craning my head to see if the guards have caught up to us. The giant sets me down, and I feel elation and fear as my feet hit the path. Is he releasing me? Is this some twisted joke?

The male stares down at me. "You stay here. I swear to the Guard himself that if you run, *you will die*."

I use this moment to catch my breath, then turn towards the oncoming guards. They're getting closer. Torrent stomps towards two trees a short distance off the path. I grab my head with both hands and bite my bottom lip in frustration. Does he *want* them to catch us?

Then I see it. A small deer tangled in a thorny vine. Its leg is bleeding, and its flanks heave as it desperately kicks against the thorns. The tall male slowly pulls a small dagger from his pocket.

"Hold still, little one," he whispers. "I'll have you free in no time."

The guards' shouts grow louder, and my breath hitches. At least four of them; I can now hear distinct voices. When they reach us, we'll die. *No.* This is only half true; they're not after me. They'll attack Torrent. I can run back to the carriage.

I sway a bit and plant my feet more firmly as I try to concentrate. If I run, Torrent will surely chase, then catch me before the guards even arrive. However, if I pick the right moment and sprint, I can meet the guards on the road and hide behind them.

"This way! Hurry!" One guard's voice carries even more now.

I slowly turn my head to watch Torrent, who's stroking the deer's cheek. The animal's round, dark eyes slowly blink at the man, a primitive sign of trust. My head tilts in awe as the massive man gently cuts through the thorny vine and then strokes the deer's wounded leg. For the first time, I see the large barbarian's expression soften. The deep, hard lines in his rough-hewn face are gone. He might even be a bit… *handsome?*

He smiles tenderly at the deer. This isn't the behavior of a brigand, a crooked thief. To stop for *anything* that could jeopardize his goal, let alone a mere animal. And then, my jaw falls open. *An animal! An animal in the woods!*

The deer is free, but it doesn't move; it only stares calmly into Torrent's face.

Torrent gently pats its head, then swivels to rush back to me. He falls flat, his chin smashing into the earth. The thorny vine that entrapped the deer twists around his ankles. Multiple vines shoot up around him and plunge across his body as I watch in horror. He can barely struggle; they hold him tight, and his strength has diminished after days of hunger.

The voices are so very close; the guards will round the curve at any moment, and I'll be saved. *I'm saved.* I'm truly saved!

Torrent's eyes meet mine.

"Please." He reaches his one free hand towards me.

My stomach flips. His usually proud or laughing eyes are pools of fear and loss. He knows he'll die, trapped against the earth. And he knows I'll be of no help. I gather what remaining strength I can and drop low to speak to him.

"I knew the gods would not forsake the Verdanians," I whisper sternly.

He sighs and grimaces as another spiny green rope latches onto his arm.

"May you finally find rest behind her mighty Shield," I say, then stand to face my rescuers. I start to shout for help, but my throat tightens. Something down deep is blocked. A heavy lump forms in my throat.

My hands begin to sear with heat. I groan, trying once more to release a shout. Nothing.

I only choke on the air.

I throw my palms up and vigorously shake them. Even if they can't hear me, the guards will surely see my wild movements. I run towards their voices, but the heat rises with each step. What is this? Another trick of The Wood? A call from the gods?

The closer I get to the men, the more furious the burning, until I can no longer bear it. I stop and look back at Torrent. The plant has almost completely covered him. His large fingers still move, stretching towards the help he knows will never come. I step towards him, and the heat lessens by the tiniest amount.

Another step, then another, until as I reach the bandit, my palms feel a blessed relief like they've been dipped in cool water. As I drop to the ground next to his free hand, the feeling in my palms is no longer pain but a beckoning, as if I am being directed by an unknown force. Terror threatens to choke me, but I scramble to unravel him from the nightmare vines.

I claw at the sentient plant, and it thrashes against me. Thorns cut into my hands and arms as I pull, trying to untangle the man. The vines slash at my cheeks, chest, and back, but I don't quit. I draw the short sword I stole off one of the guards from my cloak.

I swing at every long, twisted, curling piece of the hideous thing that also threatens to consume me. Finally, I reveal Torrent's mouth.

"My right arm!" His voice is weak, but I can see hope in his eyes. "Free my right arm!"

I saw away until I see his skin. His hand launches up, tightly palms his small blade, and he begins to stab his captor. He's now free except for the thickest bunch wrapped around his ankles. But we're too late.

The guards are speaking directly behind us. I lift myself and turn to face them. They stand in formation, except one, who races to me.

"Princess Idalia," he gasps. "Come with me! Let my men destroy this nasty beast and return you to safety!"

Something deep inside me warns me not to move. Something else implores me to collect on the promise of safety and continue my journey to Aeradian. The strongest part of me, the most overwhelming, demands that I fight.

I let the overwhelming part win.

I rush the guard and swing my blade down. It catches his shins, and he drops with a thud. The other men's faces contort in confusion.

A sound I don't recognize barrels forth from my throat as I clash my blade against that of another guard.

He swiftly parries, but my counter is faster. With an efficient circular motion, I disarm him. His eyes dart to his blade lying in the dirt, then flash to me.

"What are you doing, Princess?"

"I don't know," I admit, then swiftly send my blade towards him.

He doubles over and grabs his stomach. My hands flush with heat, but it's no longer pain; it now guides me.

Two other men approach from opposite sides.

I've trained with the King's Guards and faced off against my father, but I've never seen actual combat.

The wave of heat pulls me into a hunched position just as a guard swings mightily above my head. I tuck into a roll and shift inches to the right. I hear a grunt, and my ears ring with the dull thump of another blade as it lands heavily on the spot I'd barely moved from. It nearly sliced me in half.

I flip to my back and block the sword coming for my throat. Our blades clang, and the guard's face twists in fury.

"Traitorous whore!" He shouts, and his spittle sprays my cheeks.

I'm shaking and know I can't hold this position for much longer. I surrender to the power that compelled me to fight. I close my eyes, and my entire body listens. An intense force engulfs my legs, and I kick in a fluid motion.

My feet solidly connect with the man's knees, and he stumbles, allowing me enough space to push myself away and rise.

He grunts then advances. We parry, and I feel his skill and strength begin to outweigh mine. I can't last much longer in this fight. I won't…

A blade flies into the guard's throat, and blood splatters across my face.

He grabs the handle and chokes as he retracts the blade. His eyes veil over. Clutching his neck, he collapses to his knees, then slams face-first onto the path.

Torrent stands over him, a grizzled scowl ebbing from his face. He nods at me. A brief acknowledgment, a truce. He then braces himself to take on the seeming red avalanche of soldiers tearing towards us.

My arms are heavy. I know when, not if, the next guard attacks, I'll lose. I shift my weight to my heels and lift and hold my sword ready. I'm prepared to fight. And die. I mumble a swift request to the Lady and the Guard that they accept me into the Great Lands.

"And may my ancestors not shun me for dying while aiding dirty Baellileans, I add.

The remainder of the Aeradian guards charge, howling at the top of their lungs. Over their cries, I hear rapidly advancing hooves and creaking wood.

Lannex's carriage careens down the trail towards the soldiers, heading straight for us. Torrent and I gawk at each other. He swoops me up, and we hit the dirt with such force I cough in agony. He carries me a safe distance away and sets me down gingerly.

I stumble, push my hair away from my face, and view the carnage. The carriage has run over all but one of the guards.

"The crazy bastard has killed his own!" Torrent roars in approval. "Now, to take out the few that are left!"

"Torrent!" I grab his arm. It takes both my hands to cup his wrist, and he stares at them for a moment before he looks at my face. I stutter as worry rises in me and then get out my warning. "If the carriage is here, the Prince and Lorna were unsuccessful."

He slowly shakes his head. His eyes grow wide as my words hit him.

"And if Lin hasn't helped us yet…That means…" I continue.

He jerks his arm away, and I stumble back.

The carriage halts. The remaining guard runs and opens the door. A giant iron ball clubs him directly in his forehead.

I gasp as the mace is pulled back with malevolent force. A short, plump woman jumps down from the carriage as the guard drops. She rolls her neck and swings the gory weapon in a circle. My eyes stick to the green-hooded coachman, who leaps from his post to join the woman.

"Where is Prince Braizen?" Torrent demands as he stalks towards them. He points his sword straight at the woman.

She rests her hands on her stout hips and scrunches her nose.

"You mean the thief with the dreamy eyes?"

Torrent grunts and slowly moves in.

"Well, well. You aren't too bad on the eyes, either! You look like you're made from fine stone. Say, how tall are you anyhow?" She asks, her eyelashes fluttering.

Torrent jerks back, then spins his blade upright in his hand.

"Temptress," he hisses. "I won't be bought by your seductive body or entrancing eyes! Tell me what you have done with the Prince and the girl or meet your death!"

I inch back, wanting to create as much distance as possible if that mace swings against Torrent's sword.

"Settle yourself, Stoneman. I've seen what happens next. Don't tempt me to change its course."

"What in the hells does that mean?"

"Ah, stop blubbering, you big brute," the coachman interjects and throws back his hood.

"Braze!" Torrent lifts his friend into the air and spins. "How can this be? What happened back there?"

Braizen laughs and slaps his friend on the back as he's lowered. "It's a strange story. However, the good news is we have transport. And a great deal of alcohol."

Torrent yowls and tousles Braizen's hair. "And a new friend, I see?"

The small woman smiles widely and bows. "Nuri. Nuri Idunn. A pleasure to meet you, Stoneman."

Lorna descends from the carriage holding a delicate glass bottle. "Anyone care for some wine?" She's smiling.

Torrent yanks it from her and pulls the cork with his teeth while eyeing this Nuri woman as if she's the fine meal he means to devour with the drink. She seems to like this. A little too much.

Braizen chuckles and then looks at the dead men. His expression changes.

"Where is she?"

Torrent growls at Nuri, ignoring him.

"Torrent, *where is she*?!"

At that, Torrent pulls himself away. He glances around and catches sight of me, hiding behind some shrubs. He points.

"She's over there. Idalia, come out."

Braizen shoots him a suspicious look. He holds his arms to his sides and curls his fingers into fists, his signal to approach.

I don't want to obey. However, I also fear that at any moment, the shrubs will come to life and strip the skin from my body. I step back onto the trail.

As I reach the group, Lorna plants herself in front of me. "That's close enough, Verdanian."

I laugh straight into her beautiful eyes. "I don't plan to touch him. Only obeying orders like the rest of you."

She frowns. Freckles dot her dirty, exhausted face. It's a shame she's always scowling because she's quite pretty. She jerks her head at the dead guards and scoffs.

"It seems Torrent did a lot of protecting this afternoon. An awful lot of effort to keep you safe. The least you can do to show gratitude is to keep your mouth shut."

My hands flare with heat, but I'm now attuned to the signal and realize the angry flickers aren't in response to her sneers.

Danger is moving in. It's coming for Lorna.

Grabbing her waist, I throw her to the ground. Looking up, I see a rogue guard towering above us on the carriage roof. He leaps at Lorna, but I drive my short blade up and into his chest. I grunt as he collapses on me. The knife hilt buries itself in my stomach, and I gag in pain.

It's Braizen, his eyes blazing with wild disbelief, who throws the man from me. He reaches out his hand to help me up, but I lie still.

"Boss, she can't," Torrent reminds him, almost gently.

Braizen shakes his head and pulls away his hand.

Lorna breathes heavily on the ground next to me.

"Why…why did you do that?"

"What," I groan, lifting myself to my knees. "Save you?" I cough and wince from the pain that's now spreading to my back. "I wish I could tell you."

Torrent bounds over and pulls me up the rest of the way. He drapes one huge bicep around my neck.

"Believe it or not, you're not the first Baellilean she saved today." He beams down at me and winks.

"What do you mean?" Braizen asks, slowly moving towards us.

Lorna is on her feet, dusting off her rear. Her face asks the same question.

"She saved me earlier. First, she cut me loose from these cursed vines. I tell you, they were going to devour me! They had me wrapped up like a fly in a spider web. I couldn't breathe until she started hacking away at them. Then, she took on some of the sentries! By herself. I'd be dead right now if not for her."

I smile awkwardly as I meet Lorna and Braizen's suspicious eyes.

"I think it's safe to say you'd be dead too, Lorna," Torrent says.

The redhead spits on the ground, but for once, she doesn't look at me with her face twisted into a ferocious scowl.

"If Torrent was trapped, and the guards were here to take you back to safety, why didn't you go with them?" Braizen asks. His glacial eyes interrogate me.

I shrug. "I don't know."

He crosses his arms. "You don't know?" His voice trickles with cynicism.

I look down and do not respond.

"So you saved not one, but *two* Baellileans, giving up your chance for freedom, and you don't know why?"

I refuse to look up but shrug once more. "I guess so."

"You fought Aeradian guards, risked your life to save an enemy? *And you don't know why?"*

I offer nothing.

"Lady and Shield," he finally exclaims. "She might be a bandit!"

Lorna shoots him a furious look but Torrent howls.

"I told you! Today is the day we make history! We got the cargo, and I found a Verdanian I might actually like?! Who'd have thought?!"

"You can't be serious?! You trust her already?" Lorna's look and voice seep with spite.

Torrent shrugs his massive shoulders. "She saved my life. Why shouldn't I trust her?"

"You're too easily bought," Lorna snaps. "She's still an enemy to our Kingdom. Don't forget what happens if Braizen gets too close to her."

Braizen frowns, and Torrent pulls his arm from my shoulders. It's clear what's at stake. I know the heightened energy that still courses through my body will soon fade, and the reality of my circumstances will set back in.

Braizen looks me over, and this time, his smile reaches his eyes. "Those vines really got you, didn't they?"

Confused, I hold out my arms, which are covered in small cuts. My mouth mangles into a frown.

"I wouldn't be too worried about those. I, for one, think they suit you," he says.

My jaw drops, and I take a step back. "You think *what* suits me? My wounds?!" I ask sharply.

A small laugh escapes him as he lifts himself back onto the carriage. "Wounds from a fight are just reminders," he answers coolly. "Reminders that we care enough about something to fight for it."

Chapter Ten

Braizen

Twelve Years Previous

I hardly slept last night, too caught up in the image of her face and those fawn eyes. I wanted to kiss her when we were in the aviary. I wanted so badly to press her lips against mine, but timing is a fickle creature. Maybe it's a good thing that Theodore overreacted to her brother's tiny wound; maybe kissing the girl you like in a birdcage isn't as romantic as I thought.

My mother told me that I wouldn't like her and that she wouldn't like me. She said that Verdanian women are eyesores, and their voices are cat nails against iron. Then she said it wouldn't matter whether Idalia and I favored one another; the Princess was here to stay. Her parents were bringing her to be raised in the way of Baellileans, whatever that means, and when we're eighteen, we'll be wed.

"Marriage is a contract, no matter what you hear said otherwise," she said to me more than once. "Romance is not for royals, or the poor, or those in between, for that matter. Romance is a dead idea, as empty as a starless sky. We marry to seal alliances and make bargains. Men need heirs, and women need protection. Marriage is not based on romance or love; it is a product of duty."

I suppose my parents never felt anything but a duty to each other. They don't hold hands or steal glances like I see servants do. They don't even speak to each other unless it concerns the Kingdom. I thought that's how it would be when I met her, the Princess of Verdana, but I was wrong. Mother was wrong.

I do like her. And she isn't an eyesore, not in the slightest. Her voice isn't grating; it's like a bird's sweet melody. Verdanian or not, she's the most gorgeous thing I've ever seen. My body experienced all sorts of strange things when she was near to me. I'd never felt them before, but many of my father's guards have spent countless days speaking on such subjects. Like the way women make them feel, though, they don't always speak of it kindly. When they mention women, it's loud and rough. When I first saw the Princess, I felt light. I felt *awake*.

When we gather for breakfast this morning, I must pretend that we're meeting for the first time. I don't think this will be all too hard. Her perfect features will draw the same happy reaction from me each time I see them. I'm sure my mother will carefully watch me during the entire meal, making sure that I behave like the proper prince she's raised me to be. She prides herself on being a good tutor of etiquette. It's quite funny that neither of my parents knows much about me. They don't know of my love for trees or birds or dirt. They don't see my skill when it comes to getting into locked areas. They believe my favorite weapon is the longsword because they ignore my passionate rants about the bow.

I'm not complaining; I know this is the nature of parents, to not know their children. It's never bothered me, not really, until I saw her. When she looked at me, right before I wanted to kiss her, I felt like she knew more of me than anyone else. With one look, she stole my secrets. That's why I showed her the sparrow, the secret I guard closest to my heart. I wanted to put her right next to the bird and keep them both. All for me.

I've never felt this way. Ever.

"Braizen. Son, are you ready?" My father's voice loomed from outside my door. It's unusual that he's here; the maidens usually fetch me. But I suppose the next few days will be a lot different than what I'm used to.

She's changing everything.

"You look like a crow. Why are your eyes darkened so? Did you not rest last night?" His words assault me as soon as I emerge.

I shrug a bit, then straighten. "I slept decently enough."

He squints down at me, then inhales roughly.

"No matter; let's go."

We walk to the great dining hall where my mother stands at the entrance. She's wearing a gods' awful green dress; the skirts take up half the hallway. Gaudy pearls line the front bodice, and a large peacock feather sticks out of her pulled-up hair. She looks ridiculous.

Her neck snaps towards us, and she groans frantically and flicks her wrists. “Why does the boy look like this? He looks like one of those pesky rodents that eat the cook’s kitchen scraps! Did he not sleep last night?”

“Because, Eveline, he is a boy. He was likely up all night, nervous for today.”

Father is halfway right, I think. My mother wafts a hand towards him and turns to face the door, her nose pointing entirely into the air.

“He is a *Prince*, Vaskis. If he cannot even rest because his nerves are too high, how can we expect him to lead, hmm?”

My father joins her, his face more than annoyed. “Do not worry yourself with petty issues such as these,” he says. “The Verdanians aren’t the sort who can judge what is handsome. Even if the boy hadn’t rested for a week, he’d still far surpass the Princess in looks.”

Mother tsks. “It is a great shame that our bloodline will merge with theirs. Likely, our features will show dominance in the heirs. Lady and Guard will it.”

I step in front of them and grimace at the thought of having children of my own. Perhaps I can get Idalia to agree not to have any. A kiss would be nice, but I’m not sure beyond that.

The doors open, and two heralds blow the familiar fanfare before loudly announcing us. We walk slowly, too slowly, to the long wooden table, which is teeming with food. It stretches across the entire dais, and the Thrope and Hyland royals stand to greet us.

I catch her eye, and she blushes, making my cheeks red hot. Lachlan stands with his hands behind his back, looking straight ahead and remaining inhumanly still. I know this is because his father, who stands next to him, will hurt him if he makes any movement. Theodore, however, doesn't seem to care about her father's strictness and shuffles back and forth. Her hair is pulled back, two curls fall in front of each ear, and a large Aeradian flower, the Salva, rests in her hair. This four-petaled flower burns a rich red and is only found in the Deep Kingdom. The Aeradians guard it fiercely. No one knows why. It's pretty, but I've never seen a need to make such a big fuss. It's not *that* pretty.

King Ivar and Queen Revna bow their heads as we approach the table, though I see the Queen watch me from under her lashes before anyone else lifts their eyes. One of her brows arches, and she looks like she just smelled something repugnant. My father holds his hands out and bellows.

"Welcome, guests of Baelliles! Let us sit and feast together, to mark such a joyous occasion!"

The two queens clap lightly, and though they sit facing each other, they don't make eye contact. My father faces King Ivar, and King Lester of Aeradian sits next to him. We children sit at the opposite end, Lachlan across from me, Idalia to his right. Thedore sits at the foot as if she rules us all. I know this placement makes her feel right at home.

The servants file in and hover over us as they remove silver cloches from the platters arrayed down the table. Delicious smells immediately fill the room. We wait eagerly. Thedore's eyes are rounded like saucers, and she licks her lips. My father smiles at King Ivar and gestures for him to choose first. We all watch as he eyes the cornucopia spread before him and, all too slowly, opts for a turkey leg slathered in some thick, red sauce. We wait for his first bite, and as soon as his teeth close, the children swarm like hungry dogs.

I gather as much mutton as my plate will hold. Of course, the fish and duck are wonderful, but the mutton is cooked with a specific spice I've never found in other dishes. Lachlan's plate has only bread and a small amount of oil, but he looks content. Theodore's is a hodgepodge of everything she could reach.

Idalia's plate sits empty. I stare at it in wonder. Doesn't she mean to eat? Her face tells the story. She's waiting for everyone else to have selected their food. Her long lashes flutter over her brown eyes, and I wish I were Lachlan so that I could be as close to her as he is. The adults begin to converse, and Idalia peers at the platters to see what remains.

"Don't you find our food to your liking, Sparrow?"

Her eyes shoot toward me, and she gives me a demure smile. "Oh, no! It's not that at all! It's just…."

I think I know what's going on in her head. A lady should never be choosy, especially at a table of men. I've heard my mother say so too many times to count.

"Come on, Sparrow. You've already broken plenty of rules."

Her smile deepens into a grin, but she looks down at her plate.

"So, what will it be? Duck, venison, rabbit?"

Her nose crinkles. "Do you have any lamb?"

"Mutton," I say, pointing my fork at my plate.

Her eyes light up. "Even better."

There isn't any left on the platter, so I stab the largest piece on my plate and hold it up.

"Psst, Lachlan! Pass this to Sparrow."

Lachlan raises his thick, dark brows. He looks up the table to his father, who's talking with his mouth full, and quickly snatches my fork.

Idalia giggles when he passes it to her, then looks right at me. Her eyes are wide and bright; her smile takes over most of her face. I decide that I'll do whatever I can to make her smile like this more often.

She holds the fork out to me as if she's toasting me and then rips into the meat without hesitation. "This is wonderful!" she exclaims. "I've never had mutton with coriander and turmeric! Amazing!"

My grin widens and pulls to the right. When I'm King, mutton will always be seasoned just the way we like it.

When the morning feast ends, my father dismisses the children. Horrick appears in the corridor, and he stretches his thin arm to direct me forward. Idalia is flanked by two handmaidens, as are Lachlan and Theodore. I know we're all meant to bow to each other and then part ways. Lach is staring at Idalia, and I don't like it.

So when Horrick turns, I don't follow. Instead, I catch everyone's eyes and nudge my chin towards an opposite corridor. Lachlan seems confused; Theodore and Idalia send me wide smiles. I know they'll follow. I mouth a silent countdown.

"Three… two… one!!!"

We launch ourselves down the hallway. Horrick sends a curse after me, but I drown it out with my laughter. The girls are on my heels as we race towards the castle entrance. I look back to see if Lachlan has joined us. Sure enough, he's stumbling along, his face filled with terror. The two soldiers at the entrance look puzzled as we race past them, engulfed in giggles. Or at least the girls and I are laughing. Once outside, we pant and look at each other in bewilderment.

"What are we supposed to do now?" Theodore asks breathlessly, her curls now sticking out in multiple directions.

"I don't have a plan," I say with a shrug.

"But you're the one who encouraged us to follow!" Lachlan bellows, scanning the people who are now avidly watching us.

Idalia laughs hard, and her dark hair snaps wildly in the wind. "I don't care what the plan is. This is fun!"

Lachlan throws a hand to his brow and paces in an anxious circle. I know that he's only afraid because his father is so mean. King Lester doesn't let Lachlan behave like a child. Theodore chases after her brother pleading with him to stop worrying.

I can't look away from Idalia. I walk to her and tuck a loose wisp of hair behind her ear. Her hair is as untamed as she is, as I am.

She stops laughing and is still. Then she smiles, and her cheeks turn red.

"Is that her? The Verdanian scum?" A crude voice cuts in from behind us. Two boys around our age prance towards us. Two noble sons, based on their clothes. The one speaking is tall and stalky, his long brown hair tied back from his brow. The other is blond, with eyebrows so light he seems to have none. Their faces contort in disgust.

"My father told me Verdanians were ugly, but he didn't tell me just how foul they'd smell!" The blond boy snickers at his insult.

"She is a Princess," I seethe. "You would do well to treat her with respect."

The tall, thin boy's eyes widen in mockery. "Treat a Verdanian with respect? Did you hear that, Niklaus?" He spits. "I'd sooner show respect to the rats."

I hear Idalia's breath hitch, and anger flows through my chest.

"Then you will respect your Prince. I command you to apologize to her. At once."

The boys look at one another and laugh.

"I'll never apologize to that *bitch,*" the skinny one jeers.

A wave of red washes over me, and then I see him on the ground, clutching his nose in agony. My fist uncurls, and my knuckles ache. The boy's nose is bleeding.

"Marcel!" Niklaus cries, looking at his friend. He rounds on Idalia. "You'd have Baellileans turn against each other! Our fathers were right!"

He launches towards her, and I lunge to jump in front of her, but there's no need.

The Princess winds back her fist and strikes him under the chin, hard and true. His head flies up, and a groan leaves him as he's thrust to the ground.

The two scramble to their feet. "Our fathers will hear about this! How you chose a Verdanian over your own!"

I salute them with a cheeky smile. "Make sure you explain in great detail how the Verdanian took out the likes of you!"

The Princess smiles, but her eyes are heavy.

"Sparrow." She faces me, and I smile. "Nice hit."

"Prince Braizen!" Horrick shouts from the castle's entry.

I moan and pivot to see him clenching Theodore and Lachlan by the ears.

"I don't even want to dream of what your father would say if he saw you out here. I suggest all of you return to your chambers and get ready for tonight. *Now.*"

Head low, Idalia leads the way back inside. Before she follows the maidens to her room, she winks at me over her shoulder.

"You made his nose as crooked as he is."

Finally, it's time for the ceremony, the reason everyone was invited to our castle. I've been ready for more than an hour. My maidens bathed and even shaved me, though I'm not happy about that. I've just started growing soft fuzz around my chin, and now it's gone.

Once I'm ready, I stand by her door. I hear the maidens brushing her hair, swooning over her dress, and her uncomfortable laugh. I pace the corridor, pretending I have a destination, hoping that she hears me and appears. I flush when the handmaidens exit and close the door behind them. They curtsy then giggle.

As they retreat, I overhear their whispers. "I don't think the young Prince can wait five years! See how he stalks her room even now?"

How ridiculous. Of course, I can wait five years to get married. I'm in no rush for that. Eventually, I hang my head, accept defeat, and make my way to the Great Hall to join the crowd that awaits her entrance.

Lachlan looks handsome layered in Aeradian reds. A sparkling gold sash that mimics his father's crosses his chest. He unlocks his hands from behind his back and wipes sweat from his brow. King Lester smacks him upside the head and grunts. Lachlan's face sinks, and he resumes his former position. I don't like King Lester, not one bit. Theodore is regal in a golden gown and red shoes, her hair intertwined with more Salvas.

My mother sits on her throne, her face tense. Piles of green fabric spill around her and onto the marble dais. Her dress mimics the one she wore yesterday, pearls and all, but I figure it is intentional. At least there's no silly peacock feather this time.

She looks me over and then promptly sticks her nose in the air. I suppose she isn't impressed, but what can I do? She's hardly ever impressed. Or happy.

I reach my father's side. He's standing proud and upright. I stifle a gasp as I take in how many people are here. Hundreds are squeezed in at the long tables that stretch nearly from wall to wall. Some wear Baellilean green, a familiar sight; others are in red. The strangest sight is the Verdanian blue that cloaks parts of the room. I've never seen this color in our castle. But I like it; it matches my eyes.

The horns blow, and everyone rises, including my mother. This is it; she's here. King Ivar and Queen Revna enter, their chins held high. They wear their frosty blue outfits with pride, and I hear the guests murmur. Queen Revna's eyes meet mine. They lighten as a faint smile forms on her face. As she ascends the steps to the dais, the smile disappears.

The horns play a soft, whimsical melody. Maidens enter and throw white petals into the air, creating a delicate illusion of snow. The Princess follows. A sheer veil covers her face, and she takes slow steps toward the altar that sits on the dais. The audience buzzes. This girl is the future of Baelliles. This day will seal that truth, and everything we know will change.

As she approaches, I glimpse her features behind the mesh. She beams at me as she climbs the steps. When she stands before us, my father lifts his hand, and the music ceases.

"Baellileans, Aeradians, and honored guests from Verdana. We come together to mark the end of a centuries-long war. Today, we put away our Kingdoms' feud, and with it, we do away with any grudge. For far too long, the people of Baelliles and Verdana have suffered the consequence of our ancestors' actions. For far too long, we have held hatred in our hearts for the mistakes of our predecessors. Today symbolizes the dawn of a new era. There will be free trade amongst all our countries. There will be no more slaughter for control of the river. Even our dear friends from across the sea in Osinea have written to congratulate us on this most advantageous occasion. People of all nations, I ask that you join me in welcoming the future Queen of Baelliles, Princess Idalia, by raising your hands to the Lady and bowing your head for the Guard."

I do so but peek at her again. I can tell she's looking back at me from behind her veil.

"To the Lady and the Guard," King Ivar says, a large smile stretching over his jaw.

The audience repeats it back, and then the maidens pull the veil from the princess' face.

I suddenly need to sit down. Her dress is pure white, save for three encrusted, blue jewels that line the collar. Ringlets drape down past her shoulders. Her eyelids are painted a glittery silver, making her eyes appear even larger. Her skin glows as she looks straight at me.

I tug at my pants and shift a bit. Something is happening that I can't explain. Lachlan nudges my ribs and smirks. The crowd cheers. Theodore claps wildly, and then the Princess stands beside me. Her nervous breaths grow louder as the applause heightens. Without thinking, I grab her hand and squeeze.

She squeezes back, and our eyes meet. It's as if the room has gone silent. The Little Sparrow with her fawn eyes. How I wish I could catch her and keep her with me always.

Chapter Eleven

Idalia

Present Day

“So, there’s a village then?” Braizen leans towards Nuri, a hint of arrogance coloring his words.

“Of course, there is. Has your schooling taught you nothing of the Florian Wood?” she asks.

“Only that it’s filled with magic and terrors,” he says.

Nuri rolls her eyes and throws her hands into the air. “Of course, that’s all they’d teach you.”

Everyone is quiet for a time. The carriage wheels grate against the stones on the road, and the gold and rubies inside Lannex’s chest jostle as we sway.

Across from me, Lin gawks, as he has for some time now. Like I'm a grotesque animal he's never seen before. I narrow my stare.

"Can I help you?"

He blinks as if my question abruptly returns him to the present. He shakes his head. "I'm sorry, I'm just so confused." He massages his temples and closes his eyes. "You saved both Torrent *and* Lorna?"

I cross my arms and lean my head against the cushion.

"Yes."

"But… *why*? Why would you help them instead of escaping? It doesn't make any sense!" He looks to Braizen, who wears a charming smile.

"Maybe if you'd done your job as the lookout, she wouldn't have had to step in and save the day," he teases.

"I've already told you a hundred times! I saw something horrifying when I was on watch, and when I got back to my post, there was nothing on the path except trees! I assumed you'd all died. I thought *she* must've done something to ruin the plan."

"Well, she didn't," Braizen says matter-of-factly and tosses me a glance.

I quickly look away.

"That's what I'm trying to understand! *Why* didn't she? The Princess hates Baellileans!"

I groan and try to find a more comfortable position in the jostling carriage. I kick Lin's shin.

"I'm right in front of you, so you can stop talking about me like I'm not here."

His stare goes blank and Braizen chuckles. Nuri strokes the handle of her mace.

"The real question is why a Verdanian and a bunch of Baellileans are traveling together in the first place. Isn't it?" Nuri asks, though her tone suggests she already knows the answer.

Everyone falls silent. Lin glares at me, commanding me not to speak.

I ignore him. "They kidnapped me. For what reason, I don't know."

Nuri's eyes widen, and she blows out a heavy breath. "And you *saved* them? Now I'm as confused as the anxious one!"

Lin's jaw unlatches as he releases an agitated breath. He clearly doesn't enjoy being called that by a stranger. The woman appears gratified by his annoyance.

"Well, technically, we saved her first. We rescued her from the Obsidian Mist," Braizen cuts in.

"Is this supposed to be a joke? You kidnapped me!"

He sends me a tight smile. "Did it make you laugh?"

I scowl, wishing with everything inside me that we could touch, just long enough for my hand to strike his cocky face.

"Ah, yes. The mist is a terrible thing to witness, indeed. I'm surprised at how well you are all faring after seeing such a thing." Nuri gives a low whistle and pulls her mace up beside her, a little too casually for my taste.

"Trust me," I breathe. "I've seen worse things than the mist."

I feel him staring at me, but I refuse to look. He knows exactly what I mean.

"So, Nuri, is it?" Lin says, breaking the tension. "What exactly is the mist? How does your kind survive it?"

She laughs at him. "My *kind*?"

"I didn't mean it offensively, of course! I only meant to say, well, to ask…It's just that between the mist, sentient plants, and scarce wildlife… It makes for nearly impossible living conditions, and I was wondering …"

"We aren't enemies to the forest," she interrupts. "I'm afraid that's reserved for *your kind*." She winks, draws her mace up to her side, and uses it to knock on the carriage wall behind her. The horses halt. Lin rubs his palm against his mouth in a flustered motion, but Nuri only leans forward and places her hand on his knee.

"Magic." She says simply. "That's how we survive." Lin squints at her.

"Magic?" He repeats, the word suspended in disbelief.

The woman smiles widely. "Yes, magic. I'm sure you've heard many stories of the Wood and this one is true. Magic flows through it like a hidden web. It connects all things and weaves them together. Those who live within this web are tethered to it; we can feel its ebb and flow. We don't fear the magic because we're as much a part of it as the trees. It helps us survive."

Lin inhales deeply as Nuri squeezes his knee harder. "But should something or someone come and disturb this web… That's a much different story. Magic itself is a being, you see. It's the roots that ground the trees. Some wish to tend it, but others seek to cut and dig it out. Theirs is a dark relationship, a viscous and harmful one, and it can create even darker outcomes."

Lin's face grows even paler than usual. "How does one have a dark relationship with magic?" he asks.

Nuri clicks her tongue. "If I give you a hammer, you have two choices. You can build, or you can destroy. It's the same for those who wield the powers from the Wood. Dark magic is merely a creature that's been trained to kill. Above all, magic will try its best to preserve itself by protecting its world. It has and will always choose to protect itself. To go against this is a great evil indeed."

"Protect the world? I thought that's what the gods are for," Lin probes, his dark eyes gleaming in a challenge.

"Gods, magic… Who's to say they're not the same thing?"

I contemplate her words. What we encountered was no doubt dark magic, which means someone must be wielding it against us. But why?

"So, if magic *does* truly exist, is it how the First Prophet saw into the future?" Braizen asks, leaning towards Nuri.

"Why not?" Her grin stretches across her dark face.

When Lin realizes this is all she's going to say, he releases a frustrated breath.

"No offense, but your descriptions could use some work."

Nuri's plump face turns to him.

"No offense, but so could your people skills."

Braizen releases a hearty laugh and slaps his knee, nodding in appreciation.

Lin ignores this and lifts a finger. "The sacred texts say the gods will save us, nothing about this magic or web you speak of." His tone is accusatory, and Nuri starts to snap back, but we're interrupted.

"We've arrived!" Torrent bellows. He opens the door with such force he nearly rips it from its hinges. Lorna appears behind him and scowls. Saving her life didn't earn me her trust and I don't blame her for not giving it out as freely as Torrent does. I reserve my trust, as well. Everyone here is still my enemy.

"Look at that! Stoneman has manners! Chivalry is still alive and well In those savage lands you call a kingdom," Nuri jeers.

Torr flashes a crooked smile and then holds out his hand. "Let me help you down," he urges, but Nuri swats at him.

"There are a few things I can think of needing your assistance with, Stoneman, but this definitely isn't one of them," she says coolly. Torrent's cheeks flush. She jumps from the carriage, and we exit after her.

"Now, everyone, follow me!" Nuri struts towards a pair of arched trees. Torrent follows right on her heel, his smile growing as he watches her body sway.

"Well, this is an interesting turn of events, to say the least," Braizen laughs. He stops and shouts after Nuri. "Can we hide the carriage and our things here?"

"Of course. We won't need them where we're going."

Lin looks to Lorna, then to me, then back to her. “Are we supposed to tie her up or something?” He asks.

Lorna shrugs. “I think it would be wise.”

“Tying me up will no longer be necessary, thank you.” I stalk away, keeping a safe distance from the hatchet woman, who looks ready to swing at my neck.

The two follow, speaking in low voices. “Who’s this Nuri woman? Why is Braze letting her lead us further into the Wood?” Lorna asks.

“I’m not sure,” Lin answers. “I’m not sure about any of this.”

As we dip under the trees canopy, the very atmosphere lightens. The sky shimmers, violet and marigold hues fill its dome. The trees are different, too; they glow against the sky. Radiant, glistening blue greens and enchanting ambers cover their leaves and bark, and their light cascades onto a small village.

The first dwellings we come to are small and made of some sort of clay. Their doors are arched, and their gardens burst with vegetation. Set apart from them and down the cobbled road is a square surrounded by wooden buildings. As we draw closer, I see people of all sizes, shapes, and skin tones dressed in bright colors walk past. Laced between the tall branches, golden strings of lights illuminate our path. I take a deep breath, and a sweetness caresses my nose. Again, I notice the air. It’s lighter, better. I’d go as far as to say I feel…*calm*. I grin from ear to ear.

“Welcome to Idizina,” Nuri exclaims, thrusting her hands into the air. “Home to the Idunns. Safe Haven of the forest. Florian’s Secret Place.”

Braizen runs a hand through his curls and smiles up at the sky. "Idunns? Isn't that your name? Does this village belong to your family?"

Nuri spins and rests her hands on her hips. "Nothing is anyone's property," she snaps. "We're *all* Idunns when we are here. We belong to each other. And to the forest alone."

Lorna sends Braizen and Torr a cynical gaze. "Well, I guess that means we're Idunns now."

"Not yet," Nuri winks, skipping off into the distance. Torrent yelps in merriment; Lin is already busy assessing the tree trunks and leaves. I continue to breathe deeply.

A woman bearing a warm, inviting smile approaches me. The deep wrinkles that flow from her eyes only serve to elevate her beauty. Her hair is dark but graying from what I see under her multicolored headscarf. Sandstone eyes flecked with yellow are enhanced by her dress, the pale pink of the mallows blooming in the gardens. She reaches her hands towards me; I find myself taking hold of them. We speak no words. She nods, then leads me back down the path to one of the clay dwellings. I follow without question or worry.

Inside what I presume is her home, I sit on a bright red chair covered in material softer than velvet and shinier than silk. She steps into another room, but I don't feel fear. I'm mesmerized. Plants of wildly different shapes and sizes grow and hang from pots built into the clay walls. Their trailing vines spill like lush green waterfalls splashing to the stone floor. She carries a tray holding a cream teapot and a matching cup when she returns. Only one.

She pours a generous serving of a steaming liquid and hands it to me. Her eyes are endearing. They remind me of Nurse Lydia. They remind me of home. They make me feel safe and loved.

I thank her and blow the vapor from the surface before I sip. I swallow and moan in delight. This is the best tea, *no*, the best drink my senses have ever been blessed by. It's a heady mix of flavors and scents, yet I can call them out individually. At first, a caramel tart washes over my mouth, but soon my tongue is coated with an earthy, nutty flavor. Somehow, this merging isn't repulsive; it's invigorating. Intoxicating. It soothes my throat, and when I sip again, the palate switches to pine, then to dark, warm, and sweet. I can't explain why, but this is the most pleasurable flavor of all. I wish I could taste it forever. I take another sip.

"Ah," I scowl when the cup touches my mouth, and my head rears back. The woman cocks her head. "It stung me!" I exclaim and hold it away from my body.

She doesn't take it from me. She remains still.

I look back into the cup and am shocked that it's almost empty. My sips must have been larger than I thought. I rest it on a small mosaic glass table and nurse my wounded lip.

"How did the liquid shock me?" I ask, but she remains quiet. I rub my lip once more and lean forward. "Can you speak?"

The woman smiles, the crinkles beside her eyes deepening as she tilts her head the other way. I slowly blink, and the vines on the wall shift. "The plants…they're moving!" I warn as a vision of Torrent wrapped in those fatal green ropes plays in my mind. "You need to move! You'll die if you don't!"

The elder stays immobile; her smile doesn't falter. I breathe heavily and try to rise, knock her out of the way, and escape but I can't move my legs or my arms. I'm weighted down. My vision hazes, and my words slur. "We'll die… We're going to die. I can't save us."

The woman kneels and rests one hand on my knee. "Why?" Her voice isn't that of an older woman. It's a golden gong that could resonate throughout an entire kingdom. It's powerful; it's many women speaking at once.

My head rolls back, and I stare at the ceiling. "I can't save us because I can't move," I manage.

The many voices roll like thunder before a crack of lightning whips to the ground. "Why can't you move?"

"Because of the tea." Is this drool spilling from the corner of my mouth?

"No," they counter. "Answer truthfully."

A sensation grows, like I'm falling off a cliff, and my organs are traveling upwards.

"I can't move because…because…"

"Tell me," the voices command.

The plants crawl across the floor; Their sinister vines encroach from every corner of the room, bony fingers inching towards me to clutch my throat. They're moments away from suffocating the very life from our bodies. Then, they begin to glow. Half of the room rests in deep shadows, and the vines undulate in the darkness between them. The other glows as if it's lit by the bright morning sun, and golden tresses curl in hoops, repeating their patterns over and over. These vines stretch towards me.

"I can't move," I breathe rapidly. "Because the Lady has willed it so."

"What has she decreed?" The voices demand.

I try to take a deep breath, but I can't. I inhale shallow gulps hoping they'll keep me awake.

"She has forbidden me from saving them. The darkness will spread until all the Kingdoms fall. Her power is growing…She is almost ready." I don't even know what I am saying anymore.

"What has the Lady done that prevents you from saving them?"

My head lolls, and from the corner of my eye, I see vines snake down the wall behind me. I wait to be mercilessly entrapped and defeated.

"Tell me!" The voices hiss.

My chin finally drops; I stare at my spinning feet. "I don't know!"

"You do know!" The voices wail. "You are a Hyland woman! Search within!"

My eyelids flutter, and I'm afraid I won't be able to keep them open long enough to witness my undoing.

"Tell us, quickly!"

I feel the insidious strands inch over my shoulders, digging into my skin like nails. I'm going to die. This dark magic will take me.

"She cursed us," I sigh, accepting the death that will soon capture me. "She has made it so that we may never touch one another. The Lady…she will not let me. I cannot save them. I cannot move."

I feel like I'm choking on the words that bubble up in my throat. Without further hesitation, I concede. *"Because I cannot be with him."* My palms pulse with furious rage, and my eyelids finally close. Sleep and death overtake me.

Chapter Twelve

Idalia

Twelve Years Previous

I can't decide whether I feel silly or pretty in this dress. Despite the many choices Nurse Lydia had me try, my mother supplied a completely new dress for tonight's ceremony. It's not lacey or frilly. It's sleek and presses against my skin so tightly that I wonder why a corset is necessary. I wish I could dress like Teddy; her skirts billow around her, and gold looks spectacular against her skin. I want flowers in my hair, too. But that would require Verdana being able to grow them. We have snow and mountains, and I don't think my hair could hold either.

As I pass Lachlan on the dais, his green eyes gleam as he scrapes a barely perceptible bow. My mother seems more than pleased with how I look. Then, there is the Prince. His hair is smoothed to one side, but his curls are as rebellious as he is, and one by one, they're already breaking loose from the oil that attempts to hold them down. He smooths a cowlick as I approach. I stand beside him, and his ice-blue eyes trace the frame of my face. This is my future home; he's my future husband. I've always dreamed of weddings. The colors, the dresses, the flowers… the husband. He's exactly what I pictured for the role.

The crowd is loud, and my stomach begins to roil, my head spins. They cheer, but some faces look less than satisfied with me. Women in green grimace in disgust as if I'm a rotting carcass in their midst. Men dressed in red eye me with evident discomfort. Even our nobles dressed in blue appear vexed. My throat closes in; I've failed to make them all happy.

He grabs my hand and squeezes.

I squeeze back.

Once the adults begin to drink, I remove the blasted veil, and the celebration grows fun. Those who earlier scowled at me are now an hour into dunking their faces in Baellilean wine; they've only smiled since. Even King Lester's mood lightens with a drink, and he loudly laughs and jokes at his table. I hate that the nobles laugh when he isn't funny. My father isn't funny either, and people always laugh at his jokes.

"Do you want to dance?" Teddy swishes her dress with a giant smile on her face. "The musicians are about to play an Aeradian classic. Come with me!" She holds out her hand, and I laugh as we run to the middle of the hall, where the tables are set far enough apart for us to move freely. She braces herself and pulls me around, then clasps hold of my other hand and leans back. We spin, and her dress swells in the wind we create. As Teddy giggles and spins faster, I give in to the moment. I throw back my head and laugh as we twirl. The music picks up speed, and our whirling follows suit.

We spin and spin, and then I fly hard into someone. We drop our clasped hands as the sudden thump propels us to the floor. I regain my balance and look up to apologize. I jerk back as an old woman with one eye much larger than the other leans over me.

"What is this then? Who has done this to an old bat like me? Do you not know how easy it is for a woman my age to stumble?" She surveys us both.

"I'm so very sorry, Madam! My friend and I were dancing, well, spinning really." I stammer an apology. "We just got carried away and didn't watch where we were going. I didn't mean to cause any harm!"

Her cloudy eyes peer further into me before she pulls back.

"You are the Princess of Verdana, no?"

I gulp and nod. I pray she doesn't tell my mother.

She cackles. "Why should a Princess apologize to a nobody like me? Truly, it is I who should apologize to you, Your Highness." Her old body cracks as she bows, and I wave my hands.

"No, really! It was my mistake, princess or not; I apologize. I'm sorry, and I pray for your forgiveness on the matter."

She leans back and tilts her head. "How disappointing. You have taken after him," she mutters.

I stare at her face with its many lines and liver spots. She frightens me, though I can't say why. It's not her age; I've met many women far older who didn't scare me. But her ramblings confuse me. I quickly decide it would be best to bow and leave her with a blessing.

"May the Lady grant you health and longevity," I say.

Her thin lips spread into a grin.

"May the *Lady* do just that."

I flee, longing to return to the dais. Teddy disappeared as soon as the old woman began speaking, which was no surprise. I would've done the same had our roles been reversed. The guests slam their mugs together and whistle to the music, and I can't reach the platform fast enough. An arm reaches out and closes in on my abdomen. Before I can exhale, he's holding me to his chest.

"What happened?" Braizen whispers.

I bury my face in his chest and whimper. "Nothing. Not really. I got spooked by a guest."

"You're safe now, Sparrow," he assures me while stroking my hair. "There are plenty of strange people who roam our lands; we're bound to meet a few of them tonight."

I turn my cheek against his chest and laugh. I feel safe within his hold.

"Hey, Sparrow," he breathes into my hair.

I look up, and he smiles. "Would you want to dance with me?"

I only nod because, for a moment, I forget how to speak. He leads me back to the middle of the floor. The old woman is gone, and I relax even more. The melody is soft, light, and slow.

He twirls me in a wide circle. I've practiced dancing with my mother many times, but she didn't prepare me for the stomach flutters I feel now.

The Prince extends his arm and bows, then pulls me close. When he places my hand on his shoulder, I can almost hear his heartbeat. Or maybe it's my own heart that's unabashedly roaring. I didn't expect to feel this way for him or anyone—ever. I'm elated because he seems to feel the same. The guests are now watching us dance, and I hear their rumbles of speculation. I don't mind, as long as I keep looking at him.

He spins me twice and then dips me, and I feel like an adult. I feel like a woman.

I move my chin from side to side in low sweeps, just as I've been taught, and I see my parents raise their glasses to us.

King Vaskis and his Queen join them with full smiles. They toast each other and sip.

Braizen grabs me by the waist and briefly lifts me for a half-turn. The guests cheer, but all I see are his blue eyes piercing mine, his tan skin shining in the candlelight.

He slows his pace though the music doesn't, and I realize what's happening. He's leaning forward now, and his eyes close. His mouth puckers.

I swallow the nervous lump forming in my throat, nerves buzzing in a chaotic symphony. I am apprehensive about doing such a thing in front of so many people, but at the same time, *I want to*. I want to kiss him, and I resolve that it might be romantic to share our first kiss during our first dance. I lean in and feel his warm lips draw near.

A bone-curdling scream rents the air. More cries follow, and then two guards grab us. "Idalia!" Braizen shouts as he's dragged away.

"Braizen!" I scream, reaching out my hand.

Our fingers stretch in full extension towards one another, but to no avail.

The guard's grip is tight. I don't know what's happening, but everyone is shouting, and I see King Lester order Teddy and Lachlan to be taken from the room. The Deep's King then claps a hand over his mouth. The wails heighten.

"It's the Queen!"

"She's dead!"

"She's been murdered in cold blood!"

"Poisoned! It was her wine!"

"This was the plan all along, wasn't it? Is this why we were all dragged here?!"

I kick against the guard's shins in futile resistance until I realize I can use the crowd's frenzy to my advantage. I squirm, and when his grip slightly loosens, I push against his chest as hard as I can and thrust myself forward.

He drops me with a curse on his tongue, and I land on my hands and knees. Shouting guests now flee the room, shoving each other aside on their way to the door. There isn't enough space for me to rise, so I crawl toward the dais.

There, Braizen clings to his mother's side, and she holds him tight against her voluminous skirts. King Vaskis grips his forehead and is shaking. Where's my father? I crawl closer. He's hunched over something on the dais steps. The guard shouts my name, and I swiftly crawl under the table until I can see what he hovers above. I gasp.

My mother lies still, her face turned towards the room. Her cheeks are flushed, but her eyes…her eyes are void. Crimson wine drips down the steps in the same direction as her outstretched hand. One that seems to reach out for me on the floor. A lifeless attempt to touch me one last time.

"You did this! You killed her! My Revna!" My father flares, rising and swiveling to meet King Vaskis' stare.

The Baellilean king's face slackens in shock, and he points at my father.

"I did no such thing! Poison your wife? Are you mad?"

"You did! You brought us here under the guise of peace, but you are merciless! You have killed my wife, the Verdanian Queen, as retribution for events now hundreds of years old! You hold a grudge that knows no bounds!"

King Vaskis shakes his head and then looks around the now quiet hall. All ears listen to their quarrel.

My father continues raging. "Is this the Baellilean way? Stealing our resources that come from Aeradian and killing our troops at the river does not satisfy you? You sin too greatly, Vaskis! *My wife?* My precious Revna!"

The crowd mummers and multiple sobs break out. King Vaskis looks to King Lester, who stares at the Baellilean King as if he is a monster.

"*Oh.* I see now," King Vaskis whispers. "It is all so clear. This was the hidden agenda of the Verdanians all along." My father stiffens. "Yes," Vaskis resumes. "I always knew Verdanians to be sick people, but this… this is far worse than anything I could conjure up myself."

"What are you talking about?" King Lester asks sharply.

King Vaskis turns on his heel and strides to the Aeradian monarch's side. He points to my father.

"Do you not see? This is a trick! A vile, pathetic, morbid trick! The plan of a twisted individual! Ivar has killed his wife to make me appear the villain!"

The audience sucks in what sounds like one breath. I dare not take my sights off the dais, off my mother, but I sense all eyes on my father now.

"Do you hear yourself?" My father rages. "Do you even understand the treacherous words that your lips summon?"

"Why would he kill his own, Vaskis?" King Lester asks slowly, looking down at my mother.

"It is obvious!" King Vaskis roars. "To make Baellileans appear as monsters! To ally with you and Aeradian and destroy our Kingdom! It is an unholy strategy, but one that would surely secure a war against us!"

"You are *a snake!* A lying, conniving, evil snake!" My father bellows.

"And you are a murderer! You have killed your wife, the mother of your child, the Queen of your Kingdom!"

"It is *you* who has murdered my wife, you demonic spawn of the four hells! And you will pay greatly for what you have done on this day!"

King Lester shifts, and his eyes race between them. He doesn't seem to know who to believe; no one in the room does.

My father raises a fist high into the air. "I pray to the gods, to the Lady herself, that she vanquishes your entire kind. That she rid the world of your wicked Kingdom and that your people's hearts be pierced by the lies and deceit of their King. I *swear* it to the Lady that she *will* destroy Baelliles!" The room fills with gasps, and the murmurs grow louder. We're not supposed to swear to the gods. Ever.

King Vaskis stands taller and points a stiff finger at my father. "I pray to the Guard that he would cause Verdana to collapse into the sea! I *swear* he provides no refuge, no ships, no escape for any of your people! May they drown in your iniquity! And may he block entry into the afterlife to anyone from the North! The Great Lands will not see one Verdanian, by the Guard!"

My father's face is completely red. He draws his sword and braces himself. "To the death!" he shouts.

King Vaskis brandishes his weapon and stands firm.

"To *your* death!" They flourish their blades and advance to strike.

I look at Braizen's horrified face. As if he hears me call him, he glances down and sees me under the table. His mother doesn't notice as he slips away and joins me. Like everyone in the room, she's fixated on the two kings.

His hands cup my cheeks, and his bright eyes dart between my own.

"Are you hurt?" He whispers.

"No, but my mother…" I can't finish the sentence. I can't bring myself to utter the words.

Braizen looks like he'll say something, but a slow clap echoes through the Hall.

The Kings stop and look up. The sound grows louder, and the crowd parts as the old woman from the dance floor walks toward the dais. Her hands meet in a slow, sinister pattern.

"Very good. Very good indeed," she coos.

My father points his sword at her. "Stand back, crone, or you shall be a casualty."

The woman interlocks her fingers and tucks them under her chin with a coy smile.

"A good display of your faith, which I now see is very small. Tell me, do you often swear to the gods? Is it commonplace for you to publicly hold their names in vain? Is this truly how you wish to demonstrate your gratitude to them?!" Her voice rises with each question.

The very air stills, and I shudder. Each word bounces off the walls like thunder. "You curse each other so cavalierly. As if it is a normal practice for you to damn a person in the gods' names."

Both kings look confused; the crowd begins to murmur. Braizen squeezes my hand, but his gesture doesn't remove my fear this time. This old woman intimidated me before; now, I'm terrified.

“Enough of this,” Vaskis grinds out. “Guards, take this wench away. At once!”

A Baellilean guard races towards the woman and reaches for her. She holds up her hand, and an enormous gust of wind blasts him back. It also knocks several people to the ground, and the tables creak as it pushes against them.

“Impossible,” Vaskis breathes, his brows fully raised.

The old woman laughs. Holding her black cloak, she spins.

I’m now frozen and barely breathing.

Her hood begins to burn bright and molds itself into a gleaming golden crown. Inch by inch, she transforms. A gold dress clings to her body, which is no longer that of an older woman. Her skin glows, her face is young, and her hair is long and blonde. *She radiates light.* When she holds up a shield, I know exactly who she is. We all do.

“*The Lady*,” I whisper to Braizen, who looks as mesmerized as I am.

Everyone drops to their knees in awe; even the Kings lower themselves and hold their arms towards her.

“Lady and Shield,” my father cries. “Forgive us, goddess, most gracious!”

She glides forward, the hem of her dress barely touching the dais steps where my mother’s lifeless body still lies.

“You have been warned not to swear to me. You have been taught in the Way, yet you both blaspheme as if they are commands. As leaders of your people, you ought to be ashamed. The poisons your tongues so readily spew!"

The two kings lie flat and shaking on the marble. Mumbled apologies rise from their mouths, but the Lady isn't impressed. She faces the guests, and I hear sharp cries of fear.

"Ivar, you prayed to the Lady that Baelliles will be vanquished. To rid the world of their wicked Kingdom." She flicks her wrist; her delicate fingers point toward the ceiling. One by one, people dressed in green grab their chest as if they've been stabbed and fall to the floor. My eyes stretch as far as they can go. *She's killing them.*

"Pierced by their King's deceit," The Lady moans.

Braizen's breaths grow heavy in horror, and we watch more bodies fall into piles.

"And Vaskis, you prayed to the Guard that Verdana would fall into the sea, yes?" Her eyes snap towards the entryway, and the door flies open. A giant man dressed in glittering armor steps through. He glows, just as she does, only it's a cloud of silvery dust that surrounds him. He lifts his sword, and I wince as I hear it slice through the air. Braizen squeezes my hand so tightly I can no longer feel it. Groups of people dressed in blue clutch their throats, writhing and coughing as if they're drowning.

"Mercy! I beg of you! Mercy!" From his prone position, my father shakes his clasped fists.

The Lady turns her attention back to our fathers and smiles.

"Stand. Now."

They immediately obey her command, but they're both trembling. King Vaskis' jaw quivers relentlessly.

"I will not kill you for *your* sins, King Ivar of Verdana, and King Vaskis of Baelliles. But because of your blasphemy, I *will* curse your lands. I will ensure that your Kingdoms will not receive the peace you sought after!"

She raises a flattened palm, and heat roars through my body. Something urges me to rise. It calls to me, *rise against her.*

"What are you doing?" Braizen hisses as I crawl from under the table and scramble to my feet.

"Stop." My demand flies out of my mouth before I know what I'm doing.

The Lady, in all her glory, turns to face me. "What is this?" She muses, a golden-flaked eyebrow arching.

I hold my hands, my palms pulsing with heat, in front of me and narrow my stare.

"You won't hurt one more person! I won't let you." I wonder if her magic casts the fire that roars through me. But The Lady brings a finger to her chin and laughs.

"Are you threatening me, child?" She lifts her free hand towards me.

Braizen quickly positions his body in front of mine. He yells at the goddess. "Don't you dare touch her!"

I hear his mother cry out. From the corner of my eye, I see King Vaskis wince at his son's outburst, and he shakes his head.

The Lady, however, is amused.

"Look at how he cares for the girl already," she titters. "Do you see, Kings? Do you now understand what you have done? Your Kingdoms would have thrived under their rule and grown as a great, unmovable tree. But now? Because of your unrighteousness and inequities, they will never get the chance to bloom."

She raises another flat palm, and Braizen flies across the room. I scream as he slams into a table.

"I curse your children, the blood of your blood, the heirs to your thrones. I curse their love, and I take no pity on them!" she proclaims. She glances between Braizen and me, and a mocking smile creeps across her face.

"Don't touch her, he says, don't you dare *touch* her." A flick of her wrist and my body constricts. Invisible limbs circle me, and I can't move.

The Lady raises her arms and cries, "Should Idalia Hyland and Braizen Brader *ever* touch, they will die, and their Kingdoms will fall with them."

I scream again; the heat in my palms is now a raging fire. She can't do this! She won't! The hold around me is intense, but my body's call to let the fire loosen the invisible chains is stronger. I break free and barrel towards Braizen as fast as my leaden legs will carry me.

"Braizen!" I reach out my hands. I'm almost there. His fingers stretch towards mine. I can almost touch him.

A heavy body falls on mine, and I'm flat on the floor, my breath knocked out of me. I look up to see my father. His eyes are filled with tears.

"No, Idalia. You can't."

I shake my head and fight against him, but he's too heavy, too strong.

"Hear me, all Kingdoms and all people!" The Lady's voice ascends and echoes against the ceiling. "All of your fates lie in the hands of these two, the God-Cursed Children. Should they ever touch, you will *all die with them."*

She turns as she did before and vanishes, the Guard along with her.

Chapter Thirteen

Braizen

Present Day

I stumble out of the clay house and gasp. My head's still fuzzy from the wine the older woman gave me, but I'm starting to think clearly again. At least, I think I am. It was daylight when she invited me into her house. It's now dark, and stars glisten brightly. I could've sworn I was only inside for a few torturous minutes. What was in that wine, and what did I tell her?

Torrent barges out of a doorway and lands with a thud on the cobbles. His eyes are squeezed shut, and he rocks unsteadily on all fours before standing. Lin trips in a doorway and wobbles for a moment or two. He spies me and slaps himself. Hard.

"What's happening to me?" He's scared. The three of us share blank stares before I finally speak.

"Is everyone okay?"

Torrent raises a thumb. "I'm alive. So, good enough," he grunts.

Lin doesn't answer; he keeps smacking his cheek as if to wake himself from a terrible dream.

Lorna exits another house and quietly closes the door behind her. She observes each of us, folds her arms across her chest and rolls her eyes. She looks irritated but otherwise fine.

Next, Idalia appears. She seems disoriented, and she rubs her eyes to look up at the sky, seeming confused that it's nighttime. She fixes me with a peculiar expression, as though she might cry, and then runs to Torrent, who's about to topple again. Pushing her small, delicate hands between his colossal shoulder blades, she helps him straighten, as if unaware that if he falls back, he'll likely crush her.

"So, they drugged us," Lorna finally says, wiping her hands down on her thighs. "How nice."

I run my hand through my hair and manage a laugh. "There are far worse things they could've done."

"Far better things too," Torrent interrupts and pats Idalia on the back. "I thought I was following Nuri into her house, but an old woman was inside. I wasn't that disappointed. I mean, she was beautiful, and I do like my women older, but really? She didn't have enough curves for my taste. Besides, she wasn't much for conversation." He shakes his head and then brightens. "She did offer me rum, though!"

Lin smacks his face again and continues to mumble to himself. I don't even try to understand what he's saying.

"Anybody want to share what they saw inside the houses?" I flash a light grin to balance out my anxiety.

"Never," Lin barks, now rubbing his sore cheek. "We should get out of here and never look back."

I drop my chin to my chest and blink at him a few times before querying. "What in the four hells happened to you in there?"

Lin's only response is a glare.

"I saw myself in Verdana," Torr interjects. "Next to those foul, inescapable mountains! Only, they didn't look foul at all. They were beautiful. Tall, broad, and strong, like me." He smooths back his hair. "Next thing I know, the walls of the house start leaking like a punctured dam, and water was filling the room. I thought I was going to drown! I tried asking the lady for help, but she didn't move. She didn't seem to notice the water at all! She kept asking me questions, which were hard to answer, seeing as I was about to die!"

"She was testing you," Nuri's voice cuts in. The curvy woman swaggers toward us, wearing a chipper smile. Her hair is pulled back, and instead of the bright skirt, she now wears a silken, body-hugging dress of varying shades of blue. A gold nose ring dangles from her right nostril, and a giant red scarf wraps her neck. Torrent's mouth falls open.

"They were looking within, gauging the outcomes of what you'd see," she says.

"So, those women raided our brains without our consent? Wonderful," Lorna snaps.

Nuri keeps her composure. "Those women are the Mineas of the Herrah. The ones who founded Idizina hundreds of years ago and have kept it safe ever since. If they'd determined that what they saw in you was a threat, you would've woken up in the woods with no memory of this place."

"Wait, I'm sorry? Mineas? The Herrah? Did you just say hundreds of years ago?" Lin demands. "Surely you didn't mean to say *they* founded Idizina*?"*

"I meant what I said. I always do." Nuri grins.

Lin now seems more disconcerted than ever. "Are you telling me those grandmothers in there are centuries old?"

"Maybe. Or maybe they're not."

Lin grunts and throws up his hands. "What does that even mean!? How is that even possible?"

She only smirks and walks away. "With the hammer they've chosen to build," she calls over her shoulder and gestures for us to follow.

"Braze," Lorna says softly, her expression wary. "We need to be careful here. Don't let your guard down."

I nod. After what I saw in the house, there's no chance of my guard wavering. I follow the Idunn woman into a grove of glowing trees bathed in lamplight. Idalia walks far enough away from me to be considered safe, but I can still see her expression, bewildered by all the beauty and enchantment. It reminds me of the girl in the aviary all those years ago.

Nuri stops before a large stone arch that rests in the middle of the grove and then turns. "Don't tarry," she calls and trots through the arch.

I gasp as her body disappears into a glistening haze.

"Gods," Lin breathes. "I hate these woods."

"Lady blessed!" Torrent yowls as I follow him through the arch. Here the glowing trees nestle houses within their branches. Golden orbs light the paths and twinkle above us like warm stars. Torrent cheers and sprints towards a pen filled with four small animals. He towers over the fence but gently leans over to stroke a strange, furry creature with his large palm. It emits a docile chirp, then lifts enormous brown eyes. It clings to Torr's finger with its tiny paws. "What are you, little one?" Torrent purrs, placing a kiss atop its head.

"Torrent, really? Be careful!" Lin reprimands. "We don't know what those things are!"

"Yes, I do," Torrent grins. "I can feel it. They're pure and innocent and *small*! Just like you, Speck!"

Lin's face tightens, but Torrent smiles as he scratches the creature behind its fuzzy, rounded ear.

"That's a *grimshka,*" Nuri says. "They're harmless. Until they aren't."

Lorna whips her head around. "Until they aren't? What does that mean?"

"Don't worry. Stoneman's heart is no threat to their kind. He's safe." Nuri lightly taps her bottom lip and, for a moment, watches Torrent with soft eyes. She then flashes Lorna a sharp look. "You, however, should keep your distance."

Lorna gawks, and I laugh. I'm not alone; Idalia covers her mouth as giggles spill from her.

Lorna pushes forward in annoyed silence. Wooden buildings line the path, each lit by the beautiful glass orbs filled with fluttering golden flakes. The orbs illuminate the path to a small square.

"The lights line our perimeter," Nuri says as if she's heard my thoughts. "Don't wander past them."

Loud, wild music fills the air. I recognize horns and something like a lute but have never heard some of the other instruments that spring up around us. "Where's the music coming from?" I ask, patting my thigh in beat with the tune.

Nuri twirls, her hands swaying in the air. "The trees," she drawls, elongating the latter word for full effect.

Lin gawks in disbelief. "Don't try and make sense of it," I whisper to him, though I know he can't help it. I can almost feel his mind working and reasoning, but at least his breathing has calmed. Slightly.

Idalia is the first to leave the path and approach one of the trees. Tentatively, she rests her hand against its bark. At her touch, it ripples like water, and the melody changes. No longer an untamed clash, it now exudes a sweet song, like one plucked from a harp. Have the gods ordained that the forest play angelic music for her? She removes her hand and shoots Nuri a worried look as the harp-like notes continue to dance around.

"I'm sorry, I didn't know it would do that!" she says.

Nuri only laughs. "Why do you apologize? You have a lovely song!"

Idalia holds her hand to her chest. "*I* have a lovely song?"

"Yes, that's what's playing now—the song within you. No one knows a spirit like the trees, especially trees within the Florian Wood. They're far older than all of us combined and have seen, heard, tasted, and endured more than we can imagine. When a being touches them, they play that soul's melody."

"Yours is a tender spirit, but do you hear that?" Nuri continues. She leans in. "Just there! It changes into a different key! It's subtle, but it moves the entire song in a different direction."

"What does that mean?"

Nuri shrugs. "How should I know? It's not my song."

Idalia purses her mouth and narrows her eyes, one brow tilting down.

Lorna elbows my rib. "Stare harder, why don't you," she hisses.

I open my mouth to reply, but the music changes again. This time, drums beat in a wild tantrum. Torrent has one huge hand pressed against another tree's bark. His head nods to the beat, and he roars his delight.

"Yes! Do you hear this? It's the sound of a warrior's heart!"

I admit the trees *have* assessed him correctly. He flashes a grin to Nuri, and the drumming quickens.

She smiles coyly, then skips over to him with flamboyant dance moves.

"Now, watch this," she says, placing her hand next to Torrent's. Tambourines and clanking bells join his drums and create a fantastic tune.

People dressed in bright, multi-colored fabrics spill out of the buildings and join us. Perhaps they received word that we aren't a threat and are here to greet us properly. A tall woman of at least six feet reaches down and grabs Idalia's hands then swings her to the square, whose stones are painted with the image of a large tree. Its branches expand to the edges of the floor, and the green leaves sweep into the grass seamlessly.

Idalia kicks off her shoes and dances with the tall woman, smiling and clapping to Torrent and Nuri's song. Her laugh spills from her like liquid. If only I had a cup, I'd gladly scoop it up and merrily drink it.

A dark-skinned man races towards us, his eyes locked on Lin, who steps back and shakes his hands in front of him. "No. No, thank you. I don't dance." The man ignores Lin's protest and pulls him onto the square. "Really, I don't know what I'm doing. I'm just here to drink and fix everyone else's mistakes," Lin sputters. "I don't know what to think about this."

"This isn't a place for thinking," the man chirps. "This is a place to free your mind of its burden." Lin stares at him in disbelief.

A place where he can't overthink is one of the four hells for my friend.

"Let's see you dance, Lin! Release your mind!" I call out in mockery.

He stares back at me unamused, but the man grabs his hands and spins him. He suddenly releases him, and Lin twirls twice, then wobbles to a stop. I wonder if he'll run as far away as possible; then I see him smile. To my surprise, he even starts to tap his foot.

Torrent and Nuri twirl around, not caring who or what they may take out in their wake. His eyes are closed, and a smile stretches across his massive jaw. Another man, this one tall and lean, comes to collect Lorna. She spits on the ground and pulls out her hatchet, holding it out straight in front of her in warning.

"*No*," she says curtly. The man's eyes widen, and he promptly retreats. She looks at me, her expression oozing with disdain.

"He seems harmless enough," I shrug.

Lorna rolls her eyes, turns sharply to leave, and runs straight into a blonde woman holding two mugs of frothy ale. The impact sends the alcohol spilling over the woman's lace bodice, and Lorna apologizes and awkwardly tries to pat her dry.

"No need for all that. It's a celebration; drinks are bound to spill," the woman chuckles. Her round blue eyes meet Lorna's, and they both fall silent. The woman glances down. "You could… help me fetch another drink. If you want?" Lorna doesn't respond with words; her lips form a tight line, and she nods, then follows.

It's about time that Lorna learns to have some fun. I cross my arms and tap my feet to the music; enjoying watching these encounters all too much. Suddenly, a beautiful young woman stands before me. Her cat-like eyes rest on angled cheekbones. She smiles and stretches out her hand.

"Would you like to dance?" Her accent is thick and mesmerizing, one I've never heard. I take a deep breath.

"I would *love* to dance." I grab her palm and spin her, then catch her in my arms to slowly lower her.

She beams in delight. "So, you've done this before?" One of her brows arches high, nearly touching her hairline.

I hold her in position and wink.

"More times than I can count."

It's true. Many nights with The Cloaked were spent in a tavern or small village where Torrent and I embarrassed the entire crew with our shameless dancing and antics.

Idalia raises her hands above her head, her eyes closed in merriment as her body sways to the music. I try not to stare. To gawk. But gods, her movements…

We continue to dance with small wariness in our steps, careful not to get too close. Every so often, our eyes lock, but maybe it's for more than simple caution. Maybe they linger upon each other a little too long.

Perhaps a stare can be more deadly than a touch.

Hours pass. My legs shake. Even Torrent leans over, and Nuri stretches her arms as high as possible to fit around his waist, though they don't make it past his hips. Lin has been sitting for a while now, downing drink after drink and telling stories about our adventures. Lorna is totally drunk, which makes me happy. She's still listening to the blonde woman, Rianne. I've no idea what Rianne is saying that could possibly hold Lorna's interest for so long, but I mean to congratulate her and buy her a drink. Idalia had a few glasses herself, but left the dance circle to join the Idunn children off to the side and play.

I've danced with countless partners, and as I spin Breto, a short male with gangly teeth and mustard hair, for the final time, I know I'm at last too spent to take on another. The music stops. He bows and thanks me, and I bring him in for a hug, then stumble over to the soft grass. The orbs' light now shines a warm, dim gold. The Idunn people are tired and start to make their way back to their homes in the trees. Nuri releases Torr and approaches me, her eyes foggy from drink.

"We have an inn, but there are only two beds, and they're quite small."

I throw up a lazy hand. "I can sleep here; I prefer the ground to a mattress."

"I know," she smiles.

Torrent appears behind her; his buzzing grin says it all. "I won't fit in one of those beds. We should give them to Lorna and Lin."

Nuri's brow arches. "My bed is large, Stoneman, so that I may fit large people in it."

Torr's lips curl into a smile.

"Goodnight, Boss."

They're off before I can respond. I ease down and cradle my head in my hands to stare up at the stars, shining brighter here than they do in Nerwick. They appear only an arm's distance away—as if I could reach out and pluck them from their inky canvas. Crickets and other insects hum their nightly hymns, and I wonder how the Idunns find and keep these and other creatures alive in The Wood. A question for the morning. A question for the daylight.

"We're taking him to the inn. He asked that you make sure no one touches his crossbow."

Rising to my elbows, I see a larger woman carrying a dead-asleep Lin draped across her shoulders.

I chuckle as she leaves, and my breath hangs in the brisk air. I rest back in my hands.

Someone kicks my foot, and I'm pulled from relaxation yet again. It's Lorna. She's smiling as I've never seen her smile before.

"I take it you had a good night?" I ask.

"Something like that," she laughs, and her cheeks flush. "Okay with you if I take the other bed?"

"Yeah, I don't want it. You should know that."

"I do know that," she corrects. "I thought you might want to give it to the girl."

I shoot up. Idalia. Where will she sleep? Lorna is waiting, so I laugh lightly.

"You think I'd give a Verdanian a bed and leave one of my own without? You definitely drank too much. Get inside."

For the first time since we started this trip, Lorna sends me a look filled with gratitude, satisfied that I haven't forsaken my people.

I smile and lie back again, listening to her boots scuff against the old wood as she makes her way up the spiral stairs into the trees. No one remains outside now but me—*and her.*

I shut my eyes and try to let the gentle breeze and crisp air lull me into a deep, peaceful sleep. Any other time, this would work. Tonight, though, thoughts keep me awake. My heart thuds and my breaths are labored. I can't rest because I can't stop thinking about Idalia.

With a sigh, I prop myself up on my elbows and look to the last place I'd spied her, but she's not there. She's gone. *Good,* now I can sleep.

Though, she *is* my captive. What if she's escaped? What does that matter! She doesn't even have a map! Honestly, how far could she even get? *Still,* it's my responsibility to deliver her to my father. Yes! I must make sure she's still here, my gods! What would my band say if they awoke to a missing captive princess? They'd have my head and…

I'm on my feet before I can finish the thought. I trek beyond the square, where night swallows the trees. The moon casts silver rays that light the path. Ahead, within the protection of the orbs' light, a small cliff overlooks a gorge. I sense in my heart that she's there.

I follow this familiar feeling, hoping it will lead me to her again.

Chapter Fourteen

Idalia

Footsteps approach, and I know whose before he says anything. I dangle my feet off the ledge and stare at the looming moon and the washed, ethereal halo that hugs around it. The dark Wood sleeps. Below my feet, the dense trees stretch as far as I can see. For the first time since entering them, I'm not afraid. Without a word, he settles several feet away and throws his legs over the edge.

"Enough distance?" He smiles, and I turn to meet his arrogant stare.

"I suppose. Unless the cliff decides to crumble, and we meet at the bottom."

"In that case…" He scooches another inch away from me. "How about that?"

I expel a heavy breath that comes out as a laugh. "Perfect."

I again face the moon and let the wind blow my hair. I feel his eyes still on me, and my heart races. Why does my heart race?

"Quite a day, huh?"

I want to laugh and agree. I want to drink and spend the night going over just how wild this day was, but I can't. I must remember who he is. I must tell my heart to calm and my mind to take control. I'm not a twelve-year-old girl chasing birds any longer. I look at him.

"Have you come to make sure I haven't run away? I told you, I'm not foolish enough to brave these woods alone." He looks stunned. "Furthermore, I saved two of your people today. I think I've proven that I'm trustworthy enough to have a moment for myself."

Eventually, his brow relaxes, and he nods. "Of course, you have," he agrees and rises. "You've proven more than that. I'll leave you be. Have a good night, Sparrow." He pivots to leave, and an involuntary groan escapes me.

"I wish you wouldn't call me that."

He doesn't move. The curls on the back of his head sway lightly in the wind.

"We were friends when you gave me that name, and now that we're not, I don't think it's appropriate to use it anymore. It doesn't seem right."

He's silent, but I see one of his hands ball into a tight fist.

"If you don't want me to call you that, I won't," he bites out.

My stomach drops. I don't *not* want him to call me Sparrow. I'd half expected him to fight me for the right to use that name.

"Good," I say, and he sends back a confirming nod.

"Good."

He takes a step, and anger begins to boil in my chest and propel my words. "You *kidnapped* me. It's not like you're trying to be my friend. I'm here against my will."

"Because if we were here for any other reason, you'd consider me a friend, right?" He scoffs.

My cheeks burn. "No, I wouldn't."

He huffs as if he proved his point.

Arrogant little ass.

"You killed my men, Braizen!" I shout up at him. "Verdanian bodies rot in this Wood as we speak because of you and your bandits. Why would I ever consider you a friend? After what your crew did! After what your father did all those years ago."

"*My* father?" He breaks in and finally faces me. Holding a hand to his chest, he leans down and speaks slowly, as if I'm a child. "Really, Idalia? After all these years, you still believe that? My parents wanted peace between our kingdoms! They invited you into our home, and they were prepared for you to live with us until we were…Until you and I…" His voice hitches, and he doesn't say the word. *Married.*

"What should I believe, then? Would you have me blame *my own father* for my mother's death? He loved her, adored her! He traveled to the land he hated most with the woman he loved wholly in hopes for a better future!"

Braizen's laugh is cynical, and he wipes the tip of his nose with his thumb, a gesture of dismissal if I ever saw one. His eyes are now cold.

"So, your father is blameless while mine is a monster? Is that it? You're completely convinced my father would do something so vile?"

All I can do is laugh. "Verdana is *starving* because of your father! We can barely trade goods with Aeradian because Vaskis sends his men to slaughter ours at the river! And Lachlan won't deign to send his troops to protect us, fearing that *our* war will cost *his* men *their* lives. That's the greed of the Baellilean people and the will of your King. Your father is too evil to let us have food! He'd rather women and children die daily of hunger than pull his men back for one day! So yes, I *do* believe your father is vile. I'm convinced he killed my mother. And I believe with everything within me that he'd do so again."

Braizen stomps toward me and doesn't stop until he is dangerously close.

"My father does whatever he has to do to protect his people. Why does this make him a monster? What did *you* do when Torrent needed saving? Or Lorna, for the Lady's sake? You killed men for the lives of your *enemies*. And yet, you consider my father evil for doing the same for those he loves?" His voice now mocks me. "This is truly the Verdanian way; your tongue betrays you with its contradictions."

My head pounds in rage. I rise and plant myself mere inches from him.

"Your father doesn't love anyone," I spit. "He's a coward and a fool, unholy and unfit! He lured us with an empty promise, and my mother died trusting it! This is of no concern to you, though, is it? Because while you clung in fear to your mother's side, mine lay on the floor *dead*. When yours tucked you into bed and reassured you that all would be well, mine was buried in the cold ground. The Lady and Guard punished my family after we'd already suffered a great loss. And yet all your father could do was pledge his undying vengeance against us. *That's* how I know he did it, and that's why I hate him. That's why I hate all of you!"

His nostrils flare, and his chest heaves. I haven't been this close to him since we were children, and I see light freckles splattered across his cheeks, almost too faint to notice in the moonlight. But his eyes. The pale light only emphasizes their starkness. My neck constricts under their frosty bite. I can almost feel his warm breath against my lips. My panting grows heavier.

"Well then, it's a blessing that The Lady cursed us when she did. It would've been a tragedy for you to marry a man you hate," he hisses. "To be forced to lead a country you despise." His lids flicker, and he pulls back his shoulders. "Unfortunately for you and whatever lies you choose to believe, none of it matters. You dared to travel through Baelliles and look where it got you. Caught by a bunch of lowly bandits who took out Verdana's best men." He leans in even closer. "*How pathetic.*"

My lips clamp so tightly I can feel the blood draining from them. Then, I tilt my head back to say, "I can run right now, and there isn't a single thing you can do about it."

His eyes flare at my threat, but he lifts his chin and smiles. "You wouldn't last ten minutes alone, and you know it."

"So?" I answer. "I'd rather die than stand here for another minute with a Baellilean!" I'm too angry for thought. I turn and flee. I've no idea where I'm going, but I force my legs to kick as fast as possible. Behind me, I hear Braizen groan.

"Don't do it, Idalia!"

I hate him! I hate him and his entire kingdom. I should've let those vines kill Torrent. I should've escaped with Tawdrey and his men. I should've let Lorna die.

"Idalia, stop! The lights!"

Does he think I'll listen to him? What can he do? He can't grab me and drag me back. He should've known that I wouldn't stay after hearing him spew such lies.

I try to ignore a growing discomfort in my palms and shake them relentlessly as I press forward. Now it's hard to breathe, and my eyes overflow with tears, blurring my vision. The line of golden orbs comes to an end. *I hate him. I hate him. I hate him.*

"Idalia… Idalia! Sparrow! Look out!"

I slam into something warm and drop to the ground with an agonized moan. I rub my head and curse Braizen's name. Heaving, I try to collect myself before standing. A long, sticky substance dangles in front of me. What in the four hells? I look up and scream.

A giant wolf towers over me. No, it can't possibly be a mere wolf. It's far too large. It's something else, something more. Sleek onyx fur that gleams in the moonlight coats its mass. Above its snarling snout lie a pair of forest-green eyes that teem with hunger. The trail of saliva hanging from its fangs finally drops to the ground.

With a low growl, it bares its teeth, dark with the dried blood of the prey that came before me. It lifts a paw to strike.

"Duck!" Braizen shouts.

Instinct takes over, and my head swoops down as a small dagger spirals overhead and pierces the beast in one eye. It yelps, violently shaking its giant head.

"Get up!" Braizen yells. "I can't carry you! Get up and run back to the lights. Now!"

I stand, shaking, and see him waiting for me. I take one last look at the beast and, with my hands on fire, sprint back to Braizen.

He lets me pass him before he joins. "Don't look back! Keep running, no matter what!"

I propel my legs faster than I've ever moved them before. Exhaustion quickly overtakes me. But I don't falter, not for a single step. I run and run.

I see the square and sprint even faster until I reach it and fall to my knees on the grass, panting, and wheezing. Finally, *finally*, I can draw a deep breath. I roll onto my back.

"Is it still chasing us? Is it coming?" I gasp and hold a hand to my racing heart.

Braizen flings his body onto the ground near mine.

"We're back in the perimeter; I don't think it can pass through."

Relief washes over me. So, that is why Nuri suggested we stay within the lights. "What. Was. That?!" I pant.

Braizen sits up and drapes an arm over a bent knee. "More stories of terror, I guess," he says quietly.

It takes a while, but I can finally hear the soft rustle of leaves dance in the wind and not my anxious thoughts. I pull myself up. Braizen isn't asleep, as his silence led me to believe. He's still surveying the perimeter.

"Thank you for saving me," I whisper, embarrassment stinging my cheeks.

He looks bewildered, then his glance softens. He sends me a silent nod.

I take a deep breath before I speak. "I know you only did it because I'm your prisoner, and you need me for whatever reason. But still, it was a nice thing to do."

The soft glance disappears, and he releases a sharp laugh, one absent of any humor.

"I didn't save you because you're my prisoner. I saved you because..." He runs his hand through his curls and seems to weigh what to say next. "Well, you saved my team. I was only repaying the favor. That's what nasty, peon bandits do."

Of course, he only did what was right. I bob my head in acknowledgment. Though it's hard to believe a Baellilean would know what *right* means. A long moment of silence drags on, and I catch him looking at me.

"I'm sorry about your mother, Idalia," he says carefully.

I search his expression for any signs of malice but only see his endearing blue eyes and somber face. His words are genuine; I can tell as much. A thud goes off in my chest, and I'm suddenly too nervous to look at him, so I turn away and smile before speaking.

"Call me Sparrow."

From a sidelong glance I see a handsome smile score his face. My heart beats even faster.

"Okay, Little Sparrow," he says, playing with a loose string on his boot. "Can I ask you something personal?"

I don't know if it's the cool wind or embarrassment that now causes my cheeks to burn, but I nod before I can decide against it.

Braizen swallows and gives me an uneasy glance. "What happened to you that night after you left Nerwick, after the curse?"

I inhale and tuck a loose strand of hair behind my ear. This certainly isn't what I expected. I gather my thoughts, then plunge ahead.

"It's really all a blur," I say coolly. "I remember being in the Hall, and my father stopping me from…" My eyelids flicker. "From doing something disastrous," I finish. "We left without returning to our chambers. Without any of our belongings. I remember him yelling at me to get in the carriage. So many things were happening at once, and I couldn't understand any of them. I think I was too young to comprehend what had happened, to cope with such overwhelming feelings."

I hear what sounds like a grunt of agreement from Braizen and continue. "Finally, I found my way to the carriage, and I realized that… That it's not only the young, who struggle with their grief. My father went mad that day, I think. He spoke words I didn't understand; he barely stopped long enough to catch his breath. And then…" The following words creep from my mouth like the air pulls them from deep within me.

"He wouldn't let her body be carried behind us. He said it wasn't honorable. Nor did he trust anyone else to bring her home, not after what happened. So, he sat her next to me in the carriage, where she'd be safe."

Braizen's breath hitches, and he drops the shoe string.

"What?"

Tears threaten to spill, but I blink hard, shake my head, and keep them at bay.

"I rode the entire way home next to my mother's dead body. My father spoke to her corpse for most of the trip, whispering that she'd be avenged. I didn't look at her. Not once. But I could feel her skin pressed against mine, and it grew colder and colder. And, and… *the smell…*"

I shudder and shove the memory further back in my mind where I don't have to face it. "We buried her beneath a willow in our courtyard."

Braizen is so still; if it weren't for the sound of his deep, even breaths, I'd think I was alone. The silence grows thick and heavy but, at the same time, too loud for me to concentrate. I push on to ease the tension it creates.

"In all these years, I haven't visited her grave, not once. I can't bring myself to. It reminds me of that night and the trip home. Besides, our people suffer outside the castle walls, and the Burial Ground grows every day. There are too many graves to mourn. If I start with hers, I'll never stop. I'll never stop mourning."

Now the tears form. I feel them slide down my cheeks. I always afford two or three for my mother. When the fourth drips down, I wipe them away and straighten my back. *Why did I tell him that? What in the hells am I doing?*

Braizen's eyes lock on mine, his sorrowful stare discovering hidden places that I never wanted anyone to find. I hate that he pities me. I shift, discomforted. Besides, it's his fault—all of it. Baelliles caused this tragedy.

"*Idalia...*" He whispers, his fingers reaching for mine. When I pull away and grimace, he yanks back his hand. He stares at his palm as if confounded that he is unable to comfort me.

He can't. Not physically, or any other way for that matter.

"Let's talk about you now," I say abruptly, longing to move his attention away from me. "What happened to *you* that night? After we left?"

He's still staring at his hand, and when he looks up, his eyes gleam with building tears.

"You rode home with her body," he murmurs. "My gods. It's no wonder you hate us."

"Please, Braizen. Anything else." My mouth quivers, and I clamp my lips tight and frown so I don't break into sobs. "*Anything else*," I repeat, and my voice wavers.

He nods. "My father spent most of the night trying to convince King Lester that what happened was one of Verdana's sick measures," he says. "My mother...Well, your father wasn't the only one who went mad that night. She completely lost her mind; perhaps seeing the gods in the flesh proved too much for her. Or maybe it was all the bodies," he adds quietly.

"Horrick took her away," His eyes snap up to meet mine, and for a heartbeat I wonder if he is going to continue or not. He seems unsure of what information he should divulge. He swallows hard and resumes, "He took her to a place called Pathstowe. He used to take me to visit her until

I was old enough to go alone. I've only seen her a few times in all these years. She may not have been the kindest woman, but she's my mother. I can't bear to leave her alone for too long." His long fingers flex and dig into the dirt.

"So, she didn't tuck you in."

"No. No, she did not tuck me in," he laughs.

The frigid wind hits my cheeks, and I crinkle my nose in irritation. It's likely turned deep red by now. This is why I hate the cold.

Braizen gazes at the trees. "I spent most of that night helping the servants drag the bodies from the Hall. My father was too busy with politics to notice what I was doing. We found even more dead outside. The Baellilean council was convinced your father had somehow killed them, too. There was so much death, so much pain. I could hardly stand being in the castle after that. There wasn't time for tears, no time to grapple with what had happened. Just talk of war and strategists lined up at our gates to help guide us to victory."

He absently pulled on some blades of grass. "My father told me that leaders don't have the luxury of weeping. That we must press on and make sure our Kingdom stands tall when something wants to bend or break us. I hated it. I started to leave the castle and found myself in villages and towns far, far away from my home. I still don't want to be there. I don't want anything to do with it."

He looks at me with those last words, and I see the same look he gave me all those years ago. Deep inside, he's still the same boy who just wants to be outside and watch birds—nothing more, nothing less.

"Is that why you were in The Wood?" I ask.

His neck muscles tighten. "Yes."

"I suppose I can understand," I say. "My father did the same thing. Once we were home, it's all he spoke of. Enemies, strategy, alliances, war, war, war." I lift my hand to view the dirt caked beneath my nails and lazily begin to pick at it, anything to keep from making eye contact.

"Everything changed. I was rarely allowed to leave the castle, not even to play with the noblemen's children as before. I couldn't visit towns or wander the frosty fields. My Nurse, Lydia, was the only friend I could truly talk to. You'd think I was an enemy to Verdana; I was treated almost like a prisoner. All I was allowed to do was ride and train..."

I catch myself and bite down on my tongue. *Too much, Idalia. You say too much around him!* Slowly, I bring my head up; he's staring at me with his head cocked to one side.

"Train?" His tone is light and playful. "For what?"

To kill any Baellilean I see on sight. I manage a laugh and wipe my dirty hands against my dress.

"Oh, to be a good wife and a patient queen. My father thought I needed work in those areas. He's berated me about it for the last twelve years." It's only half a lie. My father certainly does think I could improve those skills.

Braizen laughs, and I silently sigh in relief that he's bought this semi-truth.

"I don't know why you're laughing," I say with a pointed glare. "One day, you'll take a wife of your own, and you'll regret it if her parents didn't train her for the role!"

He snickers louder, then pauses briefly. I think I glimpse despondence wash over him, but he shakes his head, so his curly locks fly. He sends me a cheeky grin.

"I'm sure the woman lucky enough to marry me will be more than prepared. And if not, it just so happens that I'm a mighty good teacher. Across all aspects of marriage, of course. But particularly in *one* area of expertise," he says with a broad wink. "If you know what I'm saying."

I groan loudly. "I shall start praying for the poor girl now; may the gods bless her soon-to-be tormented soul."

He's still smiling, and I look away to hide my flushed cheeks. I've heard servants in the castle speak about Braizen and his…*area of expertise*. How in the hells they knew about it is beyond me, but our servants loved to gossip, and I loved to listen.

I gaze into the bright boughs arching overhead and at the golden lights that warm and protect us. I sense something lives and breathes in and among these beautiful trees. I can feel it when I place my palms against the earth; I can almost hear it when the music is low enough. It's serenity and strength, as if I'm *supposed* to be here. *As if I belong.*

The thought pulls me back into the present, and my expression hardens. No, I'm not meant to be here. I'm supposed to be on my way to marry King Lachlan to save my people. I'm meant to be the Savior of Verdana. No longer a little girl forced to hide behind white stone walls while her Kingdom dies around her, but the woman who triumphs over those who seek to harm us. The one whose name will be praised and be the last thing King Vaskis will hear before he's defeated.

Instead, I've been captured by his son. Braizen is an irritating obstacle and a hindrance to my fulfilling my fate, not someone whose company is to be enjoyed. "Why did you kidnap me, Braizen?" I concentrate on playing with some stones and refuse to face him, afraid I'll fall prey to his charms yet again.

"Why were you on your way to Aeradian?" He prods back.

This time, I won't say too much. I clear my throat and start to draw in the dirt with my finger. "Because of Baellilean troops, my father was wary of attending King Lester's funeral. As I'm sure you know, we didn't go. No Verdanian attended."

"With good reason," Braizen huffs. "Our Royal King's guards line that road."

I scoff, flicking away some of the dirt under my thumb. "Yes, well. We decided now it would be safe for me to go and pay our respects. Of course, we were wrong," I add.

Braizen releases a low whistle. "After all this time, with so many years to cultivate the skill, I thought you'd be a better liar."

My eyes shoot up to meet his grin. I grab some dirt and throw it at him.

He lets out a deep chuckle as it lands on his leg. "If you don't want to tell me, I won't pry," he says.

"I asked a question first; I'll remind you."

"Well, I could just make up an answer as you did, so what's the point of asking?" He counters. "What if we start with smaller secrets and work our way up?" Braizen suggests.

His smile drains me of all reason. He scratches his facial hair, which has grown quite a bit in the last few days. His smile grows wider. "Have you ever been with anyone?"

"I'm afraid you'll have to be more specific if you want a decent answer," I laugh.

"Oh, I think you know *exactly* what I mean, Sparrow." He leans forward and winks. "Have you taken, or has anyone taken you to bed? Man, woman, or otherwise?"

At that, I throw my head back and howl. "You can't be serious! Surely, there are more pressing unknowns you'd like to know about!"

"I said we should start with small secrets, didn't I? To learn if a Princess is unbesmirched seems little enough to me."

I throw up my hands. "Trust that any man who's taken me to bed is far from *little*."

"I guess that answers that!" Braizen laughs.

"Does it surprise you to know that I'm impure?"

"*Impure?* Good gods, what do they teach in Verdana? Being experienced doesn't make one impure! I mean, if it does, then it's straight to the four hells I go."

"Indeed." My haughty tone doesn't match my smile, and as soon as Braizen notices, his relaxed grin grows.

"Your turn," he says with far too much enjoyment.

I tap a finger to my chin and ponder what small untold truth I should ask of him. I scan his face for a moment, then click my tongue.

"Where did you meet Lorna?"

He rubs his hands across his face. "This feels more like her story to tell than my own," he says. "But for the sake of the game... I met her in a small town just outside of Tranket River. It was only me, Torr, and Lin at the time. Lorna was caring for her sick sister when a hostile creature named Godfred Allim paid a visit. He was rounding up peasants to become...well, how should I say this…"

"Slaves?" I interrupt with keen interest.

He shakes his head and bites his lip.

Apparently, he believes it too ungentlemanly to proceed, so I press in closer and whisper, "*Whores?*"

His wide eyes tell me my assumption is correct.

"Are you too shy to say that word around me? *Whores*?"

He doesn't answer, though his smile slants devilishly.

"I'm plenty familiar with the profession," I say. "Women in Verdana often choose it! It pays good money, and everyone must eat, especially when food is scarce."

Braizen turns his hands over as if he doesn't know what to say, then laughs. "Oh, I don't judge the profession. In fact, I rather enjoy it. As often as I can."

I roll my eyes. "I wish I had a drink," I say.

Immediately, Braizen stands and scans the small square. He lifts a finger to tell me to wait and sprints into the distance. I can see him slowly and carefully opening a door that squeaks on its hinges. I wait, rubbing my hands against my arms to keep the cool air at bay, until I again hear the squeak.

He runs back, his hands filled with two large cups, ale spilling over the rims. I can't believe he retrieved them in so little time, and I'm pleasantly surprised by the gesture. It can be convenient to have a thief as a companion, I suppose.

He sets my mug on the ground and then backs away to his spot. I nod in appreciation and sip. The froth stains my upper lip, and the ale's strength has me smiling in glee.

"As you were saying," I thrum, swallowing another gulp.

He again settles with one arm draped on his bent knee and continues.

"Godfred came to collect people, mostly women, to be sold. In this place, men and women *don't* choose the profession; it's chosen for them. Lorna and her sister were to be collected. Had her sibling been in good health, I might not have ever met my comrade. You see, I was only in this quaint town to rob Mister Allim. But he was already dead. A hatchet straight through his throat. His pockets were already empty."

"Of course, Lorna would take out such a man," I say after a long exhale.

"She almost took the three of us out, too, till we explained we weren't any danger to her."

"What about her sister?"

He stops mid-drink and lowers his mug. "She didn't make it."

I drop my head and murmur a prayer to The Lady that Lorna's sister might find rest behind Her shield. I drink again and resolve to be more lenient on the fighter. Lorna's spirit might be harsh, but it likely wasn't born that way. Life had molded her into a fearsome warrior, and I'll do my best to respect that truth.

"It's my turn." Braizen grows serious, and he sets his mug down on the ground. "Why did you do it?" He queries, and his jaw tightens.

I tip my glass and take a generous gulp; a bit of ale finds its way down my chin.

"I'm sorry?"

"Why did you do it? Why did you save Torrent and Lorna?"

"Oh," I whisper so quietly I'm not sure he heard it.

"I've been thinking about it all night, and I can't make any sense of it. We're your enemies. We're Baellileans, and we captured you. You had the chance to let both of them die, yet you didn't. You had a chance to escape, and yet here you are. I want to know why."

I slide more ale into my mouth, knowing damn well that I've already had too much of it. I can drink glass after glass of wine, but this is a much more potent concoction. I smack my lips and consume a great deal more.

"I wish I could tell you," I say plainly.

I extend my legs and point my toes. Sliding my tongue across my teeth, I wonder how I'm going to answer. How do I explain an unknown force that urges me to do things, appeared just as his friends were about to die? And that I must do as it demands, or I become drenched in insufferable discomfort that only grows with denial?

I take another ill-advised drink before declaring, "I don't have any friends."

The retort jolts us both back. Braizen's brows are knit; he expects me to elaborate. Gods, this drink is much too strong.

"It's just… It's… Well, it's as I said. I've been alone for a very long time. I don't have any real friends. Teddy and Lachlan might count, but I've only seen them twice in my life because your father would have me decapitated before letting me travel to Aeradian freely. Seeing you all together, you and your bandits, made me envious. I think I saved them because I'm lonely."

Immediately I bring my cup to my mouth, but there are only a few measly drops left. I lean back and shake them onto my tongue.

Braizen stares intently at me. I don't know what to do. I squirm and will myself to stare back.

"Next question," I cough and pretend not to be humiliated by the honesty in my response. "Do you still think of me as an enemy?" I lean forward, squinting like a lunatic. Surely this new question will make him forget the last one.

Braizen seems to feel the heat of this examination and straightens himself to answer.

"Hmm," he muses. "Yes."

I blink a few times, then let out a sharp laugh. He's not wrong, yet I can't help but feel wounded by his blunt answer. A roll of nausea uncurls in my gut and I rub my sleeve against my mouth. Perhaps I shouldn't have drank so quickly.

His words pull my attention back. "But only because you *want* to be. I think you want to hate me, and I suppose it's easier if you think I hate you too."

I've no idea what to say. The ale begins to drag me under, and my mind floats; it's all too excited at being close to him.

"You're wrong," I state, though I didn't give my tongue consent to say this.

He studies me closely.

"I am?"

I nod profusely and blurt, "*So wrong.* I hate what Baelliles takes from my people, and I hate it even more that you're a part of it." The uneasy wave roams through my stomach, yet the words still somehow make their way out.

"I hate that I have to hate you."

Hot bile inches its way up my throat, and as Braizen opens his mouth to say something back, I vomit onto the grass. I heave, and the bile flows in unrelenting droves. I'll never drink ale again. *Ever.* Well, maybe I will, but at least not as fast.

I collapse, and my cheek slams against dirt. I can't hold my eyes open a second longer; it's dark.

Gasping, I quickly push myself up when I hear voices. I reach for my dagger. It's gone, of course, and bleak reality washes over me as it has each morning I've awakened since my kidnapping. I rub the heels of my hands into my eyes and stretch my limbs. They ache from calling the ground a bed, and I wonder if I'll ever get a good night's rest again. I touch my hair, disheveled and tangled, and reach to pull threads from my cloak to tie it back. But it's not my cloak covering me. This one is far thinner and pine green—Braizen's cloak.

With a huge yawn, I scan my surroundings. I don't see him. Only Idunns, whistling, humming, *skipping*, dear gods, as they go about their sunrise duties. Some smile and wave, seemingly unperturbed by my ghastly appearance. I pluck a green string from Braizen's cloak and wrap it as many times around my hair as I can. It won't hold long, but it'll have to do for now.

"Good morning. Idalia, is it?" A silken voice greets me. I look up to see a blonde beauty smiling down. It's the woman Lorna spent the night with. She reaches down and helps pull me to my feet. "I see you slept well. That's good."

"I slept. I don't know how well," I say with a weak laugh.

Her light eyebrows rise. "Apologies. Had we known you'd sleep on the ground, we would've offered you one of our own beds."

"Oh, no. I wouldn't want any of you to do such a thing." I follow her to one of the large tables in the small square. I don't know what to do with the cloak. I'm afraid even to hold it; it's something that constantly brushes against *his* skin and feels almost blasphemous to wear against mine. I place it next to me on the bench. "Do you know where the Prince went this morning? I believe he slept near me."

She chuckles. "We found him sleeping in a tree. Lorna took him to the river so he could bathe." Her large eyes peer at me with great sincerity.

"Perhaps you'd also like to bathe? We can offer you a fresh change of clothes if you wish."

Embarrassment washes over me. Until now, I hadn't stopped to consider how I must reek after surviving in these woods.

"A bath would be lovely."

Chapter Fifteen

Braizen

Whatever the Idunns put in their rivers, I want endless vials of it. The moment I dipped my toes in the water, my entire body felt refreshed. When I dunked my head and let the current flow over it, I realized I have never bathed truly in my whole life. Not like this. As I step out of the water, my body tingles as if I've been lathered in mint.

Lorna says that she feels as if she's wrapped in eucalyptus, and her hair burns a brighter red than I've ever seen. Yes, something truly magical exists in these waters. I wrap the linen sheet she left me around my waist and am shaking water from my hair when the seraphic plucking of strings rises from a nearby glade. Idalia must have touched a tree. The music is divine, a perfect melody for such a heavenly morning. She'll want her privacy. I quickly gather the ivory tunic Lorna also left; I can change elsewhere. But as I turn to leave, Idalia spots me.

Her cheeks blush, and her fists clutch her sheet.

"Good morn—"

"I left your cloak with Rianne—" We speak in unison, then stop in unison.

She laughs and then says, "Good morning."

"Thank you." My words almost trip over hers, and I let out a humorous sigh. "I'm sure it could use a heavy washing, too."

She shrugs and swallows hard. "I appreciate the gesture," she says.

"When you passed out, you were shivering. I couldn't do much to help, so, I just kind of…threw it over you."

Her laugh harmonizes with the tree's harp.

"I decided it was better not to sleep right next to you, so I climbed the nearest tree. That way, I could keep watch without, you know, endangering us." I'm rambling. I need to stop, but I can't. My tongue continues to betray me. "I would've carried you somewhere more comfortable if I could've."

"Really, the cloak was more than enough. I hate the cold, and I have a strikingly low tolerance for ale," she says, pushing her hair from her face.

"Well, don't let Torr or Lin hear you say that. They'll make it their life mission to grow your tolerance. I should know."

Her cheeks are still red, and she doesn't respond. I gulp, then give one heavy nod. "I should leave you to it then." I gesture towards the water, offering her the entire river as if it were my own. She's staring at my body. Her eyes glisten, and I remember that save for the thin linen fabric wrapped around my waist, I'm naked. A laugh rolls off my tongue, and she joins in before lightly saluting me with two fingers to her forehead and making her way to the river. When her back is to me, I realize my heart is racing, and for a second, I could swear it beats in unison with her song.

Torrent struts to the table that evening. "How do I look?" He asks. His heavy blond hair is slicked back with oil, and his beard is trimmed so closely that I can see skin. In all my years of knowing him, I've never glimpsed a trace of his chin.

"I hardly recognize the brute," Lin scoffs, licking sauce from his fingers. The Idunns have prepared us a massive dinner, and it's all I can do not to kiss every one of them. I'm clean, and I'm in fresh clothes. Idalia is wrapped in a white, oversized tunic. I can catch the sweet fragrance of peonies mixed with gardenias from it even across the table. Periodically, she drapes her sleeves over her hands, presses them firmly to her face, and breaths in the scent deeply.

"I think he looks wonderful," Nuri sings, grabbing and shaking Torrent's chin as he sits next to her on the bench. "Although, I didn't mind the untethered look either, Stoneman. Beard kept or unkept; you exude a rugged force I can't keep myself away from."

"Oh, *temptress…*" Torr croons. They must've passed a wonderful night in her *large* bed, though I stop myself from imagining any of the details for my own sake.

Rianne sits down between Lorna and Lin and pours herself a healthy glass of wine. Music fills the air, and the orbs begin to glow with the coming of night.

"Is it always this happy here?" I ask.

"Why wouldn't it be?" Nuri's smile stretches from ear to ear.

I shrug as Breto pours ale into my mug. "It's hard to believe, is all. It just seems a little too good to be true."

Nuri blows an exasperated breath and releases Torrent's hand.

"How sad you people are! The misery that binds you is a powerful spell indeed! You haven't yet been here two full days, and you already assume the joy you feel must be running out."

"That's not it," I protest.

"No?" She probes. "Then what is it? Do tell."

"I only mean it's *odd*. Everyone's always smiling; music's always playing, and the food is delicious. It doesn't seem possible..."

"Why not?" Breto chirps from the other end of the table. "Are your kingdoms truly so dispirited that you feel everyone else must be too?" He digs into his meal and nudges the man sitting next to him.

"May I remind you that most of the Florian Wood lies within Baelliles," I say. My mother would've approved of my haughty, princely tone. "Idizina sits in the very Kingdom you speak ill of."

Everyone, save my companions, howls. "Have I said something humorous?" I take a pull of ale and try to regain my composure.

Nuri waves her hands and titters. "Very humorous! 'Tis a great joke to believe the Florian Wood belongs to anything but itself. We're Idunns, not Baellileans. Not Verdanians and not Aeradians, no matter what imaginary lines these trees may take root on. The Others would mock you as I do."

"*The Others*?" Lin repeats, eyes riveted on her.

"The Idunns aren't the only ones who've made their homes here. The powerful Minea who make up the Herrah may protect us, but others are out in the Wood too. I'm sure you've heard of them in your stories. The tribe of white, the tribe of black..."

"And the tribe of many colors," Lin whispers, his eyes now fixed on me. "It seems King Vaskis wasn't wrong in his tales."

"Oh, he was definitely wrong," Nuri cuts in. "Those tribes don't exist."

"Then who are The Others?" Lin asks.

Nuri's face grows grim, and she eyes her fellow Idunns before staring coldly at Lin. "These white and black tribes are how outsiders have come to think of the powers that live here."

Lin eagerly leans forward, and his eyes race between hers; he doesn't seem to notice her severe expression.

"The Herrah siphon the forest's magic to do good, to protect it. The ones who wield magic in this way are the Holders of Light. But, as I told you before, there are those who seek to disturb the network. They're called The Others or the Keepers of the Dark…"

"They're the followers of The Dreaded," Rianne finishes, then closes her mouth in a thin line.

Lorna glances at her, then focuses on Nuri.

"The Dreaded?" She probes, tapping an overwrought finger against her mug.

Nuri hums.

"Yes. Surely you've heard of The Dreaded?" When no one answers, she scoffs. "It is worse than I had imagined out there. How little you all know of your own history."

"Then teach us more of it," I say steadily, hard focused on her every expression.

"The Dreaded is an awful, powerful force. One that uses the forest's magic for its own sinister means." She answers directly.

"Is that who sent the Obsidian Mist? The Dreaded? The Keepers of the Dark?" Lorna asks.

Nuri inhales deeply, stabbing at her food with a fork.

"I'm afraid so. Many who live within these trees know better than the outside world that sooner or later, we must all make a choice. We either choose to uphold the light, or we embrace the dark. We can build, or we can destroy."

Idalia shifts uncomfortably, and we lock eyes before she turns to Rianne.

"Why did they send that mist after us? What do they want?" She asks timidly.

Rianne's eyes skirt to Nuri before she answers.

"You."

The table falls silent. "Why do they want Idalia?" I demand of Nuri.

The plump woman stares me down.

"The same reason your father wants her. Power. Why do you think he sent you to collect her? Baellileans have always been a greedy sort and it seems you are no stranger to the characteristic yourself."

My breath hitches, and Torrent abruptly stands. Whatever lust brews between these two is no match for his loyalty to our group and his devotion to me.

"Down, Stoneman," Nuri instructs, her hand lifted in a warning.

He flicks his eyes to me, then to Lin and Lorna, both tensed, awaiting my command. I lift my palm slightly, and Torrent slowly lowers himself. His eyes teem with warlike readiness.

"Your father?" Idalia finally says.

I can't bear to look at her and see the dawning comprehension in her fawn eyes, which I know can warm to dark pools of honey when she's upset.

"Is that why you kidnapped me, Braizen? To take me to Vaskis?" Her face is calm, but her voice rises in anguish.

Something sharp and deep pierces my gut. I grip my mug so tightly that I think it might break. "You crossed into Baelliles territory, Idalia. Verdana knows the risk."

"So, it's true," her voice shakes. "You *are* working for him."

"Why else would we steal you?" Lorna barks. "For the thrill of it?"

Idalia blinks slowly as if trying to remember what she did once believe.

Anger now steams inside me, a kettle ready to be poured. "Torrent, did you tell the Idunn this information?" I murmur, staring down at my plate.

"No, Boss. I wouldn't do that," he answers, confirming what I suspect. Unhurriedly, I sip, then gently set down my cup. I fix my eyes on his companion.

"Well, she had to find out somehow," Nuri says, and her brow flicks up in amusement.

"I heard Lannex speak of your visions," I return. It's as if no one else is at the table. "Tell me, might *you* be one of the legends we were fed of this Wood when we were children. A heretic perhaps?"

Her smile is sharp and vixen as she lowers her chin.

"Very good, Prince. I wondered when you'd catch on. However, we don't like to be called heretics. Prophet is as good a title as any."

"Like the Woman of the Woods?" Lin asks as his gaze pounces on each person at the table.

Nuri nods in agreement. "Much like the Woman of the Woods."

Idalia's brow is wrinkled, and I sense her rapidly thinking. Before I can open my mouth, Lin presses on.

"So, wait a minute. Are you her, then? Are *you* the Woman of the Woods? The First Prophet?"

Nuri laughs and drinks straight from the pitcher in front of her. "I'm afraid not."

Lorna crosses her arms and stares at Nuri. "Then are you a prophet for the gods, like her?"

"No," she answers in a bored tone.

"But the sacred texts say she's the only prophet! Anyone else is a heretic!" Lin sputters, though Nuri doesn't pay him any mind.

Idalia looks sick, her fair skin turning even paler as the conversation goes on. I can barely stand the sight of it.

"Is this how you do it?" I cut in, unable to restrain my irritation. "You have visions of people passing through The Wood, so you meet them and seduce them into coming here? Do you cram the magic you speak of into your trees, the lights, and liquids all to trap people here?"

The table falls deadly silent. "There's no wildlife outside of this place," I continue. "Explain that! Did the Minea, or the Herrah, or whatever the hells they're called, cast a spell over the rest of The Wood so that no one can survive outside of Idizina?"

"Watch your words, ranger," Nuri says slowly. Rianne and Breto shift in their seats.

"How do we know that the Minea are Holders of Light? What's to stop us from believing that they–and you—aren't the Keepers of the Dark?" I ask.

"You know nothing about us," Nuri hisses, her eyes now cloudy.

"And you think you know us?" I laugh, throwing up my arms. She gives me a long stare as if reading my thoughts, then smiles like a wise fox.

"Aye, I've known plenty of proud archers in my day. Long-range fellows who don't seem to understand that from a distance, anyone might feel brave."

My face heats, and from the corner of my eye, I see Idalia twisting and pulling her fingers on the tabletop.

"Do you truly think that I don't know you and the name that you bear, Braizen Brader, Prince of Baelliles? Or the curse that follows you and the Hyland Princess?" She points a stiff finger at Idalia, who squirms.

"Oh, I know you. I know the exact number of curly, brown hairs upon your head. I know you can name each bird that soars above us. I know you created this pathetic band in an attempt to run from what you can't escape! And above all, I know your feelings, which you hush deep down—passionate, terrifying, *treacherous*. Don't think for a second that you entered this territory with secrets, young Prince. We've known of you for a long time. We know how your line began, and what's more, we know how it might end." She draws in a mighty breath. "How *we all* might end."

Idalia pushes back from the table, and her chair crashes. She runs towards the cobble path that leads back to the clay homes.

I slam my mug to the table and rise, glaring at Nuri.

"You don't scare me with your heresy, nor does your possessed village," I growl.

Nuri laughs, throwing a hand onto her belly. "Tell me what you saw then, dear Prince? What did the Minea reveal to you that you refuse to accept? Have you told your friends their fates? Which one will die serving you?"

I scowl, then turn on my heel to follow Idalia.

Lin jerks up next to me and grabs my arm. "What do you want us to do, Braze?"

I pull from his clutch. "I'm going to find her. Stay close to the others."

Lorna shoots up; her face is devoid of emotion. "What are you talking about, Braizen?" Her voice is heavy and calm. "You can't catch her and bring her back. Let me or Torrent go after her. You stay here and figure out what in the hells is going on."

Rage flares and I want nothing more than to command Lorna to sit down and shut her mouth while I find Idalia. But I know she's right. I don't know what's overtaken me. I tilt my chin and send Lorna and Torrent after her. Lin stands at my side, and we guard each other against the sorcerers that line the table.

"Your anger for her sake is admirable, but it's misguided," Nuri says calmly, scooping another bite from her plate.

"What's your game here?" Lin glowers, palms pressed firmly on the table.

Rianne chuckles, and those next to her refill their cups.

"There's no game. There's only the truth," Nuri says.

"Then what is it?" I grind out. "What's the truth?"

Nuri gestures to us to sit and holds her hands over the food as if to summon peace.

"The truth is a stallion, set loose on the grassy knolls."

"Enough riddles," Lin spits. "Speak plainly."

Nuri huffs a laugh. "The truth is ever-changing in its direction. Like a wild horse, it charges one way for a moment, then chases a new course in the next. I can see things that are guided by the Light. But *the Darkness* grows and shrouds the view in its murky haze."

My mind is transported back to my youth, when Horrick would lecture me for hours over the sacred texts. The endless pages written by the First Prophet, the Woman of the Woods.

She spoke of the Great Darkness, and made mention of how the Lady would save us all from its impending arrival. Nuri folds her arms and leans back in her chair. "All I know for sure is that Idalia Hyland is caught up in both. She holds the key."

"The key to what?" I demand, about to lose my patience.

"The key to the end," Nuri declares.

Lin and I fall silent, and he leans in closer, his expression calm. He stares down the bridge of his nose at the Idunn.

"We're listening."

Chapter Sixteen

Idalia

I don't know where my legs are taking me, but I bolt even faster when I hear Braizen call after me. *The Idunn woman knows nothing about me! These crazy stories about the Light and the Dark, they mean nothing! Braizen captured me for his father. The bandits are no more than ill-dressed guards, working for the evilest man I know.* Pain hitches in my side, but I keep going. Tears stain my cheeks, and my foot snags a rock, propelling me forward. I land hard on my hands and whimper as I berate myself.

Why am I so angry? What did I expect? They were my enemies, and I was their prisoner. Why is the anger more intense now? Because he means to take me to Vaskis? Because he stole my Kingdom's chance for freedom?

I grunt, picking away at the tiny gravel imprinted in my palm. I'm embarrassed for the way I spoke too freely last night, utterly humiliated I let him into that secret place. All the while, he was planning on hand delivering me to his father. Gods, I hate him. *I hate him!*

I beat my fist against the ground. "Why have you chosen nothing but pain for me, Lady?" I shout. "Why won't you hold me behind your Shield, and why won't the Guard fight for me?"

"Idalia," says a soft, firm voice above me. I crane my neck and see the elderly woman who gave me the tea yesterday. The Minea. Her smile is gentle, despite my obvious contempt.

I clench my teeth and face the ground.

"Leave me. All of you! Leave me alone!"

I feel it again: that annoying call from within. It tells me to take her hand, to allow her to help me. I thrash against it, trying to deny its force, but it only grows. Discomfort blasts through my chest, and I feel sick to my stomach. The longer I fight it, the more pain I feel. Grudgingly, I stop fighting and eye her with disdain.

She only nods and extends her hand. I drop my shoulders in defeat. These wretched woods. This wretched place!

With a scowl, I reach my hand out to take hers.

The trees and the path shoot past me as our skin meets, though I remain in place. The sky rapidly expands into the distance. I cannot even take a steady breath before the world around me contorts into a thousand twists and turns. The woman is no longer beside me. I am being sucked backwards, though my feet do not budge.

Suddenly I jolt forward, falling onto a marble floor. My chest tightens as I try to level my breathing. *What just happened? Where am I?*

I look at the ground, stabilizing myself. I recognize it; it's the floor of my castle. But it's brighter, as if it's new. I draw shallow, escalating breaths. I'm in our entrance hall, but so many things look different. The chandelier that holds over one hundred candles isn't the dull bronze I know it to be, but instead sparkles with flaked gold. The stone steps of the twin staircases that curve to meet each other on the next floor gleam white. It looks exactly like my home, yet, completely different at the same time. Nothing here is worn with age. How did I get back to Verdana?
I can't seem to catch my breath. Footsteps approach, and I scramble behind the nearest pillar. Two maidens carrying piles of soft toweling walk towards me.

"The babe is a boy; praise the Lady and the Guard. Queen Adelaide has produced a fine new ruler. Healthy as a horse." The two ascend one staircase and continue gossiping. I press my back against the pillar.

Adelaide? The Traitorous Queen? What in the four hells is happening to me? More footsteps disrupt my thoughts. When I see the male, dressed in royal Verdanian blue and flanked by two guards, I *really* can't breathe.

I recognize his face. Paralyzed, I remain flattened against the pillar.

The men walk straight towards me; there's nowhere to hide. The guards' eyes don't meet mine.

"What's this?" The man I recognize speaks in a deep voice and raises his chin in suspicion.

I cry out and stumble to the floor.

"Idalia Hyland, the Princess of Verdana! My mother is Queen Revna Hyland, and my father, Ivar, is her King consort. Please. I'm so confused. The Baellileans have captured me…"

"An old friend, you dolt! I hear it is a son!" Another voice rises from the entry.

I lift my head through my sobs only to see the guards' and the man's legs stride past me. I blink rapidly and fear I have no sanity left. I watch the guards join others at the castle entrance. They stand in a wide formation as the male and his visitor greet each other. The guest is dressed in the pine green of Baelliles' people, and he kisses the cheeks of the male in blue. Have I gone completely mad?

"It is a boy, indeed! The gods have truly shown me favor on this day."

"And Adelaide?" The visitor queries, slapping the other on the back.

The male in blue laughs and joins in a hearty embrace. "Perfectly fine. Beautiful as ever. Although, I don't have to tell you that, do I, Seraph?"

"Seraph," I mouth silently, although I can't believe my own words.

"Still the same old mule, aren't you, Novak? Regardless, you won her fair and square, so I cannot mock you too much for it," Seraph laughs.

"Novak!" I shout, realizing why his face is so familiar. I slap my hand over my mouth and face the floor again, terrified the guards will restrain me. But no one moves. No one hears me. Can they not even see me?

I slowly rise and walk towards the men, still laughing and chatting. I wave my hands by their faces. No response. When I reach my hand to grab Novak's arm, it passes straight through.

Ghosts?

A scream rises in my throat, but my vision distorts. The castle's entryway pulls and stretches, and the image spins, all I can see being wrung out like a wet cloth over a basin. My hair flies out of control, though there is no actual force of wind to cause it to do so. I fall through the coiled reality until I finally land somewhere else. There are trees everywhere. Perhaps I'm back in the Florian Wood?

An eerie, heavy silence hangs around me, and a thick mist cloaks the forest floor. The trees are dark; their dense, almost black canopy closes out any chance of sunlight spilling in. It feels...*haunted.*

Wrapping my arms around myself, I shudder at the ominous energy surrounding me. I scan in every direction for some semblance of life. More silence. A twig snaps close by, and I hurl myself towards the base of a tree. I curl behind its mass and try to stifle my heavy breathing. I hear a female voice, fragile and frightened. I peek and see a young maiden, no more than sixteen, who looks terrified.

Her face is soiled from dried tears and dirt; sticks and leaves tangle her long reddish-blonde hair. "Please! Anyone? Can anyone tell me where I am?" She cries into the void.

My heart thuds. She's so much like me. Alone, afraid, and confused beyond belief. Still hugging the tree, I rise and prepare to face her.

"Anyone!" she calls again, "I do not know where I am or how I got here! Please! Please!"

I move carefully around the tree until I face her.

"What is your name?" I ask.

She doesn't look at me. She can't see me either! A sob catches in my throat. Am I to be a faceless ghost for the rest of my days?

"Child," another voice hisses, this one old and dry. An older woman.

The girl and I whip our heads, and through the thick fog, a dark silhouette appears.

"Why do you cry so loud? Do those who slumber not concern you? Have you no pity for those who seek to rest?"

The girl wipes her eyes and examines the dark figure. "I am lost. I have no idea where I am! Please, can you help me?"

The withered voice cackles, and the form disappears. "Lost, you say?" This time the voice is much louder. A figure in a dark cloak appears a few trees away from me.

The young woman backs away with outstretched arms. "Do you truly have no recollection of how you got here?" The elder woman croaks.

The girl, now visibly shaking, doesn't answer.

"Spit it out, girl!"

"It is true! I have no memory of this place. The last I remember, I was at home, speaking with a friend about finding… about finding…" The young woman falters.

"Finding what, child?"

"I cannot remember what. I only recall that I spoke to him about finding *something. Somewhere.* The very next moment, I was here, in the woods."

The cloaked woman emits a shrieking laugh and loudly clicks her tongue. She vanishes and then reappears next to the girl.

We both scream. Fearfully, I cover my mouth though I'm sure neither can hear me.

"Let me have a look at your hand," the woman urges, and tentatively, the girl offers her one. "Ah, yes. Yes, indeed. I see now."

"What is it?" The delicate female pulls back her hand and presses it against her chest.

The cloaked figure removes her hood, revealing an old woman with a face as gnarled and ancient as the trees. I recognize it, somehow.

The girl gasps.

"There is a darkness in you, deep and unsettling. Though, you are in luck. I do not scare as easily as the Herrah."

"The *what*?" The girl asks.

The old woman laughs. "Come with me, and I will show you all the things you sought from them."

The girl lunges back, shaking her head.

The old woman shrugs. "Then die out here alone. The choice is yours," she says and walks back through the mist towards the trees. The forest has almost swallowed the woman's silhouette when a howl sounds in the distance.

The girl jumps and calls for the elder to wait, that she is coming. Before she leaves, she turns her head in my direction. Her eyes widen, and I swear she sees me, but before either of us can say a word, the earth warps again, bending and wrapping around me.

My stomach protests, and I gag on bile. I slam to a stop. I'm still in a forest, though it's now daylight, and the trees' lush canopy is a lighter green.

"Now what," I huff, bending over to catch my breath.

Another call for help; this time, a male voice cries in the distance. I almost don't care. Surely I've found one of the four hells! This must be a punishment from The Lady for my complaints about my life. She's thrown me into worlds where I can't be seen, heard, or understood. I resolve to settle next to a tree and rest while waiting for the next vision or whatever these journeys are.

A gust of wind whips against my face, and the young female from the dark wood flies past me.

"I am coming! Hold on!" She cries.

Despite my determination to rest, I'm overcome with curiosity, and I follow. We dart between trees, dodge shrubbery, and sprint down a hill before I see who's in distress. It's a young male with round cheeks and bright eyes that dart wildly.

I stop in my tracks, horrified. He's stuck under his horse and is gasping for breath.

"Please," he begs. "I cannot move. He is too heavy!"

There's nothing that I can do to help, and judging by the mount's size, the young girl can't either. My face collapses as I realize I'm about to witness this young man's death.

The young woman isn't as convinced. She stumbles over to him and holds his head in her hands. I observe her more closely. She's different. Before, she exuded terror; now, there's confidence. Her confusion has grown into a deep understanding. She is older now, by a few years at least. She leans down and brushes the sweep of the young man's hair from his brow. His skin is turning a pale gray-blue; breath is leaving him. The horse struggles but can't lift itself.

She carefully lowers the male's head and, removing a ribbon from her wrist, uses it to tie back her hair. She's concentrating intensely and I wonder if she'll attempt to push the horse off him. A futile gesture, but I can't blame her. If I believed I could touch the horse, I'd offer to help too. She steps back, and I notice the boy's face grow still, his eyes hazing from the coming of death.

I slowly exhale and find comfort in reminding myself that this is only a vision. That this tragedy isn't real and I've simply lost my mind.

What happens next only confirms the thought. Closing her eyes, the girl stretches her hands towards the horse. A dark, glowing smoke of some kind spirals from each palm.

My own palms burst with heat as I watch the dark smoke wrap itself around the horse and see its body rise a few inches. The girl braces herself and grimaces as if she feels its weight. The horse now floats…*floats* in the air until it's away from the male's still form. It drops to the ground with a thud, and dirt flies as it scrambles up, shaking its muzzle in distress.

The girl flings herself at the male and holds his face in her hands. He's so still. But just as I begin to lose hope, the young man gasps.

Praise the gods! He made it! I walk softly on my toes towards the pair. The male stands, disoriented, staring in awe at the girl.

"You saved my life." His eyes twitch as he takes her entirely in. She's beautiful and so young. She smiles, and her cheeks blush, but she remains silent.

He steps closer to her. "I am indebted to you. Pray, take me at once to your home so that I can meet your father."

She tilts her chin up and swallows hard.

"I have no father, sir."

He shakes his head. "Then to your mother."

Her mouth tightens. "I have no mother, either, sir," she replies.

He closes the gap between them. "Your guardian, whomever…"

"It is only me," she says quietly.

He straightens in shock. "You live out here alone? In these woods?"

She gently nods.

"Then I will gladly assist you home." He grabs her hands. "Pray, tell me, do you even know who I am?"

She peers up at him through her lashes while her neck and face bloom pink. She shakes her head, and he laughs.

"While I am sure your kindness is not limited to those with titles, it is not a common boy that you saved. I am Prince Novak of Verdana, and I am in your debt."

An unintelligible sound escapes her, and she retreats a few steps. My mouth is agape. From a lifetime of gazing at the portraits on our castle walls, I know he speaks the truth. That is Novak, again, albeit the younger version.

The first vision; now this one. *What is this?*

"Your Highness," she says and curtsies. "I had no idea."

"Please, rise," he protests. "It is I who should bow to you." Her eyes flare, and she giggles.

With an answering chuckle, he asks, "How can I repay you?"

I listen as they go back and forth. She insists that his being alive is payment enough. He insists that he must reward her act.

Realizing that the Prince won't concede, the girl takes a deep breath and closes her eyes.

"One day, I would like to have a home in your kingdom. A good home. One that I can be proud to care for and that people will not turn me away from."

He howls, then throws his hands onto his hips.

"Milady, though I am not yet King, I promise you that you will have your home and more the moment I ascend the throne! Not only will you come to live in my Kingdom, but I invite you to my court. You will reside in the castle and be taken care of for all your days."

Her smile spreads, and she flings her arms around the Prince's neck.

He looks shocked, but his face softens, and he returns the embrace, squeezing her tightly. "I must return now," he says as he pulls away.

"But in two days, I will return and bring food and gifts. Will you meet me here?"

She nods vigorously. "Yes. I will meet you here, Prince Novak."

"Good," he says, and mounting takes up his reins. "Two days. Wait for me."

She smiles, holding her hands behind her back.

He turns his mount and then throws up a hand. "Gods, forgive me! I did not ask your name."

The girl laughs in delight. "My name is Cyra, Your Highness. Cyra Hyland."

What? The vision blurs, and I fly down a contorting tunnel of colors. Without warning, I hit the ground, landing solidly on my rear. Heaving, I open my eyes. I'm back where I started, and the older woman, the Minea, has released my hand.

"Come," is all she says. She turns from me and makes her way back to the village.

I remain on the ground panting for a few more moments before my palms begin to hiss with their now-familiar dissent.

I *will* follow her to her home, but this time, I'll be the one asking the questions.

Chapter Seventeen

Idalia

She settles into the red chair and crosses her ankles. The house looks much as it did the day before, although now, I hear soft music and the plants don't appear ready to strangle me. I stand stiffly by the door, and we stare at each other as if waiting to see who'll speak first. But I'm too tired, too confused to play this game.

"What was that?" I demand, moving to stand directly in front of her.

"What was what?" She returns with a shrug.

"*That!* The vision! When I touched your hand, I traveled somewhere. When you released me, I returned. How?"

"That was no vision." She smiles and calmly takes a teacup from the table and briskly stirs the liquid. "A Minea possesses magic, as you've been told, but you don't understand what kind. We have a rather special ability, one that allows us to see into the past."

"The past?" I gasp in disbelief.

"Precisely. Just as a prophet can see into the future, a Minea can see into the past. But just as you had no control over what you saw, neither do we. Neither does Nuri. The magic reveals what it wants when we're ready to see it. What it showed you were memories from your own family."

"You expect me to believe that?" I laugh. "That somehow, I went back hundreds of years and saw my dead ancestors?" She nods, then sharply knocks her spoon against the rim of her cup.

"I expect you to believe whatever you want."

"You're telling me that the Minea's power is to send people into memories?"

The woman takes her time sipping. She sighs contentedly as the liquid goes down her throat.

"Absolutely not. A Minea cannot send anyone back but themselves." She sips again. "It is extremely difficult for one to do alone, you see. But it is quite simple when more than one Minea harnesses the energy together."

She leans forward and smiles encouragingly. "You, dear, are a natural! Tell me, how many memories did you see? I felt more than one. Was it two? Three?" I stare at her blankly, and she pulls back her chin. *"Four?!"*

"Are you saying *I* sent myself into the past and saw the memories?" I blurt out.

"Yes," she says. "With my help, of course."

"But if Mineas can only send themselves back, that would make me…" I pause and hold up one finger as if to stop my thought.

She chuckles under her breath. "A Minea? Yes, I suppose it does."

My hand drops to my side.

"Is it truly so shocking, Idalia, that magic runs through your veins?" She rises and glides around the room, her eyes never leaving me. "Or is it more of a relief to know that there is a reason for that feeling inside you? The one that calls out, desperate for your attention, your obedience…"

"Stop," I demand, holding my palm out towards her. I can't seem to find my breath. "You deceive me; you trick my mind."

She laughs and continues to pace. "I have no time to deceive. What I say is true. You are a descendant of a Hyland, which means you wield magic, more so than you know. I sensed you the moment you crossed into this forest, as could The Others. When I peeked into your soul, I saw even more. You are a powerful Minea, pure enough to be a part of the Herrah. Not like the one who came before you."

I'm dizzy from following her around the room. I speak as plainly as I can.

"You're mistaken! I'm no magic wielder; I've never conjured anything in my life! I didn't even *know* magic existed until I was kidnapped and taken further into these woods!"

She releases a sharp tsk of annoyance and continues to pace.

"Now, who is the deceiver?"

My mind grows hazy, and my palms begin to burn. Did she serve me tea, and I've forgotten? I stumble towards the red chair but collapse on the floor and press my hand hard against my brow. I squeeze my eyes shut and begin praying to The Lady. For forgiveness. For safety.

"Do you often spend your time praying to gods who do not answer?" The woman cuts in.

I look up from under my lashes; she's towering over me.

"The gods *do* answer," I say on a half breath. "I've seen it with my own eyes."

"You poor girl. The delusions you will believe," she says, and her voice drips contempt.

"They answered! They came down–"

Effortlessly, silently, she drops to the floor next to me. I don't hear a single creak; not even my young knees are that strong. Her unwavering stare unnerves me.

"They came down when their names were sworn in anger. But do they come when their names are invoked for mercy? For health? For food?" Her eyes gleam. "You count Baelliles' King and his people as your enemies, do you not? Because he decimates your troops and slowly starves your people. Yet, you humbly serve gods who do worse! Your gods lord above you all from a secret place, watching thousands die each day! Women and children suffer before their eyes, and what do they do? They remain silent. They remain hidden. Tell me, why should anyone worship such a thing?"

My palms simmer, and my body flushes with a white heat. The sacred texts flood my mind. My mother used to make me declaim adages from their pages, but once she passed, my father's desire to teach them died with her. "It is their promise of the afterlife that we set our hopes to," I recite on a shaky breath. "The affliction we face here cannot cross into the Great Lands. There, we will know no pain."

"Then why are you still so angry about your mother's death?" Her voice cracks against me like a whip. "Why mourn the dead at all? Why brew vengeance for those taken? Should we not all wish for swift death? Tell me, Idalia, if pain only exists in the life we now live, then why is our most basic instinct to preserve it?"

Distraught, I try to follow her words. "I'm no philosopher or teacher of sacred texts," I stammer. "I can't answer those questions. But I saw them. I saw the Lady and the Guard kill people. And I felt it when She cursed me! I don't care if you think I'm stupid or if you think I am lying!"

"I know you are not lying."

"Then why are you hounding me like this?!" I cry.

She tilts my chin until I meet her gaze. "I have witnessed many people see countless things they do not understand, and unfortunately for us all, none more than you. I do not pity you for having faith in such things; I pity you for not possessing the same faith in yourself."

I don't know how much time has passed. There are no windows, and I'm so tired I can't trust myself to guess whether it's still day or night. "I don't understand," I whisper, my body slumped in the red chair. "I don't understand why you won't answer any of my questions."

She shifts in her seat to face me. She holds her lips in a tight line as she smiles.

"It is as I have told you before. One day I will answer your questions, but it is not the right–"

"*Time,*" we say in unison. Her wrinkles deepen with her smile.

I let out a swift groan. She's given me the same answer to each of my questions: '*It is not yet time for you to know that*' or '*You will find that most of these answers will be given in time.*' I push myself deeper into the chair and scowl. "I still don't understand. I don't understand any of this."

"Exactly," she smiles. "One day, when you gain more understanding, come and ask me again."

"Nothing you say makes sense," I remark crossly. "Nothing that's happened to me since I stepped foot into these gods forsaken woods makes any sense!"

For the first time, she laughs. "One day, it will. Now, why don't you go find your friends and have a nice night with the Idunns?"

"My *friends*?" I scoff. "Those people are my captors, not my friends! Prince Braizen is going to take me to his father! To the man who killed my mother! I'd sooner die here, in this chair, than have a nice night with him."

The Minea doesn't say anything to that. She only tilts her chin downwards and rests her warm eyes on my face.

I cross my legs and settle back. I don't like the weight of her stare, and I don't like that I have no idea how long I've been in her cottage. "I need to see what time of day it is," I say to break the silence and start to rise.

"I do not think that is at all what you need," she returns and folds her hands in her lap.

"Oh?" I drop back into the soft cushions. "What is it then that I need?"

"I think you need to find the spirit of forgiveness."

I release a crude sound and shake my head. "Forgiveness? Seriously? Why would I ever forgive him for what he's done?"

"I didn't say the forgiveness was for him," she says. Her eyes stab me like daggers.

My hands prickle, and my legs begin to shake. My throat is dry.

She stands and smiles. "I think it is now time you go."

"I'm not going back out there with him. I won't do it."

She chuckles, and her laugh reminds me of Nurse Lydia's after I say something idiotic.

"Why are you so angry, Idalia?"

I blink at her in confusion. "What do you mean? They captured me! They stole my future!"

Her mouth twists in mock sorrow. "*They* stole your future?"

I stomp my foot. "Yes! Yes, they did! My fate was to be the Queen of Aeradian. To have a chance for love, and to save Verdana!" I stand and shout the rest. "They took it all from me!"

For a long moment, I hear only the sound of boiling water. Then, the Minea draws a long breath and moves to the door.

"Your fate? An interesting idea, that you think you know anything about fate at all."

I don't move, even as she reaches for the door handle.

"Go see for yourself, child, about this fate you claim to know." She pushes open the entrance, and cool air blows in. Dusk is near. I study her new expression, cold and unwavering.

"Why won't you tell me anything? Just one thing? Help me, please!" I step forward.

Her lips barely part. "I will tell you this, Idalia Hyland of Verdana. As much as you thrash against what you know is true, you cannot outrun it forever. You *will* come face to face with the cacoethes of your soul, and you *will* have to decide. Until then, know that whatever secrets the Herrah may keep is for a reason larger than us all."

The door creaks open further, and the orbs' golden light spills across the entry. "And if you think you can face what comes for you without him, you are as daft as you are stubborn."

"What's coming for me?" I almost crash into a chair as I run towards the door. "Nuri said it was The Others. What do they want with me? Why are they after me?"

The Minea's face reveals not one ounce of pity. Her once warm eyes are now hard and impenetrable.

"The Others seek to snuff out all light, and they know that yours burns too brightly."

My body twitches with malaise. I sense that she's finished talking. I feel her magic pull me from the house. In defeat, I stride towards the door. As my foot crosses the threshold, her hand lands on my shoulder.

"Drink this," she instructs, holding a small cup in her hand, but I snort.

"So that I can hallucinate again? You're mad. A mad, old woman!"

She doesn't react to my outburst; she only pushes the cup forward.

"You might find that this tea will be more to your liking. It helps to… calm the nerves."

"Calm my nerves?" I ask suspiciously. The last thing I want is to lose my senses again. However, I can't deny the eager delinquent within me who's enthralled by the prospect of leaving sobriety and its discomfort behind.

Her face betrays no emotion as she nods.

I squint, still wary, then chug it down. Immediately, a pleasant lightness, a powerful happiness, consumes me. Perhaps I can have a fun night with those rowdy bandits and their insufferable leader. Yes, I *can* enjoy another night of drinking and dancing.

It would be a far cry from the lonely nights I spent in Verdana, hounding the most handsome stable boy I could find to enjoy a night of thrills. Not that any of them lived up to my expectations. None wanted to drink as much as I did, laugh as loudly, or talk as much. None were like *him*, the bastard. That rotten, filthy tongued, uninhibited, untamed, undeniably gorgeous bastard.

I take a weightless step out of the door, and the Minea calls out. "Idalia. One last thing about your fate."

As her words wash over me, I wonder if I am imagining them.

"The Great Darkness is in your blood, Idalia. Should you choose to face your fate, you will not survive it. However, should you choose to ignore your fate, the world will be swallowed whole, and all light shall pass away."

Chapter Eighteen

Braizen

Lin tosses me a look as the Idunns leave the table. I turn away, watching Nuri walk towards one of the wooden buildings. Breto joins her and tugs her close. Another male walks with Rianne back to the grimshka pen. When they're out of earshot, I turn back to Lin.

"Well, what the hells are we going to do?" He says instantly, his eyes brimming with panic. "We need to go home, Braze. We can take some food from here and buy more with the money in the carriage. We'll make it just fine."

I stare at my plate and clench my jaw.

"Come on, Braizen! I know that you don't want to disappoint your father, but this, this is too much! He doesn't know a single name of The Cloaked, and I doubt he'll go blabbering about our failure. He wouldn't want the Kingdom to know he hired a bunch of thieves to do his dirty work. We need to go. We'll get a good rest tonight and leave first thing tom—"

"No." I cut in.

Lin stops and jerks back.

"No? *No*?! What in the Lady's name do you mean *no*? If Nuri's telling the truth and The Others are looking for us, we likely won't survive. We can't continue with the mission!"

"No, we most certainly can't," I say, bringing my ale up to take a sip.

"Right," Lin says slowly, though he looks confused. "So, you agree then? We leave tomorrow?"

The cool liquid slowly slides down my throat, and I take in its delectable taste with unhurried appreciation. When it hits my stomach, I set the mug down lightly and face Lin.

"The rest of you will leave tomorrow. I'll stay."

At that, Lin jumps from his seat. "Are you mad?! Has the ale already intoxicated you? You want us to leave you behind to finish the mission *alone*?!"

I say nothing. Instead, I grind my back teeth.

"Braizen, are you listening to yourself? The Wood is full of dark magic, aimed right at the girl, no less! A girl you can't even touch! Do you seriously think we'd let you go on by yourself?"

"I didn't ask because if it were up to you, I know that you wouldn't."

Lin leans toward me with a sour expression, and I stiffen.

"I'm ordering you—not as your boss, but as your Prince—to return without me."

He slips down to the bench, shoulders slumped.

Torrent and Lorna fly around the corner a few moments later, without Idalia.

"Where is she?" I demand. My voice is harsh, but they don't seem to notice.

Lorna points behind her. "One of the old witches took her into her house. We tried to follow her in, but there was, well, something stopped us, like an invisible wall. Another witch came out and told us to wait back here." She leans over to catch her breath.

Torrent scans the area as if searching for Nuri, then looks at me and shrugs.

"It's true, Boss. We tried."

Lin hasn't moved; he hasn't even looked up at them. He's still staring at me, dumbfounded.

Lorna approaches the table, takes a swig of my ale, then slams it down next to Lin; froth splashes his cheek. He doesn't flinch.

"What's his problem?" She jerks her head, and her brows rise.

Torrent leaps towards us and tousles Lin's hair. "He probably just realized that I'm smarter than him. Took you long enough, Speck!"

Lorna sits and takes a bite of her food, eyeing Lin through narrowed eyes. She meets my gaze and swallows. "What's going on, Braizen?"

"You're crazy," Lorna hisses violently. "And a total jackass if you think for one second, I'm leaving you with *her.*"

"It's not up to you," I counter with a sigh.

"Like hells, it's not!" She yells and flings her cup onto the table. "Since when did you decide to be our *Prince?* Last I checked, we were a band. A family. We make decisions together." She stands and walks away, her arms crossed tightly. "She's gotten to you. I *knew* she would. That's why I said you shouldn't have come in the first place."

"Lorna," Torrent warns, his voice low.

"Don't *'Lorna'* me, Torr. You know I'm right. I said it at least fifty times. Between their past and their curse, it made no sense for him to come. And now look! He wants to send us away so he can complete the suicide mission all on his own!"

I take even breaths and let Lorna release all the aggression she needs. I don't blame her; I expected her anger. I'm surprised her fist hasn't yet landed somewhere on my face.

"Tell us how this is going to work, Braizen. How do you plan to get the Princess from here to Nerwick? Have you two grown so close that she'll gladly follow you? Or do you plan to hold hands and skip through our corpses and your fallen kingdom as ghosts?"

I remain silent, but Lin sees the look in my eyes and draws a long, unsteady breath. "Lady and Guard," he whispers. "You don't plan to take her to your father, do you?"

Lorna's emerald stare darts from Lin to me, then back to Lin.

"What are you talking about?"

Lin closes his eyes. "He's taking her to Aeradian."

"*What?!*" Lorna glares at me, and I swear, for a moment, her freckles are ablaze.

Torr, leaning against a nearby tree, straightens.

Lin slowly shakes his head. "Nuri told us why Idalia was traveling through The Wood. It wasn't to pay respects to King Lester. She's to marry Lachlan and become Queen of Aeradian."

Lorna laughs wildly and throws up her hands. "Oh, for the Guard's sake! How wonderful! Well, Braizen, I don't see what the holdup is. Go ahead and kiss her now since we'll all be dead soon anyways!" She spits, wipes her hands on her thighs, and paces.

Torrent slowly walks over; unlike the others, his expression isn't flustered or angry. "I'll go with you," he says simply.

Lorna spins. "Oh, hells Torrent, not you, too!!"

"You don't understand, Torrent," Lin says and places a hand on our large friend's arm. "There's more to the story. The obstacles we've faced: the Obsidian Mist and the deadly vines, are *because* of her. The best thing we can do, for all our sakes, is to return home. Without the girl."

He looks at me. "If you want her safe, Braizen, you'll convince her to stay put. Nuri said the Minea Herrah protect Idizina and that no evil will befall her if she stays here."

"She said Idalia's safe *for now.* That's not the same thing," I rumble, making eye contact with each one of them. Lin breathes heavily.

"But it *is* enough. It has to be!"

"If you go with her, the Keepers of the Dark will come after you too," Lorna interjects. "That's not a risk we're willing to take."

"We don't know that," I say slowly. "All Nuri told us is that The Others are in the forest and that their main goal is to capture Idalia. She never said they won't try to hurt us if we don't have her."

"What do they want with her?" Torrent asks.

"I don't know. Nuri can't see the answer because of the Darkness. All she said is that she's seen many outcomes and most end with Idalia in The Wood. That's it."

"That's not all she said," Lin catches my eye, and he jerks his chin toward me. "Tell them." I rake my fingers down my face.

"There was also something about me. The last she saw of me was in The Wood, too."

"So, the last the prophet saw of you both was in this Wood?" Lorna grinds out. "And now you want us to leave you in them, *alone with her*? Are you truly this much of an imbecile!?"

"Tell them the rest," Lin says, his expression bleak.

"She also said…" My chest tightens, and I struggle to finish. In the distance, music begins. A lovely clanging of metal bells erupts; someone must've touched the trees. I twist the cup in my hand. "Nuri also said that this is the only way, the way it must be."

"The way what must be?" Idalia's question seems to spring through the air.

Lin jumps, and I whip my head to see her standing on the path. The sleeves of her tunic are pulled down, and her hair is half pinned back. She looks stunning. She looks *dangerous.* I eye the others, signaling them to say nothing of our conversation.

"Where were you?" I ask and walk towards her.

She shrugs. "Busy."

"Busy with the Minea again?" I chuckle. "Did she give you more wine?"

"I was given tea the first time, not wine. Not that it's any of your business."

"You know, you're pretty fast for someone so small," Torrent says with a wide grin as he joins us.

Idalia coughs out a laugh. "I'm full of surprises, as you should know by now."

"Aye, I do know," Torrent cheekily agrees.

I hear a scoffing laugh and turn to see Lorna scowl and Lin grimace. Without a word, they walk away. Lin looks back once with a somber stare.

"How have I angered her this time?" Idalia blows loose hair from her cheek and almost skips to the table. She isn't scowling or even frowning. A promising sign, I hope.

"Lorna just takes time," I say and decide to press on. "Which now that we're here in Idizina, we have plenty of."

Torr throws me a glance before he sits down hard next to Idalia, causing the bench to quake.

"Oh, so you plan to stay awhile?" She picks up her cup and frowns when she sees it's empty.

There's something different in her tone. Almost as if she's been drinking in the Minea's house. I flash her a cocky smile and shrug. "I don't see why not. A few days here wouldn't be so bad. Why? Are you in a hurry to get somewhere, Little Sparrow?" I eye her, not knowing where we stand. Surely she's still furious that I was working for my father, but her face looks calm. Happy, even.

She shrugs one shoulder and scrunches her nose. "No hurry at all, Braizen."

Night falls once more. Music thrums through the thickets and briars, and Torrent is dancing again. Of course. The man couldn't say no to a celebration even if he tried. Lin and Lorna haven't returned, but after a few queries, I learn they're still within the orbs' perimeter and safe.

Nuri speaks with Rianne in hushed whispers. Idalia is smiling, perched on the grass beside the dancers. She claps her hands and laughs as the

Idunn villagers twirl, and Torrent almost squashes them all. I don't mean to stare at her, but I can't help it.

Everyone cheers as Torrent downs an enormous barrel of ale. When he finishes, he chucks it over to the side and wipes his mouth on his forearm, sending Nuri a crooked grin. She appears receptive, which only the gods can explain.

Idalia's eyes turn to me. With its golden undertones, her smooth skin gleams in the light from the orbs. Her nose is a deep red from the cool wind. I shiver, even in my cloak.

Breto interrupts my gaze with a shove. "Ale in a bottle?" He holds out a skinny glass container.

Puzzled, I take a gulp. "This is amazing. How's it so cold?" I exclaim.

"We chill the bottles all day in the stream. It makes all the difference, no?" He smiles proudly and plops down next to me.

"All the difference in the world! Say, I'm sorry things got so tense earlier; we really mean no harm."

Breto waves a careless hand. "We know how little Baellileans appreciate being called names. It was an expected response. Besides, if any of you even try to do something funny, you'll be taken care of before you even swing a fist."

"I believe you. Nuri alone terrifies me," I laugh.

"As she should. She terrifies us all. The way she lugs around that mace, and her visions…" He shudders. "It's enough to scare any man."

I drive an elbow into Breto's arm.

"Those visions, are they an Idunn thing? Are you all prophets or part of the Minea Herrah?"

"Oh, no! Prophets are pretty rare around here, and the Herrah don't collect many new members. In fact, Nuri is the only prophet Idizina has known in ages. As for the Mineas, only one has joined since I've been here."

"I thought the Herrah were all hundreds of years old?"

Breto claps his hands for the dancers before answering. "Honestly, I don't ask too many questions about them. They protect us with the magic they harness from The Wood. That's all I know."

"So, prophets are that rare, huh? I wonder how accurate Nuri's visions are. Has she ever mentioned any of them to you?"

Breto works his tongue around his teeth and then spits some bit of food on the ground.

"Never. She doesn't really tell us about them. Only the Minea. And Rianne."

"What about you? Do you have any special powers?"

"I'm just a man, like you. Only, I'm no Prince, and I didn't arrive here with a bunch of friends." Breto barks a laugh and slaps my back.

"When did you come here?"

"Oh, I'd say it's been about eight years now. Eight years! I didn't even realize until you asked. Almost a decade…" He lifts his bottle and swallows a good portion.

"It's still hard to believe this place exists," I say and hand him my bottle when I see he's finished his. "I've scoured Baelliles my entire life and never even heard of it. We know so little about The Wood."

"In Aeradian, we knew even less," he says. "But I suppose it's more strange for you since most of The Wood runs through your Kingdom."

"Aeradian?"

"It's where I hail from. Not that it matters now. I'm an Idunn, through and through." Breto declares brashly, smoothing down his mustard hair.

"So, how did you find this place? As you say, Aeradians know even less than Baellileans about The Wood."

"The only thing I knew about the Florian Wood is that most people who went in never came back out." He lets the remaining alcohol slide down his throat and then grunts. "I didn't enter the trees to find Idizina. I entered them to die."

"What?"

"I lost my family. A wife and two children. Twins, if you can believe it. Nerry and Nimwe. The two loveliest little girls you'd ever seen! And my wife!" He gives a low whistle. "So tall and so beautiful; I was a very lucky man to have married her. I still can't believe she chose an imp like me."

A heavy weight settles in my chest. Breto watches me and pats my leg. "My wife, rest her soul, was a medic. She was the best at what she did. My little girls, well, of course, wanted to follow in her footsteps. They were thirteen when they began their training. They took right after her, they did. Not like me. I'm just a brute who was good at chopping wood.

One day, eight years ago, we learned of a mass slaughter by the river near the North Kingdom's perimeter. We heard some Verdanians were still alive there, but barely. The ones who survived were limbless, screaming, bleeding out…" He clears his throat.

"My wife just couldn't stand the thought. Her and the little ones set off to help. They even got a written safe passage from the Prince! Can you believe that? Prince Lachlan… What a man."

I smile, remembering my old friend. What a man, indeed.

"But Baellileans don't care about permission, do they? My wife and my daughters were killed trying to help wounded Verdanians. Baellilean troops considered their aid a breach of our truce, fighting for their enemy, or something like that. Only, they weren't fighting. They weren't taking sides. But that's war, Braizen. That is the cost of kingdoms."

I stop breathing. "Breto," I whisper.

He holds out a hand. "I don't need anyone's sympathy. Truly. As much as I miss them, as much as I still love them, I *have* healed. The Idunns took me in. I drank that blasted tea. I work every day, and each time the sun sets, I feel lighter. Like somehow, my girls are still with me. Yes, I can feel them. Say it's the trees. Call me a lunatic; I don't mind. They're here, and they don't want me to be angry forever."

Without waiting for a response, Breto stands, salutes me with his empty bottle, and makes his way back to the dancers. I don't dare call after him, and anyway, I don't think I can. A giant lump sits in my throat, and I know I might break into sobs if I try to expel it. He joins Torr on the dance floor with a broad smile that exudes a carefree spirit. I watch him blankly for a time, and then I feel it. Her stare. *Her.*

She's watching me, and I can see from her expression that she heard the entire conversation. A single tear drips down her cheek. She sits near the lavender thickets, her legs curled to the side, her hair uncoiling over one shoulder. I'd paint this image if I knew a damn thing about art—the fair snow maiden who comes alive in the trees.

I walk toward her, but her face doesn't change. Only when my toes nearly touch hers does her gaze flicker.

"What happened to his family isn't your fault," she says.

"Yes, it is," I whisper and sit a safe distance away. "I didn't know that… I don't believe my father would give orders like those. Slaughter innocents? Murder children?!" She stays quiet, and I suppose she's reveling in the satisfaction that she was right about my father.

"There must've been a mistake! He wouldn't… I know him. I know my father!" Guilt slips off my tongue with the final words. I've rarely been at the castle, much less spent time with my father in years. How could I know him?

I hear her scoot closer, and the sweet scent of gardenias envelopes me. I look up to find her face beside mine. *Gods.* I strain to prevent my body from moving forward. We're already too close.

"I can't do it," I say, and my voice breaks. "I can't be what my father is… I'm not made for it. How can I be King?"

Though her eyes are solemn, she smiles lightly, and it's all I can do to not take this beautiful creature into my arms and make us both forget, even if only for a moment, the horrors we've faced. To apologize and tell her that she's no longer a prisoner of Baelliles.

"Let wisdom be your staff," she murmurs. "Grip it firmly. Let compassion be your crown; wear it proudly. And above all, bring joy with you wherever you go. Cling to it with all your might."

Chapter Nineteen

Idalia

My head slams into ice. Eyes shooting open in panic, I extend my arms to brace myself for what's to come. I don't know where I am. The glacier wall knocks against my skull once more, and I can't stop it. I'm surrounded by frozen walls of water, inside a glass-like fjord that illuminates all that moves within. I see that I'm traveling in a boat, but the bottom is leaking. It does me no use to cry for help; each time I attempt to do so, my head thuds again into the ice walls.

'You did this to us!' A woman cries from a distance. *'It is the Verdanian Princess. She has come to finish what they started.'* Wildly, I look around to see where the voice is coming from. But I can't see anything beyond the ice. The boat approaches a drop-off. My heart pounds. A cliff? A waterfall? *A trench.*

"Ahh," I hiss as my head slams into the ice again. Though, this time, it feels different. I rub my brow and peel my eyes open. It was a dream, that ice-bound fjord, but I feel no relief when I realize where I actually am. I'm back in the carriage and can see trees quickly passing through my blurry vision. Wherever I'm going, I'm headed there fast.

All I remember is falling asleep in the grass, the same as before. How did I end up here, wrapped in my blue cloak, neatly tied beneath my chin? Who put me in this carriage, and where am I going? My head bobs as the terrain grows bumpier, and I stiffen my neck to prevent my head from slamming into the window again. My grogginess disappears as fear overtakes it. I fling myself against the front of the carriage and press my ear against the wall to listen. At first, there aren't voices, only the scream of a harsh wind blowing against the coach, but then a familiar laugh breaks loose.

"Do you think Lachlan will be pissed about Tawdrey?" Torr sneers.

"Probably, but who cares?"

It's Braizen. He's kidnapped me yet again. I rear back into the cushioned seat and, panting, search for a weapon, but the carriage is empty. The alcohol, the food, and even the box of salva petals I saw on the way to Idizina that were stowed here are gone. Nothing remains save a piece of crumpled hemp on the floor. I'm totally alone and completely defenseless. If I want to escape, I can only do one thing.

I scooch to the door to see how fast we're traveling. It's fast, very fast. Too fast. But I have no choice. I take a deep breath and push down the door handle.

The wind hits me like a stone hurled from a sling. My hair slaps at my cheeks in vehement rage, and then the breath is knocked from my lungs. I'm tumbling, rolling against the dirt, and I wonder if I'll ever stop. Gravel pierces my skin, the cold wind settles around my body. A few more rolls, and I'm staring up at the sky. It's only then that I realize my decision's toll. My bones ache, and my neck screams in defiance. I bring my hands to my sore ribs and wince, though I don't suspect I've broken anything. Not that it matters. I must get up. I must run. They'll notice the door swinging sooner rather than later, and I need to put as much distance as I can between me and the carriage. *Between me and Vaskis.*

I roll over onto my stomach. With an agonizing exhale, I pull myself to all fours, then will myself to stand. Though my entire body pleads with me not to, I start to run back down the dirt road. It's more of a wobbly stumble, but I must do whatever I can. Each breath is a torment, each thrust of my legs harrowing, but I'm moving, and that's enough.

I'm not sure if I hear horses or if my mind is playing a foul trick on me, but I manage to run faster. I want to go home. I need to go home. The safety of my castle walls is the only hope I can cling to now. Nurse Lydia's sweet voice plays in my mind. I'll run through the door, collapse in her arms, and she'll cradle me. She'll bring me a caramel tart and draw me a bath. The mountains will again crowd my windows, and I'll be calm. Even the constant snow I once loathed will seem serene. Home. That's where I'm going. That's where I'll stay forever.

The cold autumn air burns my throat. I've only run for a few minutes, but they draw out like years. Perhaps my father was right to demand I build my strength through endless sprints carrying weapons. My lungs are bruised and begrudge my air, and just as I think I'll collapse, I glimpse something spin near the ground. Something snaps around my ankles, and I trip. I land hard, and my chin crashes into the dirt.

The pain of slamming into the ground again is almost too overwhelming to bear, and I can't decide which hurts worse, my head, torso, or pride. I don't try to fight; I can't. I'm too weak. I can only wait for my captor to retrieve and likely kill me. Could it be one of The Others Nuri spoke of? Or a Baellilean soldier? There's no telling how close Braizen got us to the border while I slept. My mind skitters through the possibilities, heart racing in fear.

The daunting sound of footsteps closes in. A pair of dirty boots appears near my cheek.

"You look terrible." A female voice breaks the tension. "But then again, you've always looked terrible."

"*Lorna*," I whisper in resignation. She drops to her haunches, and I can barely turn my aching head far enough to peer up and see her fiery red hair.

"Verdanian," she greets me with a coy smile. "Looks like we just can't escape each other."

I sigh heavily, blowing the dust on the road into soft ripples.

"Come on, Lorna. No playing with your food." Lin stalks out of the trees and joins us. His eyes latch on to mine, and I see smug arrogance. He releases a dramatic breath.

"Idalia, I *really* want to like you, but seriously? Jumping from a moving carriage? I expected more, even from a Verdanian." He shakes his head and tsks.

Lorna elbows him. "We should get going. You know, before the forest tries to eat us or something."

Lin nods, and they both grab my shoulders.

I moan as they raise me, and Lorna shakes her head. "You really beat yourself up, didn't you? Shame. I thought I'd be the one to do it."

I roll my neck to look at her and stick out my tongue.

She laughs, a sound I don't think I've ever heard from her, and readjusts her grip.

"Relax, Verdanian. We're here to help you."

There it is, that dreadful sound I've been waiting for. The horses' hooves pound the road as the carriage approaches. Torrent is yelling my name at the top of his lungs. Lin and Lorna wave their free arms, prompting Torrent to smile widely and cheer. Braizen's eyes are on me, though. No joy lingers on his expression.

Tossing the reins to Torrent, the Prince jumps from his seat. He lands effortlessly, which I try not to resent, and rushes over.

"Well, well," Lin teases. "Nice to see you, Braze." He releases his hold on me. "Now, I don't want to say I told you so … But, I told you so." His face beams as if he's waited his entire life to say this.

"He's right," Lorna chuckles. "We told you that you'd be an idiot to leave us behind." She shakes me gently. "As always, though, we are here to fix your mistakes. What would you do without us?"

Braizen doesn't smile back. Instead, he walks closer to me and doesn't break eye contact.

"Are you okay?" He scans the scratches and dirt on my cheeks.

I drag my head higher, though it feels so heavy I want to cry. I spit. My saliva doesn't make it far, but the message is perfectly clear.

Braizen's face sinks, and he runs his fingers through his hair. He looks at Lorna.

"Take her to the carriage. But be careful."

She nods and pushes me forward. Torrent has climbed down and playfully shoves Lin.

"So, what happened, Speck? Did you miss me too much to stay away?"

"The time we spent apart was the prime of my life. I don't think I'll ever achieve such happiness again," he scoffs.

"Don't lie," Torr growls. "I know you followed us because you can't live without me. A day without my handsome face would be too great a loss."

Lin grumbles and swats Torrent away. "If you and Braizen could ever do a job correctly, I'd leave you instantly. Unfortunately, you're both idiots, and it's up to Lorna and me to do the heavy lifting."

"Heavy lifting!" Torrent howls. "How much is that for you, five pounds?"

Lorna hoists me up, placing a sturdy hand behind the small of my back to rock me inside. I fall forward and squirm.

"Hold still. Let me untie your feet."

"What's the point?" My voice is devoid of energy. "You might as well leave me be. I'm a prisoner, after all."

She loosens the rope, climbs in, and sits across from me. "Don't you understand what's going on here? Braizen is taking you to Aeradian."

I blink but remain quiet.

"He's taking you there so that you can marry King Lachlan."

I laugh.

"Oh, I'm sure. What will you tell me next? That you're starting to like me?"

Her knee hits mine. "I'm serious, Princess. We're headed to the Aeradian border now. In a few days, you'll be wed, and we'll be gone."

Slowly, I survey her face. She doesn't appear to be lying, but I can't be too sure. I don't know her well enough to decipher her expressions.

"And to answer your question, no. I still despise you," she says with a smirk.

Though it hurts, I lean forward. "Why would he take me to Aeradian to marry King Lachlan? He knows what that would mean for him, for all Baelliles."

"I learned long ago to stop trying to figure out why Braizen does what he does," she says and rests her neck against the plush seat. "When his mind's made up, that's it. There's no swaying him, no matter how hard we try. The rest of us just need to choose whether we'll suffer through those decisions with him or not."

"And so here you are," I muse. "Stuck in a box with the Verdanian Princess, your mortal enemy. What could've possibly convinced you to suffer *this* decision with him?"

She closes her eyes as we hear Torrent and Braizen settle into their perches on the driver's seat. Lin braces himself on the footboard to my right, brandishing his giant crossbow like a trophy. They're all cursing and mocking each other. Lorna clears her throat and points a finger toward their voices.

"Because of that right there," she smiles.

"Their bickering?" I cross my arms.

Her smile stretches. "The sound of a family. One that decided long ago that it's better to die together than it is to live apart."

"Tomorrow, we'll reach the border," Braizen calls down. He's already at the top of the hill and is staring into the distance, a torn map in his hand. Earlier, we found a small clearing, and Torrent and Lorna are already gathering wood for a fire. Autumn is truly breaking across The Wood, and her coldness shows us no mercy.

I join them and, for a moment, enjoy the beauty of the scenery.

"It's risky," Lin says. "A fire is more of a beacon than anything else. We'll give away our position, Braze."

"Shall we freeze to death instead?" Though he faces away from me, his curls dancing in the wind, I know precisely the grin that marks his face.

Lin raises his chin. "I only mean it isn't wise to press our luck. We've survived thus far; do we really want to invite trouble in on our last night?"

I listen closely, pretending to search for small branches to kindle the hypothetical fire.

"There are other ways to stay warm," Lin says.

Before Braizen answers, I chime in. "Lin is right."

Both men turn quickly, their expressions making it clear they'd forgotten I'd trailed them up the hill. When Lin realizes I agree with him, his eyes widen.

"A fire risks The Others finding us," I continue. "If what the Idunns say is true, they're already looking for me. Best not to give them aid."

Braizen nods slowly. Disbelief still washes over Lin's face. He is truly not used to being agreed with, I note.

"So, what do the two of you propose then?" Braizen asks.

Lin braces his hands on his hips. "Well, I… There are a few options. Uhm. So, the first thing we could consider, possibly, after a vote, of course," he stutters, and his cheeks burn red.

"Body heat," I state.

Lin sighs, all too relieved he didn't have to be the one to say it.

"Body heat," Braizen repeats.

I feel warmth lance through me but ignore it. "We can all tiptoe around the obvious, but it's growing cold. What do you think Lorna and Torr will say?"

Braizen's face pulls back in shock. "*Torr?!*"

I hadn't realized I'd used the nickname. After a moment of paralysis, I clear my throat.

"What? I can save his life, but I can't shorten his name?"

Lin's eyes crinkle, and he snickers. Braizen stares at him then turns to me. "Call him whatever you like. Hells, call us all whatever you'd like."

Lin raises a finger. "Uhm, I suggest you refrain from doing so with Lorna," he cautions. "She won't be pleased. Trust me."

I release a lighthearted laugh, and we clamber down the hill.

Nerves consume my sore body when I hear them approach. First, Lorna arrives, her arms filled with wood that she dumps on the ground. Sweat beads across her flushed face, and hundreds of loose hairs escape her braid. She spits, then, like us, focuses on the giant pile of wood wobbling behind her. Torrent is a bark mountain, carrying at least fifty pounds of wood in his massive arms. He releases the load and sends us a devilish grin.

"Good news," he announces proudly. "We cut tons of branches, and none of them came alive!"

"Better news," Braizen counters. "We're all going to sleep naked together."

Chapter Twenty

Braizen

"What's the matter, Lorna? Never been naked with a man before?" Torr teases as he yanks off his tunic. His massive chest is covered in golden hair. The man is pure muscle, so much muscle that I sometimes wonder how much space is left for a brain. He tosses the tunic at Lorna, and she growls.

"I have been with a few men, and you're an asshole for reminding me." Lorna's shoulders sag, and she turns a desperate face to me. "I think we should risk the fire," she states.

"Relax, Lorna. You don't have to fully strip. Besides, you're sleeping with Idalia and Lin. The big boy's all mine."

Torrent releases a barbaric yowl, winks, and sends me a sinister grin. Lin shivers, wrapping his arms around his fully clothed body.

"I never agreed to that arrangement," he says.

"Didn't have to," I say between bites of an apple. "You three are the smallest, so you'll need more of each other's heat. Torr's a bear; his heat will do fine for me."

Lorna clutches Torr's tunic to her chest and continues to argue. "I can't believe you lot agreed to this ridiculous plan. To the Lady, I'll never forgive you," she huffs.

A laugh springs up behind me—her laugh.

Lorna is unamused. "Oh, I'll bet you think this is hilarious, don't you?" she shouts at Idalia. "Verdanians love frigid weather. After all, they do say your bones are made of ice."

I turn around. Idalia holds her red nose high in the air, though she doesn't look upset by Lorna's jeer. Her lips press tightly together before she speaks.

"Actually, I've always hated the cold." She unbuttons her trousers, and I can't move. I can't look away. "So, I highly doubt my bones are frozen." She briskly pulls them down without so much as a thought. Though the oversized tunic still covers most of her thighs, I'm surprised by her lack of shyness.

"Truthfully, I'd say that if my bones were made of anything, it would be branches. Like a tree. I've always loved trees. Especially the ones that hover over the Baellilean castle…" She abruptly stops.

"Was that a compliment…about Baelliles?" Torr asks with a cheeky grin. Idalia blushes and then throws her trousers on the ground.

"A slip of the tongue," she smiles. "These woods must've bent my mind."

Torrent also removes his trousers and stands before us in nothing but a brown loincloth.

I choke on my fruit. "Gods, Torrent. That can't possibly be all you wear!" I yell, catching coughed-up apple in my hand. Lin is almost hysterical with laughter; Lorna grimaces. Torr's skin is layered in goosebumps, but he stands straight and pretends not to notice.

"Shall I remove it?" His fingers trace playfully over the small cloth.

"For the love of the Guard, no!" Lorna pleads. "If you have any ounce of respect for me, you'll leave it on!" We all buck in laughter. Even Idalia.

"Well, I, for one, will change in the privacy of the carriage. After all, that's where we'll be sleeping," Lin says, stalking away.

He flings open the carriage door and gives us all a once over, his eyes briefly resting on Torrent. He rolls back his shoulders. "You bear an uncanny resemblance to the creature I saw when I was on lookout. If I hadn't known you for all these years, I'd shoot you stone dead and return us all home."

"Well, Speck, if that's your plan, you're in luck! I saw an anthill just over there," Torr says, pointing. "It seems your home is only mere steps away!"

Lin clicks his tongue and disappears into the carriage. Before entering behind him, Lorna turns to Idalia. "You're sleeping in the middle."

Idalia scowls but nods. "More warmth for me, I suppose," she says.

Torrent finally breaks his facade and growls at the wind. "I'm going to run for a while. That way, I'll get nice and hot for you," he says to me.

"I'm getting excited just thinking about it," I quip, taking the last bite of fruit.

Torr winks and then sprints off towards the perimeter of the clearing, his massive strides kicking up loads of dirt. What a sight: a giant in nothing but a flap and boots.

Now, only the half-dressed Sparrow remains with me outside the carriage.

"I'd better get in there," she says timidly. "Before Lorna kills Lin."

"He'll likely die before she gets the chance. I don't think he's ever seen a woman in just her undergarments."

Idalia laughs. I pull my tunic over my head, and my skin immediately rebels at the cold air. I ball it up, preparing to make it my pillow and notice that Idalia isn't laughing any longer. She's staring at the point where the trail of hair disappears into my trousers. I smile. "Do I have a poisonous bug on me or something?"

Her eyes jerk back to my face. Quickly, she shakes her head and scoffs. "I wouldn't tell you if you did."

She opens the carriage door and lifts herself, but I see her scan me again before she enters, and I smile even wider. In addition to her nose, her cheeks are red, and I know it's not from the cold.

For the most part, the night's chill hasn't found me. Though, each time Torrent twitches in his sleep, the protection of his arm falters, and my teeth chatter. My cloak only covers a small portion of his body. Never in my life have I encountered such a shrill wind. I assume that whatever magic powers The Wood holds must exaggerate the weather within it. Leaves rustle, and I crane my head to look for danger, but Brax sleeps soundly, and if I know anything about this horse, it's that if there were a threat, he'd be the first to alert me. I haven't slept much, but I don't need much rest to operate. Besides, every time I close my eyes, I see the same scene.

First, I imagine birds in flight, their relentless pursuit for freedom. Then, I see her eyes. She lies next to me, our noses almost touching. Golden sunlight falls across her face, gilding her fair cheeks. We tangle further into silken white sheets, laughing at something I've said. Her hair briefly spills over her face, and I move it away. I can touch her, hold her. It's as if there were never a curse, and we're in love and happily wed.

The same melody I heard from the Idizina trees surrounds us, but now a delicate, rippling wave sings alongside the harp; the two meld in perfect harmony. "*Braizen,*" she hums, and her voice makes the golden rays illuminating her face shine brighter. I've heard a thousand melodies in my lifetime, but none as beautiful as the way she says my name now. Her hands run through my hair, and when she smiles, I'm in the Great Lands, finally at peace.

"Get up," she whispers.

I laugh and tug at her hands, forcing them to wrap around my shoulders.

"Get up," she repeats, only her smile has faded this time. Mine disappears as I search her eyes.

"*Get Up!*" She yells. "*Get up! Get up!*"

I feel a tug at my arm and see Torrent standing over me.

"Get up!" He shouts, pulling me to my feet. I'm barely conscious when I see Lin, in only his braies, firing his weapon into the trees.

"What's going on?" I ask, struggling to balance. Torr grabs his trousers and sword as he replies.

"The Others."

My mind spins, then I snatch up my bow, run to the carriage, and yank open the door. Lorna is almost dressed and holding Nedson. Behind her, Idalia sits with her knees tucked against her chest. She looks frightened

"I'll protect her," Lorna says shortly. I nod, look once more at Idalia, then slam the door.

"Where are they?" I call as I join Lin and Torrent in our circle formation.

"Not sure. They're using magic, so we don't even know how many there are," Torr responds, waving his sword high.

Lin is still aiming at the trees, squinting one eye over his crossbow when he adds, "They're trying to get her. Lorna and I both felt it."

"Felt what exactly?" I ask, readying my weapon.

Lin sucks in air. "It was like someone was inside the carriage. First, I heard a voice. Then, I felt a pair of hands. They were trying to rip Lorna and me away from her. Trying to get her alone."

"What did the voice say?" I knock my bow and swivel, aiming in different directions. I see nothing but the empty clearing and the dark trees surrounding us.

"I was half asleep, so I'm not too sure. I think it said, *'Now.'*"

I blink. "Now? That's it?"

"Like I said, I barely heard it. I was asleep. The hands are what got me, naked, standing here. Then I saw a dark smoke spiral in the trees. I shot at it. Not sure I got anything."

"Like the mist from before?" Torrent stammers.

"No," Lin emphasized. "Like a spirit."

I flash him a concerned look, then immediately return my focus to my section of the tree line. I study the base of the trunks and then slowly move my attention to the canopy.

Nothing. It's so quiet.

Braxton whinnies and bucks. I lower my weapon. "We need to leave. Quickly." Torr and Lin nod. I grab my cloak and throw it at Lin, who does his best to cover himself. Torr is already patting the horses, gearing them up for the run ahead of us. At least this time, they've slept and eaten. I pound on the carriage door, yell that we're leaving, then pull myself into the driver's seat as Torr quickly hitches the horses. As soon as he climbs up next to me, we're off.

We push the horses through the night. I try to ignore the frozen air that whips against my face and pray we aren't far from the Aeradian border. If this spirit doesn't kill us, the weather might. I flick the reins and urge the horses to run faster.

Lin calls from his perch behind the carriage. "Braze… Braze!"

I don't have to signal Torrent, he is already climbing across the carriage roof to meet Lin. "What in the four hells?" I hear him sputter. The carriage sways, and it's all I can do to keep the horses moving forward.

"Uh, Boss. We have a problem!" Torrent shouts.

I barely turn my cheek towards the disturbance behind me.

"What is it?"

"I… I have no gods damn clue."

"Oh shit!" Lin screams, and then the carriage topples over.

I throw my arms out, bracing myself for impact, and then smash into the ground. There's a blur of darkness and boughs that slap at my face as I roll down, down, down. I finally stop, then scramble up to look for the others, ignoring the pain searing through my chest. Torrent and Lin are nowhere in sight. A few yards away, the carriage is upside down. The horses are no longer hitched and have fled. I run to the gig and shout through the broken door.

"Lorna! Idalia! Are you okay?"

A hand reaches out and grabs my boot. "Braze," Lorna coughs. "I'm stuck."

"Lady and Shield—hold on! I'll get you out of there. I promise I'm coming back!" I drop to the ground and search through the tall grass for my bow. There's little moonlight to aid me. My palms pat every inch around me until finally, I feel a handle and raise Torrent's sword.

"Good enough," I breathe and launch myself up the hill. I call out but don't see or hear them. Finally, I reach the road. My breath ceases momentarily when I see what stands there, as if waiting for me. The dire wolf. The same one we faced back in Idizina. One of its eyes is sealed shut.

It lowers its head and snarls. My breath clouds around me. The horrific animal rears back on its haunches, ready to leap. Its vengeance will likely not be quenched until every part of me is torn to shreds.

"Come on, then!" I shout, waving Torr's blade around me. "You big bastard! Come on! Kill me!" I swear I see its lip curl into a smile. Then it whips its head to focus on something behind me.

I spare a glance. Idalia crawls towards me, and even in the dim light, I see her hands are bloodied. "Sparrow," I cry. "Go back!"

The wolf flicks its head toward me and lurches for Idalia. A bellow discharges from deep within me as I charge the beast. I'm ready to drive the sword deep into its ribs when it swings its snout toward me and snaps.

Idalia screams, and for a brief, blessed moment, all I feel is the biting air. The wolf draws back, its snout dripping blood. My blood. I glance down and see a growing, crimson stain cover my right shoulder. Pain unleashes itself, and I fall to my knees. I can't move my arm. I'm not sure I still have an arm. My eyes lock on Idalia, who's crying uncontrollably.

The beast turns to her again and opens its mouth to devour her.

At this moment, before our deaths, I reach out my hand. If we die here, die now, I will not have her pass alone.

I will die with her skin on mine.

A battle cry sounds and something strikes the wolf with a thud. It whimpers, and as it thrashes, I see a thick bolt sticking out of its side.

"Lin," I whisper.

The beast suddenly barrels over on its side as if an iron wall crashed into it.

"Braizen, go!" Torrent, his face distressed, stands over the creature. "We'll hold it off. Take the girl!"

The wolf flails its legs and growls. I want to help them. To stand and fight by my brothers' sides and die next to them. But it's no use. My arm is hanging, barely connected to my body by slivers of muscle and skin. "What about Lorna?" I manage to get out. "She's stuck beneath the carriage!"

"We'll get her," Torrent assures me. He squats and puts a hand on my cheek. "For whatever reason, these crazy demons want you and the girl. We'll die before they get their way."

"No." I resist, even though I'm breathless just trying to talk. "I won't leave you. It's better to die together than to live—"

"Not this time, Boss." I've never seen my large friend so serious. His eyes gleam, and his lips are tight. Then, he lifts his head and sounds a barbaric howl into the wind. Snatching his sword, he swivels and swings at the wolf's leg.

"Limb for limb, you filthy bastard!" He screams, and the enormous canine moves as if to rise. I know I must run. *Now.*

"Idalia, come on!" She's slow to stand, but I can't grab her. I can't force her to move faster. I can only run and hope that she has enough sense to follow.

Finally, she reaches me, and the two of us sprint down the hill and back into the trees. I see Lorna's hand sticking out helplessly as we race past the carriage. My stomach drops.

"She'll be okay," Idalia says in between breaths. "I've seen it."

We keep running.

Chapter Twenty-One

Idalia

Dappled sunlight skirts across the forest floor and splashes on our faces. We ran and stumbled through the night, and now I can barely breathe. The lace chemise I'd stripped down to in the carriage is ripped apart from catching on branches. There's no room for me to complain, though, as Braizen clutches his bleeding shoulder. My palms flicker with heat. When the sun rose, I looked at his wound; I haven't been able to stomach looking at it again. His arm is lost. It will have to be amputated, and that's only if we can reach a medic in time. An infection will likely spread before then.

"We need rest," he finally says. "I think we've put enough distance between us and the creature."

I nod my head and drop to the ground.

"We need to find the path back to Aeradian, though I don't know how we'll manage that," I say.

"I can find it," he says confidently. "I'll get you to Lachlan. Don't worry about that."

"You think I'm worried about getting to Lachlan?" I scoff. "How little you must think of me to say such a thing."

His eyes dart to mine, and I almost gasp at the dried blood covering his chest.

"Aren't you?"

"No," I retort.

Braizen hisses as he moves to sit, and I wince. "I'm worried about you."

He follows my gaze to his shoulder and snaps the fingers of his left hand.

"This? Just a scratch. I'll be fine." He smiles, but I don't join him. "Really, Sparrow, losing an arm isn't the worst thing that could happen to me. Besides, I'll still have *two* left."

I wrinkle my brow until I see that gods awful, cocky grin on his face.

"Gods!" I throw up my hands. "How can you even joke at a time like this?"

He shrugs. "Because I'm stuck in the middle of the Florian Wood, mortally injured by a giant dog, with the Verdanian Princess whom I can't touch. Hells, we aren't even fully clothed! This entire situation is a joke, and I'm sure the gods have been laughing at us every step of the way. Might as well join them in their entertainment."

I wrap my arms around my knees, and a reluctant laugh escapes me. "I suppose you're right," I allow.

His face grows serious. "Besides, it's my fault we're all here. My father wanted us to capture you, and we did. You've been my prisoner this entire time, and everything that's happened to you since..."

"Whatever lurks in these woods was hunting me, whether I was kidnapped by you or not," I interrupt. "It's unlikely my Verdanian guards would've survived all the obstacles hurled at us." I take a deep breath. "I think I've only lived this long *because* I've been your prisoner."

"Well then, I guess we're even. Except I think you've saved my team more times than they've saved you."

I smirk and playfully dust off my shoulders. "Just another day of Verdanians being better than Baellileans."

His brows rise, and he chuckles. "I wouldn't go that far."

I throw myself backward, landing softly on the dirt, and close my eyes.

"What are we going to do, Braizen?" I ask. There's only the sound of our quiet, matching breaths. The still trees keep their ominous secrets. I rest my mind for a few minutes. I barely hear his whisper.

"We're going to keep going, Idalia."

"What about Swan?" I ask, stepping over a thorny plant that threatens to jab me. Braizen shifts his arm in the rudimentary sling we constructed from supple branches and vines, then protests loudly.

"*Swan*? Surely you jest!"

"You've made fun of every name I've offered! You're too hard to please!"

He shakes the long stick he carries in his free hand into the air. "On the contrary, my dear! I'm quite easy to please. But your nicknames are atrocious. Swan? Woodpecker? *Cuckoo?"*

"I thought that one was fitting!"

He stops walking and squints a warning. "Easy, Sparrow," he says.

"Fine, fine. Let's see… What other kinds of birds are there? Hmm…" I tap a finger to my chin and scan the sky, though I know I won't see any here. "What about Raven?"

"Raven?!"

I grunt at his displeasure and roll my eyes. "Maybe I should just call you a parrot since you repeat everything I say!"

"It's just that…Well, a nickname should be personal! What do I have in common with a raven? If you can name three things, I'll gladly accept the name."

"I don't know anything about ravens," I say and admit defeat.

"Well, that's your first mistake," he sighs, shaking his stick at me. "Ravens are incredible. Did you know that they can imitate humans? Once in the aviary…."

"Shh," I push my finger to my lips.

He immediately falls silent and follows my gaze.

A cottage sits nestled in the trees. The path that leads to it is overgrown, and its door is little more than rotting wood. Perhaps it's abandoned; maybe it's filled with deserted food and clothes. I glance at Braizen, and he nods. We weave our way between the trees.

I pray to The Lady that we find tonics and elixirs inside to help Braizen. He's making a valiant effort, but I know he's in great pain. The sweat on his forehead and bags beneath his eyes give him away. His usually tanned skin is turning pale. He needs more than his jokes to succor his wounds. Both the physical and internal ones. We approach slowly, and once at the door, I press up against it to peer through a small hole. I don't see much. Turning to him, I whisper.

"On three?"

He nods, then lifts his stick like a sword. I mouth, "*One, two… Three!!!*"

The door catches and scrapes loudly against the stone threshold, and then we're inside. The interior spills over with knick-knacks. At least a hundred jars of jam cram the shelves, and piles of dried herbs lie across a large, wooden table. I walk closer and touch their brittle leaves. They've been dried out for years, it seems.

A black cauldron hangs in the stone hearth, and its contents emit a putrid smell. Long, tapered candles, their surfaces ribboned with melted wax, are scattered around the room. Cracked ewers and branches line the floors. In one corner, a mattress displays two body indentations. Perhaps a couple once lived here, and that's where they slept. Beside the bed, I see a wardrobe, and I fly towards it. I open its doors and scream with excitement.

"What is it?" Braizen asks worriedly and starts towards me.

I snatch some of the hanging garments and spin around.

"Clothes! For men and women!" I say through tears of joy.

His nostrils flare, but then he smiles.

"I call the dress," he says.

Some of the jams and preserves are still edible. I take one of the two spoons from the kitchen and pass the other and a jar to Braizen, who looks even more tired after dressing himself in the clothes we found.

He grabs the spoon and begins shoveling jam into his mouth. His blue eyes light up, and he licks his lips. "This is delicious," he declares. His spoon dives back into the jar.

I take a spoonful from another, and the flavor of peach erupts over my tongue. He's right; this is wonderful. I try not to spill any on the old white dress I'm now wearing. I finish my jar and clasp my belly, satisfied.

"We need to find you some kind of ointment," I say, surveying his arm. The blood has crusted over, and it's still a grotesque sight. "Do you know anything about plants?"

"Oh, sure. Baellileans are known botanists," he answers, flinging his spoon to the ground.

"Truly?"

"No, of course not. I don't know one damn thing about them. I'm a bird man, remember?"

I huff a rude breath and search the cottage: every drawer, every nook, and cranny. There's nothing.

"We need to go," Braizen says as he stands. He stumbles and grimaces.

"Not till I find something that can help you."

"Idalia, there's nothing here," he sighs. "And even if we find tonics, they'll probably be so old they'd do me more harm than good."

"I don't care. We aren't leaving till we find something." I scramble around the room and begin to open old books; dust rises as I flip through their pages.

"Sparrow…"

"No!" I yell and open drawers for the second time. "Leave without me if you want, but I won't go. You'll die before we reach Aeradian, and you know it."

"Wouldn't that make you happy?"

"That's not funny," I say, my face beating with heat. "None of your jokes are."

He hangs his head with a grin, then drops onto a chair. "Last night," Braizen begins as I rip apart the cottage like a madwoman. "You said Lorna would be okay because you saw it. What did you mean?"

I stop and consider his question. I did say that, didn't I? I resume foraging and shake my head. "I don't know how to explain it."

"Try."

"It wouldn't make any sense." I move towards the bed.

"You're probably right," he shrugs. "But look around. Nothing makes sense anymore. Humor me."

I take a deep breath and shake the bed covers. I suppose he's right about that. I drop to all fours to search under the mattress and decide that I feel sorry enough for him to share.

"Last night, I had this dream," I say. "Only, it didn't feel anything like a dream. I could've sworn I was awake. It felt so real." Nothing lies under the bed but more dust. I scowl. On to the wardrobe.

"First, I saw Lorna, then Torrent and Lin. But it was so dark..." I swing open the doors and check each piece of simple clothing. On the wardrobe floor lies a coif and some ripped pieces of black cloth. Absolutely nothing of use. Now, I'm angry.

"Anyway, Lorna looked me dead in the eyes and said, *'Torrent lifted the carriage just in time.'* Her hair was covered by black fabric. Then,

I started going in and out of sleep and heard Lin say something about a spirit. Or phantom? I don't remember. I woke up to Lorna standing over me with her hatchet, telling me to be silent."

Braizen is quiet.

"What, no quips about my stupid dream?" I ask without turning around.

He doesn't answer.

"Oh, really? Have I convinced you that easily? That's a first," I mutter.

I finally stop my frantic search. The cottage contains nothing I can use to help him. "Looks like you were right," I concede, shoving the last drawer closed. "Maybe there's a garden, and we just try different things." The eerie silence is deafening.

"Braizen?" I turn and gasp.

He's slumped in his chair, his pale body drenched in sweat.

"Braizen!" I scream, lunging towards him. My hands shake, mere inches away from his body. I don't know what to do. I can't touch him! I can't help him! "Lady and Guard," I breathe and grab the dried herbs from the table, then kneel in front of him.

I press the herbs against his wound in a fit of chaotic dread. His face betrays no reaction. "Oh gods," I cry under my breath. "Please… *Please* don't die."

Even though my first search didn't unearth any, I wildly scout the room for spirits, or anything that might help disinfect the wound. I turn in circles and wring my hands in growing panic. Hot tears stream down my cheeks. Braizen is dying, and I can't even hold him as he does. *He's dying.*

My hands flare, and I drop to my knees, burying my face in my hot palms. I sob, praying as reverently as possible for The Lady to help. My hands throb, and a roaring heat cloaks them.

"Lady, I beg you! I beg you to help! You made it so that I may not touch him, so I plead that you do so for me! Heal him! Please!" I sprawl on the floor. "I beg of you! Guard, protect him from death!" Tears drip into my mouth. My eyes are swollen, and my head pounds. Is this truly the end for the boy who led me into the aviary?

My palms rage. Now each sob is followed by a stabbing pain in my chest. I hear the Minea speak.

'There is a reason for that feeling inside of you. The one that calls out, desperate for your attention, your obedience.'

I stop crying and wipe my face with the back of my hand. I swallow hard and raise myself off the floor. My fists clench. I'm out of options, out of places to run and people to hide behind. If the Minea's words are true, if this *feeling* is more than only a feeling, let it prove itself now. I lean back, point my face at the ceiling, and inhale a shaky breath. I exhale steadily and release my fists, stretching my fingers wide.

I listen.

The calling tells me to move. *Go to him.*

I take a step, and the pain in my chest instantly eases a notch. *Closer.* I shuffle my way to Braizen until our feet almost touch. *Reach out to him.*

As I move my palms toward him, their seething heat transforms into something bright and refreshing, like stepping out of a cold room into the sun's warmth. With my eyes closed, I press my palms out harder. I can feel him. I can feel his arms around my waist as if we're dancing together again. I hear his laugh and see his light blue eyes pierce mine.

"Idalia." I can hear his voice, too. That disastrous voice that ruins me each time it says my name.

"What are you doing? *How* are you doing this?"

My eyes snap open, and I realize I'm not only hearing him inside my head.

He's staring up at me, wide-eyed. Golden streams of light pour from my palms and wrap around his shoulder. My mouth drops open as I watch the illuminated ribbon work its way in and out of his wound. His face returns to its normal color, and the sweat that coats him dries.

I drop my hands, and the gleaming strands uncoil, then extinguish like a candle flame. I collapse to the floor. I look up. His shoulder—it's completely healed.

He touches it lightly with his opposite hand. Then, his head snaps down. His eyes glow with speculation.

"What are you?"

I run through the trees. How often during this past week have I found myself doing this? But I don't care. I run faster and faster and hear Braizen pound after me. He wants answers, and I can't give him any. He wants to know things that I don't know myself. Things I can't even think about. Mud spatters the once white dress, and more branches tangle my hair with each stride.

I've no idea what I just did or if the Minea woman was right about me. I only know I need to run. I don't even know to where. I only hope that if I'm quick enough, maybe my thoughts won't be able to catch up to me. So, I take longer strides and push my legs faster and faster.

When I can no longer run, I slow to a walk and hold my arms above my head, taking deep, controlled breaths of the frigid air. It's so gods damn cold, and I left my cloak in the carriage. Safe to say, I'll never see it again.

"Good Guard," Braizen wheezes as he closes in on me. "Torr was right. You *are* fast." He leans down to catch his breath, "Seriously, Sparrow? How many times are you going to make me chase you through these damned woods?"

"I've never asked or forced you to chase after me," I huff.

Braizen brushes the tip of his nose and smiles. "Just like I didn't ask you to save me. And yet, here we are. Both doing things the other didn't ask for."

"I don't know how I did it! There. Are you satisfied? I don't know how any of this is possible. So, please, don't ask." I breathe in the biting air. My nose must be as red as the Aeradian flag by now.

"I wasn't going to ask how you did it. I was going to ask…"

"If I knew that I could? If I'm capable of anything else? If my father can do magic, too?"

"I was going to ask if you're okay," Braizen finishes slowly.

"Oh." If the cold didn't make me red before, my embarrassment does now.

"Oh." He repeats sharply.

I look down and kick up the soil under my feet before raising my chin.

"Honestly?" I ask.

He steps closer, but I don't retreat.

"Honestly, I think I'm fine. I just need to get out of these woods."

Braizen hesitates as if he wants to say something, then his shoulders relax, and his face lightens.

"I couldn't agree more. Thankfully, we'll be out of here soon enough. Especially with you running so much."

I manage a weak laugh. "If only you could run as fast as you run your mouth," I tease.

He cracks a handsome grin. "If only."

We rest for a while longer, Braizen rotating his shoulder as if unable to believe it's healed. "For what it is worth, thank you. For saving my arm, and my life," he says.

"It's the least I could do after you tried to take on that dire wolf for me."

"I know that you're overwhelmed by it all, but I think it's amazing that you can use…magic. Or, whatever the hells you did back there. One moment, I could feel myself dying, and all I could hear was…" His throat bobs. "All I could hear was you singing." The air between us stills for a moment, then he quickly continues.

"Next thing I know, there's a golden light spiraling towards me. At first, I thought it was The Lady, coming to take me to the Great Lands, but then, it was you. Amazing."

I blush. What happened is amazing, but I'm still confused by it all.

"I wish I were magic," he whispers, shaking his head.

I stand. We need to reach the border before nightfall to avoid more deadly encounters.

Braizen jolts up. "Ready?" He asks with a dashing smile.

I only nod as he takes the lead. "Do you know where we're going? I think the map is back in the carriage."

"I memorized enough of it to get us the hells out of here. Don't you worry about that."

I look back at the ground we've covered. Crossing the border means leaving behind everything that happened to me, and I don't know if I can. I don't know if I want to.

A heavy weight drags in my chest. A clod of reminders: I must save Verdana. I must go to Aeradian. I *have* to cross that border.

"I tell you," Braizen shouts back at me. "Lachlan better have good alcohol. I need a drink."

Chapter Twenty-Two

Braizen

M*aybe the gods are tired of torturing us,* I think as I take my final step out of The Wood. Idalia is close behind, and as soon as her feet cross that invisible border, I hear her begin to cry. I don't look at her or say anything. I could cry, too, thinking about how lucky we are and about everyone I had to leave behind.

Her sobs break my concentration.

I wish we could hold each other and share the victory that comes from surviving the evil that lies within those trees, the triumph that comes from crossing through that invisible veil. But I can't and I'm not convinced she'd let me touch her even without the curse. So, I stare off into the distance and wait out her sniffles.

"How far from here, do you think?" She asks after some time.

"By foot, we should arrive at the castle a little after sundown. Less time if we can find a ride." She nods and, without a word, walks past me. I quickly reach her side, and we walk in unison. My neck itches as the wool tunic from the cottage pricks at it, and I pray that no looming magic crawls within the stitches. I don't want to carry an ounce of the Florian Wood with me.

"Look!" Idalia smiles and points. Ahead, horses graze in a small, fenced pasture. My heart aches. Did Braxton make it out safely? Can he track the paths as well as we did and exit the Wood? I pray Torrent finds him and leads him to safety, that *they all* make it to safety. The alternative…

No.

I shove down the dread and bury it deep. They're all safe. They have to be. Torr and Lin alone could have finished off the wolf and Lorna…She'll be fine, too. I can't spend another second imagining otherwise because I know a second will be too long, and I'll surely break.

Idalia sprints towards the pasture, waving wildly at a man standing by the gate. "Good sir," she cries, and I see his eyes immediately light up, even from a distance. A feral, oddly dressed, yet outstandingly attractive woman is flailing her way toward him. Of course, he's excited.

The tall, lanky male holds a lute but lowers it as Idalia draws near. He reaches out a hand. "Milady! Are you all right? You look like you've just escaped a dungeon!" His eyes move to me, and his dark brows furrow. He pulls Idalia behind his back and lifts a cautionary hand. "Is this man causing you distress? If the answer is yes, I'll have to show him that a lute is a powerful weapon if swung hard enough!" He rears back his instrument and braces himself.

I laugh, and his brown eyes sizzle.

"I'll have you know, to laugh at a musician is a dangerous gamble! We often have nothing to lose," he says.

"No, no!" Idalia finally chimes in, moving around him to join me. "I'm with him!"

A gust of euphoria waves through me at her words, then Idalia continues. "I mean, I came here with him. I'm not *with him*, with him. We're friends. Well, not even that, really. We're together, but not together in *that* way."

"We escaped the Florian Wood together," I interject, crossing my arms. "Is what she's trying to say."

"Ah, I see," the man says with a grin. "Survivors of The Wood, are you? That's no easy feat! They say there's a path that the Verdanians sometimes use, but even that's perilous, no? Tell me, are you Verdanians?"

"I am Princess Idalia of Verdana," Idalia announces, smoothing the loose fringe on the front of her dress.

"Ha!" He squawks, pointing a finger. "That's a brilliant jest!"

"I tell you the truth! I am who I say I am, and I must be taken to King Lachlan at once!"

"Oh, yes! Of course, *Your highness*!" The male only laughs harder. "I'll get you to the new King in no time, but first, allow me to introduce myself." He bows stiffly. "It is I, the ghost of King Lester! What a wonderful reunion this is! I say, just look at these fine clothes you donned this morning! You swapped lace for dirt! Only the best wool for Princess Idalia of Verdana." He slaps his leg and snorts. "And that must make you?"

He points at me, and I shrug.

"Prince Braizen of Baelliles."

"Brilliant, brilliant!" He howls. "The whole court is here then! Now, what will you be needing from me, Princess?"

Idalia huffs. "I need a horse I can ride to the castle. If you provide one of yours, I will gladly pay you more than what's fair."

"Two horses," I cut in, glaring at her. "We can't touch each other."

The man whistles. "That's right! The Lady's curse! Spooky stuff, eh? Well, let's see… I have two horses to spare, so if you hand over the silver, I'll gladly let you be on your way."

Idalia lifts her arms and then slaps them against her sides in frustration.

"I don't have any coin on me. But once we get to the castle, once Lachlan sees me—"

A click of his tongue interrupts her. "A Princess with no coin to spare? How very unlike royalty to withhold your treasure trove from the poor! Well, that's a shame because as much as I want to serve Your Highness, I'm afraid I can't be doin' no favors for free." He scopes her lush body and shrugs. "There *are* other methods of payment I'm willing to accept, of course."

"How about, if you grant us the horses, I won't kill you for saying that," I say softly.

Idalia's eyes flick to mine, and a hesitant smile crosses her porcelain face.

I step closer and fold my arms across my chest, the incredibly irritating fabric scratching against my skin.

The male squints, sizes me up, and then spits.

"Is that supposed to scare me, Prince Man?" He steps closer, puffing out his chest. "Because, as I said before, I'm a *musician."* His lips twist as we close the distance between us. "You don't want to know the horrors I've faced."

I give him an easy smile and shake my head. "What's your plan, then? Are you going to sing me to death?"

The male scoffs, then strokes his chin. "Perhaps not, but my songs can make you feel so much pain, you'll be wishing you were dead."

"Is that so?"

"Yes, that *is* so." His nose nearly touches mine, and I almost gag as I smell his breath. It alone is enough to kill a man.

"I don't think you understand the severity of what you're walking into, Lute Boy."

"A man with no weapon, threatening an armed combatant? Are you that daft?" He holds his lute high and gives it a violent shake.

"Your little instrument doesn't scare me."

"No, but the power of song should."

Our jaws clench tightly as we stare deep into each other's eyes, waiting for the other to strike first.

Idalia's loud laugh breaks my stare. I turn my neck to see her almost in tears, holding one hand to her belly, the other to her forehead.

"What is happening?!" Her voice cracks as deep laughs roll from her. "Is this how men deal with things? Guard and Sword, what a joke!"

I immediately step back and point at her. "Don't involve yourself, Sparrow. I'm going to kill this man."

"That's right, little lady, no sense in you being so close to danger. Why don't you sit on the fence while I take care of this tone-deaf savage?"

She slaps a hand to her mouth and then drags it down her throat. "Fine! Go ahead, boys. I'll be right over here, waiting for the victor." She strolls to the fence and sits, nestling her chin in her palms and glaring at me.

I watch her for a few seconds before turning back to the weasel.

"I'll have you know; I'm *not* tone deaf. I've been told countless times that my voice is pretty good."

"Please." The man rolls his eyes and steadies his footing. "I can tell with just one look who's got the gift, and I'm telling you right now, Prince Man, you don't got it."

"You calling me a liar?"

"So, what if I am?"

I release a breathy chuckle. The male may be taller, but I must have at least forty pounds on him. This fight will be over before it starts.

"You might be a singer, but you don't want to join this dance. Trust me."

He leans close. Too close.

"I can assure you… *I do*." He pulls back his fist.

A horse whinnies, and I bolt my head around. Idalia is mounted and already on the road. She peeks back to catch my eye and smirks.

"*Hiyah!*" She kicks the horse's ribs, and they're off.

"Should've seen that one coming," I say with a large sigh. With one last look at my opponent, I scramble over the fence. A brown stallion with white patches grazes nearby, unperturbed. He'll do just fine.

"Where are you going?" The man shouts, but I ignore him. I'm already flinging myself onto the stallion as he runs towards me.

"Where all Prince Men go!" I flash a cheeky grin. "To the castle."

I grab mane and lean forward, bracing myself as we clear the fence. I hear the idiot burbling behind me, struggling to mount a horse.

He calls out as I race down the road toward her.

"You know, this would make an amazing song!"

Chapter Twenty-Three

Idalia

Six Years Previous

Nurse Lydia rests her large, wrinkled hands on my shoulders and leans down to meet my eyes in the mirror. She saw my grimace; she knows what I'm thinking.

"He's going to think you're beautiful, Idalia. He always has." Her smile is soft and warm, and despite my nerves, some comfort finds me.

"How can you be so sure?" I ask, rubbing my face. "The last time he saw me was in the middle of a massacre. I'm not sure his first thought will be how pretty I am." Then, I take a deep breath, pick up a small brush, and gently stroke powder on my cheeks. "He probably resents his father for making him come here, and he'll leave as soon as he gets the chance."

Nurse Lydia clicks her tongue and straightens. "Nonsense, child. Prince Lachlan would never do something so rude." She turns towards the bed and holds up one of the dresses she laid out for me. "Now, that Theodore girl, on the other hand."

I run to my bed with a dramatic whimper and collapse onto the fine outfits.

"Up! You'll wrinkle them!" She swats at me.

I ignore her and groan loudly. "It's hopeless. I'm doomed to become an old spinster. No man will ever want my hand in marriage."

She rolls her eyes, pushes me, and frees a frock. "Believe me, not being tethered to a man your whole life is more of a blessing than you could know."

"Well, if *I* were a servant, I wouldn't trouble myself with marriage!" I roll onto my belly and prop myself on an elbow. "Unfortunately, that's not how it is for a princess. We're raised from birth to marry royalty, forced to move to an entirely new land with an entirely new castle! All my servants will be strangers one day!"

She stops smoothing the dresses for a moment and sends me a cynical gaze. "*How tragic for you.*"

"Hopefully, my new handmaiden will be more charming than my nurse." Nurse Lydia's expression doesn't change in the slightest, of course. "I guess I'm not that upset at the prospect of moving somewhere new," I admit. "Anything would be better than being here, buried in the snow."

Nurse Lydia grunts a half-hearted agreement of sorts.

"Besides! I'm an adult now! I shouldn't have to count a nurse as my closest friend!"

Finally, she stops and faces me. "A closest friend wouldn't make my job so difficult. Have you even brushed your hair today?"

"I just get so bored, retracing every step I've taken since I was a child. I've counted every stone in the corridors. Every panel in the windows. Trained with every guard. What else is left but get married and escape this dull prison?"

"Women don't marry because they're bored, Idalia."

"No? Pray, then, tell me why a woman gets married. I'm dying to know your thoughts."

"If I tell you, will you get off the bed?" My simple nod is enough; she knows me well.

"There are a few reasons a woman will marry. Political alliance, an offer of peace, a rise in station…*an heir.* Things of that nature. As for women eager to marry, I've seen only two reasons. One isn't boredom; it's loneliness. Sometimes castle walls, and an old nurse aren't enough for a girl with a wild curiosity. Sometimes, her heart leaps and yearns for something more, something new."

She pats down her apron and then gestures for me to leave the bed. I shake my head. "The second reason," I demand.

Her face is blank for a moment, then she smiles and gives a weak laugh.

"Love. If you believe in such a thing."

We smile at one another, and I wonder if Nurse Lydia has ever loved.

But she cuts off my thoughts. "Up!"

As promised, I fly off the bed. I twirl around the room in my midnight blue chemise.

"Do you think that Lachlan will want to dance with me tonight?" A low grumble is her only response, but I continue. "You know how I love to dance! Oh, I hope he asks me. I hope he dances with me the entire night!"

I hear another annoyed noise before she hands me a gold gown with blue ribbons that tie in the back.

"Here, put this on. I believe if you want to impress the Aeradians, you'll need to be dressed."

I laugh, clutching the soft gown to my chest. "Can you believe I'm already eighteen? It feels like yesterday that you had to put my skirts on for me."

"Indeed," she mutters. "Now, you should be more interested in who takes those skirts *off*."

"Lady and Guard! You shouldn't speak so openly about such things!"

"Then you shouldn't be so open with them. Sneaking into the stables late at night. Tell me, which horse do you wish to visit so desperately?"

My face heats, but I only flash her a sideways smile. "Are you living out your youth again through watching me?" I croon. "Because I know some older men and women in this castle find you very attractive."

Nurse Lydia's head knocks back, and she makes a rude noise. "Perhaps you're right. We should definitely *not* speak of such things. Now, get dressed, and I'll send the ladies to do your hair."

"Is Harea one of the ladies?" I tease. "Because I think she'd prefer to visit your room instead."

"Gods. Please make a good impression tonight, so some poor Aeradian servant will have to endure you and spare me my remaining years."

"Love you too, Nurse Lydia."

She closes the door, and I launch myself to the standing mirror in the corner. I hold the gossamer gown against my chest and swish the skirts back and forth. "It's such a pleasure to see you again, Prince Lachlan." I bow my head to the glass. "Oh! A dance? Of course, Your Highness. A dance would be quite lovely." I prance around the room as if Lachlan is next to me. We execute our steps flawlessly, and the entire hall murmurs at how picturesque we look together.

"You're a wonderful dancer; I had no idea." Another spin, and the crowd coos even louder. "What's that, Prince Lachlan? You wish to make me your wife and take down the Baellilean kingdom together? Why, I'm not sure what to say!"

I turn again, making sure the hem of my dress flies up into the air, then I press my back against a wall. I glance up, then lower my eyes. "I suppose, since you've wooed me with your superior dance skills, I've no choice but to accept."

I smile as I see Prince Lachlan kiss the top of my hand and lead me to the dais, to a new world. One where Verdana is, at last, safe.

I look amazing in the gold gown Nurse Lydia picked, I must admit. And from the expressions on some faces, as I pass through the ballroom, I can tell I'm not the only one who thinks so. King Lester and his children stand on the dais at one end of the room. Behind them, steps lead up to my father's throne, where he sits and watches me, smiling.

I haven't seen Lachlan or Teddy since *the incident,* but we've written several letters. For a time, Teddy and I wrote to each other about our plans to escape together to the Osinean Kingdom, where we'd become ladies of the court, drink copious amounts of wine, and visit the male brothels at each turn of the week. Then her letters changed drastically. She used words that I didn't understand and wrote about subjects in such depth that I could hardly keep up. I still sent her notes of admiration, but as for long letters, it's been years.

To Lachlan, I only sent two messages. The first was a simple note: "*I hope all is well with you and your family. Verdana sends our best wishes to the Aeradian people. Princess Idalia.*" The other I wrote on a day when I felt rather brave, thanks to the plant one of the stable boys had fed me. I saw stars when I wrote the cursed thing. I can't remember the exact words, but it was something along the lines of:

"Lach, Lach, quiet, old Lach! Do you remember that bird that hurt you in the aviary? I think about it often, and it makes me laugh. Have

you spoken to Prince Braizen? How is he? Did he grow up to have warts and bad skin? I hope so. Do you know we almost kissed? Ha! Can you believe it? That despicable, traitorous Prince and I were to be married. I, for one, am glad we are cursed. Now I never have to see his ugly face again! If you are ever in his territory, please tell him I am not thinking about him, and I never have. Verdana wishes you water and good wishes and bread and also, water. -Idalia."

Lachlan's sage-green eyes glow as he watches me approach. I swallow hard and pray he never received that humiliating letter, that his father burned it before it ever reached his hands.

I look at Teddy, and my mouth almost falls open. She's as tall as her father now—and her dress! It's wildly extravagant, with red and purple fabric slipping into a pool at her feet. The neckline clutches her throat, and a huge gold necklace falls almost to her waist. A tiara rests perfectly atop her braids, and her lips are stained a dark berry. Her citrine eyes blaze beneath thick lashes. She slowly scans the chamber as if considering how each stone is made. For a moment, I forget which Thrope I'm to impress.

Between his children, King Lester stands with his hands behind his back. His constant frown and light, pasty skin stick out in contrast to his children. Their mother must have been the most beautiful woman to have ever existed, and, in the womb, the Thrope children were smart enough to have chosen her features.

King Lester's nose lifts as he turns his head to glare at his son. Lachlan doesn't seem to notice; his eyes never move from me. His burgundy tunic has gold buttons the same shade as my gown. A fully bloomed Salva rests under one shoulder. He's so still, a marble statue dressed like a King.

I stop before the platform and curtsey.

"Verdana welcomes Aeradian's royalty to our home," my father booms. "We celebrate the kindness of King Lester for remaining neutral in our fight against Baelliles. We honor his wisdom and his reign. Tonight, we acknowledge our future as kingdoms and people who can trust and appreciate each other!" Wild applause spirals through the ballroom, and Lachlan finally smiles at me.

He's so disturbingly handsome.

Although the feast is absolutely brilliant, I stop eating long before I'm satisfied to avoid bloating in this tight dress. I don't want to be uncomfortable as I dance with Lachlan. I play with what's left of my food and decide to ask the kitchen to send my leftovers once I'm back in my chamber. Just then, a pea pelts my cheek and lands on the table. I touch my face and look around to see Teddy watching me with a wide smile.

"So, the Verdanian Princess is all grown up! I can't believe it's been nearly seven years since I saw you last," she says.

I pick up my wine glass and grin. "Shocking indeed to see how the two of you have grown over the years. Tell me, what is your age now? Fifteen?"

"Sixteen in two months," she winks. "Which makes Lachlan near thirty. Isn't that right, old man?"

I turn to face Lachlan, who shifts in his chair and sends a shy smile. "Not quite, Teddy. You're off by a few years."

"You're nineteen now?" I ask him and sip some wine.

The way his cheeks flush at my question, I might have asked him how many people he's bedded. He stares at his half-empty plate and slowly moves his knife around the rim.

"Twenty, actually. I'm two years older than you, by four months and twelve days. You were born during Verdana's second snow of that year under the Flore constellation, and I was born just on the cusp of spring to summer." His eyes catch mine for a moment, and he looks flustered. "Of course, I only know that because of the records in our library. I didn't intentionally search for your name! I mean, *I did*, but not in an intrusive way. I search everyone's names. Well, maybe not *everyone*, but enough people for it to not be unusual that I searched yours."

I cover my mouth to mask my breaking smile.

Lachlan clenches his knife so tightly I'm afraid he'll snap it in half. "I did deduce the time difference between our dates of birth, though, so that happened. I don't know why I'm telling you this. I did the same thing with you and Braizen! He's a year older than you. A year and two months, seven days..."

Lachlan trails off, and his eyes skirt to his sister. A plea for help.

"Well, that went much better than I thought it would," Teddy says, and we both laugh.

I stop when I see him rubbing his earlobe and not meeting our eyes. "I'm fascinated by birthdays," I say encouragingly. "My mother used to tell me that the day we're born says a lot about our lives. That the stars are arranged in certain constellations, and that we can determine how..."

"The stars!" King Lester scoffs from two seats down. "You must jest! The stars are old Kings who have passed away, taking their rightful place in the Great Lands! Have you not read the sacred texts, girl? Do you mean to take away the glory from past Kings?"

I lean back and fold my hands in my lap. "Not at all, Your Majesty. I did not mean to offend."

"*Offend*? Do you think you can offend me? Surely you do not believe that you hold enough power to do so?"

Before I can protest, my father slides into the conversation.

"Lester, you must forgive my daughter and her rambles. As a child, she was read one too many stories by her mother. And after the incident, I fear she might cling to them as a form of comfort."

My hands tingle. I clutch them tighter.

"Right, you are then, Ivar!" King Lester nods with a chuckle, then tears into another slab of meat. "I sometimes forget the coping mechanisms of women. The silly things their minds come up with to distract from reality."

My lips tighten as he continues to spew hatred, my father nodding his head in cowardly agreement. My hands roar a message to my body, begging me to stand. *If it's a fight he wants, then a fight he shall—*

"Pay him no mind," Teddy whispers. "He's just mad that women are smarter than him."

Lachlan chokes on his wine and thumps a fist to his chest. "Theodore," he hisses. "Mind your tongue. He's still our father."

She rolls her eyes and pops a grape into her mouth. "Lachlan is mad about it, too," she adds as I hide a smile behind my napkin.

"Besides, stars are made up of gasses. Elements only a few wise scholars understand. If Lach dared to read anything other than people's birth charts, he might know that."

"I'd love to read books like those," I admit. "Our library doesn't have anything of the sort."

"When you visit, I'd love to give you a tour." She lifts her glass in the air, and I clink its rim with my own.

The dancing begins, and our guests stream to the floor, moving in tandem with the music. I patiently wait for Lachlan to ask me to dance, understanding that it may take him a while to work up the courage. He's a nervous creature, and it's hard to get a good read on him. But I think he likes me. I remind myself that he memorized my birth date.

I wait while our musicians play song after song into the night. I wait and watch Teddy spin and laugh with her partners as if no can see her.

I wait even as my stomach drops, and I feel a frown set itself snugly on my face.

I wait, but he never comes. He never asks me to dance.

I hear my father murmuring in the hall to the lady's maid who helped me prepare for bed. He enters and sits heavily at the foot of my bed, tracing his finger across the intricate designs carved into the wood frame. His lips form into a bitter frown.

"Lester forbids Lachlan from marrying outside of Aeradian," he finally says in a low voice. He doesn't look up from his finger. "He does not wish to ruffle any feathers. If Lachlan marries you, Vaskis will consider it a breach in their allyship. If we wish to keep ours with Aeradian, we have no choice but to accept this."

"But Baelliles sabotages our trade with Aeradian every day! Is this of no concern to King Lester? Does he not consider that a breach of our allyship?"

"I am afraid not. He has stated that any quarrel between Baelliles and Verdanian remains between us. He came to declare his friendship with our Kingdom, nothing more. Nothing less."

I breathe evenly even as my eyes brim with tears.

My father steps away. "There will be no marriage between you and Lachlan, so there is no need to waste any time wallowing over it. Get your rest, we train early tomorrow. Do you understand this, Idalia?"

"Of course, Father." I nod weakly.

There's a moment of complete silence before the door opens and shuts. I turn my face into my pillow and sob. My heart does not ache because I cannot marry Lachlan, but because I again must face a harrowing truth that I've tried my best to run from. That a life filled with love and partnership, a life without loneliness, has been denied. It will always be denied.

I don't believe I deserve to love anyone. Maybe I don't believe in love at all.

Chapter Twenty-Four

Idalia

Present Day

After a moment of confusion, I'm lucky that two older palace guards recognize me and finally convince the younger ones to allow me inside the gates. Otherwise, I would've been thrown back into the bustling streets of Senlow, Aeradian's capitol, and left to fend for myself. Or worse, tossed into an Aeradian prison, which I've heard is filled with brutish men who hold no respect for any woman, whatever her title. I likely wouldn't survive the night. I feel relief and ease I haven't experienced since leaving my home.

This feeling doesn't last long.

First, they bind my hands in iron cuffs. I'm then deposited in a small, dingy chamber that smells like cat piss and told to wait. I gag, barely able to stomach the stench. I glance at a narrow cot with a stained mattress and then lower myself onto the one chair that creaks as I sit. Wherever I am, it's not where favored guests wait.

The guards must be searching for a way to verify my claim to be Princess Idalia, especially given my filthy state and attire. I steady myself and count each frill that runs across my bodice. I repeat this count seven times. Then I count the stones set in the floor, the same way I've done hundreds of times back home.

It seems like hours before I hear scuffling outside the door. I stand, my heart pounding in anticipation of seeing Lachlan's eyes again. I strain to hear his voice, but there's only an indignant yelp as the door swings open. My heart sinks.

Braizen and the lute-playing horse owner stagger into the small room, iron cuffs shackling them together. The door slams shut. I roll my eyes and plop back into the chair.

"Great. You followed me."

"Missed you too, Sparrow."

I point at the other man. "And you? You came all this way because I stole your horse?"

The musician raises their bound hands and lifts a finger.

"Technically, *three* horses were stolen."

"Yes, sorry about that," Braizen says and drags his companion towards the cot where they sit.

"It's quite all right, seeing as they aren't even my horses, to begin with."

"Those weren't your horses?!" I almost screech.

"Nope. Truth be told, that was only my second time ever on one. Scared me to the four hells and back it did, racing as we did today. Thought I might die," he grins.

I huff and slam back into the chair. I close my eyes. *Please, old guard. Please hurry and fetch the King. Please.*

"Then why did you give us such a hard time?" Braizen asks between laughs.

I try to ignore them, but it's impossible in this tight, smelly space.

"I figured I could get some coins out of the ordeal. Like I said, I'm a musician. Money is not something I see a lot of," the man says, "Hope you aren't too angry about my deceit."

"Not at all! That is something a bandit would do!" Braizen approves. "You ever steal anything of greater value?"

The male chuckles, glances in either direction, then narrows his eyes. "You see this lute?" He nudges his head towards the instrument hanging down his back. "Worth over five hundred… *Silver.*"

"Impressive!" Braizen cheers. "Once my friend Lin stole a pan flute that he thought was the same price. It turns out it wasn't worth the rope that held it together. He still tried to master it, though. That was a bad week for all of us."

His face drops, and a twinge of pain creeps through my chest. I wonder if Lin survived the dire wolf. If Torrent got Lorna out of the crushed carriage.

"The name is Ranstig," My attention returns to the idiots on the cot, who are shaking their bound hands. "Ranstig Belton. Though most call me Stig. Stig the Euphonious."

"Oh, I like that name. *Stig.* Yes, I enjoy it quite a lot, actually. A quality name for a quality man!!" Braizen says with a wide, easy smile.

"I think I preferred it when you hated each other," I groan.

Braizen gives me a pointed look before turning back to his new friend. "Do you think you could play it if I got it off your back?"

Stig contemplates the question, then shakes his head in defeat. "Unfortunately, my playing will be useless without freedom of the limbs. A shame, really. I'm actually quite good. Though, I've always wanted to be a bandit. The missions, the high stakes, it all sounds riveting."

"I believe that you're good," Braizen assures him. "And you were right about me earlier. I can't sing a note to save my life. However, I could teach you my ways if you teach me yours."

Their excited voices flood the room. I squeeze my eyes shut and try to block their chatter as they prattle on about their respective passions, but to no avail. I managed to survive the Florian Wood, but their insufferable conversation may be what takes me out.

"By the way, miss." I open my eyes, and Stig jerks his chin towards me. "I didn't mean what I said earlier. You know, about *other* payments. I was bluffing. I've heard bigger, more disgusting men say things like that to get their way. I figured I'd give it a shot."

Braizen grunts. "Next time, leave the disgusting remarks for the disgusting men."

I can't decide which is more unbearable: the pain from the shackles digging into my wrists or the sound of those two getting along. I'm no closer to an answer when the door opens. I could cry at the sight of the room's new occupant.

"Teddy," I say with a shaky voice.

She plants her hands on her hips and squints, taking in every inch of me. "So," she muses with a devilish grin. "The Princess of Verdana has finally come to see my library."

Chapter Twenty-Five

Braizen

Theodore is an absolute sight to behold. I haven't seen her in years, and how she's changed. I try my best not to gawk at her swaying form as she strides down the hall ahead of us and yells at the guards who cuffed and threw Idalia and me together in an enclosed space. I even try to dismiss the odd feeling that dares to consume me when I notice features on her that look shockingly akin to her brother's. They have always been an insanely beautiful pair.

Finally, we stop before a set of double doors. She looks over her shoulder at me.

"Still good at picking locks, Prince?" The thick lashes lining her round eyes flutter a bit, and I stutter.

"I, I think so. I do locks all the time. So, I could. I can. Pick it. The lock."

Idalia glances at me; her expression leaking embarrassment and scorn.

I clear my throat and continue. "What I mean to say is that if you want a lock picked, I'll do it for you." Theodore smiles. "If you want me to…" I finish with a tight grin.

Ranstig elbows me. "*Smooth*," he whispers from the corner of his mouth.

My face twitches, and I stand straighter.

"Good to know. I'll keep that in mind," Theodore says and reaches for one of the gold knobs. The open door reveals towers of bookshelves, climbing to the glass-paned ceiling. Sunlight splatters the spines of thousands of volumes. Idalia slowly twirls, taking in every inch of the room.

"I didn't know you had such a passion for books," I say, breaking the silence.

Her eyes don't leave the shelves as she answers. "There are many things you don't know about me, Prince Braizen." She saunters to a table and picks up a thick volume, thumbing through it with an untamed urgency.

Theodore joins her and seems elated with Idalia's pleasure.

"Didn't I tell you this place was impressive?"

Idalia chokes on a laugh. "I'm afraid you didn't do it justice. It's *huge!*"

Another elbow digs into my ribs, and Stig's brows bounce. "If I had a gold coin for each time I've heard that," he snickers.

I smile, but only because I can hear Torrent's howl fill the room. Of course, Lin and Lorna would groan at the joke. *Gods, I miss them.*

"When our father died, Lach permitted me to do as I please here. I sent men across the world to gather these texts. Some even come from the Far Kingdom," Theodore explains.

"Osinea? But how did you get them here when no one can cross the Trench?" Idalia asks, flipping through another codex. "Letters are easy enough for birds to travel with, but books?"

"There's a species there that *can* travel with larger objects. I called in for a few favors, and they delivered."

"Bigger birds?" I ask. "Are any still here?"

"Oh, Lady and Shield! How did I forget your infatuation with birds?!" Theodore claps her hands in delight. "I always underestimate just how peculiar men's interests can be."

At that, Stig pokes his chest forward and strides towards the Aeradian Princess. "Men's interests run far and wide, Your Highness. That's why we've accomplished a great many things."

"A great many things you say," Theodore says with raised eyebrows. "Do tell, whoever you are, what has a man accomplished that is so *great* in your astute opinion?"

Stig shuffles his feet before her unwavering stare and clears his throat. "Why, everything, of course. That's why men run this world."

An almost unbearable silence follows until, without looking up from the book she's scanning, Idalia cracks a laugh.

Theodore looks first at Idalia and then back at Stig, sending him a cool smile.

"Well, then. It's no wonder the world is in shambles."

With beet-red cheeks, Stig laces his hands behind his back and studies the bookshelves, pretending the insult did not critically hit him. I only hope he can sing better than he can act.

"Theodore," I ask. "Is Lachlan here?"

She sends me a wide smile. "He is, and he'll be so happy to see you. Both of you," she says.

A thud rings through my chest. Two old friends reuniting should be a blessed thing, but I can't forget why Idalia is here. I can't accept why he'll be so happy to see her. The Sparrow has found her permanent nest in a new aviary.

Theodore leads us down at least twelve corridors before we arrive at a ladder resting against a wall. She gestures with her chin for us to climb to the simple trap door in the ceiling. Idalia begins her ascent, and Stig moves forward, but Theodore shoots out her arm and shakes her head. "This is for royalty only," she says.

Stig gazes so hard into Theodore's eyes I wonder if he remembers how to speak. Eventually, he blinks and looks back at me.

"Sorry, I didn't believe you, Prince Man, about the whole royalty thing. What are the chances?"

I laugh and haul myself up. As I reach the top, I see Idalia rushing across the room. My stomach twists in knots.

Chapter Twenty-Six

Braizen

There are times in a person's life when a singular moment seems to last longer than it should. As if the gods themselves plucked it straight out of time and lengthened it between their hands like string. Stretching and pulling until mere seconds extend into what feels like an eternity. Depending on what you're doing at that exact moment, this can be wholly wonderful or completely unbearable.

I watch Lachlan's face, at how his eyes glow as Idalia runs towards him, and the gods stretch time for me.

She flings her arms around his neck.

This singular moment is not wholly wonderful.

Chapter Twenty-Seven

Braizen

As Idalia throws her arms around his neck, Lachlan tightens his around her waist without hesitation. The two embrace for several minutes before he pulls back.

"Idalia?"

She throws herself at him again and cries into his chest. "*I made it.* I'm alive."

Lachlan appears more confused than welcoming, but he caresses her back. His eyes meet mine as I walk towards them.

"Braizen!?" He mouths silently.

I nod, trying to ignore the heat rippling through my body at the sight of him touching her.

"The two of you came here… together?" He says aloud.

"Yes," Idalia says and finally pulls away.

Lachlan blinks slowly, then places his fingers to his temples. "So, the curse? Is it…?"

"I can assure you the curse is still perfectly intact," Idalia says. "Braizen… well, he helped me get here. He helped me get to you."

Her words sear like a hot iron against my skin, but I hold a calm smile.

"But Verdana and Baelliles, you're enemies. You hate each other. Don't you?" Lachlan asks, his puzzled gaze darting between us.

"Well, he *did* kidnap me," Idalia says. "So, there's that. But eventually, something changed."

"*What* changed?" Lachlan asks.

Idalia opens her mouth and then shuts it. She finally speaks. "I… I don't know." Her eyes meet mine as if searching for an answer.

Lachlan looks at me straight on. "Is it true, Braizen? You helped her come here?"

His question drains me, and I fight an urge to hit him in the face. So, I nod and wink. "It's true, Lach. I helped her get here safely."

A grin slowly stretches across the King's face. Behind him, I see Idalia examines me as if waiting for something else.

"I wouldn't get too excited about it, though," I add with a shrug. "She's a real pain in the ass once you get to know her."

Chapter Twenty-Eight

Idalia

I've taken for granted the simple pleasures in life. Eating a hot meal, kindling a warm fire, bathing more than once a week. It's only after Teddy wraps me in a silken, red nightgown and splashes my face with a rosy tonic that I remember to give thanks for small joys. I curl my toes beneath the fine sheets and fluff the pillow behind my head.

"The Lady has finally shown grace," I whisper, gently stroking my cheek with a soft, vermillion blanket.

From her perch on the edge of my bed, Teddy smiles. Her braids fall loose, framing her delicate face. "You were kidnapped and then lost in the Florian Wood! It's *only* grace that the Lady has shown you! That you'd survive any of it is unheard of!"

I nod in agreement. I haven't told her about Idizina and am not sure I ever will. I'm where I'm meant to be. Finally, I can lay to rest the horrors of the trees. It's over.

"Are the stories of The Wood true?" Teddy's voice is halting, and she refuses to meet my eyes.

I scoot back against the plush headboard and roll my neck. Perhaps the horrors aren't *entirely* over.

"It depends," I sigh. "What stories have you heard?"

She picks at the covers before she answers. "Many, actually. I spend most days reading in the library or making those." She gestures to shelves lined with small bottles filled with colored liquids.

"What are they?" I squint, but I can't read the labels, and I'm too tired to rise.

"Some are medicinal; some for cosmetic purposes. Then others have…a different purpose," she says and gazes down at her hands. "Lach refers to them as potions. I prefer to call them Teddy Tonics. But the Wood. I want to know more."

"Trust me, Teddy," I interrupt sharply, and she finally looks at me. "You don't want to know. There are terrible, terrible things within them. Braizen and I survived by chance alone. We should be dead."

"But the trails," she continues. "The trails for Verdanians to use are said to be safe. At least, for the most part."

"Let's talk about something else."

Her eyes twitch, and for a moment, I think she'll wish me good night and leave. Instead, she scooches closer and rests a gentle hand on mine.

"Fine," she concedes, and I'm grateful. "So, you and Braizen?"

I'm no longer grateful. I let out an uneasy laugh. "What about me and Braizen?" My body floods with embarrassment.

"How about you tell me." Her voice trails off softly, but her smile grows.

I shuffle my feet under the blankets.

"There's nothing to tell," I state. Her expression doesn't change. "I'm serious! He kidnapped me and dragged me through the four hells so he could take me to his father. What else do you want to know?"

"But he *didn't* take you to his father, did he? Instead, he brought you here."

"Yes, he did. I can only assume that my prayers were heard, and the Guard changed his mind for him," I say.

"I'm not sure I'd give the Guard credit for that decision."

I huff and roll my eyes. "Thanks be to the Lady, then."

"How did you two manage to do it, though? Travel all this way without touching?"

"Easy. I hate him, and he hates me. Keeping our distance was the easiest part of the entire journey," I say, grabbing a pillow and hugging it to my chest.

"That's hard to imagine. I remember a time when the two of you longed to touch. I mean, I can't blame you! Those heavenly blue eyes! That jawline!"

Her eyes shut as if she's imagining them now. "I've heard stories, you know? Many servants frequent the taverns, and the women talk a great deal about the Baellilean Prince." She leans in and smiles widely. "They say he can go again and again."

"Teddy!" I fling the pillow straight at her head.

She catches and tosses it aside. "They also say that it isn't necessary because he does the job right the first time."

I scramble out of bed and make a gagging sound. "Enough! I've heard enough! Change the subject, or may the gods take me to the Great Lands now!"

She snickers and waves me back to the bed.

I hesitate, making sure she's quite finished with tales of Braizen, and return to my comfortable spot.

Her smile disappears, and she grabs one of my hands. "Tell me what you saw in the Wood, Idalia." Her voice is a near whisper.

My eyes race between hers, and slowly I release a deep breath. She's not going to let it go.

"Fine," I say reluctantly. "The first night I was taken, there was a mist, like a cloud of smoke. It raced out of the trees like a great wind was pushing it. It…It devoured a lot of people."

"The Obsidian Mist," Teddy murmurs. "I've read about it, though it's only mentioned twice in all the books I've studied. Do you think it was sent by *them*?"

"Them?" I repeat, matching her stare.

"The Keepers of the Dark. The Others."

We speak simultaneously.

"How do you know about The Keep—"

"What do you think they want?"

My chest heaves, and my eyelids flutter as I remember what Nuri told me.

"Do you think they want to know about The Pass?" Teddy's voice is steady.

"What's The Pass?" I ask and shudder.

Teddy taps her chin. "Why don't we strike another deal? You tell me what you know, and I'll tell you what I know."

I think, then stick out my hand for a shake.

"Fair enough."

"So, the festival is tonight?" I ask, pushing the last biscuit into my mouth. Deria, the Thrope's scandalous aunt, smiles and moves the empty plate to a nearby sideboard where quiet servants set steaming dishes and remove empty ones.

"Yes, and we're so glad you came all this way for such a special occasion! My nephew loves this festival, and this year he'll honor Sera."

"Sera," I say quietly. "I was heartbroken to hear what happened."

Deria's mouth tightens. "Yes. The Gray is a nasty disease. I'm shocked my brother didn't die from it." She sips on an orange concoction that she brought to the table, smacking her lips at its intensity, and continues. "Although, dying from a hunting accident is just what he deserved. Vile brute. May the gods rest his soul, of course."

"Of course," I agree and stifle a laugh.

"Tonight, Lachlan will honor Sera's memory. He won't tell us what he's planned, but he's been tucked away in that attic of his for weeks now. So, we know it's special." She takes another sip and then gently places her cup on the lace cloth.

"If he's planning something so extravagant, he must have truly loved her." Discomfort crawls over my body like ants on spilled food. I don't know why the thought of him loving her bothers me. It would surely bother me more if he hadn't loved his wife.

Deria clasps her hands and sighs. "Oh, yes. He loved her very much. In the way that only Lachlan can."

"What do you mean?"

"Lachlan is very… *hushed* about his feelings. He always has been. I blame Lester. None of us were allowed to express much while he was alive. Shameful pig. May his spirit find refuge and solace in the Great Lands." She dabs her mouth with her napkin.

“Then again, I suppose each one of us loves differently,” she says. “My first husband was terribly handsy. I detested it. I couldn’t go anywhere or do anything without him grabbing me. But that’s how he showed affection. It was all *very* physical. My second husband…” She trails off and flicks one wrist. “He was a man of few words, and even fewer sentiments, but showered me in jewelry and fine clothes to make up for it. Now, *that’s* the kind of love I can get behind.” She smiles and reaches for her glass.

“How many times have you been married?”

She swallows and sighs with pleasure. “I stopped counting after five,” she says with a wink, and we laugh.

I gesture towards her drink, and she nods. “Oh, gods,” I choke and cough as the liquid hits my tongue. “It’s potent.” My eyes water and I smack my chest, trying not to wheeze.

“My own recipe,” she says and flashes me a proud look. “Helped me tolerate husband number four.”

“Do you think Lachlan still loves Sera?” I ask when I can breathe again, surprising myself with the question.

Deria’s expression softens, and she stares into the distance as if caught in a daydream. “Yes. I think he’ll always have love for her. She helped him a great deal with his father, when he was alive and in death. She was a wonderful girl.”

I beam, happy that Lachlan was supported by someone he loved. “Do you think it might be too soon for him to remarry?”

Her eyes snap to mine. “Whatever do you mean?”

"Good morning, beautiful castle. Good morning, beautiful food." We both startle as the doors slam open. Stig strides in with a cocky grin and gazes lustfully at every object he passes. "Good morning, beautiful women." He wiggles his brows as his smile grows.

Deria laughs behind her hands, but I'm less than amused. I've no idea why he's still allowed here.

"Perhaps you could write a song about their beauty," Braizen calls as he enters. I roll my eyes. The last thing I want to hear on this peaceful morning is these two blathering, yet here they are.

"I could," Stig says as he grabs a platter of eggs from the sideboard and sits next to me. "But not on an empty stomach." He begins to devour the food with his hands. I frown and slide a fork towards him, and he acknowledges the cutlery, but continues to eat like a barbarian.

Deria holds a hand against her chest and eyes Braizen as he settles himself next to her. "And who might you be?" She asks flirtatiously.

"Prince Braizen, son of King Vaskis," he says, staring deep into her eyes. "And you are Lachlan's aunt, correct? Deria Thrope?"

I shake my head at his blatant display of charm, but the older woman laughs hysterically.

"I haven't been called a Thrope in years, darling. I've taken many names in my day. I can't even recall which one I'm using now! Though, you aren't mistaken. I'm Lester's sister, aunt to Theodore and Lachlan."

"Ya know, I'm wondering something," Stig says. He looks at the noblewoman. "How are King Lachlan and Princess Theodore so dark while you're so pasty?"

Braizen chokes and coughs into his fist.

"My seventh husband once called me pasty!" she says. "In fact, he told me that if we ever visited the mountains of Verdana, he'd lose me in the snow." Deria heaves an exaggerated sigh. "He died not two weeks later. *Shame*."

The musician's eyes widen, but Deria only sends him a dangerous smile.

"May the Lady offer him serenity in the afterlife, of course." She adds.

The two men resume gobbling their food with feral intent until Braizen speaks.

"Do you have any children? Any cousins Lachlan hasn't told me about?"

"*I hate children*." The woman's face is perfectly serious when she answers.

Stig lets out a fit of giggles. "You and me both, Aunt Deria!"

Deria quickly downs the remaining alcohol in her glass and clears her throat. "So, if you're the son of Vaskis and Idalia the daughter of Ivar, that means you're the infamous gods-cursed children."

"Here in the flesh," Braizen says and lifts his glass. He turns to Stig, who's gnawing on an apple core. "Now there's a good title for a song. *'The Gods-Cursed Children!'*"

"You've traveled together all this time and haven't touched? Not once?" Deria fans herself with one hand. "My, that must've been hard!"

My face flushes. What is it with these Aeradians and their curiosity? I clear my throat and try to sound nonchalant. "Why would it be hard? We kept our distance, for the most part. Besides, it's not like I *want* to touch him."

Braizen looks up from his plate, flashes me an unreadable look, then goes back to eating.

"Well, of course not!" Deria exclaims with a breathy chuckle. "A Verdanian and Baellilean wanting to do *anything* together is unheard of. Let alone desiring each other's touch! I only meant to say, traveling through the Florian Wood with an added challenge? Good gods, the two of you must've come close!" She fans herself faster.

Braizen stares down at his plate.

"Have you tried wearing gloves?" Deria asks plainly.

The Prince and I both snap up our heads and gape at her.

"You've never thought of that? Does the curse even work if something is between you? A cloth of some kind, something thick and sturdy?" She glances between us.

Braizen retches and struggles to swallow. I stammer a bit before I manage to answer. "With our Kingdoms on the line, it's not worth finding out."

"She's right," Braizen agrees. "Especially when neither of us *wants* to touch each other anyway." Deria chuckles and reaches yet again for her decanter of orange poison.

"The two of you sound just like me and husband number three. Or was it number five?"

I hang my head and shake with laughter. Something within forces me to peek through my lashes at Braizen.

He's staring at me intently.

He's not laughing.

"And I'm telling you, the red will look best," Teddy states.

The gown in question is positively....salacious. Its bodice is tight, and the neckline plunges down the entire front to the navel. "There's *no way* I'm wearing that tonight," I say, flapping my hand.

"Why not? It's gorgeous! And perfectly vermillion!" Teddy presses the gown against my chest. "Trust me; you want to be wearing Aeradian colors tonight. *Everyon*e will be."

I push the gown away and pull at the ends of my braid.

"I just... It's getting colder each night. That's hardly enough to cover me."

"You're Verdanian! Weren't you born in ice?"

I roll my eyes. "How about something with long sleeves?" I say, opening her massive wardrobe. "Let me see. Oh! What about this?" I hold up a lacy white gown.

"No. Not that one," Teddy says abruptly. She grabs the gown and pushes past me to return it to its place. She then half disappears among the dresses, muttering to herself as she evaluates options. Finally, she emerges and hands me a silver gown.

"It's perfect!" I cry. Long sleeves, a jewel neckline, and billowing skirts. The fabric shimmers as I hold it up. I'll look like a beam of moonlight cast onto snow *and* stay warm.

"I have a question," Teddy announces, holding up the red dress and looking at herself in the mirror. "You said the Minea can go back into the past, right?"

I join her and pose with the silver dress, wondering how to wear my hair tonight.

"Correct." I say, and decide a low chignon would look best.

"And prophets, like Nuri, can see into the future…"

Dangling earrings will pull the whole ensemble together delightfully. I wonder what options Teddy might offer.

"Do you think you could do both? What you said about Lorna seems to have been some sort of premonition, right?"

I catch her eyes in the mirror and spin to face her. "I told you," I breathe. "I've no idea what I can do. I healed Braizen, but I don't know how I did it! I had no prior knowledge that magic even existed outside of the gods and legends of The Wood."

"And you really don't know what The Pass is for? Or why anyone would be interested in it?"

The conversation hurts my head. "No! I'd never heard of it until you told me. Trust me, Teddy, if there were an opening between the mountains of Verdana, everyone would know. My kingdom is suffering! Our only way out is to the south. If there were a way to leave without going through Baelliles, wouldn't we know?"

"It just doesn't make sense. The books clearly state there's an opening."

"Books can be wrong, Teddy," I say and wince as it's clear my words wound her.

She flings herself into a plush armchair. "Maybe you should take a tiny peek into some memories? Then, we could know for sure."

"I don't want to go wandering through the delusions of the Herrah," I huff. "Those women do *not* like to answer questions. Besides, according to them, I can't see into the past alone. More than one Minea is required, and as far as I know, they're all stuffed away in a hidden village deep in that demonic Wood."

"Perhaps you could try it alone? Isn't it worth finding out if The Pass exists?"

"Teddy," I say as my head pounds. "If you wish, the next time we visit Verdana, I'll cover every inch of its borders with you. We'll search the Shouldered Mountains for openings. Is that enough?"

She sticks out her hand for me to shake. Another deal. With a weak laugh, I grab it.

"You know, I've read about prophets. There aren't many, at least according to the books," she muses. "Most people that call themselves prophets are actually heretics. So say the texts."

I can't believe I'd thought Teddy had finished her interrogation. I straighten my shoulders.

"Yes. True prophets must be incredibly rare."

Teddy jabs a finger in the air. "Exactly what I'd deduced! Although, there was one legitimate prophet I read about. I'm sure you've heard of her."

I face her with a blank stare.

"The Woman of the Woods, of course," she says proudly. "The First Prophet."

"I don't know much about her," I admit. I spent my youth training with blades, not books.

Teddy is clearly looking for some kind of response from me. She drapes both her legs over the chair arm and strokes a finger along her chin.

"Well, even though you show no enthusiasm, I'll have you know most of my research focused on her. She's the reason we know about the Lady and the Guard in the first place. All the sacred texts were written after her prophecies."

"That much I do know." I hesitate for a moment. "In your studies of Verdana, did you run across a Cyra Hyland? Around the time of Novak's reign?"

Teddy taps a steady beat against her thigh. "Not that I recall. The records of the Hyland lineage start with Novak and his wife, Mallory. I mean, there was Queen Adelaide before her, you know, the Traitorous Queen. Nothing on a Cyra Hyland, though."

I nod again, consenting to the mystery. I may never learn what those Minean visions mean, and I remind myself that I'm at peace with this. The visions don't matter, not anymore. Teddy's eyes glow with her passion, so I ask the question I know she longs to answer.

"What else do you know about the Woman of the Woods?"

"Oh, plenty! I have her first prophecy nearly memorized: what she taught about the gods and the Great Darkness. The one to end all things, or whatever."

My skin prickles and crawls. Although I told Teddy much of what happened in The Wood, I didn't share what the Minea said about my fate as I left her home the second time.

"The Great Darkness is in your blood, Idalia. Should you choose to face your fate, you will not survive it."

Teddy jumps up from the armchair and holds up the vermillion gown. "It would be a shame to let something so perfect go to waste. I'm wearing this." She sends me a quick grin. "If you're ready, I'll send for the maidens."

"Yes, I'm ready," I say brightly, hoping my trembling hands don't give me away. Thankfully, she leaves the room. My shoulders fall, and I let out a heavy breath.

I'll dress for the festival. I'll honor Lachlan's late wife and dance the night away with my future husband. I want no part of what The Wood showed me. Marrying Lachlan is my chance to save my Kingdom, and I won't let the mysteries of the Florian steal that away.

I grab the silver dress. The rest of the Minea's words drift around me like a plume of smoke, filling the room.

"However, should you choose to ignore your fate, the world will be swallowed whole, and all light shall pass away."

Chapter Twenty-Nine

Braizen

Lachlan fiddles with the cuffs of his sleeves, staring at them with a fixed expression. He seems more anxious than I am. I can't blame him; he's in complete regalia, and the fur collar of the robe resting on his shoulders would make any man miserable. I smooth down my auburn tunic, adjust the cravat clinging to my neck, then rub my freshly shaven chin. My hair is tied back so tightly it pulls my face. We're in a small room preparing for his annual parade through the streets during the Aeradian Festival.

Lachlan and I haven't spoken much since we arrived, and I *certainly* haven't brought up his future wedding. Perhaps it's time. It would be wise to ascertain Lachlan's loyalties and ensure that Aeradian and Baelliles will continue as allies after he marries Idalia.

My father would've already done this. Though, to be fair, my father would've made sure this wedding would never happen in the first place. I face my old friend.

"Maybe after all of this, the two of us can grab a drink. What do you say, a couple of old Princes getting blindly drunk and discussing days past?"

"One of us is a King now," he says, and his smile wavers.

I give him a mocking bow. "But of course! Forgive me, Your Majesty," I exclaim and Lach chuckles. "I don't suppose Your Majesty would allow someone lower on the food chain to buy him a drink later this evening. To make up for such a silly remark?"

I hear cacophonous instruments and loud voices piling on top of each other until it's a cluster of noise that seems to shake the earth. Now, I'm nervous.

Lachlan slaps my back. "A drink will be much needed, friend. I accept."

I smile, ready to toss him another witty quip, but the doors swing open, and even my jokes get lost in the frenzy. The festival has begun.

The ladies are sorted into a separate palanquin. Four stout men carry Theodore and Idalia ahead of us through the crowds lining Senlow's streets, parading them like gorgeous birds perched inside a luxurious cage. The masses cheer when they see Theodore, and many citizens throw tiny, wrapped scrolls her way. I scan the rabble, a small part of me hoping their familiar faces will appear. That I'll see Torrent towering above the rest, a grin plastered across his face. But the reality is, he won't be there. The reality is, they probably didn't even…

"So that you know," Lachlan drops a hand on my shoulder and interrupts my thoughts. I sway as Aeradian warriors lift us into the air and onto their shoulders. "This is an excited group. Keep your eyes peeled; they'll be throwing a lot of items."

I blink a few times and swivel my head. "Has there ever been an assassination attempt?"

Lachlan shrugs, removes a small flask from his robe, and takes a generous swig. "Probably. But my guards are well trained. Plus, Aeradians have lived in prosperity for a long time. There wouldn't really be a reason for that." He hands me the flask. "Besides, it's well known that the Baellilean Prince is a looker. If anything, we should be more concerned about naked women trying to climb in." His lips quiver, and he rubs his earlobe. "Lady pray none of their husbands mind."

I laugh, take a pull from the flask, and then we're off. We bounce atop the thin cushions as the warriors carry us down the stone streets. Lachlan was right about objects flying at us. At one point, a bottle of spirits tied with maroon ribbons is launched into our cart.

Every so often, Lachlan digs his hand deep into a purple pouch and pulls out gold coins that he throws into the crowd. His people cheer. A twinge of guilt swarms my gut. *Tawdrey Lannex.* Perhaps I should tell him.

"Now, the real fun begins," Lachlan's tone is light, but his face betrays nervousness. Our palanquin is lowered to the ground, and the beastly men help us exit. We're on a large stage built in the middle of Senlow's main square, looking over a sea of Aeradians, all thrusting celebratory fists into the air.

"Long live the generous King!" The crowd chants in unison.

Baellileans have never known such unity in their lifetimes. Not even on the battlefield. When Theodore exits her craft, the crowd's roars grow even louder.

"Nosis Magis! Nosis Magis!" She bows to them and walks slowly across the platform, gliding her cupped palm through the gentle breeze. When she nears me, she leans in.

"Wave," she says sternly.

I oblige, which sends the horde into near hysteria.

It isn't long before I hear their newest chant: *'The Gods-Cursed!'* I look to my left and see her, a porcelain dream wrapped in silver. Her long, braided hair is twisted into a coil that rests on her neck. Curled wisps of hair frame her heart shaped face. Long earrings dip to tickle her shoulders. Her eyelids glimmer, and her lashes are coated in a thick, black paste. I almost kneel at the sight.

I'm still staring at Idalia as Theodore moves between us and lifts our hands. The people descend into madness. I've never heard a sound so loud.

Word will surely travel back to my father now, and I'll no doubt be labeled a traitorous son. A sinner who fell victim to the lure of a Verdanian. A dead man. But when I look at Idalia, fear seems to elude me.

Her joyful smile means that she's alive and that she's safe. It means she's happy. The wild cheers melt into a muted symphony, like music playing in a distant room. Her eyes find mine, and her look sends a frisson through my body. A dead man I may be, but that look, that smile…*that* is a sin worth dying for.

"I can't believe this," Idalia laughs, a skip in her step as we make our way down a market street. "It's beautiful! The people are so warm and welcoming!"

Lachlan smiles shyly and lowers his head to speak to her. "It's their favorite time of year. We feast, dance, sell, and trade. It's a true celebration of our Kingdom. The people love Aeradian, and they love to celebrate it."

"My brother's being modest," Theodore says from beside me. "The people love *him*. When our father reigned, this festival wasn't nearly as fun."

Lach's face tightens, but he bobs his head at his sister in gratitude before adding, "They love you too."

"I know. I never said they didn't."

It's hard to pay attention to their conversation; Idalia's amorous glances at Lachlan are wearing me out. The way she stares at him, the way her hand lightly brushes against his. It's difficult to regain my focus and impossible to apply it to anything else. Lachlan grabs Idalia's arm and pulls her towards a vendor selling flower arrangements. Gods, don't let him buy her flowers. Don't let him even think about it.

Theodore tugs on my sleeve. "Let's give them some time alone. Won't you assist me to this tent over here?" It takes everything for me to break my gaze away from Idalia, but the Aeradian Princess is relentless. "Oh, come now, does a girl really have to beg for your companionship?"

I shake my head and manage a laugh. "Of course not. Where do you want to go?"

I follow her inside a turquoise tent. "Bottles," I say flatly, looking around. "You wanted me to look at bottles with you?"

She picks up one and cups it into her palm. "I wanted you to come with me so that you'd stop looking so pathetic."

"Pathetic?"

"Mm," she hums, putting the bottle back before selecting another. "Like a dog that hasn't been fed in days. I'm surprised you didn't start salivating."

I draw in air as silently as I can. "I don't know what you mean."

Her thick brows arch even higher than my own. "Fine then, play dumb if you like. It's not my business anyway. Let's talk about something else, shall we?"

"What does *Nosis Magis* mean?" I ask as we meander deeper into the tent.

Theodore nods at the shopkeeper, who offers her a satchel for the many bottles she now holds. "It doesn't have a direct translation. But in short, it means someone very wise."

"So, you're the Wise, and Lachlan is the Generous. And the entire Kingdom adores you both. Not an easy feat."

Theodore continues shopping, pointing at some of the larger containers behind the seller. "It's easy to be liked when your Kingdom isn't at war all the time and easier for a Prince to be praised when he does his duties instead of fleeing."

I grab a glass carafe and force every muscle in my face to relax. "Ah, yes. Royal duties. Well, it's hard to do those when your King doesn't trust you enough to give you any."

"Even harder when one runs around with a bunch of bandits," she says.

I gently set the decanter on a table. "How do you know about that?"

Theodore takes coins out of her pouch and slips them into the seller's hand. His eyes widen at the amount, and he blows kisses and begins to bless her.

"I know many things. I'm The Wise, remember?"

We both know her wit far surpasses mine, so I concede. "Fine, you got me. It's true, Theodore. Some of us just weren't meant to be royalty." I dig my hand into my pocket as we leave the tent and pull out a small glass vial. "Some of us were born to be thieves."

She only laughs at my smug expression. "That's your problem, Braizen," she says. "You're so busy thinking that no one is paying attention that you forget to do so yourself. Why do you think I paid that man as much as I did? You're good, but you're no ghost. If you want to be the best, you'll have to make sure your moves go completely undetected."

"Impressive that you caught me, but why are you so concerned? I don't mean to rob your land blind. I won't even be here much longer. I have business that I must attend to. People I need to find." A thud quakes inside my chest, and Nuri's words spill over me. I'm drenched in the memory of what I saw in the Minea's house. I roll back my shoulders to shake the dread that follows. No. I'll find them.

Theodore sighs and tugs at her neckline, which plunges so low I think it rude to stare for too long. "I'm concerned because I need a favor."

I stop walking and smile, crossing my arms, "Aye?"

"And for payment, I'll do you one in return."

After hours of shopping and mindlessly dumping coins into pockets, we meet at the massive temple towering over the center of Senlow. At the base of its stone portico, people throw petals and sing hymns and chants as we walk past. Children laugh and play with wooden animals while their parents bow. Idalia locks arms with the King, and she waves to the people, soon to be her people, with an effervescent expression.

Inside, white marble pillars curve into giant arches. Walls of an ivory pearl shimmer under the light of chandeliers whose bright candles cast shadows across the intricately painted ceiling. "Gods," I breathe, astonished by all my eyes drink in.

"Funny you should say so; that's who it was built for, after all," Theodore says, picking up the pace to join her brother's side.

The ceiling holds my attention, its mural stealing it from other ornate statues and art. The Lady holds her shield high and proud on one side, and the Guard courageously brandishes his sword on the other. In between them, the artist painted the entire world. Near the feet of the gods, Aeradian is outlined in bold red, and its interior blooms with a field of Salva flowers. People who are holding their hands out are painted between the petals.

Above Aeradian, Baelliles is depicted as a great tree. People dressed in green are laced between its branches. A few strange creatures I've never seen before are perched on a few of the limbs. I concentrate on them for a long moment, unsure of what they have to do with my Kingdom, unless Aeradian has made up its own folklore concerning my home.

Near the head of the gods, Verdana is painted as a giant, glistening blue mountain. At its base, a group of people stand at a river; in the middle is a large boat with a giant sail. Atop Verdana sits a golden crown. Light, like the sun itself, shines over the entire rock.

Osinea isn't shown, but that's understandable since no one has ever crossed the Trench of Arborlow. In the shadows, the people in all the kingdoms seem to move as if they're sentient. As if, while I stare up at them, they stare back at me.

I'm only pulled away as the music begins. Lachlan stands in front of long tables and holds his hand high. Idalia is at his side, beaming in all her beauty. As I approach, I see his forehead twitching, and he pulls on his earlobe.

"If I may have your attention," he says, but the space is filled with too many cheers. He swallows and tries again. "Aeradian, it is my great pleasure…"

"Everyone, be quiet!" Theodore bellows. Silence falls.

Lachlan flashes his sister a grateful grin and then addresses the room.

"Because the gods have honored us so greatly, so plentifully these last few seasons, we take great pride in giving honor back. Tonight's feast shall be held in the Lady's and the Guard's good names. We eat to give thanks; we give thanks because we can eat." His voice quavers as he takes a long look around the room before nodding. "Uh, that's it. Thank you." Despite his wavering confidence, his people dispatch loud applause.

At our table, servers lean down and ask us what we'd like to eat. Directly across, Theodore and Idalia are already drinking wine and laughing.

"The herbed salmon," Lachlan requests, looking to me next. I've never ordered food like this before. In my castle, food is presented, and I eat it without question. Before I can even think of what I want, the server leans closer and whispers to his King.

"The Princess Idalia asks that you order for her. She said that whatever you wish for her to eat, she will. She also said she looks forward to learning what you recommend."

Lachlan's hands shake as he stammers incoherent words to the server.

A ball of nerves, this one.

I lean forward, place a steady hand over his, and smile. "Do you have any mutton?"

"Yes, Your Highness. We have whatever you wish."

"Good," I say. "Bring her that, and make sure that it's seasoned with coriander and turmeric."

Lachlan slumps in relief.

"Right away. And Your Highness?"

I wink and nod at the King. "I'll have what he's having."

After waiting a short amount of time, Lachlan starts on his recently delivered salmon with a small groan of delight.

When Idalia receives her dish and the scents waft up to her nose, she releases a sigh of pleasure. When she takes her first bite, her eyes light up. But not for me. *For him.*

"How did you know?" She asks with a euphoric smile. "The gods surely have brought me to you," she praises, taking another bite.

I push my plate away as I watch her bat her thick lashes and blush like a smitten youth.

"Aren't you going to eat?" The nobleman next to me asks.

I shake my head, looking up once more to see her eyes still on Lach.

"I've lost my appetite."

Chapter Thirty

Braizen

It's time for dancing. While we ate, a crowd gathered in the square. Musicians stand nearby, readying their instruments. A familiar face slinks out of the crowd.

"Prince Man," Stig yells, holding his lute high above his head. "Nice to see you again."

"You've come to play?"

"A special thanks to Aunt Deria for making it happen. I'm pretty sure in return she wants me to be her next husband," he confides.

"Not too bad," I say. "For a musician."

He slaps my back and roars. He and Torr would get along just fine. After I'm sure that Aeradian and Baelliles are truly safe, I'll see that they meet. Lorna is going to detest the friendship.

"Ladies and gentlemen!" The bard calls out and climbs to the stage where the musicians are ready to play. "A special treat for you on this day. A special treat, indeed! I've written a song just for this occasion and have been asked by Deria Ferdal to perform it for you now! Please, quiet. *Quiet!"* Most of the onlookers lower their voices, apparently interested enough to see what the King's aunt has approved for the day.

Idalia moves closer to Lachlan, wraps her arm through his, and rests her head on his shoulder. He looks down and flashes an unsteady smile before turning back to the stage.

Stig holds his instrument high, closes his eyes, and mumbles a prayer.

I do my best to focus on him and not glare at Lachlan. At their touching skin.

"Sing then, Bard! We haven't all day!" A man shouts from the crowd, but Stig's eyes don't open. He slowly brings the lute to his waist and strums a chord. The song begins with a slow melody. Finally, he sings:

"Once a man had no bread, he lost his home.

He lost his head.

And nary for him was there a tear shed."

My mouth drops open in disbelief. I hear her laugh and see Idalia holding her hands over her red face as she gasps hysterically.

"Gods, he's *terrible,*" Theodore whispers over to me. Her face is contorted and likely mirrors mine. "My aunt must've been very drunk when she heard him."

Stig prances across the stage on his lanky legs and thumbs the lute strings.

"Give him a coin or give him ale! Or his insanity will prevail! Give coin to the bard that sings of his tale!"

No one realizes that the ditty is over, so Stig stands on the stage in dead silence, heaving as if he's just returned from battle.

Idalia eventually breaks into applause, her face still pink. I join her and whistle loudly in appreciation.

Stig's voice is *atrocious*, but his confidence is a sight to behold. He proudly bows multiple times before one of the musicians pushes him from the stage. When he joins me in the crowd, I throw my arm around his shoulder.

"Well, Stig. That performance was… Well, it was…"

He throws a stiff hand into the air. "At a loss for words, are you? That's to be expected. As I told you, Prince Man, some just have the gift."

"Whatever gift you have, I can honestly say that I don't possess it."

Stig gives my chest a sympathetic pat and darts towards the dancers, ready to be greeted by his adoring admirers. A plump brunette with light blue eyes meets him there. She's very drunk, and I'm not sure she even knows what's going on. I gaze at the dancers, watching couples and merry citizens move in joyful tandem to the music.

Idalia pulls Lachlan to the floor; his smile is wide and full of wonder. She places his timid hands around her waist and begins to sway to the melody. I can see him gulp when she folds her hands around his neck and pulls him closer.

My stomach sinks. A pit in my chest burrows deeper. This might be one of the four hells.

I dance with a few women, Theodore included, who ever so kindly informs me that getting naked to stay warm is a myth. I won't be filling Idalia in on that anytime soon. Though, I wish I could tell her *anything* right now. The music is slow and romantic, and she and Lachlan are laced into each other's bodies in a repulsive display. The moon rises above us, making her silver dress glow like the Lady herself.

I can't stand watching any longer. I finish my third glass of wine in a single gulp and stalk toward them. Lach sends me his dashing smile. *The prick.* Where does he get off being this handsome? Idalia's expression reads somewhere between scattered excitement and confusion.

"Come to join us, Braizen?" The King chirps. He must've had a few drinks by now, and his usual nervousness is covered by liquid courage.

"Don't be silly, Lachlan," Idalia says and sinks her fingers into his arm. "Braizen and I can't dance together. The Gods-Cursed Children, remember?"

"Nonsense!" Lachlan throws back a laugh and twirls Idalia under his arm. "You don't have to touch to dance!"

With that, he releases her and moves to the musicians. I can't hear what he asks, but the music changes almost immediately. It's even softer than the intimate tune that preceded it. Lachlan weaves his way back through the doting crowd and slaps a hand on our backs. "Are you two familiar with The Desiderium? It's the perfect dance for this peculiar situation."

Without waiting for an answer, he begins swatting people away from our position, ordering them to give us space, so we don't accidentally bump into each other. People retreat but then form a giant circle around us. Lachlan waves his hand in an affable gesture, signaling us to begin.

I swallow. Of course, we know the dance; we learned it when we were young so we could celebrate holidays with our cousins and noble children. It's more of a mockery than a dance, made for drunk parents to coo over their precious children.

Idalia's neck is tight, but she clears her throat and stiffly lifts her hand. I roll my neck and glance again at Lachlan, who's still motioning for us to start. Reluctantly, I raise my hand to mirror hers and turn in step. For a while, the audience gawks, ogling Idalia's beauty, then falls into the dance themselves. Theodore is partnered with Stig, which he'll undoubtedly talk about for the rest of eternity.

"Well, this is fun," Idalia says dryly, her eyes anywhere but on mine.

"I'm having the time of my life."

"I'm sure you are. After all, this is your greatest pleasure, isn't it? To make sure I'm miserable." Her tone is sharp.

"You think *you're* the miserable one here? Trust me; I don't want to be doing this any more than you do."

"Really? Then why did you interrupt our dance?" Her stare captures me like a gust of wind takes up leaves.

"I…I didn't…" We swoop to the left, and a rogue curl sweeps against her cheek. "I didn't come to interrupt you; I came to tell the King goodnight." Inwardly, I groan. Surely I could've come up with something better. Too late. I've said it and, therefore, must commit to it.

"To tell him goodnight?" she says, her eyebrows high. "Who are you, his grandmother? Do you also want to wish him sweet dreams?"

"Actually, I'm a gentleman, Idalia. That's what gentlemen do. We bid each other goodnight."

"Please," she snorts. "You are anything but gentle. Everyone knows that."

"So, it seems my bedroom tales have caught up to you then?"

"You're disgusting."

"And you're an ass."

When she's silent for long enough, I wink. "Stalemate," I whisper.

She groans. "Can we please just finish the rest of this dance in silence?"

"That might be the smartest thing I've ever heard you say."

We turn again, hands still parallel. With both of us now quiet, the music is easier to drink in. Its melody is calm water effortlessly sweeping over smooth rocks—delicate, soothing. I look into her eyes. The warm golden circles that rage in the lamplight of the square. The darker shades that surround them, as if protecting that inner pool. Her lashes grace them like the thick canopy of trees that hover above Baelliles' castle.

Her eyes demand to be looked at. They demand to be adored.

Our bodies shift again. We're face to face, and our arms are raised high above our heads. Her lids flutter as we're forced to stare at each other. Slowly, we lower our arms to our waists.

I picture my arm sliding to the small of her back and pulling her into me. I imagine her chin resting in the crook of my shoulder. I can almost feel her body fusing into mine and can faintly feel her heartbeat reverberate off her palms.

Everything has gone silent. The chattering crowd, the music. All I hear is her breaths, a symphony of its own, in unison with mine.

We're the only two people here. We're the only two people who've ever lived.

Though she may be Verdanian, she is not made of ice. No, she is a fire. An unholy, consuming flame that is setting every inch of me ablaze.

How long can she look at me before I completely turn to ash?

Chapter Thirty-One

Idalia

There's something different in his cool stare tonight. His eyes glimmer under the stars in a violent hue. He's not just looking at me; his gaze is palpable. Visceral. *Terrifying.*

We turn in slow circles, nearly reckless with our movements. I almost feel his arm around me for a moment, and a shiver scales up my back. I swallow hard. My body responds to the *thought* of his touch more strongly than it ever has, even in the thick of intimacy. Why?

Someone clears their throat next to us, and I take a giant step backward, blinking myself back into reality. The musicians are already halfway into another song, though no one else is dancing. Lachlan smiles nervously.

“I didn’t want to interrupt; however, I can’t keep the audience at bay for too long,” he says. “This next dance includes a lot of movement, and I fear you two touching. Would you both like to go inside?”

“Not at all! We were just…It was very hard to hear the music change over all the noise. Sorry about that.” I see Braizen’s face from the corner of my eye, and my gut turns in discomfort.

“Of course, all the noise. I’m sure—” Lachlan says.

“How about another dance?” I ask sharply, stepping on his words.

Lachlan rubs his earlobe. “Surely, you’re tired of dancing after all these hours? Wouldn’t the two of you like to sit for a minute, fill up on a drink?”

“No!’ My gaze trails back to Braizen, whose eyes remind me of a raging storm. “I wish to dance with *you,* Lachlan. If you wouldn’t mind just one more?” I can’t let my dance with Baelliles’ Prince be my last. I must wash away this uncomfortable rush of longing that our closeness sparked.

Lachlan’s face pulls into a playful frown as he leans into a bow. “Of course, Princess. Another dance will be no trouble to me at all.” He straightens and looks at Braizen. “How about you? Would you like to join us or get another drink, perhaps?”

Braizen shakes his head. “I’ll pass, old friend. I think I’ve had my fill of dancing for one night. I’m going to find the nearest tavern.”

“Are you sure?” Lachlan presses. “I have something spectacular planned! I’d hate for you to miss it.”

Braizen raises a hand and smiles. "Really, Lach. I have some things I need to figure out. I'll see you later for that drink?"

"Braizen!" I call out as he leaves. His expression is unreadable. I'm not sure what I want to say or why I even called his name. I gulp down my confusion and grin.

"Thank you for the dance. Not bad for a bandit."

His lips twitch upwards, but his smile seems anything but genuine. Two fingers to his forehead, and he lazily salutes me. "You too, Little Sparrow."

He effortlessly braids his way through the swarm of people who call out and pat him on the back. My neck strains as I watch until he's completely lost in the crowd.

Lachlan coughs, and I turn to face him. He's rubbing his ear again.

"Are you ready?" I grin, holding out my palm. His brows raise, but he nods, and we dance our merry little steps. But as we hop and skip, I wonder where Braizen is and what he's doing. Not even the loud music can drown out the sounds of my thoughts.

The sound of his voice.

The sound of his skin calling out for mine.

Lachlan is all smiles as he leads Teddy, Deria, Stig, and me onto the temple's balcony. We overlook a sea of red, Aeradians still burning with energy and erupting into cheers when they see their king. Teddy sips her wine while Stig hovers, taking in her scent like a starving street cat. She looks like she doesn't mind, or perhaps she's too used to the attention to care. I can't tell if Deria is drunk or incredibly tired; her eyelids droop, and her smile is crooked. Now and then, I hear her mutter unintelligible whispers to herself, followed by a low laugh.

Lachlan doesn't tell us what's going on. He doesn't even say a word to me once we reach the balcony; he only gazes at the night sky with childlike fascination. The crowd eventually falls silent, and we wait.

"I suppose we're about to see why you've been up in that attic for months," Teddy smiles. Lach beams at her.

A squeal zips through the air. My heartbeat quickens, and I clutch the railing.

"Are we under attack?" I snap, my eyes darting in every direction. No one answers. I spot a trail of fire zooming high into the sky from the corner of my eye. My neck whips towards the burning ball, and my eyes widen in panic. Have the terrors of The Wood followed me here? Do they seek to destroy Aeradian's capitol to flush me out? Where is Braizen? Without warning, the flame disappears, and all is still.

Bam! Across the night's canvas, multiple streams of colored fire disperse from all angles. An involuntary laugh leaps from my throat as I watch the fiery lights form what looks like an opening palm made of stars. A crackling follows, and then another fireball whizzes to greet its predecessor. Again, it explodes; only this time, warm honey-colored lights fall like the limbs of a weeping willow. A thousand lightning bugs fly in formation, twinkling like individual tiny suns.

Another launches, and then another. At least fifty tiny missiles impale the air, only to burst into multicolored shapes stretching across the heavens like a cosmic root system. Their embers drift to the ground, vanishing before reaching the crowd's outstretched hands. Children's delighted laughter and astonished exclamations soon fill the square.

So many flares fire at once that I can't contain my joy and giddiness. I move to Lachlan's side and rest my head on his shoulder. "This is the most beautiful thing I've ever seen," I say excitedly.

"It's all for her. She loved the stars," he whispers.

I remove my head and tilt my face to watch him.

"Sera?"

He nods. "My father always said that when Kings die, they become stars. Legend further states that only a righteous man can become one, king or not. But I like to think that *anyone* can become a star if they're kind and good enough," he says. He points a finger. "That's where I think she is. Up there, shining brightly over our darkest times. I pray she knows that I look to the sky each night, searching for her in every constellation."

His voice catches on a slight sob. "All of this is so that hopefully, she can see me too. I want her to know the world still burns bright for her. That I still…" His voice drifts, and his green eyes lock onto the sky—onto her.

I place my hands on my churning stomach. If the dead do become stars, I wonder if my mother is up there too. Perhaps she can see how Lachlan scours the heavens for his love while her own daughter can't even bear to look at her mother's name carved into stone.

And if the good become these wonderful, shimmering lights that cast their beauty across the night, I'll surely become the dirt, forced to spend an eternity trampled under heedless feet. Because I'm a coward. And cowards deserve the heels of those greater than them.

"I must go," I say to Lachlan, but he doesn't hear me. He's preoccupied, as is the rest of the party. So, I slip away and kick off my heels.

They're much too fancy to wear in a tavern.

After two failed attempts, I finally find the right tavern. He's at the bar, tracing his finger lightly around the rim of his cup. Three women behind him point and gawk, most likely stunned to be both in the presence of royalty and someone this handsome. The elder barkeep doesn't seem impressed that he's waiting on a prince, or perhaps he doesn't recognize Braizen. Like the other taverns I tried, the place is packed full and plenty busy. The festival appears to bring out most of Aeradian.

I take a deep breath, gather my skirts, and tell myself not to think too hard about why I'm here. I plop down next to him and tap two fingers on the wooden slab. The leathered-faced elder gestures and rolls his eyes. I huff, crossing my arms.

"What does a girl have to do to get a drink around here?"

Braizen's eyes peel off his glass. "What are you doing?" His tone is sharp, almost fearful.

I rest my elbow on the bar and exhale an exaggerated breath.

"Whatever do you mean? It's the night of the most fabulous festival in the Deep Kingdom, and the King has launched fiery mirages into the sky.

Naturally, a dingy alehouse is the only place to be." I stretch my smile thin and bat my eyelashes.

Braizen snorts and takes what appears to be his first sip. "I've heard about you runaway brides," he says. "And to be honest, I love the theatrics of it all. But don't you think it might bother your husband that you ran away *before* even seeing the altar?" He then thoroughly looks me over and strikes his forehead. "*Barefoot*, no less."

I wave down the ancient barkeep, who continues to ignore me.

"Oh, Lach's probably very torn up about it. I'm sure he's rubbing his earlobe twice as hard right now."

Braizen throws his head back and roars. I love the sound of his laugh. It's rich, like an aged liquor. I could drink it all day if given a chance. I inspect his profile as he drinks, fully observing what his loose hair usually hides. Sharp, angular features that match his sharp, angular personality. How dreadfully annoying for someone to possess both.

I wave again and exhale loudly. There are far too many people crowded in here for me to grab the barkeep's attention.

"We should just find the cellar and borrow a few bottles of whatever we want," I suggest.

"You mean *steal* whatever we want?" Braizen shrugs. "I'm a bandit, Sparrow."

A bandit indeed. I toss one last futile glance down the bar and then meet Braizen's stare.

"Okay, thief. You win this round."

Chapter Thirty-Two

Idalia

Thievery proves to be more exciting in theory than it is in reality. We easily snake our way through the drunks and bar wenches and, even more disappointing, past the tavern's security, a lone balding man slumped over in his chair, dead asleep. Braizen descends the spiral staircase leading to the cellar.

I leave three steps between us and take careful note of the loose curls that revolt against the leather tie that dares try to hold them back.

He claps his hands in celebration as we enter a damp storage. The room is lit by two sconces that send dim light across the mossy stone walls. We waste no time.

Braizen starts on a wall of shelves, and I take the one opposite of it. I drum my fingers against the bottles, squinting to read the labels.

"Did a child write these? I can barely read what they say!"

"Who cares what they say? Any one of these will eventually get you to the same destination."

I roll my eyes even though he can't see me.

"Is it truly so wrong to want to enjoy the ride to that destination?" I slide my fingers across the bottles as I make my way down the aisle. "Besides, I shouldn't have to remind you how quickly ale affects me. I much prefer wine. More drink, less puke."

"Fair point."

After another minute or so of searching, I throw up my arms. There's no wine that I can see. I don't know why I'm surprised; it's a tavern for brutes, not princesses.

Braizen responds to my relentless sighing. "For the love of the Guard, Sparrow. Just pick one."

I turn to see him pull a cork from a bottle with his teeth.

"I don't know which one!" I return to my perusal and tap my chin, "Which one do you think Torrent would like best? I could tell he had the best taste for these things."

I realize what I said and quickly swivel.

Braizen's face is ghostly white; the bottle hangs limply at his side.

“I’m so sorry,” I whisper, moving forward an inch. This is the first time any of their names have been said out loud since being here.

He doesn’t respond; he doesn’t move.

Guilt swirls through me as if I’ve drunk the ale. I take another step. “Braizen…” I whisper.

“What’s there to be sorry for?” He says, breaking his gloomy trance to flash me a cheeky smile. “He did have good taste—the best taste of all of us—except for me, of course. Here, let me look.” He strolls past me, picking up bottles as quickly as he sets them down.

“Not this one. Oh, no, *definitely* not this one. He’d never drink this piss.” He fiddles with more choices as I slowly approach.

“Braizen,” I say, even softer this time.

“Now, what in the four hells?” He shakes one of the bottles and grimaces. “I think this one might actually be piss. I’m not joking; look at the foam.”

“You don’t have to do this, you know.” I stop a few feet behind him.

He turns his cheek slightly toward me. “I’m fine, Sparrow.”

“No, you aren’t.”

He moves to the next beverage. This time, he uncorks it and sniffs.

“Not piss,” he reports. “But not what we’re looking for. Torr would want something stronger.”

I take another step forward.

“I said I’m fine, Idalia.”

My chest aches; I wish more than anything that I could touch him if only for one second, to bring him some form of comfort.

"I know you're hurting, Braizen. I know that while you tease and joke, your heart is breaking for them. You can leave now if you want to. I'm safe."

"Leave?" He's perfectly still.

"Yes, you can go and try to find them. I know that's what you really want to do."

Braizen takes a swig and laughs without turning around.

"You have no idea what I want."

"Maybe not," I concede. "But I at least know how deeply you're hurting. When I lost my mother—"

"This is nothing like that," he bites out.

"Braizen, my mother died right in front of me! How can you say that?"

"Your mother died because your father is a crazed tyrant," he says coldly. "My friends are dead because they were saving *you*."

My nostrils flare along with my hands. He's lucky I can't touch him, or I'd have him by his throat.

"My mother died because of your—" Before I can finish the sentence, my tongue begins to scald against my teeth. It's the calling. The magic. I shake my head. "She's dead because of your—" The flames rage up and down my windpipe.

It does not want me to say it. It does not want me to fight him. Not now.

Braizen finally turns on his heel and faces me, waiting for my curses against him and Baelliles.

I swallow and squeeze my eyes shut. "There's no need to act like it doesn't hurt you. You don't have to pretend, not in front of me. I understand the pain. I understand losing someone so close..." The flames immediately fade.

Braizen's mouth turns down into a snarl. His eyes are a void as he snaps at me. "What are you talking about, Sparrow? The pain of what? Torrent, Lorna, and Lin aren't actually dead. I don't know why I even said that, so spare me the lecture about what you know of grief. It isn't necessary."

I bite down on my lip as the reality of his sorrow crashes over me. I may know some about grief, but I'm a downright expert on denial.

"Braizen," I whisper, and a cool draft wraps around me. Since we stepped out of The Wood, I've noted his anguish. The way his eyes sink in the middle of a laugh, or how he shakes his head after plunging too deep into his thoughts. I've done the same since my mother's murder.

Instead of facing the pain, I doused myself in drink, slept with stable boys, and irritated Nurse Lydia until she couldn't stand to stay in the same room with me. I push down the guilt. Down, down, down in hopes that it can be forgotten. So deep and far away that I can chase my temporary distractions without feeling pain.

Braizen looks at me expectantly, waiting for me to finish my sentence, so I say quietly, "Our friends wouldn't want us to ignore their sacrifice."

"*Our* friends?" He all but spits at me. "You think they're *our friends?*"

I step forward to stop him, to ward off the venom I feel him injecting into my soul, but he doesn't give me a chance.

"They're not *our* friends. Is that clear? They're *mine.* My family. My beating heart. You barely knew them! They didn't care for you. The only thing that *they* knew about you was how much strife your very existence has caused our kingdom. If anything, Idalia, they only grew to hate you more."

A lancing pain shoots down my arm. It's not the discomfort that commands me to strike. It's the recognition of this other side of grief: Anger.

He stares at the bottles behind me. "You can't possibly know what you're saying right now. You don't know them. I do. They aren't dead. They're fine, do you hear me? *Fine.* They are. They have to be."

"Of course. We'll just keep pretending if that's what you need."

He laughs, a stark, arrogant sound that echoes off the stone walls. "That's ironic coming from you." He turns his attention back to the bottles behind him and takes generous gulps while he searches through the shelf.

"What's that supposed to mean?"

"That's all you do, Sparrow. *Pretend.*" He selects a bottle, studies it, then removes its cork with his teeth again. He sips, then jerks back around. "This one," he says and holds it out. "Torr would like this one."

Cautiously, I grasp the base of the bottle. I turn my hot face as he strides past me.

"Don't look so pathetic," he scoffs. "You know exactly what I mean."

"I don't, actually," I say softly and inspect the dark lager in my hands.

"There you go again… *pretending*. I can't blame you, not really. It is a Verdanian trait. Heads stuck so far up in the mountains—you play dumb for the rest of the world, hoping it might save you."

"Why are you being so mean?"

He snorts, then pours the remainder of his first bottle onto the stone floor. "Because we're enemies, Idalia. Why should we pretend we're anything else? It's like you said, we aren't even friends."

"You're such a coward," I hiss.

His head whips to the right, revealing his sharp profile.

"What's that?" He demands.

"You heard me." I step towards him. Any kindness I felt is gone. "You're a coward, Braizen. A lowly, selfish coward. You heard what your father and his men did, yet you still defend him. You act as if losing your friends doesn't bother you because you're afraid that showing your wounds is a weakness. But I can assure you; it's not. Hiding your wounds is idiotic; they can't heal when you stuff them away. You cannot grow from them if they're left in the shadows."

The bottle drops from his limp hold, and the rattle rings through the storeroom.

"Even now, you cower behind the guise of our being enemies, acting as if we could never be friends because you're still scared of him, your father. Though a hundred miles separate you two, you still fear him. His disappointment, his shadow…his crown." I move in closer.

"That's why you ran away and created that gods damn circus you call The Cloaked," I continue viciously. "It's why you rob the richest noblemen in your precious kingdom and spend your reaping on booze and whores. Most consequentially, though, it's why they're gone."

My face hardens as the cold words fly from my tongue like a blizzard. "They're dead because you dragged them into this pitiful masquerade to flee from under your father's thumb. And then you bailed on them. All for your enemy. All for the little bird whom you despise. I'd be angry if I were you, too."

His jaw grinds so roughly that I swear he might break his teeth.

I smile, then take a deep gulp of the lager. With an obnoxious sigh, I commend him. "You're right. Torrent would've loved this."

"Get out." He nearly breathes the muted command. The room is void of air, void of sound. The heat returns to my hands, so I cross my arms and point my nose in the air.

"No."

He growls under his breath. "You need to leave. Now."

My heartbeat escalates, but I hold firm. "You can go if you like. I'm enjoying my drink."

His lips curl into a snarl, and satisfaction ripples through me.

His icy blue eyes pin me like frozen spears of rain. "I will throw these bottles at you, Verdanian. Do not tempt me."

I laugh and take another swig. "I'll just throw them right back at you, *Baellilean*." I watch him intently; he now knows my words can cut more sharply than glass. The liquid tickles my throat as it goes down. "Besides, it's not very bandit-like of you to waste alcohol, wouldn't you say?"

His expression is positively feral, one I've never seen and very well may never see again.

"*Idalia.*"

My name sounds like a threat.

The hair on my arms rises, but I won't show my trepidation. I can't show it. Not now.

"I'm going to ask you one more time…"

"Or what?" I place the half-empty bottle on the ground. "What are you going to do, Braizen? If you touch me, you'll die before you can take out your anger. Not that we *need* to touch for you to hurt me. You've done plenty of that in our time together."

His face softens for a fraction of a second before it twists back into rage.

"The gods blessed you the day they cursed us, because if I *could* touch you right now, I'd…"

"You'd what?" My tone is frigid; an unmovable stone rests behind each word.

His gaze darts up, locks in on mine, and his pupils dilate. Another burst of heat lances through me. *Closer,* it whispers.

Slowly I bring my foot forward, monitoring his reaction. The light from the sconces warms his face, but his eyes reflect their flames. He's so angry with me, and to be fair, I am livid too. It's *his* fault we experienced the horrors of The Wood.

I was better when I didn't know him. When he was just a memory.

"What would you do if you could touch me, Braizen?" My question is a tiny breeze, one that also carries my scent.

Closer.

His eyes are narrow slits as he watches with an ungodly concentration as I draw nearer.

"Are you afraid?" I ask. Another step.

Closer.

Another.

We're six inches apart. I can hear his breath quicken.

"I'm not afraid of you, Sparrow," he says finally. His shoulders sink, and his jaw unclenches. To my surprise, he shuffles forward.

Five inches apart.

"I'm utterly terrified."

I can't feel myself breathe, but I hear the heavy pants that escape my mouth.

We're supposed to be angry. We're supposed to hurl wildly inappropriate insults with wicked grins and keep our distance until one of us storms off into the night.

We're not supposed to be this close.

But the magic trickles through me in tiny rivulets, spilling words that I'd never before admit to him.

"I want you to tell me," I say, trying to steady my breathing. From the sound of it, he struggles to do the same.

"Tell you what, Little Sparrow?"

"What you would do to me." My answer nearly trips over his sentence.

My skin prickles as if I've jumped into one of Verdana's icy lakes, but I know I must keep moving if I wish to stay warm. "I want you to tell me where to put my hand as if it's your own."

His brows dive deep towards the bridge of his nose, his breath is jagged, and his eyes rove over me with wild hunger. Like a starving feline that's just spotted a lone fawn. A predator that can't play with his food.

Bringing my hands behind me, I begin to untie my dress. As the fabric loosens, I whisper, "Tell me where you'd touch me first."

He stumbles back, a hand over his heart. For a moment, I'm sure he'll flee up the stairs, leaving me in a dim cellar to face my humiliation. Then his hand shakes as if it's caught in a flame. He stares at it, his expression unsure, and all at once, his eyes are back on me, and it's *my* turn to stumble back a few steps.

His stare is a commandment.

"I would undress you faster." He smiles arrogantly, breaking the tension immediately.

I grin, and a light laugh tumbles from my lips as I wrestle with the ribbons behind me. I'm not used to undressing myself.

I keep my eyes on his as I work the strings, knowing damn well the corset beneath will be the real trouble. My body calls out to me: *Faster. Faster!*

He stands completely still. Anticipation floods his eyes, and I feel a spark leave my fingertips. His stare widens as my dress falls to the floor, the corset neatly dropping with it. My chest heaves as he feasts on the sight of me in my chemise. His lip curls, and I sense his need to devour. His plea to ravish.

"Little Sparrow," he whispers. His voice is low and rough.

My back arches, and my breasts push forward, beckoned by the very sound of it.

He moves his hands down to his trousers and unbuckles his belt.

My eyes drop to his pants and then back up to his face. They can't decide what's more pleasing; I can't decide what's more pleasing.

The sound of fabric hitting the stone fills the cellar. Braizen slowly raises his tunic above his head. As he stretches, his muscles ripple in the dim light, and I follow their deep lines to where they disappear into his braies. Heat surges through my lower body. How badly I wish I could be the one to take off his clothes. How I wish I could trace those hard lines with the tip of my tongue.

Playfully, he places two thumbs under the remaining cloth and smirks. "Your turn," he says.

I take another deep breath; my lacey white chemise is the last thing that hides me from him. It's only now, as we stand half-naked in this dingy place, that I realize what I am about to do. My hand rests on one of the straps and stays there. I fear I might not have drunk nearly enough to summon the courage to skim the strap down my arm and fully reveal myself to him. My hand lays there, awaiting instruction. I swallow and close my eyes.

"Take it off."

My lids snap open.

He pulls down his linen braies, nothing but authority in his gaze. My mouth drops open. The sight of him, hard and ready for me, is almost too much to take in.

That confirms one of the rumors I've heard over the years.

"Idalia," he interrupts my gawking and tilts his head downwards. "That hand belongs to me now. Do as I say."

My back arches again, and before I'm even aware of it, my hand pulls down the strap. Then the second strap. The silk glissades down my body and pools at my feet.

He draws in a deep, long breath. I wait for a compliment—or anything resembling one—to soothe my nerves as he studies every curve of my body. He looks at me in the same way he once gazed at the rare sparrow in the aviary. The prize that carefully selected him. Something rare.

His gaze returns to my face, and I hold my breath as I wait for him to say anything, *anything* at all.

"Let down your hair."

As if I have no control over my own body, my hands snatch at the pins that hold up my hair, and it falls effortlessly to my shoulders and down my back. I shake out the curls as best I can until they frame my face.

"Good," he whispers. "Now, I want you to slide your palm down your chest."

My breaths are shallow as I trace my fingers gently along my collarbone and then lower them into the crevice between my breasts.

"Stop," he orders.

I freeze, eyes locked below his waist. My heart races as his hand glides down and clasps his taut member. One slow stroke and I see his entire form tremble.

"I want to feel your breasts in my hand," he instructs.

Without breaking contact with my skin, I skim my hand to my right side. His breaths are louder now as I take a handful of my breast.

"Put two fingers in your mouth," he says next.

His strokes pick up pace as I lift my free hand to my lips. I watch him wait for me, a desperate urgency in his eyes. I graze each finger with my tongue as if thick sap falls from them. His gaze is set keenly upon my flesh, and his lips tremble. Then, my fingers are in my mouth, and my tongue swirls over them as I watch him beg for more.

He gives his orders through labored breaths. "Move the other hand lower."

I drop my hand from my breast. "Slowly," he intercedes. "I'm in no rush to skip over any part of you."

I curl my fingers and brush my skin with my fingertips. Before he tells me to, I lie down on the floor and look up at him.

He doesn't stop me. His eyes glisten in frantic fascination when my back is against the stone. A ferocious flare spirals through me, and I spread my legs wider for his enjoyment. A groan pours out of him like he's tasted food for the first time in years. His leg muscles tighten, and his torso constricts to keep him standing upright.

I stop just before I reach my hips and dance my fingers around my navel.

"What would you do to me next?"

His eyes are entranced beneath lowered hoods, his strokes quicker, longer. He finally speaks through gritted teeth.

"I want you to bring my hand lower until I can feel the warmth that comes from you."

I follow his directions and gasp as my fingers, *his fingers,* touch me there.

"Now," his tone is more animalistic than human. "I don't want you to feel your hand anymore. I don't want you to feel mine either. Instead, you'll feel my tongue." He moans lightly as he adds, "I want you to drag it over every single inch of you. When you find the place that feels best, let me know so that I can stay there."

I massage myself in circular movements. I keep my eyes fastened to his as he squints, and his face tightens in pleasure. I use the tip of my middle finger and rub against the hood, and immediately my body floods with an intense bliss. My loud moans meet his groans, and the sounds of pleasure fill the cellar.

"Right there," I say breathlessly. "Keep it right there."

I move my fingers fast and faster, and when I close my eyes, I can feel it; I can feel *his tongu*e slide over me in rapid licks.

"Do you like it, Little Sparrow?"

"Yes." Our voices are equally strained.

"Tell me you can feel me."

I moan again, then release a high-pitched squeal that's never come from me before.

"I can feel you, Braizen. I can feel your tongue all over me."

His voice flattens. "I can feel you too, and I want more. I want to be inside of you."

My body shakes against the cold stone; wetness drenches my fingers as I lower them.

"Idalia, let me inside of you."

I slip in two fingers, breaking the tight seal, and enter the threshold of my inner self. I whimper as he spreads me open and forces himself deeper. Taking in every inch of me, he slides in and out, both raw and graceful, as if I were made for him and him alone.

His breath is hot against my cheek, and his scent lingers with mine as he seems to hover over me. Thrust after thrust until I can't possibly take it any longer. Heat twines around my limbs, and I convulse as the tip of his cock sweeps against the top half of my canal. A spot so sweet, a place so delicate…I can't…*I can't breathe.*

His blue eyes burn above me, and I see a gold-laced trail of sparks shoot across his irises. The sky fires that Lachlan ignited for Sera pale in comparison to the explosions building in me.

Braizen shouts my name like a vow. I join him, repeating his name like an unanswered prayer.

I've never felt anything so good, so real, *so…*

Together, we shatter.

Slivers of emotion flitter to the ground, shards of the pleasure and anger that once made up an imperfect mirror, one that reflected our broken silhouettes and forbidden desires.

I lie empty on the floor, my arms limp. Pebbles of sweat from my brow coast towards my eyes. Thoughts of his body lying so close to mine pull at my flesh like the roots of a tree desperate for moisture.

The Lady's words ring in my head, a reminder of our forbidden fate.

They could have been a strong, unmovable tree, but they will never have the chance to bloom.

Chapter Thirty-Three

Braizen

I don't move as Idalia gathers her dress. I stare blankly at the crumbling stone walls and the water droplets lingering amidst the moss. Not the most promising place for a first encounter, but certainly not my worst.

Once she's somewhat clothed, I grab my trousers and focus on breathing normally, so I don't give away how desperately my mind is searching for clarity.

She stands still, her dress loose around her, corset in hand. We stare at each other; our faces are utterly void of readable expressions.

What are you feeling, Little Sparrow? Talk to me.

She must be silent out of embarrassment, so I save her by speaking first.

"How are you…" I cough nervously. "How was that?" *Oh, gods.* I can't find the right words. "Do you think…"

"My father once told me that anger is the hardest emotion to overcome," she interrupts, keeping her eyes on the floor in front of my feet. "He says that it can make a person blind to everything around them and that people will seek out many ways to diffuse its flames. He also says we do much the same to counter guilt." She takes a deep breath and plunges on. "I understand why you participated in… *that,* with me."

My breath hitches, and her voice breaks slightly. "You were angry with me. I said terrible, *terrible* things. I felt guilty. We both absolved ourselves in the only way we knew how."

"Idalia, that's not—"

"Please." Her flattened palm is raised to me, but her face is turned away. "I need to get back. I'm sure Teddy is looking for me. I don't wish to scare her."

"Sure," I scoff. "*Theodore* is who you must get back to."

"Lachlan, too." Her words are deflated, as if she's resigned to my disgust.

"Well, how nice of you to want to go running back to him so soon." A boiling pit is forming in my gut.

She fumbles, searching for her hairpins on the stone. "Braizen," she whispers. "You know why we came here. And you know that I'm betrothed to him."

"Of course, Princess. I know that. So, when you return, do let him know that I'll be right behind you. Just have to clean the cum off my pants first."

Her eyes finally meet mine, wide with the faux innocence I once believed. "Oh, don't worry, Little Sparrow. I won't tell him that it was your cunt that did it to me." She winces, but I don't relent. "Besides, it's not like I didn't guess how this would turn out. Soon you'll be the precious Queen of Aeradian, and I have no doubt that you'll dispatch an army to my Kingdom before I can even step foot out of your new one."

"Braizen, you can't be serious."

"Deadly serious, little one," I drawl. "You think I haven't seen the plan all along? I know why your father sent you here. Baelliles doesn't stand a chance if armies from the North *and* the Deep come knocking on our door. My Kingdom will be burned to the ground before I can even make it back to the castle. My home will be gone; my titles will be rubbish and my friends…" I choke, then straighten myself. "My friends will have died for *nothing*."

"*Braizen*," she says in a weak murmur. I see her tears build up, promising to wash over her cheeks.

"Want to know what the *real* kicker to this is, Sparrow? Do you want to hear the worst part of it all?"

She hugs herself like a child, her lips quivering as if she gives a damn about my cursed fate. As if she gives a damn about me. The next words come out despite my apprehension.

"It's that I would do it again, Idalia. All of it."

Her neck tightens, the veins on either side constricting like I've stabbed her. My heart aches, but I can feel Torrent's arm draped across my shoulders. I sense Lin, eyes full of nervous energy and honesty upon my face. And Lorna's judgmental glare, its ferocity only subdued by her irritating compulsion to champion my happiness.

"If I never see the castle in the trees, my parents, my people, or my friends again. If I die as a traitor at my father's hands because—all because I brought you here, to live and be happy, *to be with him,* I'd do it again. A hundred times over. For you."

A single tear drips down her cheek. She's trembling and appears tortured, but I can't fall for it again. Another thud sounds off in my chest. I grab my tunic and pull it on, then finish my message.

"But as you said, anger and guilt are blinding. Thank you, Idalia, for I can finally see."

I grab another bottle and leave. As I ascend the spiral staircase, I shake out my hair and uncork the bottle. With a bountiful swig, I swallow the strong contents with one thought.

It's time for that drink with Lachlan.

For the first time in my adult life, I'm surrounded by people who are drunker than me. I push my way through the crowd, which no longer seems to care who's royalty or not. My father would never let his people behave this way. I suppose that's why the Thropes are adored, and my father is only revered. It's a fine line between love and respect. Both rarely exist at the same time when it comes to those in charge.

"Braizen!" I hear his familiar voice and turn to see him making his way toward me.

King Lachlan. His cheeks are red, and his eyes sport a glassy glaze. He tosses his arm across my shoulders and tugs me into his side. "Where've you been? You look as if you've traveled to the ends of the earth and back."

I want to laugh hysterically, to tell him exactly why I look so wild, but I refrain. I'm too grateful. I've found the Aeradian King before Idalia could. I throw my arm across his back.

"It seems you've been having all the fun without me, Lach! Let's change that."

He winks, though I'm not sure he fully understands that I intend to make him drink even more with my invitation. I pull him away before he has a chance to say no.

"Quite a party, is it not?" Lachlan queries as he blows into his scotch. The brown liquid ripples in the small glass. I raise an eyebrow, and he chuckles. "An old trick. It's supposed to quell the burn." He pours a small dollop onto his tongue and immediately spits it out. "No, no," he says in coughs. "It doesn't work. The trick is a myth."

"I could've told you that, friend," I say, laughing and slapping his shoulder.

He nods tightly, then presses the glass firmly to his lips. With his eyes squeezed shut, he downs half of it.

"I never drink," he hisses, his lips curled in distaste. "If that isn't obvious enough. Twice a year, I make an exception. The Aeradian Festival is one of them."

"I'm sure your people are grateful for your sacrifice." I raise my drink to salute him, but he doesn't join me. He's far too vexed, still battling his drink's aftertaste.

I lean in as if to share some advice. "You'd do well to gain some tolerance. After Idalia moves in, she'll want wine all the time. Make sure she stays away from ale, though." I shudder at the memory of her bile coating the grass. "It doesn't sit well with her."

Lachlan nods and dumps more drink down his throat. After his body involuntarily bucks, he cocks his head.

"Wait. What do you mean?"

I flag down the rosy-cheeked barkeep, who isn't too busy considering everyone in here is on their last legs. I gesture for a mug of water, and she nods.

"I mean, she may not drink as much as I do, but Idalia knows how to put back a couple of bottles," I explain.

"No, not about her drinking habits." Lachlan lifts a finger, and mouth closed, discreetly burps before finishing. "Which I advise both of you to exercise better self-control over. I meant the 'moving in' part. Is Idalia moving in?"

My head jerks back, and I wonder how much he's truly had to drink. The barkeep sets a clay cup of water in front of me, and I slide it towards him, but he waves it away, opting for another swash of scotch.

"Well, I'm not too versed in the Aeradian way, but in my world, when a couple gets married, they usually live together," I say.

"Idalia is getting married?! How wonderful!"

Oh, gods, he's past drunk. I let out a rough laugh and place my hand against his back in case I need to stabilize him.

"Wonderful indeed," I nod. "To you, no less. When you're sober, I'm sure you'll remember that."

His body leans back heavily onto my hand and then thrusts forward.

"I'm not marrying Idalia! Guard and Sword, Braizen. I might be boozed up, but I'm not *that* boozed up. I think I'd remember proposing to someone tonight!"

"You didn't propose tonight, Lach," I say patiently. "You sent her a letter asking for her hand."

"I did no such thing," he says vehemently, shaking his head.

A cold chill races up my spine; it's not the alcohol speaking.

"Yes, you did."

"Braizen, you jest too much for your own good! These silly pranks were more amusing in our childhood."

"You wrote her a letter." I say, my voice rising in frustration.

Lachlan neatly sets down his glass and turns his entire body to face me.

"I have not written to Verdana since my father's death, and Idalia hasn't written to me since… hells, since I was a youth! A note filled with incoherent ramblings about *you*, if I remember correctly. I assumed that you and Idalia came here because you heard the news about my wife and wished to offer condolences."

I take the water and chug it down. Perhaps *I'm* the one who's too drunk.

Lachlan shifts his attention back to his drink and rubs his earlobe. "In all honesty, I thought the two of you were together. Only Braizen Brader and Idalia Hyland would brave the Florian Wood, forsake their families, and break all the rules just for the fun of it. I mean, you look at each other the same way you did when we were children! No, no. To be clear, I put away any feeling I might have ever had for that girl the moment we left the aviary. It was obvious she only had eyes for you."

My palm grips the clay cup, and my jaw tightens before I manage to peel it open enough to speak.

"Lachlan, she's here to marry you."

"Well, I don't want to marry her! I'm in love with my wife! *My wife*, Braizen. She's only been gone for a moment! Do you believe me to be someone who would move on so quickly? You think I would remarry this fast just to have a queen by my side?" He quaffs the rest of his drink and slams down his glass.

"I already *have* a queen, dammit! The whole world thinks my father chose her for me, but that isn't true. I loved Sera! She was gentle in speech, even gentler in touch. I wasn't nervous around her—not once. She…she was my steady breath. She *is still!"*

He rises and stands straight. "You and Idalia are welcome to stay if it brings no harm to my people. But as for this heresy, this marriage you speak of, I will hear no more of it. I love my wife, and as I promised in my vows, I will love her even in death. Till I join her in the sky."

He stalks out of the tavern, leaving me no chance to stop him. I stare blankly into my empty cup.

"You want another one, sweetheart?" The server asks.

I throw down too many coins for her to collect with one hand.

"Keep all of it. I have to go."

There's no trace of her in the masses that still swarm Aeradian's cobbled streets. I move recklessly, not caring that I could bump into her without realizing it, and join Sera in death before Lachlan does. I call her name, but my voice is lost amidst the frenzied echoes of the revelers. I overhear a man with a slurred voice say that the castle gates will close at midnight. I must get back and find her. I must tell her that she's been deceived. Lachlan did not send the letter.

Her father, that sinister man, has tricked her. Again.

And if it's the last decision I'll ever make, I'm going to find out why.

Chapter Thirty-Four

Braizen

"Where are you off to?" Stig stumbles a bit, then matches his pace to mine as I frantically stalk down corridors and scan each room of the Aeradian castle. *She must be in the next one, then.*

"I can't tell if I'm very drunk or if you're just walking really fast." The bard wipes his forehead and lunges forward with each step. "Is there something I can help you with?"

I throw my body against the door frame of an open room and look in. Nothing. She's nowhere to be found.

"Braizen?"

Finally, I turn towards him and throw my hands on his shoulders. "You want to help me? Go find me a bow and arrows—and fast. If you see Idalia, tell her I'm looking for her."

He winces at my barked orders but then smiles and claps his hands. "A mission! Just like a *real* bandit." He raises a stiff hand to his brow and salutes me. "You got it, Prince Man. I won't let you down!" He quickly pivots and scurries down the hall.

I roll my eyes and continue my search. I'm at the second to the last door on the right side of the corridor, about to lose my mind, when I shove it open with my shoulder.

Theodore stands at the foot of a bed, the red dress hanging around her waist, her bare breasts revealed to me. She doesn't try to cover them.

I slap my hands over my eyes. "Lady and Guard, Theodore. I'm so sorry. I had no idea this was your room. I was looking for, I mean, I *am* looking for Idalia. Have you seen her? Oh, gods, I saw your breasts. I saw them, and they're really nice. I'm sorry."

She laughs, and I hear a loud tsk. "You've always had a knack for opening doors you weren't supposed to," she says.

My chest rises and falls as I sort through my emotions. *Tonight is not my night.*

"I think I saw her in the square just before your singing friend escorted me home. She said she was looking for Lachlan, and I told her I didn't know where he was. She's probably still in the town, looking for him. I'll have guards retrieve her at once if it bothers you that she's out there alone."

Though they're still behind my palm, I squeeze my eyes harder and nod. "Yes, I have something important to tell her. I'd be very grateful if you could send them to find her."

"I will. As soon as I finish dressing, I'll send out the order."

"Great. Thank you. Um, well, goodnight then, Theodore. I'll see you tomorrow. Fully dressed, of course! Not that I would mind you not being fully dressed–Uh, goodnight!" I fumble blindly, searching for the doorknob until it's within my grasp, and close the door. When I hear the click of safety, I lower my hand and force myself to breathe evenly.

"Now, off to pretend like that never happened," I whisper to myself as I retreat. I'm halfway back up the corridor when I hear a door open behind me.

"Braizen," Theodore calls.

A nervous wave etches itself across my abdomen. I stop in my tracks but don't dare face her.

"I'm dressed now; you can turn around."

My lips depress into a line, and ever so slowly, I turn.

She's leaning against the doorframe, dressed in a silken, creamy nightgown. She smiles coyly.

"I think it's time you do me that favor."

My mouth drops open, and I bob my head. What else am I to do while I wait for Idalia besides drink myself stupid or walk in on Aunt Deria in a similar undressed state?

"Sure," I say and resign myself to the night's surprises. "I think that's more than fair."

Theodore leads me into a vast bedchamber. Fireplaces are carved into the north and west walls, and giant, arched windows line the rest. An enormous dark wood, four poster bed, its canopy swathed in white cloth that sweeps to the floor, rests against the east wall.

I rest my hands on my hips and gaze at Salvas, connected by gold branches, painted as part of a fantastic mural. "Is this Lachlan's room?" I ask, noting that the chamber is bigger than even my father's.

Theodore only shakes her head in response; her eyes are fixed on the marble floor. She's looking for something. "This was my father's room," she finally answers.

I let out a low whistle. Lester, for all his many faults, had good taste. A shock indeed.

"Neither Lach nor I wanted this chamber after he died. He was a wicked and cruel man, especially to my brother. We'd have this room burned if it wouldn't harm the rest of our home."

"Yes, I do remember him being exceptionally unpleasant."

"You don't know the half of it," she scoffs.

I can't imagine how dreadful Lester was behind closed doors. I shake my head, remembering their father. Lachlan's nervous disposition undoubtedly springs from Lester's mistreatment. I snap out of my memories and turn my attention back to her.

"So, what exactly are we doing in here?" I say briskly. "Do you want me to try and burn it down or deface some of these hideous portraits?"

She snaps her fingers and gestures for me to move closer. She points down. "There," she says. "Just by the crack in the stone. Do you see?"

I lean forward and squint; I can just make out a slight crevice. "So, the floor has cracked. Really, Theodore, all castles age."

"Watch, will you?!" She hisses and drops to her knees. Reaching into a pocket, she pulls out a curved pin connected to a length of fine wire. She slides the pin into the crack, and it clanks softly against something metal.

"What is that?" I whisper and wonder if Lester's ghost haunts us at this very moment.

She doesn't respond, only lowers herself further towards the floor and keeps fishing for whatever lies beneath.

"Almost have it," she says between gritted teeth. "There!" She gathers the fine wire until a small key appears. She jumps to her feet and bounces onto the bed. Balancing on the pillows, she pushes the key into the frame of a portrait. Besides watching her succeed in whatever plan she's concocted, I've no idea why I'm here. A click, and the entire portrait gently swings away from the wall.

"Remember when I asked if you still picked locks?"

"Yes, but it seems you don't need me to. You have the key."

"Wrong. I have one key. I need two. My father was a very secretive man." She pushes the frame back further, and I see a safe built into the wall. A gold lock seals its hasp shut.

"What in the Guard's name…" I murmur as I climb on the bed. "A double-locked safe? What's hiding in there?"

Theodore flings herself onto the mattress and crosses her ankles. "Triple-locked, technically," she says. "First, I had to find the key to his room, then the key to the portrait."

"Why don't we look for the third key?" I ask, fiddling with the metal. "This looks like no easy task."

"I know it isn't. I've tried many times myself. As for the third key, my father had it buried with him. So, unless you want to go to the guard-infested King's cemetery and unearth my father's corpse, this is our only chance."

"Only chance for what?" I ask, still contemplating just how hard this lock will be to pick.

"To get what I need," she says. "My whole life, I've spent my days reading, researching, and making things. While he was alive, Lester only allowed me to read certain books. But after he died, I could access the entire library. I've had endless days of studying, sleepless nights of creating…Then I realized that I had every text except one."

"One?" I ask, looking down.

"I've studied the inventory, and there's only one book missing. I've scoured the entire castle and can't find it. Lester took it, kept me from reading it, and put it in there," she says and gestures to the safe.

"Must be a dangerous book if he went so far as to be buried with the key."

"Knowledge is deemed dangerous by the wicked. They don't want those beneath them to learn too much because wisdom threatens power."

"So, whatever's in this book is that important to you, huh? Well, I'll try my best. Give me that pin." She hands it to me and settles her back against the bed frame.

"I keep journals, you know. I write down everything I find and then study it. I've even written a few books myself."

"Is that so?" I slowly push the pin into the keyhole.

"It is. I've written much on the First Prophet, and I have an entire thesis on the Salva plant and its true nature."

"Uh huh," I acknowledge, hardly paying attention; my total concentration is centered on the blasted lock.

"Two weeks ago, we hosted a dinner for nobles. Afterward, I looked for a particular journal, but it was gone. Stolen from my very chamber."

"That's awful, even to me, a bandit who enjoys stealing. A private chamber is completely off-limits! Unless the person is dead and buried with the key, of course."

She ignores my joke.

"It was an entire book of notes dedicated to Devil's Mirages and The Pass in Verdana. Ever heard of it?"

Frustrated, I huff and shift the pin in different patterns one after the other, but to no avail. "The Mirages, yes. The Pass? Never," I answer absently.

Theodore can barely contain her excitement. "Supposedly, there's a narrow channel between the Verdanian mountains that leads towards Osinea. I've asked a few people, but no one has ever heard of it. But it's there. I know it is. And now someone else does, too. I asked Idalia–"

There is a strange pull in my hands at the sound of her name. Tiny sparks shoot through them as I picture the pain that i'll see in her stare after I tell her the truth. That Lachlan has no intention of marrying her. The truth about her father, that he…

Click.

"*No gods damn way,*" I breathe as the lock unhitches.

Theodore jolts up on the mattress, steadying her hands on my shoulders to stare at my victory. The rusty hasp creaks as I gently test it, then face the Aeradian Princess. "The pleasure is all yours," I say gallantly and motion to the safe.

She kisses my cheek, gives a small squeal, then takes a deep breath. She pulls the door fully open, and we gaze in. An ancient, wrinkled volume rests amid the dust swirls that arose when she opened the door. Some of its fragile, disheveled pages slip away from their binding as she lifts the book. Carefully she brings it to her nose and takes a few sharp breaths. "Can you smell that?"

"Dirt?" I ask, jumping to the floor.

"*Knowledge,*" she muses with a childlike grin. "There's so much for you to teach me," she whispers and then sinks onto the bed. With another deep inhale, she opens the book to the first page.

I cross my arms and smile. "Well, if that's all you need from me, I'll get going. Don't forget to send the guards. Let me know when Idalia is back, would you?"

"Oh, Braizen! Wait!" She stretches an arm towards me. "Didn't I tell you I'd give you a favor in return?"

"I thought sending the guards for Idalia *was* the favor. If not that, then you know," I tease as I wave my hands vaguely across my chest, "walking in on you could also count."

"Men are truly disgusting," she sighs, scrunching her nose. "But no, the guards are not your favor. I want Idalia safe, too. Sending them is more for her sake than yours. And as for the view," she mimics my hand waving, "consider that a blessing from the gods."

I laugh and nod in approval.

"My favor is far more consequential to you," she says hesitantly.

"What is it? Are you going to make Stig's voice bearable?"

Her face is serious as she leans forward and drills her eyes into mine.

"I think I know a way you and Idalia can break the curse."

Chapter Thirty-Five

Idalia

"I'll have you know, in Verdana, forcing a Princess to stop drinking is considered punishable by death! How else are we to keep warm in the snow?" I squirm between the two Aeradian guards' grasp as they drag me into the castle's guest wing. I glimpse Stig, who's carrying an Aeradian quiver. When he sees me, his eyes light up, but he continues to sprint down the corridor. "Who in the hells is letting him stay here?" I demand of the guards. "You know that stranger swindled one of your farmers out of his horses! Yet, he gets better treatment than I do!" I humph as they toss me into my room.

"Apologies, Your Highness, but our orders are from Princess Theodore. The Aeradian festival can get a little rowdy after midnight; it's in your best interest to stay here," the older guard says.

"I was looking for the King, you peons!" I cross my arms and scowl.

"King Lachlan is asleep in his bed. Your search would've been meaningless, Your Highness. Please get some rest," he says as he leaves the room. At the door, he turns and stiffly reenters. "Also, Princess Theodore asked that I give you this. She said it will stifle any lasting effects of alcohol." He hands me a small vial containing a sparkling liquid within.

"What?" I pout. "I don't want the effects of my drinking to be gone; that's the whole point of drinking!" He shakes his head and laughs.

"For the morning, Your Highness. Trust me; we've all used it a time or two."

"Or twelve!" The other male shouts from the hallway. The door closes, and though I whine to myself, I begrudgingly unscrew the vial and drink the shimmering purple liquid. It tastes like sweet berries. Though the lovely haze of the alcohol cloud remains, my throbbing head does feel much better.

I pull the remaining pins from my hair and toss them on the dresser, where they almost land in the ivy growing in an Aeradian red pot. I wobble to the bed and fling myself onto it. I'd left my corset in the tavern cellar, and now the only thing between me and the fine linen sheets is a half-undone dress and my chemise. I yawn. *Tomorrow. I'll get ready for bed tomorrow.* My eyes close, and I drift into sleep.

The door slams, and I jerk up from my hard sleep, drool staining my pillow.

"Idalia."

I scowl, although a larger part of me swarms with embarrassment. "What do you want?" I hiss, pulling my knees to my chest.

Braizen's eyes flare. "I need you to listen to me, fully and without interruption. Before you say anything–"

"Excuse you?!" My entire body goes rigid. "You burst into *my* chamber without warning, wake me from my slumber, and now you assume you can make demands? I think not!"

"You don't understand–"

"I understand plenty," I retort. "We're enemies, remember? You said so yourself. Why should we act like anything different? Now, if you don't mind." I motion for him to leave.

"Sparrow," he says with bared teeth. "I *really* need you to listen."

"No, Braizen, I need *you* to listen! Go away!"

"Sparrow…" he tries, but I dismiss him again.

"Get out of here this instant, or I'll call for the guards."

"*Shut up, Idalia*! I'm trying to tell you that we can break this curse!"

I freeze. Have I gone mad? Did Teddy's elixir cause delusions? "What did you just say?"

He moves closer. "The curse. We think it can be broken."

"*We?*" I ask cautiously.

"I helped Theodore find this forbidden book, and in return, she gave me information. The Woman of the Woods, the prophet who can speak to the gods, can break the curse. Or at least, tell us how to."

I rub my forehead. Indeed, Teddy's tonic does produce a madness, albeit one where I don't suffer from headache or nausea.

"You and Teddy… found a book?"

He strides closer, stopping mere inches from the bed.

"Not just any book, Idalia. The book of all books, apparently. Theodore says it was written by the first people, or something like that. Though, that's not as great a concern to us. The Woman of the Woods knows all about the gods, Idalia. How to see them, how to communicate with them. If we can find her, we can–"

"You found a book?"

"If we find her," Braizen continues without a hitch, "We can learn how to speak to the gods ourselves. We can ask them to revoke the curse."

"Why would we want to revoke the curse?" I slowly tilt my head to face him.

Braizen lurches back, his eyes dark, the excitement on his face gone.

"I mean, does it matter now?" I ask. "You're setting off for The Wood, and I'm going to marry Lachlan. We don't need to touch or fear being too close. All Baellilean affairs can go through my husband. Truthfully, we needn't ever see each other again after I marry."

His jaw clenches. "Is that truly how you feel, Sparrow?" He asks quietly. I only nod in response, remembering how quickly he left me in that tavern.

He stands inhumanely still for a heartbeat, then says, "Fine. If that's really what you want, I'll leave you with your decision."

Heat streaks through my fingers as he walks towards the door.

"How dare you," I spit. He doesn't look back as I add, "That's the entire reason I'm here!"

His shoulders lift, and he gives a weak laugh. "Of course, it is. Whatever brings you happiness, Idalia." His voice is dry and cynical.

"Happiness? Is that why you think I was sent here? Is that why you think I'm marrying him? For my *happiness?* How ignorant can you be? I must marry him, Braizen. My Kingdom is dying! I haven't gone through all this just to smile and play someone's wife. My duty is to my people, and they *need* me to marry Lachlan!"

He's too quiet; his stiff back gives me no indication if he'll turn to face me. A sharp pain impales my chest, but I'll take the discomfort this time. The last I obeyed it, I was abandoned in a dingy cellar. I'll not be so foolish as to repeat my mistakes.

He reaches for the doorknob and takes a deep breath; his head lowered as if he's waiting for me to stop him. I do no such thing.

He leaves the room, and the door shuts behind him with a resounding thud.

"Good riddance," I sulk, lying back on the pillow. "Break the curse. Ha! As if anything is more powerful than the gods!" Heat flickers through my hands, and I shake them with a snide grunt. "Especially not some old woman hidden away in the woods. If she's even still alive! The Minea would've told me about her. Nuri would've seen her."

Another sizzle webs through my torrid palms as my thoughts race between the memories I saw when I held the Minea's hand. *The old woman, the younger girl...could that have been her?*

"Fine, maybe there *is* a Woman of the Woods. But they would've told me if they thought there was a way to break the curse."

My fierce headache returns. I need another Teddy tonic, and quick. "Besides, even if there is a way, what's the point? It's not like Braizen and I could ever be. Our Kingdoms are at war!" This time a severe pain rustles down my spine, and I yelp.

Go to him. Find him now.

"No." I counter the feeling and cross my arms. Anguish burns deep in my chest and prevents me from taking a satisfying breath. "Are you going to kill me if I don't obey? Is that what this is?" I wheeze as the pain travels up my neck and thumps against my skull.

A nasty headache that even Teddy's solution can't lessen. A headache just like the ones I saw my mother grapple with…I stop squirming.

I hold my throbbing head in my hands and slowly set my bare, dirty feet on the floor.

"You know, I'm growing quite exhausted from this." I complain to the phantom urge that compels me to run down the hall and find him. "What do you want from me? Why are you pushing me towards him?! Answer me if you want my obedience!"

Slowly, the ivy on the dresser begins to fidget. They are tiny movements, but I swear the ends of the sprouting vines turn golden and curl into a circle. I hear Nuri's words, and raging heat consumes my hands.

Above all, magic will try to preserve itself by protecting the world it lives in.

Go to him!

Without a second thought, I'm charging towards the door. I fling it open and nearly crash into him on the other side.

"Braizen!" His hand is poised to turn the knob, and he carefully returns it to his side. I pull my weight back onto my heels to prevent a collision.

"What are you doing?" He whispers, and there is hope in his confused stare.

"What does it look like, you jackass? I was coming to try and stop you from leaving."

His grin pulls to the right of his face. "I was coming to try and make you leave with me." Light is restored in his gaze.

"I guess you were right about something all along," I say. "Verdanians *are* fools. I'll go with you. I'll brave the Florian Wood again, track down a myth of a woman, and help look for our friends. Like any fool would." My headache subsides, and the pain in my hands is now only a soreness.

Braizen's body drifts forward, and his hands twitch. They battle the thought of embracing me now, damned the consequence. Instead, he offers a warm grin that wholly consumes me and then turns to flee down the hall.

"Braizen," I call out as rational thoughts flood me. He turns back immediately. "What if it doesn't work? What if the curse can't be broken?"

"It'll work, Idalia. It has to," he says, his smile full of comfort.

"But what if it *doesn't*?" I need him to answer the hypothetical; I need his reassurance.

He's only one step away when he lifts his hand and strokes the air lightly as if brushing my cheek. I can feel his hand. *I can feel him.* I cup my cheek atop his hand, even if it is only a figment of my imagination, and let his touch bring me peace.

"If we find the Woman of the Woods and discover that she can't help us, I won't care," he says gently. "We would've tried everything, and we would've tried together. That's all that matters to me."

"Then what?" I sniffle, pressing my cheek harder into my hand–*his* hand. Tears fill my eyes, and I long to fall into his arms and sob until I'm drained.

"Then we find our friends and come back to Aeradian. We'll live on a farm and watch Lorna herd cattle and mock her every step of the way. We'll get Lin a job at a shop and take bets on how long it'll take for him to argue with a customer. Or maybe we'll travel with Stig as a singing group. Torrent has a wonderful voice; we'd just have to convince the bard to shut up if we want to make any coin. Or *you* could sing. I heard you in the woods. Your voice is mesmerizing."

I blush, then laugh as I envision Lorna trying to herd cattle. It's one vision I'd certainly love to one day turn into reality. But my heart still thuds, a slamming fist trying to break down a door of steel.

"What about us?" I ask quietly, somehow feeling both embarrassed and frightened. I sense his hand under my chin, tilting it up to meet his stare.

"Little Sparrow," he muses with a gleam in his eyes. "You needn't worry when it comes to us. I'll take care of you. Whether it's a malevolent mist that comes after you or a bad day where all you need is to laugh, I'll be there. I'll be whatever it is you need me to be."

"But we won't be able to touch Braizen, not ever. How will you manage? I've heard what women say about you, the stories about what kind of lover you are. I don't want—I *wouldn't* take that away from you."

"I think we've already discovered how that can be managed," he smirks and flutters his long dark lashes.

"Maybe," I concede. "But other forms of touch are just as important, and you'll be robbed of them all by choosing me. Your fate will be a lonely and grim one."

"My fate has already been chosen for me, Idalia. The day I laid eyes on you, it was sealed, and I was yours. Wholly and true. I don't need to touch you to know that I love—" His hand drops to his side, and he lets out a shaky laugh.

"You also have to choose me," he continues. "I'm not the only one who'll sacrifice. You'll never feel an intimate touch or be able to have children. We both must consider the price we're willing to pay if this doesn't work."

My heart sinks. I've never given much thought to being a mother, but to have the option stripped away before I've had a chance to consider it hurts more than I could've imagined. I won't have a lover I can kiss or hold hands with, and neither will he. I swallow hard.

"If it doesn't work, we'll focus on finding our friends. Once we know they're safe, we'll return to our homes. Separately," I say.

"No."

"Yes, Braizen. I need you to promise me this. You cannot live a life without touch."

"I can and I will."

"Then it's I who can't!" I look away, my eyes brimming with tears. A wall of shame slams into my chest. I am being selfish and cruel, but the truth remains. A life without being held by him, a life without feeling his lips against mine would be torture.

I hear him release a deep quiet breath. "If you *need* to be touched, Idalia, if that's your requirement," he says softly, "then no matter what happens in The Wood, I'll oblige you."

I shoot my gaze back to his, but he continues before I can ask what he means.

"I will touch you as much as you will let me. As I said before, I'll be whatever you need me to be."

"Braizen, no. We would *die*! Our entire Kingdoms would fall!" I turn and face the room. "Surely you don't believe that a single touch is worth all of that!"

"I do," he cuts in from behind me. "I'm starting to believe it's worth every gods damn flame, every crumbling stone, and rotting vine."

My breath is shallow and uneven as I hear him step closer.

"Idalia, I haven't been able to sleep in these last few days. I'm kept awake by the thought of you, of your skin. Jealous of the hair that drapes over your shoulders. Envious of the wind and how often it wraps itself around you. I would choose death—*gladly* choose death—if only to touch you. Just once. To hold your cheek. And trace your lips. To drag my tongue over every single part of you. Because if you really want to know what I believe, it's that a life of being robbed of your skin against mine for even a second longer is a fate far worse than death. To not have you by my side, a misery far worse than the grave."

His breath is warm on my nape, and I feel heat around my hips. His hands hover there, mere inches away from me. For a suspended moment, I feel them holding me. How do I always feel him? He's waiting for my response. Slowly, I turn and lift my chin.

"So, we are both fools then." I say softly.

The stare from his ice-blue eyes is a tidal wave sweeping over a helpless city, and I stand on the shore, knowing I can only watch as it folds over and carries me away. Our breaths meet in the tight space between us, and I know I should be fighting with every fiber of my being not to feel this way.

I know to be near him, to desire his closeness, is to choose death. But when he looks at me like this, time slows. My heartbeat quickens, and tears threaten to spill down my cheeks. My limbs burn; the truth lingering in the back of my throat thrashes and begs to be spoken aloud.

To be with him is to die. But to be without him is no way to live.

Chapter Thirty-Six

Braizen

I've spent most of my life wandering Baelliles' forests. I've scoured beneath trees and observed all forms of life. But I've never witnessed anything as precious as the Little Sparrow. I feel her warm spirit reaching out to me. I want to snatch it, and I would…I would hold it close to me if I could. But this is not her gentle way. She would not risk the lives of our Kingdoms, nor would she risk my beating heart.

She draws closer, the weight of the world separated by only a breath. I know the risk of her standing so close to me; I've considered it hundreds of times in the last week alone. But gods know, and kingdoms be damned, if she ever looks at me like this again, I won't hesitate. I'll spend eternity in the four hells begging for my people's forgiveness if only to have her in my arms for a second. To comfort her, protect her, and love her into our shared, accursed deaths.

"Where's Teddy?"

Her question breaks the tension, and I can finally breathe again. I stutter for a second before answering.

"Back in her room. She's studying the book we found."

"We shouldn't bother her then. Have you put together any travel supplies?"

"I have two knapsacks full of food and a fresh change of clothes. Even found some Aeradian cloaks to keep us warm."

"We'll need a bar of soap, as well. Actually, make it two."

As I watch her calculate what else we may need, I smile. She reminds me of Lin, always thinking ahead for the good of our band. "We'll get soap. I'll have Stig bring me some more arrows, and we'll supply you with a dagger. No one will be unarmed," I assure her.

"I have my magic too," she says, then stiffens as if the words involuntarily flew out of her mouth.

"That you do." With that, I turn to stride down the corridor.

"Braizen," she says weakly. "I should explain to Lachlan. I can't just leave without telling him why. He deserves to know; he's lost so much already."

Her gentle way. My heart fractures into small pieces. "He knows," I lie, knowing I can't bear seeing her face if I tell her the truth. "Theodore already told him. She assumed you'd accompany me on the journey. She has a great intuition, that one."

"Oh?" She fidgets with her fingers. "Did she say how he took the news?"

I hate that I can lie so well. Years of swindling wealthy nobles means I can do it with ease. I now vow to use this skill to protect her heart, not wound it.

"She said he only wants your happiness. He only ever wants people's happiness." That part isn't much of a lie; Lach *is* the generous King.

"I suppose that's true," she agrees quietly. "Then it's settled. We'll find a few extra supplies and set off for The Wood."

"I'll get them; you wait here," I instruct.

She looks as if she'll agree, then squints, thinking again.

"Better yet, I'll change my clothes and then find a jar of Aunt Deria's special breakfast drink. We'll most certainly need that."

"Good call." We laugh a bit before I see her frown.

"What if…" She swallows hard. "What if we die out there? Before we find the Woman of the Woods? Before we find Torr and Lin and Lorna?"

A valid question. One I've known the answer to for a long time.

"You were right in the tavern when you called me a coward," I say. She opens her mouth to intervene, but it's vital I say this, so I quickly resume.

"I *have* been a coward, Sparrow. For a while now. For as long as I can remember, I've run from my destiny to be a King. I've lived in fear of my father's expectations. I've visited my mother in secret, pouring gifts and money on her as if they'd make up for lost time or heal her troubled heart. I got involved in Torrent's and Lin's affairs, and eventually, Lorna's, too, because I wanted to live apart from my world forever. And for a time, it worked. I was free of responsibility, and I found a new family to share my life with. The crown grew smaller and smaller in my mind." I pause for a moment, shaking my head at how I'd honestly believed I could outrun who I am.

"When I saw you again, that all changed. Everything changed. Even after all these years, in my heart, it was like only a day had gone by. You were the same Little Sparrow. The one who'd punch a boy in the face for name-calling and break the rules for a laugh. It scared me. Terrified me, really. And so, like the coward I've always been, I hid. But I'm so tired of hiding, Idalia. I can't do it anymore."

A lone tear slips down her cheek. Oh, to be able to wipe it away. What I'd give to wipe away every tear she'll ever cry. I finish softly.

"I'm prepared to lose my life in that Wood as long as you're by my side. It's better to die together than to live apart."

Chapter Thirty-Seven

Idalia

Stepping over the invisible line that separates The Wood from Aeradian is a very foolish thing to do. We should be smart and contemplate all the horrors we'd already faced. But time has a funny way of making us forget.

"Are you ready, Little Sparrow?" Braizen's question cuts through my thoughts.

I've just enough resolve left to smile. "After you."

I motion him across the threshold. His boot strikes the Florian path, and just like that, we are back in the hell we'd barely escaped.

Night draws near; the speckled sunlight wanes above the dense tree canopy. Braizen walks ahead and holds his bow ready at his side. I turn my palms out, unsure of what I can do if trouble appears, but nonetheless, I'm prepared.

"Do you remember where Idizina is?" I ask, fear rising as the path ahead of us grows dark.

Without looking away from his scrutiny of the forest, he shakes his head. "The landscape leading to Idizina changes each time a person leaves," he says and readjusts the quiver strap over his shoulder. "Nuri told me when I took you to Aeradian. But I remember where that old cottage is."

"Good, we should rest there." I release a relieved breath and ignore the cold wind slapping against my face. "It's nice to know that your banditry hasn't been for nothing; at least you learned how to track."

"Among a great many other things. What about you? Any other skills I should know about?" He tugs his cloak closer against the wind.

I shiver and brush cold strands of hair from my face. "Other than restoring someone's torn-off arm? No, none I can think of."

His bellowing laugh echoes through the trees.

"Not a bad trick. Not a bad trick at all."

"I don't understand," Braizen huffs as he paces in a circle. The moon is our only light source, and the air holds a frosty sting. "It was here. Right here! I'm sure of it. Don't you remember these trees?"

"I'm afraid I wasn't paying much attention to my surroundings last time," I admit.

"I swear it, Sparrow." He curses and points. "Right there, see how the trees form a circle around us? The cottage was right here, at the center!"

The grove does seem to encircle the open space we stand in. The area may have once held a structure. But there's nothing here besides a mound of dirt.

"Braizen, it's dark. Likely you didn't remember exactly where it—"

"No," he interrupts. "I'm not mistaken. I may be an ardent, insufferable buffoon at times, but my memory serves me well, especially in the woods! The cottage should be exactly where we stand."

The wind wails around us, and I shudder. "Well, where the cottage may or may not be doesn't matter. It's night, The Wood is awake, and I'm freezing! We need to find somewhere to sleep."

Braizen strokes his chin and then stomps around the clearing picking up small branches.

"What are you doing?"

"Making a fire," he answers without looking up. He continues his collecting.

"You can't! You know what will happen if we give away our position!"

He ignores me and grabs handfuls of dried leaves.

"Braizen, stop! If we light a fire, The Others could come!" Still, nothing. I grab a small rock and chuck it at him. When it hits his arm, he jerks up and stares at me.

"Last time, we didn't have a fire, and The Others still found us!" he barks. "I won't let you freeze to death, so let them come and do what they will. This is what we signed up for, remember?"

I rub my numb hands together and scowl. "You're so stubborn. Once we break this curse, I'm going to wring your neck!"

His face is the perfect picture of calm as he trots along his course. It's as if I've said nothing! I plop onto the dirt and twigs and hug myself for warmth as Braizen starts a fire.

"So, then Torr walks up to the woman and tells her that what Lin lacks in height, he makes up for in size somewhere else!" Braizen howls, splashing some of Deria's special mix on the ground.

"I'm sure Lin *loved* Torr trying to set him up! Does he do it often?"

Braizen rocks his body towards the small fire to warm his hands. "Absolutely! Torrent is the biggest believer in true love. He's tried to fix Lin up with just about every person imaginable. Even Lorna when we first met her! Poor lad does *not* pick up on things fast."

We laugh some more until I stop to produce a wide yawn.

"Sleep, Sparrow," Braizen says with a smile. "I'll wake you when it's your turn to keep watch."

I want to resist the offer, but my eyelids are so heavy I can barely focus. I didn't sleep much after the Aeradian festival, and after trekking all day, I'm exhausted. Before I can say goodnight, a thick slumber comes to overtake me. Through my blurred vision, I watch our fire's timid flickers. As sleep fully pulls me in, I see a woman framed between the trees that stretch into the night. She watches me.

A dream, I'm sure.

"My sweet Idalia."

My eyes open slowly, and I'm blinded by the bright morning sun that sneaks through the cracks between the tree boughs. I stretch and yawn to shake off the grogginess and see that our fire is now only burned wood and embers.

"Braizen?" All that remains is a small divot from where he had sat last night.

"Braizen!" I jump to my feet. What horror swept him up during the night, my poor boy from the aviary?!

"Braizen!" My cry pierces the wind with a shriek so urgent the gods must have heard it.

"Idalia, I'm here."

I jerk around to see the bandit bounding down a small slope and holding our water skins. "I only went to fill these. After last night, I needed water," he says.

I could slap him and tell him to never scare me like that again. I could kiss him and thank the Lady that he still lives.

"Why didn't you wake me for a watch? I slept through the night!"

"You looked like you needed the rest. I couldn't bear to wake you," he says with a nonchalant shrug.

"You mean you stayed up the entire night?! Are you mad?"

Tossing me my water, he chuckles. "Blame Aunt Deria! Whatever she puts in that breakfast special is powerful! I couldn't sleep even if I wanted to!"

I'm not amused, and I roll my eyes.

"There's a river, just a few meters over that hill if you want to bathe," he says, skillfully changing the subject. "I can sleep while you wash up. Unless, of course, you'd rather me watch you."

I scowl at him and swat away his idiotic proposition.

"Sleep it is then," he says with a smirk.

I wait until he dozes before I set off. Mumbling, I weave through the crowded trees and down the slope towards the sound of flowing water.

What an absolute clod! Letting me slumber through the night, and now he's sleeping when daylight is the safest time to travel? The water's rush grows louder as I approach, and the stale, pungent smell of mildew coats my nostrils. I swear under my breath as I step onto the narrow rocky riverbank and remove my boots. A quiet breeze tickles my ears, and I relax as I listen to the water burble past me.

"*My sweet Idalia...*"

I clutch the vermillion cloak around me. Are the trees playing tricks? I can't be sure in this Wood.

"Idalia." The voice is louder, and I freeze. I recognize it. My teeth begin to chatter as I scan my surroundings.

"Who goes there?" I release one hand and point my palm outwards. "Are you a Keeper of the Dark?" Only after I ask the question do I realize its ignorance.

"My sweet," it breathes again. "My sweet Idalia, can you hear me?"

I shuffle in a tight circle, almost tripping over my own feet as I gaze up and around me. I know this voice. I'd know it anywhere.

"Mother?" I cower behind my raised hands as the river rushes faster. Its surface ripples are gathering and forming a shape. I would scream, I should scream, but my mother's voice calls to me once more.

"Sweet Idalia," she says. "I am here now. Believe in me, and I will come to you."

I wait for my hands, or my limbs or even my gods forsaken head to give me a signal. For the almost now familiar discomfort and pain that will tell me what to do. But there's no heat, and my hands are cold as I watch the water move and grow into a tall, translucent figure. A shadow of a form I once knew so well.

"Can you hear me, my strong and brave daughter? I do not have much time!"

My heart pounds. Disbelief wanes in my chest, and a flood of sorrow fills its place.

"Mother! It's you!" My throat spasms, and I hold one hand against it. It can't be...How can it be?!

"Yes, my sweet Idalia!" She cries, and the transparent figure grows clearer. Revna Hyland, my mother! She hovers above the river in a watery form. Below her waist, the water rushes back into the river's flow, so her skirts swirl as if they're made of a furious storm at sea. She extends her arms.

"Mother! My gods! Mother, is it truly you?" I fall to my knees, tears soaking my cheeks. I'm distraught. I'm excited. I'm *ashamed.* What will she think of me?

"It is."

"How can it be?" I sob, unable to look at her.

"You are realizing your power," she says. Her distinct voice makes me weaker by the second. "The power of the Hyland women. I am here now, and I have been with you all along."

"I'm so sorry, Mother! I never visited your grave. I never left you flowers or said a prayer for you. I never glanced your way the entire ride home. Forgive me. Forgive me and my weakness. I'm a coward!" I wail with the guilt that has plagued me for all of these years.

"Idalia…"

"No, Mother. It's true! I see body after body dragged to The Burial, and I've never visited one grave. I'm too…too haunted by yours. I just couldn't."

The rapid waters quieten, and I hear her light, soft hum. Her beautiful singing. Immediately, my body is at ease.

"I do not hold you at fault, Idalia. You were a child when I died; you were not properly taught how to deal with grief. And you were never shown how powerful spite could be. It is not your mistake, my beautiful child. It is my own. For leaving you too soon."

I sob into my hands as I rise to meet her. *My mother.*

Her lithe frame and gentle face, her eyes—The same ones that visit my dreams so often, though I still cannot make out their color.

"I can't believe that I can see you. The Lady has blessed me!"

She smiles at me. "The Lady has indeed blessed us, but I am only here for a short time. I have come to warn you, Idalia!"

I step forward until I feel the icy water flow across my toes. "Warn me about what?"

"*Him*," she says. Her brow knits, and her faded eyes narrow. "The traitor you are with."

"Braizen?" I stumble back in confusion, and her body swirls towards me, though it stays a good distance from where I stand.

"Yes, Braizen, of the Brader line. The Traitorous Prince."

"No, Mother! It isn't like that anymore. I know him now. Though he was once an enemy to Verdana, he isn't any longer! We're here, *together*, searching for the Woman of the Woods. Do you know of her?"

"The First Prophet? She has been dead for over half a century!" Water spatters violently as my mother scoffs at my question.

My heart drops into my stomach.

"I must tell Braizen. We're here on the small chance she could tell us how to break the curse."

"*He lies!*" My mother swings her fist down and raises a wall of water. It collides into the river hard enough to spray droplets around me on the stones.

"He knows that she is dead! He knows there is no way to break the curse! He has tricked you into coming here, don't you see?"

"No, Mother! You don't understand. Braizen and I…we're…Well, the way we feel about each other…He wouldn't lie!"

"You poor girl." Her rippling eyes drill into mine. "The Braders are ruby-covered snakes. He has lied to you, and now you will suffer for it. Unless you leave at once!"

I don't understand. I look up at her, my heart fraught with colliding emotions.

"Do you see, my sweet Idalia? He has ensnared you with his charm and coaxed you with his deceit to bring you here! He has used your heart against you!"

No! It can't be true. She can't know what she speaks of.

"Braizen led me to Aeradian, Mother! He would've allowed me to marry Lachlan. It was *my* choice that brought me back here. If the Woman of the Woods doesn't exist, if what you say is true, I must tell him. We'll return to Aeradian together and live out our lives there…happily," I struggle through the sentence, still an embarrassed child yearning for her mother's acceptance.

"Together!" There's a small moment of silence before the water rages again, and a heinous laugh leaves her lips.

"You poor, insolent child. I did not realize the magnitude of your father's failure until now." Fear snakes up my spine as she ascends, towering above the river. She points a stiff finger at me.

"How easily you have been swayed towards the enemy, like a sheep drawn to a wolf. He has swindled you, just as he has many before you! The Braders seek to be your undoing, and he is succeeding! He took you to Aeradian so that he could write to his father and ask for more men! While you slept through the night, he led his father's troops straight to their prize. They have come for you, Idalia!"

"He wouldn't do that."

"Ha!" My mother scoffs from far above me. "Look for yourself; then you will know! Just there beyond those trees!" She snaps her finger towards the east.

The distant trees bend and break on her command, creating a clear path for me to see, if only for a moment.

The moment is more than enough. I see the sigil of the Baellilean Kingdom blow in the wind. A camp of men in green, sheathing their swords and awaiting orders.

"It can't be," I whisper. "Braizen wouldn't…"

"He would, and he has." My mother's voice echoes across the water. Her hands reach towards me.

"I am glad you have realized your power in full so that I could appear to you and help you see his betrayal. You must end the Brader line and, in doing so, end this war between us. Do not fall victim to their fraud as I did. Be vigilant. Destroy them before they destroy you!"

I pant. My heart races. I realize I may very well have fallen prey to Brader lies. But I also know The Wood. I know it can play tricks on me.

"Mother. Will you answer one more question?"

Her stare is a stern one. "Yes. But be quick about it. I have only a short time left with you! My power is diminishing."

"What did you used to do every night before I went to sleep?" I am confident that only my mother would know the answer.

She blinks and sends me a warm smile.

"Why, I used to sing to you, my child. Every night before bed. For that is the Hyland way."

I let out a relieved breath. It *is* my mother.

"Yes," I grin weakly. "That's exactly right."

The waves start to slap over each other, and her face grows worried.

"Idalia, you must go! Flee The Wood and never return or end the Brader line now." She is quickly fading, but I hear her final words: "For that is your fate, Idalia."

There is a large ripple, and she is gone. Again.

I trudge up the rise back to our camp. His men aren't far away; I must quickly decide whether to flee or kill. My hands answer with a swarm of scalding heat. I won't be another Hyland victim. I won't let another Brader win.

To kill, then.

Chapter Thirty-Eight

Braizen

A tickle at the base of my throat wakes me. I feel as though I just closed my eyes. Annoyed, I grunt, hoping to scare away whatever insect has landed on me. The tickle morphs into a sharp prick at my jugular, an all too familiar sensation in my line of work. Tensing my muscles, I fling open my eyes.

"Don't move," she snarls.

Her heavy, disheveled curls almost cloak her face, but I see enough. Her feet are planted firmly near my head, and she holds one of my arrows stiffly, pressing its tip ever so slightly further into my neck.

"What are you doing, Sparrow?" I ask quietly.

"Moving your traitorous mouth counts too, Baellilean. I won't warn you a third time."

My breath hitches as I watch her stare grow malevolent.

"I should've known," she spits. Her chest heaves as she takes in shallow breaths.

I part my lips to speak, and the arrow digs deeper. "That tongue is done spilling lies, Brader!" Her ferocious hiss is barely human. "I'm done being your pawn in this stupid, little game. It ends now."

Any further, and she'll break through skin. I study her frantic eyes, no longer those of a fawn gazing across a green meadow. They are now those of a huntress, and she'll stop at nothing to claim her kill. The barb drives deeper, deeper…

I grab the arrow, yank it away, and roll forward in one swift motion. Idalia tumbles face first, landing in my place.

Already on my feet, I look to where I'd left my bow and other arrows; they're gone. Now I point the arrow down at her. She groans, throwing her heavy cloak away from her legs and swipes some of the hair from her face. I swear I hear her growl; her face is tight with fury.

"What is this?!" I ask loudly. "What are you doing, Idalia? Has The Wood driven you mad so quickly?"

She spits and scrambles away from me on her hands and feet.

"Stop moving! Tell me what's happened! Have the woods possessed you, Sparrow?"

Her hair covers her face, but whimpers escape the thick strands that do their best to shield her.

"Answer me, Idalia!" I yell, walking closer. "Have the trees poisoned your mind?"

"The only thing that has poisoned my mind is you!" She shrieks, but I hear her choke on the words. *She's crying.*

"Look at me, Idalia! Look at me and explain what you mean!"

"You won," she says. She drops her face into her hands and sobs. Her muffled cries soon fill the air around us.

"Baelliles has won. Please, kill me now. Don't take me to him!" Her eyes are swollen, and her fragile face crumples in defeat.

I throw the arrow as far as I can and fall to my knees before her.

"Idalia, talk to me. What's wrong? What are you saying?"

"It's too late," she mumbles. "It's too late for me to run."

Anger rolls through me like a wave gaining traction in a storm.

"Talk to me, damnit! What's going on?"

Her wet lashes stick together, but her stare still pierces me. She wipes her hand across her nose.

"How could you do it, Braizen? Before they come, tell me. How could you!? Was it all a lie!"

The Florian Wood has her mind in a terrible hold, this much I know for sure. I shuffle towards her, and her sobs grow louder.

"Just kill me, please." Her words seem to be dragged out of her throat. "Kill me before they get here."

"Before who gets here?" I whisper, my heart breaking as I watch her mind crumble under whatever evil spell has been cast upon her.

"Idalia, who's coming?"

She rolls her neck, a guttural noise erupts from deep within her, and she hangs her head.

"I couldn't kill him. I couldn't…" she mutters.

Distorted voices echo a short distance away. I whip around to find their source and hear more voices, clearer now, and the clomp of hooves against dirt.

"Everyone has it wrong. It's Baellileans who are made of ice," she says, choking on her spit.

Glimpses of my Kingdom's flag ripple between the trees; armor gleams in the morning light. I stand as Baellilean troops break through the tree line. Horrick leads the way on a brown stallion. Following him are at least two dozen men and a cart pulled by a small mare.

"Prince Braizen," he calls, his chest puffed to make him appear more significant. As always, his attempt fails.

"Horrick!" I gasp. "What are you doing here?"

He smiles tightly and grips his reins. "I think that should be obvious. We've come to collect the girl."

"What?"

The skinny man lets out a weasel-like laugh and rests his hands on the pommel of his saddle. "Gods, if only you could grasp reality as quickly as you can catch birds!"

The men behind him snicker; Idalia continues to mumble under her breath.

"You are the future King of Baelliles, the sole heir to the throne!" Horrick continues. "The real question is, why are *you* here? After years of disappointing your father, have you come to capture the Verdanian yourself? Do you truly think this will make up for all your failures? King Vaskis would be mortified to find you out here, this close to the one who can bring down our entire Kingdom! Now, step aside and let us do what we came to do."

He angles his head towards two of the guards, who move forward.

I raise my clenched fists, and Horrick laughs again.

"Oh, please! Do you mean to punch our entire force away? Don't be a fool, Braizen. Move. Our business is no longer with you."

"No," I grind out. "I won't let you touch her."

"Not this again! Do you not remember what happened last time? It is the entire reason you cannot touch her now! Move, by order of your father, King Vaskis!"

Something rolls down my shoulders, veining through my limbs like fire catching a fuse. Lachlan's confusion over the marriage proposal rushes through my mind, and my stomach drops.

"Horrick," I say slowly, my eyes trained on the two guards. "Did my father write the letter?"

"Letter? What letter?" The man snorts.

"The one that brought her here, to The Wood." The odd sensation in my arms surges.

"How am I to know every piece of paper that leaves your father's hands? He is a King, Braizen. A King at war with the likes of the grotesque one behind you! Now move, or I will have no choice but to arrest you."

"Come any closer," I say quietly. "And I'll have no choice but to kill you."

Horrick's chin sinks into his chest.

"You threaten your countrymen to protect the crown's enemy? What does she hold over you that would possibly–" He stops mid-sentence and sighs with an exaggerated grimace. "I see… So, you have fallen for the Verdanian." His horse jolts back, and Horrick pulls the reins with a disgusted frown. "How pathetic, even for you."

He called my mother the same thing when he removed her from the castle.

"Honestly, Braizen, we thought you had sauntered off to fuck whores or gamble, the same as any young noble with too much responsibility! But *this?* Gods know if your father ever discovers the true reason you were gone, he will send you to that crazy bin with Eveline! Guards, seize her! Restrain the traitor! Do not let him touch her, or it will be all our deaths!"

A low snarl escapes my curled lip as the two guards steadily approach. The first man's gloved hand reaches to snatch me, but I dip to my haunches and easily dodge his grasp. The next clunks over and goes for his blade, but I grab a large branch and swing it up as I rise. Wood thuds against metal, and the guard topples back a few steps. I hear at least ten swords swish from their sheaths.

"Idalia," I hiss. "I need you to come back to me now!"

There's no answer, and when I glance back, she's still on the ground, crying.

"I couldn't kill him, Mother," she whimpers.

I groan as the first guard stomps toward me again. I kick with all my strength and shove him back a few feet.

"Idalia!" I shout, jumping to my right to avoid the large man's swing. "A little help!"

Another breathy grunt as I dart forward, charging the plated man's legs with all my weight. Even if I can bring him down and retrieve his sword, what then? There are twenty others, and Sparrow's mind is too far gone. Whatever happened while I slept has rendered her useless, a state she's never exhibited before.

I grapple with the guard for a moment, his armor inflicting pain each time I move my hand. The second guard creeps back, and a few more stand ready for Horrick's orders. There's no hope. I can't defeat them without her.

"Idalia!" I cry, knowing this is the last chance I have for her to join me.

Nothing.

Her sobs grow harder, and she cries out to her mother as if she's somewhere close.

Too many hands to count are now on me; they pull my arms rigid until I have no choice but to relent.

Horrick laughs and orders the guards to seize Idalia. Two rush her and easily haul her to her feet. She doesn't even try to fight. The Wood has defeated her, and it's all my fault.

"Princess Idalia of Verdana, I speak on behalf of King Vaskis and all Baellileans." Horrick's eyes cut to me. "Well, all but *one* at least, when I say you made your final mistake by passing into our territory. You are now a prisoner under Baellilean law, and you will meet your fate at His Majesty's command." He whistles, and the men drag her to the cart and toss her in. I wince as she lies lifelessly within it.

"I will kill you all for this," I grind out. "By the Lady and the Guard, I swear it."

Horrick's thin face pulls tight, and he nods his head to one of the guards who hold me. A fist lays into my cheek, and I spit out blood and saliva.

"We are not supposed to swear to the gods, boy. How dare you."

In the cart, Idalia's body moves.

"Nonetheless," Horrick continues, turning his horse to leave. "You'll have plenty of time to pray for their forgiveness as you wander The Wood alone."

He makes a clicking noise, and the soldiers shift to retrace their route. "Your father always said you were one for the trees. If you can survive them now, you'll have earned the right to come home. Of course, by then, your precious Verdanian will be long dead."

Idalia's face rises above the side of the cart.

"Braizen?"

I lunge forward. Horrick makes another clicking sound, and my arms feel like they're being ripped from my body. The larger guard grabs the thick branch I'd tossed aside earlier. His beady brown eyes gleam through the thin holes in his helmet as he smashes the branch against the back of my head.

"Braizen!" I hear her scream before darkness floods my vision.

Chapter Thirty-Nine

Braizen

The last time I visited my mother, she sat, as always, facing the single stained glass window in her room. I coaxed her to eat the cakes I'd stolen in Treden, a bustling town known for two things and two things only: outstanding bakeries and even better brothels.

With shaking hands and trembling lips, she refused the food. The nurses I pay to care for her told me that she'd barely eaten in days, and often she wouldn't even drink water; they usually had to force it down her throat. The acrid smell of ammonia penetrated the room; she regularly soiled herself in the chair she rarely moved from.

I was young when the curse happened, but I recall the smell of death and carnage that permeated our castle for years. My father never allowed the blood-stained marble floors to be replaced; he wanted us always to remember what Verdana had done. Her room held that smell, too.

I sometimes brushed her dry, wiry hair and sprayed her with lilac tonics to remind her of our home. Nothing ever worked. After the night of the curse, she never smiled again. And since my father banished her, she's only uttered a handful of sentences. Most are gibberish, the ramblings of a woman who's lost her mind. I know them by heart.

"She can be anyone; she can be anywhere!" Or, more often: "She will devour them all, and then nothing can stop her from tearing our world apart."

The last time I left that stifling room, so many years ago, I called out, "I'll see you soon, Mother. Warm up a smile for me until then."

Before I closed the door, her meek voice responded with something I'd never heard her say before.

"The golden ring is fading; the world will be swallowed whole."

I open my eyes, fighting against the pain. Light is fading from the forest, which means I was unconscious for most of the day. I gingerly rub my aching head; a large knot sits where the tree limb crashed into my skull.

Idalia. I jump to my feet and immediately sway.

"Idalia!" My head throbs. The woods are still. Lifeless. Silent.

I yell again, ignoring the discomfort. I repeat her name over and over. Useless.

"No," I whisper, my voice shaking. "Have I lost you, too?"

The sun dips lower, and leaves fall as the wind rises from the trees. I can't move. I'm broken.

"*Braizen!*" Her scream pierces the silence, a dagger cutting through flesh. "Braizen, please! Help!"

Before I can draw a breath, I'm pounding through the woods. Trees are a blurred brown smudge as I fly past. When I hear her cry again, I kick my feet so quickly I can hardly feel the forest floor beneath them. I'm a bird cloaked in red, soaring on a great wind. I keep going, but her voice doesn't grow nearer. Perhaps I'm running in the wrong direction, but no, I hear her again, and I know this is the way. She's still here, not lost forever.

Horrick must have made camp, or Idalia could've used her powers to stop them. I don't know, nor do I care. She's still here, somewhere.

I hear her sobs in the distance; she screams my name into the wind. I don't stop running, even when her voice fades into a whisper and then into silence.

I keep running. Running. Running.

It's the dead of night; a waxing crescent moon bleeds over the woodland, capturing all the eye can see in its muted tones. The only sound that dares challenge the eerie silence is my heavy breath, which falls from my mouth in steamy clouds. Everything is cold except the warm trail left by tears that run down my cheeks. Everyone I've ever loved is gone. Dead, captured, or a prisoner of their own mind. I am utterly alone.

The voice called me deeper into the Wood, but there is no sign of her anywhere.

My leaden legs wobble, and I rest my back against the trunk of a large tree. Looking up at the dark branches pressed against a starry sky, I wipe my face with a damp sleeve.

"I sure could use a drink with you right about now, Torrent," I say softly. "Or a good idea, Lin, if you have one. Hells, I'd even take one of your reprimands, Lorna. Gods know, that's probably what I need most."

I lean my head into the bark and sigh heavily. "Are you still here? Do I search for you? Or are you up there…in the heavens, laughing at me?"

The wind whips through a pile of leaves in front of me. They dance wildly before they're off to their next destination. I can't help thinking this is a sign, the answer. They're truly gone.

I swallow the sticky lump in the back of my throat. They died for me. Died so I could save Idalia and take her away from this cursed darkness. And I failed. I couldn't even protect her from my own men.

How badly must they be treating her? The ones who taught me to hate her, to loathe her Verdanian blood.

"Sparrow," I almost choke on her name. "Little Sparrow, forgive me. Forgive me for taking away your chance for freedom. For believing their lies and for not seeing you sooner."

I miss her scent, her inappropriate laughter. I miss her eyes and how they change when she's angry or embarrassed. The way she dances, her startling singing that I only got to hear once, and how her skin glows when sunlight laps over her face like it, too, wants to spend its days caressing her skin.

"And the thing is," I whisper at the sky. "That I'd rather spend the remainder of my life hoping, begging, and dreaming of the day I could touch you than live a moment, even a moment, without you here with me. Close enough to risk the world."

"Who is there?"

The mouse-like whisper sends me scrambling behind the tree. I hold my breath and hear the phantom voice again.

"Hello?" It's a female, that of a young woman. She sounds hesitant and afraid.

A figure emerges from the trees. She's small, and her long hair blows in the sharp wind. She draws closer, and I see blushing cheeks and a small nose that rounds out a perfect face. She's no older than Idalia, and she's frightened.

I jump out, and the woman stumbles back, her eyes wide with terror.

"Who are you?" I ask, holding up a fist. Usually, I'm above hitting a woman, but not here, where nothing is as it seems.

She raises her hands and shakes her head. "No enemy of yours, I promise! I heard a noise, and I never hear noises! So, I came to look. Who are you?"

"Not likely that I'll tell you, knowing you're probably a mirage of this evil Wood!"

"A Devil's Mirage? That is what you think I am? Here, feel my hand. I am real!"

"Don't touch me!" I warn and rear back as she reaches her palm toward me. "Or it'll be the last thing you do!"

One brow curves up, and her eyes gleam in a familiar way that I can't place.

"Fine," she says curtly. "Stay in the woods and freeze. I was only going to offer you a place to stay, but I now see that you have it all figured out." She doesn't give me a second look as she retreats.

I don't trust one thing within these trees. She could be a mirage or one of The Others. But she's offering shelter from the cold. If I stay here, I risk whatever else The Wood sends or contracting the Gray. It might prove to be the dumbest decision I've ever made, but I lurch forward.

"Wait!" I cry out to her, then swallow whatever pride I might have left within me. "Fine. Let me feel your hand."

She huffs a breathy laugh and walks back, one arm extended.

Hesitantly, I brush my hand over the top of hers. Skin. Delicate, soft skin.

"Okay," I concede, shoving my hand beneath the Aeradian cloak.

"Not a mirage. That's a promising start. So, where is this place of yours?"

Chapter Forty

Idalia

I don't know how many days passed before we arrived at the castle. It's not beautiful, as I once thought; the vines that sprawl over its stone grow weak and diminished. Where it was once vivid with rich colors, it is now a fading gray. The guards drag me by my arms down three staircases. It grows darker with each passing floor. I haven't eaten in days; I've been given little to drink, and my mind is tired. So very, very tired.

"Welcome home, icy bitch," one of the men says as he throws me into a murky cell. I land on my back and stare at a dark, stone ceiling covered in mold.

"This is for Queen Eveline," he says and drives his plated boot into my side.

I cough, and a metallic taste fills my mouth.

"And this, this is for King Vaskis…"

I brace myself for the pain.

"That's enough," a steely voice intervenes.

The guard immediately stops.

"There are plenty of other ways to break the girl, Diglian."

"Yes, Your Majesty."

I groan, and the air punches my lungs as it leaves. He must have broken a rib or two. Or three. I hear King Vaskis approach, but don't turn my head.

He snaps his tongue against the back of his teeth in slow, exaggerated movements until he stands over me. When I look up, I don't see his face. Not clearly, anyway. Instead, images of my mother's dead body flash across my vision.

"You," I cough. Gods, it hurts. My ribs squeeze in dissent.

"*Me.*" The King's lips curl into a wry grin.

I close my eyes, listening to drips of water leak from the ceiling. "You're going to kill me, aren't you?" I wheeze. "Just like you killed my mother."

His cold hand grabs my chin, and he jerks my head up. I open my eyes to see him squatting next to me.

"I didn't kill your mother, that little cunt. Although not a day goes by, I don't wish I had." He flings my head down, and it thuds against the stone.

I groan and try not to move.

"If only I had been the one to do it," he coos. "Then I could better deal with the curses Baelliles has endured since. But no, it was not me. I do not lie. Your father killed her, Idalia of Verdana. He killed your mother. Because of him, we all suffer."

Ruby-covered snakes.

"So, now you're going to finish me off…for revenge," I manage.

"That *is* a possibility, but it is not why I brought you here." The King laughs as he stands.

Bile rises in my throat, and I do my best to swallow before replying. "Then why am I here?"

"Do you truly think I will reveal my plan to you, the riffraff of our world? You foolish girl. There are far more powerful things in this world than revenge."

My hands jolt, but I'm too weak to lift them, let alone obey them.

"Your father has kept many secrets from you, but that is neither here nor there. I have you now, and if he wants you back, he will have to pay the price," he says.

My body is growing numb, and my eyelids droop so heavily that I can barely keep them open. My stomach groans with hunger and my ribs ache in agony when I speak.

"Verdana doesn't have much. You'd do better to kill me and laugh at him for it, because whatever price you desire, he can't pay."

"Daft bitch," Vaskis sneers. "You think I brought you here for coins?"

He stands to leave and motions for Diglian to close the iron-barred door behind him. It clangs shut, and a lock clicks.

My heart sinks.

"Then what do you want?" I call. My dry throat aches like rough nails are being dragged down it each time I speak.

He pauses in the dim light of a single sconce; his form rests in the shadows.

"I want what everybody wants, Idalia. *The world at my feet.*"

Chapter Forty-One

Idalia

On day four of captivity, I can sit up. Barely.

Once a day, the guards leave what I assume is a bowl of pig feed, or rather, what the pigs refuse to eat, and a small glass of putrid water. On day six, they throw a rag, one already soiled in another prisoner's sweat and blood, into the cell. I use some of my water to wash. My ribs are painted black and blue, and each breath is an excruciating chore. My only form of sanity is using a small, chalky rock to tally the days. I draw six lines.

Chapter Forty-Two

Idalia

Nine lines.

Chapter Forty-Three

Idalia

Twenty-seven lines.

Chapter Forty-Four

Idalia

On day thirty, I stop drawing lines. The rock dissolves in my hand, and I'm too weak to search the corners for another. My ribs jut out from my chest, and I see that one has healed poorly. King Vaskis hasn't returned to my cell. The only company I'm graced with is a black-hooded guard who leaves me my barely edible slop.

I am days away from death. I feel her draw near. Her cold, hissing shadows whisper to me at night.

I'm ready. I beg her to take me. How I long to be saved from this wretched life and be taken to the Lady, to rest behind her shield. I can run into my mother's arms and only worry about which dress she'd have me wear.

I picture Braizen's stunned face as he fought his guards for me, and I search for what the truth might be. Did he betray me as my mother accused? Did he mean to save me?

My head thuds. Death mumbles something to me again.

I wonder if Braizen still lives or if I shall meet him in the Great Lands where we can share our very first embrace.

Chapter Forty-Five

Idalia

“Come get your food, scum,” the guard calls, only this time it’s a female who shoves the slop bowl under the bars. The bowl slides, frantically spinning on the stones as half its content spills over its rim. I huddle in one corner, knees drawn close to my chest, shaking profusely.

“Princess,” she says. “Eat your food. That’s an order.” Her voice reminds me of something, but I can’t think; my brain is all but mush. I don’t answer; I can’t. My bones continue to rattle within.

“Princess?” For a moment, her voice sounds sincere.

I part my dry, crusted lips and summon every ounce of my strength to respond.

"Death…She comes today."

I close my eyes, ready to be met by death's sweet warmth.

There's movement. A sound. Creaking.

Hands are on me now; they turn me over.

I smile. *Yes, Death. Take me.*

Hot liquid spills down my throat and spreads a fire throughout my chest. This is what it feels like to pass over. I'm coming, Mother.

A muffled voice calls my name. I twitch and trace my tongue along my teeth. There's moisture in my mouth, actual moisture. My skin doesn't feel clammy.

I jolt upright, surprised at my body's strength. I must have entered the Great Lands.

"Lady, did you save me?" I murmur and open my eyes to greet the goddess herself.

I stare into a pair of emerald greens.

"Not quite the Lady you were hoping for, I'm sure," Lorna says. A black hood covers her hair.

"I've died," I whisper, reaching for her cheek to see if she's real.

"I should be so lucky," she says and swats my hand away.

Torrent laughs, and I gasp when he rides up beside us and grins.

"You think we'd let you die that easily?" He asks. "After all we've been through?"

Ignoring her frown, I pull Lorna into a tight embrace. She's the first human I've felt in months, the first familiar face. And she lives! Torrent is alive!

I'm alive.

"Uhm, just a quick reminder that we're still in Baelliles, and I think it best if we, you know, shut up," Lin's familiar voice chirps anxiously. Over Lorna's shoulder, I see Rianne riding behind us with Lin clutching her waist.

"Oh, come on, Speck. We just pulled off the greatest robbery of all time, and you want us to be quiet?"

"Yes, I want you to be quiet. More than anything I've ever wanted in my life."

"Well, too bad!" Torrent howls. "I have to revel in my plan working! The greatest plan in history, I think."

"*Your* plan?!"

The two quarrel over who came up with what, and Lorna grins and shakes her head. We bounce up and down as she directs her mount over grassy knolls.

"Lorna," I whisper. "How did you get out from under the carriage?"

Her fierce eyes look into mine from beneath the black cowl, and for the first time, I note how light her lashes are and how perfectly her eyebrows are sculpted for permanent contention.

"Rianne saved the boys from the dire wolf. Then, as I was taking what I thought was my final breath, Torrent lifted the carriage to save me."

My hands flare.

"How did Rianne save them from that beast?" It's all my tired brain can think of to ask.

Lorna shrugs.

"Remember those grimshkas? Turns out they aren't always cute and fluffy."

"Turn left there, next to that bent tree," Rianne instructs.

Lorna tugs the reins, and we shift direction as Torrent and Lin continue to bicker. My heart and mind race with a thousand questions, but the night is cold, and I'm alive. That's enough for now.

"Where are we going?"

"Where do you think?" She answers without looking at me. "We're going to save him."

"Him?"

She huffs a laugh. "Braze. The idiot himself."

"He's in danger?" My breathing escalates.

The horse neighs as Lorna pulls on the reins and lets Lin and Rianne lead the way into a small village. A worn sign creaking in the wind reads: Pathstowe.

"We aren't sure. Nuri said the last she saw him, he was in The Wood, chasing after you and screaming your name."

"Chasing after me? Why would he do that? Unless…" I murmur. The question I've been plagued with all those days in the cell finally answered.

He didn't betray me.

I grab the horse's mane as we begin to trot.

"Then what? After he chased me, what happened?"

There's a long moment of silence.

"Then…darkness," Lorna finally says. "Nuri can't see him anymore."

"Oh, gods," I breathe.

Torrent trots up beside us and looks me over, his hazel eyes alight.

"So, now it's his turn to be saved," he says and flashes his audacious grin. "Are you in?"

I look around and then up to the stars. A radical heat flushes through me.

"Yes," I say and nod. "I'm in."

Torrent howls into the night sky, and I sense Lorna break into a smile.

I'm coming for you, Braizen. Wherever you are, whatever has happened, no matter what it might cost.

It is better to die together than to live apart.

Acknowledgements

Writing and creating stories has been something I've wanted to do since I was a toddler. It's true. I would present my mother with books I wrote with crayons and she would also encourage me to keep it up. (Thanks, Mom! You are THE BEST.)

As I got older, I never stopped writing and reading, but the dream of actually publishing a book got thrown out the window. Thankfully, due to a lot of people in my life, that dream came back full swing.

I want to thank Booktok, more than anything, for giving me the opportunity to put some fun characters on the page and for championing this story. I could not, and *would not* have done this without you! I can't believe I get to sit up at night and write fun little stories for you! WHAT IS LIFE?!

Thank you for all the accounts that constantly hype me up, even when it isn't warranted and I have done nothing to deserve it.

To my Found Family group chat, you know who you are, I love you so much.

I want to thank everyone who is about to roast this book too. I can handle it. I get it.

And lastly, I want to thank my super hot husband for always gassing me up and calling me pretty, even after hours of staring at a computer screen, consuming nothing but coffee (and beer). You are my Braizen. You are my fate. I love you so much, and it's equally because of you that I could make this story possible.

Thanks to all my characters for bringing this story to life, but especially Torrent.

He's going to have so much fun in the next book.

-Kaven

About the Author

Kaven Hirning is a first time author who is trying her best. She lives with a very attractive male escort, who she also married, and they are currently very happy raising their six children. Two dogs, and four cats.

Kaven is excited to adopt even more children, and hopes her writing career can take off so she might do just that. In her free time, Kaven likes to create stories, write two of them, forget the rest of them, then cry because they were *really* good ideas! When she's not crying over her own stories, she's probably crying reading someone else's. And if she's not doing that, she's definitely crying over the TV show she just binged in 12 hours.

And if she is not doing *that*, she's probably dressing a Corona Premiere and speed talking about all the behind the scenes facts of LOTR to a new friend who couldn't care less. She's also very thankful for those of you who read her first book!

Thank you so much!

Printed in Poland
by Amazon Fulfillment
Poland Sp. z o.o., Wrocław
08 October 2022

51d1f3d9-8008-426e-85ab-bee99144938bR01